Also by Lucy Gilmore

PUPPY
Christmas

LUCY GILMORE

sourcebooks
casablanca

67360388

Rom

Published by Sourcebooks Casablanca, an imprint of Sourcebooks
P.O. Box 4410, Naperville, Illinois 60567-4410
(630) 961-3900
sourcebooks.com

Printed and bound in the United States of America.
OPM 10 9 8 7 6 5 4 3 2 1

chapter
1

Lila was going to kill her sisters for this.

"Lila! Lila Vasquez!" A voice hailed her from across the crowded ballroom floor. It was followed by the bustling of a woman in a tasteful two-piece dress suit. A pang of envy flooded through Lila for that neat, pearly-gray fabric, but it was a short-lived sentiment.

Mostly because it was immediately replaced by embarrassment. And despair. And the overwhelming urge to throw herself out the nearest window.

She changed her mind. Death was too good for her sisters. Nothing less than lifelong torment would do.

"Aren't you so brave," the woman cooed as she came to a halt. Her sweeping gaze took in the full glory of Lila's billowing bubble-gum-pink ball gown. If the color wasn't bad enough, the fact that she was followed by a trail of sparkles everywhere she went *was*. She'd left the ladies' restroom looking like a glitter bomb had gone off in one of the stalls. "I wish I could wear something like that, but at our age, you know…"

Yes, Lila did know. No one over the age of twenty-one should ever leave the house in this shade of pink. Unfortunately, Sophie and Dawn had interpreted the

Once Upon a Time theme literally. Instead of the costume party she'd been *assured* awaited her inside these
doors, Lila had found herself inside a nonprofit event
as upscale as it was elegant. She stuck out like a sore
thumb.

A giant, pink, puffy thumb.

"It's so nice to see you, Kathy," she said, forcing a
smile. It probably looked about as plastic as she felt,
but she was determined to stay put. She'd been invited
to this ball as an established and vital part of Spokane's
hearing services community. Its purpose was to raise
funds for the hearing impaired, largely for the purchase
of medical equipment, implants, hearing assistive tech…
and service dogs.

Lila might look silly—and feel just as ridiculous—
but her dogs deserved a seat at the table, metaphorically
speaking. She'd give them that even if it meant she had
to stand here all night, shedding glitter into fifty-dollar
glasses of champagne.

"I'm excited to hear who will be getting our puppy
donation," she said in what she hoped was a casual
tone. "So are my sisters. I'm supposed to text them
the moment I find out. Do you know when they'll be
making the announcements?"

Kathy waved an airy hand. She was one of the ball
organizers, but she had less to do with the details and
more to do with squeezing large donations out of the
city's finest. "You'll have to ask Anya. She has the full
schedule. I only came by to ask where you got that gorgeous dress. My daughter's winter formal is coming up,
and they're doing Candy Land this year. That's exactly
what we've been looking for."

It was enough to send a lesser woman fleeing for the nearest hiding place. Lila had spotted several already, each one more appealing than the last. There was a huge banquet table she could crawl underneath to wait out the evening's events, or a swan ice sculpture dripping in the entryway that might provide an adequate shield. In a pinch, even that pair of waiters with giant silver platters could help her make a quick getaway.

But Lila stood her ground. Lila *always* stood her ground. Neither snow nor rain nor heat nor extreme social embarrassment—

"Oh God." Catching sight of a familiar man by the entryway, she whirled around, her skirt ballooning around her legs. "This can't be happening."

"What can't be happening?" Kathy asked, her brows raised. She took a sip of her champagne, a wayward piece of glitter clinging to her upper lip. "Are you sure you're all right?"

No. Lila wasn't sure of anything except that no number of waiters with silver platters would be able to help her now. What she needed was for the ground to open up beneath her, for the world to swallow her whole. Risking a quick peek over her shoulder, she scanned the entryway again and... *Yep.* It was happening. It was happening, and there was nothing she could do to stop it.

She dashed a hand out and grabbed Kathy's forearm. "Quick—what's the easiest way out of here?"

"I think maybe you should sit down," Kathy said, frowning at where Lila was crushing the silk of her suit. "You look as though you've seen a ghost."

On the contrary, it was no ghost that had caught

Lila's eye. That flash of white coming from the opposite side of the room was blinding enough to be supernatural, but Lila had never believed in that sort of thing. Ghosts weren't real and bogeymen were make-believe, but a smile as toothy and brilliant as her ex-boyfriend's had caused her plenty of sleepless nights.

"The kitchen?" Lila asked, mostly to herself. "No, I'll never make it that far. It'll have to be the emergency exit."

She knew she was babbling, but she could no more stop the words from leaving her mouth than she could still the sudden thumping of her heart. *Patrick Yarmouth.* Of all the men to saunter through the door looking as though he'd dropped in straight out of a toothpaste ad, it had to be him.

She could brazen this dress out for the sake of her company, Puppy Promise. She could smile and sparkle for as long as it took to woo the people who had the power to take that company to the next level.

But she could not, would not, *dared* not risk exposing herself to the man who'd accused her of perfection like it was a four-letter word. Especially since he hadn't spotted her yet. *There's still time to make my escape.*

"I'm sorry, Kathy," she said as she lifted her skirts and headed for the bright red exit sign. "I have to leave."

"Does this mean you aren't going to tell me where you got the dress?" Kathy called, watching her go. "My daughter will be so disappointed."

"I'll email you the details tomorrow," Lila promised as she pushed through the door to safety. *Better yet*, she thought as she navigated the steep flight of steps leading down, *I'll shove the dress in a box and mail it to you.*

After tonight, there was nothing on earth that could induce her to wear sparkles again.

It was only cowardice if she hid *behind* the potted plant.

"I'm standing next to it," Lila said to no one in particular, if only because there was no one in particular to say it to. She'd escaped the emergency stairwell to find herself on some kind of first-floor landing. It offered a fountain and a ficus and a complete absence of other people—all three of which were serving to calm her rattled nerves. "I'm taking a break, that's all. Getting away from all those dark suits and demure gowns. I'll be back to my usual, capable self in a few minutes, and then I'll be able to face him."

Her attempt at boosting her own confidence failed. In truth, it was only her inability to pull her skirts in far enough that kept her where she was. There was no way she *could* fit behind that plant.

A soft sniffling sound stopped Lila before she could make the mistake of continuing her one-sided conversation. It wasn't like her to flee at the first sign of danger; even less to self-soothe with a running dialogue. She was supposed to be the unflappable Vasquez sister, the one everyone else turned to in times of emergency.

In other words, the *perfect* one.

The sniffle sounded again, this time accompanied by a hiccuping sob. Her own worries cast aside, Lila picked her way out from her hiding spot next to the plant and surveyed the room. As far as she could tell, it was still empty. There was a possibility that sound might carry through one of the vents, but—

A small voice sounded behind her. "Are you a princess?"

For the second time this evening, Lila found herself whirling around, startled. This time, however, her gaze landed on a small girl standing just a few feet away.

The first thing she noticed was that the girl appeared to be wearing a dress that was identical to her own. Bubble-gum pink. Sparkles. Tulle. All things that made a grown woman look like she was one magic wand away from a starring role in *The Wizard of Oz*, but looked perfectly at home on a six-year-old.

The second thing she noticed was that the child had a pair of twin cochlear implants, one on either side of her elaborate updo. The small, purple-colored plastic pieces behind her ears attached to even smaller nodes via looped cords. They were, in Lila's line of work, a fairly common sight. They were also a clear sign that this girl's parents couldn't be too far away.

Upstairs in the ballroom, probably. *Where Patrick is*.

"Oh, hello," Lila said, somewhat taken aback. Surprise rendered her voice harsher than usual—a thing she regretted as soon as the words left her lips. The poor girl was obviously lost, staring up at her with wide, blue eyes that were swimming in tears. "I didn't know there was anyone in here with me."

The girl didn't respond, her breath once more catching on a sob. Lila's experience with children wasn't vast—she was much more of a dog person than a kid one—but even she could tell that a situation like this one called for tact.

She fell into an unladylike squat so they were level with each other. Not only was getting down the first thing a puppy trainer did when approaching a wary animal, but the girl was watching Lila's mouth with the intensity of long practice. Lila had enough experience with hearing service dogs and their owners to recognize that the girl most likely used a combination of her cochlear implants and lip reading to communicate.

"Are you lost?" she asked.

The girl nodded, her arms wrapped protectively around her midsection.

Lila held out a hand with her palm up to show she meant no harm and held it there. That was another good puppy-training trick. Maybe this wouldn't be as difficult as she'd feared. "Then you're in luck. I'm not lost at all."

"You aren't?" the girl asked, blinking at her.

"Nope. I have an excellent sense of direction." She held a finger straight up. "You go thataway."

The girl's gaze followed the direction Lila was pointing, but she had yet to take Lila's hand. "Through the ceiling?" she asked doubtfully.

"Well, no. You have to take the stairs, I'm afraid. There's an elevator around here somewhere, but I'm not sure where to find it."

That caused the doubt in the girl's voice to increase. "You mean this isn't your castle?"

The Davenport Hotel, where the event was being held, was about as fancy as Spokane architecture got, but it was hardly what Lila would call a *castle*. "Oh, um. No. I think it's owned by local real-estate developers, actually."

Apparently, that was the wrong answer. The girl's arms clenched tighter around her stomach, a fresh bout of tears starting to take shape in her eyes. "I thought it was your castle."

Lila had no idea how she was supposed to respond. It wasn't in her nature to lie to small children, but she didn't know what else to do. Her sister Sophie would have been able to comfort the girl with kind words and a smile, and Dawn would have had her laughing within minutes, but Lila had always been better with adults than children.

Then again, she'd also always been the kind of woman to dress sensibly and stand her ground when faced with an unexpected encounter with an ex-boyfriend. Clearly, today was an anomaly.

"My castle is much bigger than this one," she said, casting her scruples aside. "And it's located in, um, a faraway kingdom?"

It was the right thing to say. A look of relief swept over the girl's face, the beginnings of a smile taking shape in the perfect bow of her mouth. "You *are* a real princess," she said. "I knew it."

She finally slipped her hand into Lila's. For some strange reason, Lila had expected the girl's hand to be sticky—children were usually sticky, weren't they?— but the palm pressed against hers was perfectly clean. And soft. It was a nice surprise.

"I'm not allowed to talk to strangers," the girl confided with a shy smile. "But a princess isn't a stranger."

"Oh dear," Lila murmured. It wasn't her place to lecture children on stranger danger, but for all she knew, the girl would take this one successful venture and run off in the future with anyone claiming to be royalty. "Actually, I *am* a stranger. It's important to be wary of grown-ups no matter what they're wearing. You know that, right? A fancy dress doesn't automatically make someone a princess. Just like a tuxedo doesn't automatically make someone a prince."

In fact, now that she thought about it, there were lots of warning signs that could be worn on the outside. Take, for example, a man's blinding smile across a crowded ballroom floor.

"It's all too easy for a person to hide their true nature behind clothes," she added. "Clothes and makeup and shoes and a smile you know better than to trust, if only because no man has teeth that white unless there's something wrong with him. I don't care what anyone says or how many times they say it. You shouldn't be able to see your reflection in someone else's molars."

The girl tugged on Lila's hand, pulling her attention down. She pointed first at her own ears and then at Lila's lips before blinking expectantly.

"Oh," Lila said, dismayed. "I went on a bit of a tirade there, didn't I?"

"Emily might not have had the privilege of catching all that, but I sure did," a male voice sounded from behind them, causing Lila to jump. *Again.* "And I, for one, am dying to meet this man. Does he gargle with bleach, do you think, or is it that new charcoal toothpaste everyone is going on about?"

"Daddy!" The girl—Emily—dropped Lila's hand and ran to the man, wrapping her arms around his knees. Her words were muffled by a sob. "I got lost."

He lifted the child into his arms and waited until her head was level with his before speaking. "Yes, I noticed that. But I see you found your time-traveling adult self and came to no harm. Strange that you never ended up buying a different dress. I thought for sure you'd outgrow pink sparkles."

Lila stiffened. He was making fun of her. This man, this stranger clad in a socially acceptable tuxedo, was making fun of her.

"Daddy, she's a *princess*."

"Is she?" He cast a scrutinizing look Lila's way. "I didn't know princesses could time travel."

"She rescued me."

"Well, that is what princesses do."

"I know." Emily nodded as if that made perfect sense. "That's why I let her help me."

"A wise decision," the man said. And that, it seemed, was the final word on the subject. There were no lectures about wandering off on her own, no words of warning about what could happen to a little girl who trusted any crackpot in pink tulle. He merely shifted his daughter to his hip and continued his appraisal of Lila.

It wasn't an *unappreciative* appraisal, but she wasn't sure what she was supposed to do about it. There was something about the man's glinting blue eyes and slow, spreading grin that shot like an arrow straight through her. Okay, so she wasn't some six-foot underwear model in a well-cut tuxedo. Her jaw wasn't a chiseled shadow that had been timed to remain steadfast at five o'clock. She didn't have the sexy beginnings of gray starting to take over the winged sides of her well-sculpted brown hair...

"I'm sorry—did you say something?" She blinked as the man's grin deepened.

"Yes. I asked your name, but you weren't finished

yet." He cast a look down at himself and gave a rueful shake of his head. "Ridiculous, isn't it? I feel like a penguin. But the invitation said black tie, so black tie it is. Emily's a stickler for the rules. So, what is it?"

She blinked again. "The dress code?"

"Your name."

"Oh, um. It's Lila. Lila Vasquez." Aware that her usual demeanor—the careful, upright professional she was in all things—was slipping, she stuck out her hand. And then was forced to keep holding it out. She'd somehow forgotten that the man was using both arms to hold his daughter, which meant he had to shift and shuffle before he could return the gesture.

It didn't help that the hand he eventually extracted was his left one, which bore no signs of a wedding ring. His palm was cool and dry, his handshake firm. He might be holding a kindergartner and masquerading as a penguin, but he did it with a level of confidence Lila could only admire.

"Ford Ford."

"I'm sorry?"

"You're Lila Vasquez. This is Emily Ford. I'm Ford Ford."

"You're Ford...Ford?"

He bent in a slight bow. "The one and only. Or so I hope. If there's another poor *b-a-s-t-a-r-d* wandering around out there named Ford Ford, he has my deepest sympathies. And a heartfelt wish to give his parents a strong talking-to." His smile warmed as he continued. "I recognize your name. Are you one of the organizers?"

"Not an organizer, no."

"She's a princess," Emily interjected.

"Yes, moppet. We've already covered that. She's a princess and she rescues lost little girls and she doesn't like men who smile with their teeth."

"I never said—"

"She lives in a faraway kingdom," Emily interrupted with all the certainty of a six-year-old safely ensconced in her father's arms. They were strong arms, too, not wavering under their burden even once. "Were you at the ball, too?"

"As a matter of fact, I was." Lila glanced at the clock on the opposite wall and held back a sigh.

As much as she would have preferred to stay hiding down here for the rest of the night, she was eventually going to have to suck up her pride and face the ballroom. Patrick would still be there, of course, but some things couldn't be helped.

"I should probably get back there before anyone notices I'm gone, but…" She cast a look down at her attire and bit her lip.

"But you can't possibly go without an escort?" Ford offered. Even though his arms were already taken up with Emily, he managed to crook an elbow at her. "It's the least I can do after you rescued my daughter. She doesn't take to just anyone, you know. You must be something special."

"Oh, I'm really not—" Lila began, more flustered than she cared to admit. She couldn't tell whether it was the girl, her father, or the dress that was making her feel most out of her depth, but the room was definitely spinning around her.

"If it'll help, I promise not to smile any more than absolutely necessary," Ford said with a shake of his elbow. "It'll be nothing but frowns and glowers as far as the eye can see."

Because he wore a particularly attractive smile as he said this, Lila wasn't fooled. She didn't have a chance to call him on it, however, since he winked and turned his face toward Emily. "I specially requested The Hokey Pokey from the orchestra. It'd be a shame if we missed it."

"Daddy!" Emily protested with a giggle. "You did not."

"Of course I did. Why do you think it took me so long to come find you?" He gave up on the elbow and dropped a liberal kiss on Emily's cheek instead. "I also asked them to play the Macarena, YMCA, and, I'm sorry to say, Gangnam Style. Emily doesn't have the most sophisticated taste. I, on the other hand, am an arbiter of great music. I made sure to add the The Chicken Dance to our lineup."

"The Chicken Dance?" Lila echoed. She thought of the string quartet that had been hired for the evening and suppressed a laugh. She'd known the violinist to throw his bow at anyone requesting a composition not written before the eighteenth century. "I don't believe you."

She should have known that playing into this man's nonsense was a mistake. The moment the challenge left her lips, he turned to her with a lift to his brow. That debonair arch was all that was needed to take his tuxedo from attractive to full-on devastating. "Are you sure about that? I can be very persuasive when I put my mind to it."

She didn't doubt it. She also had no plans to stick around and find out for herself. Even if she was in the

habit of picking up strange men and their daughters—
which she wasn't—there was the small matter of work
to get back to.

"Well, I don't know The Chicken Dance, so it's no
good asking me to join you," Lila said primly. "And
before you ask, I don't know Gangnam Style or the
Macarena, either."

Ford gave a gentle *tsk* and shook his head. "You seem
sadly unprepared for a dance party like this one. What
do you know?"

She thought quickly. "The waltz."

"How very princessy of you," he murmured with an
appreciative twinkle in his eyes. As if suddenly realizing
he was still holding a child in his arms, he gave Emily
a light shake and added, "Isn't that right, moppet? All
royalty should waltz."

Emily's only response was a giggle and a request for
her father to put her down. "I'm okay now, Daddy," she
said as she began wriggling out of his grasp. "I promise."

He allowed Emily to slide down his side until she was
planted on her own two feet. That, apparently, was yet
another mistake, because she immediately bounced over
to Lila and grabbed her by the hand. She gave a strong
tug, which meant that unless Lila was willing to wrench
a child's arm out of its socket, she had to take a liberal
step in Ford's direction.

If Ford Ford looked good, he smelled even better. He
wasn't, like so many of the other men upstairs, doused
in expensive cologne. Instead, he carried the light
scent of aftershave and what she could have sworn was
peanut butter.

She was so distracted by this bizarre yet compelling

combination that she missed it when Emily took her father by her other hand. Without waiting for either of them to guess what she was up to, she took herself out of the equation. That left only the pair of them, standing much closer than was appropriate, their fingers lightly touching. Every instinct Lila had warned her to jump back, but something about Emily's wistful expression gave her pause.

"Pretty please will you waltz with my daddy?" she asked. "I never saw a princess dance in real life a'fore."

There was something especially beguiling about the way Emily made the request. She didn't wheedle or plead, the way Lila always assumed children of her age did, and she didn't resort to a tantrum. She just blinked up at them with an expectant look in her big blue eyes. Her face was still puffy and red from her earlier tears, her careful hairstyle now falling around her ears.

Waltzing in a pink ball gown with a man she didn't know was the last thing Lila wanted to do right now— or, you know, ever—but at the sight of those innocently tumbling curls, she felt herself faltering. She caught Ford's eye.

Had he turned to that easy flirtation again, said something dashing and ridiculous, she would have turned him down. She had places to go and people to avoid, and it wasn't in her nature to place herself in situations where she felt this far out of her depth.

But he looked almost as embarrassed as she felt, his grin turned rueful. "I'm not very good, but I'm game if you are." He gave a tiny shrug of one shoulder. "What can I say? She's never seen a princess dance in real life before."

Lila didn't bother demurring further. How could she? At this point, she had nothing else to lose. She was already wearing the dress. She'd already fled the ball in shame and disgrace. And she already knew what—or who—was waiting for her upstairs.

It's not as if this night can get any worse.

"Why not?" she said and gave what she hoped was a regal bow of her head. "I'd be delighted."

She was rewarded with a dazzling smile from Ford and a yank on her hand. She was propelled into his arms, which came up to provide a frame worthy of any dance teacher's beginning waltz instructions.

The music from upstairs was too quiet to trickle down, and Lila had never been very good at humming, so the only backdrop to their movements was the shuffle of their feet and the trickle of the fountain in the distance. There was something acutely disconcerting about doing a music-free waltz with a strange man, especially when his daughter stood a few feet away with a look of pure rapture on her face. Lila felt stiff and awkward, but at least her footwork was solid.

Well, it was solid until Ford started gaining confidence in his own steps. As they reached one side of the room, his hold on her waist tightened. That firmer touch, the press of his hand on the narrowest part of her, his body so long and lean against hers—it was impossible not to feel a little light-headed.

Matters weren't helped any when Ford leaned close to her ear and murmured, "Thank you for doing this. I know you're probably itching to get back, but you're the only reason Emily's not sobbing into that ficus right now."

Her breath caught. "But I didn't do anything."

"Are you kidding?" he countered. His mouth was so close to her skin that she could feel the whisper of his words on her neck. There was an intimacy about it, a warmth she hadn't been expecting. "You made her night. *H-e-l-l*, you probably made her whole week. This sort of thing might be ordinary for you, but we don't run into beautiful princesses every day."

It went against all of her scruples—and even more of her common sense—to reward a heavy-handed compliment like that, but her eyes snapped up to meet Ford's. What she saw there wasn't flirtation or amusement or even laughter at her predicament. He looked, well, *sincere*.

"Oh." Her heart gave a flutter, her body gliding and moving with his. "Um. You're welcome?"

This time Ford did laugh, but it was a soft chuckle that was reflected in the light of his startlingly blue eyes. Lila thought that perhaps their steps slowed, that the music— was there music?—came to an end and the dance was over. But he still had his hand wrapped around her waist, his torso pressed lightly against her own.

As if drawn forward by some power outside herself, Lila leaned closer. Her head tilted up and her breath caught, and for one long, suspended moment, she could almost taste the touch of his lips against hers.

Until, of course, a loud cheer and a burst of applause pulled her feet back down to the ground.

"That was like magic!" Emily ran to her father and beamed up at him, her arms held up in supplication. "Like real princess magic."

Without a moment's hesitation, Ford let go of Lila

and swooped his daughter into his arms. "It was, wasn't it?" he asked.

There was nothing flustered about him, none of the awkwardness Lila felt at finding herself standing all alone in the middle of the tile floor. She still had her arms up as if he were holding her, her lips parted in anticipation of a kiss that was never coming.

"I enjoyed the dancing, but I'm not so sure I'm ready for the part where I turn into a pumpkin," he said. "Does it happen right away, do you think, or do I have a few hours before I begin my transformation?"

"Dad-dy!" Emily cried, clearly delighted at this piece of nonsense. "That's not how the story goes."

"I'd like to be a jack-o'-lantern," he said, ignoring her. He rubbed his chin thoughtfully. "One of those scary ones with flashing eyes and sharp teeth. Then you can roll me out every Halloween to delight the neighborhood."

Emily giggled obligingly, but Lila was still rooted where she stood, unable to shake the feeling that she was standing on the outside of a joke never meant for her ears. As if to prove it, Ford turned to her and swept a bow.

"Thank you, Princess Lila, for saving my daughter— and for the dance." His eyes met hers, and he lifted his shoulder in another of those awkward half-shrugs. She assumed it was a prelude to more playful commentary, but all he did was frown slightly and add, "We won't take up any more of your time."

And that was it. Without waiting for her to say any-thing in reply—which was probably for the best, since she had no idea what she *could* say—he whisked his daughter toward the emergency stairwell and allowed the door to fall shut behind them.

The echoing silence they left in their wake had Lila feeling even more unsettled than when she'd come down here in the first place. Ford and Emily might not have been accustomed to running into beautiful princesses every day, but Lila had even less experience with cracking jokes about The Chicken Dance and waltzing with dashing strangers in tuxedos.

And by less experience, she meant none whatsoever. Men didn't normally sweep her off her feet before running away like Cinderella hightailing after her footmen. In fact, if it weren't for the floor dusted with glitter from their waltz, she'd have thought she imagined the whole thing.

But glitter was there in abundance, and another glance at the clock on the wall reminded her that she'd spent far too long down here already. They'd be making the announcements soon, if they hadn't done so already, and there were several people she needed to see before the night was through.

In other words, it was back to business as usual. Now that she was done with the mortification down here, there was no use in delaying the mortification waiting for her upstairs.

"It's not like you'll ever see the pair of them again," Lila told herself as she picked her way over to the stairwell. She was still feeling a little breathless, but that could easily be blamed on the tight bodice of her dress.

Yes. It was definitely the dress. Not the touch of a man's hand on her waist, not the whirling sensation that had almost swept her into an indiscretion. Even if everyone upstairs knew that she looked like a fool, at least they'd never know that she *felt* like one.

She counted to sixty before she started up the stairs,

careful to give Ford and Emily plenty of time to clear out before she followed. With any luck, it would be nearing the girl's bedtime, and Lila could safely put the interlude behind her where it belonged.

There was no sign of either Ford or Patrick as she stepped through the door and reentered the ballroom. Her luck held while she chatted with a social worker who very kindly made no reference to her dress whatsoever. It even lasted long enough for her to take a stuffed mushroom from a passing waiter.

But just as she was about to pop the buttery morsel in her mouth, the emcee stepped up to the stage to make the announcement Lila had been waiting for all night.

It's about time. Finally, her agonies could come to an end. Finally, she could smile graciously and make one more dash for the emergency exit—this time for good.

Or so she thought.

"Please give a warm round of applause for the recipient of a generous donation from Puppy Promise for a service dog and six weeks of personalized training." The emcee made a big show of looking around the ballroom. At first, Lila thought he was looking for her, but he passed her over, not stopping until his gaze landed on the only other female in the room wearing a sparkling pink ball gown.

What? She reared back, her mushroom falling to the floor with a *splat*.

It wasn't possible. She'd heard rumors that their donation was going to a nice old man from Cheney. Not him. Not her. Not…

"A big congratulations to Emily Ford!"

chapter
2

"That's a terrible shade of lipstick to wear on a beautiful winter morning." Dawn sat cross-legged at the end of Lila's bed, watching as she put the finishing touches on her makeup. "Come to think of it, that's a terrible pantsuit you've got on. You look like a cross between a politician and a Golden Girl—and I don't mean that as a compliment."

Lila took a step back and surveyed herself in the mirror. She *did* look awful, what with her long, dark hair pulled back in a tight bun and her makeup better suited for a jail warden than a day of playing with puppies. When added to the generous features of her face—which she'd always felt were a touch too large for anyone who wasn't a marble statue—she looked downright medieval.

"Good." She clipped the lid on the matte mauve lipstick. "I want to look as blandly professional as possible. If you saw me on the street, what would your first impression be?"

Dawn tilted her head and considered the question before answering. Her middle sister's no-nonsense approach to honesty was one of the things Lila loved about her, since she could always count on Dawn to tell her the truth no matter what.

"I'd say you were trying your hardest to look like the opposite of a princess."

Okay. Maybe she didn't *always* love the honesty.

"I do not. The opposite of a princess is a pauper. I don't look like a pauper."

"No, just like the evil villain who created all those paupers in the first place." Dawn laughed and unfolded herself from the carefully made-up bed. She left all kinds of creases and crinkles behind, but it would have been fruitless to complain. Lila had been complaining for almost three decades, and it never seemed to make the slightest difference.

As if to prove it, Dawn sidled up next to her and placed her chin on Lila's shoulder. Everything about the two of them spoke of shared DNA—the wide-set brown eyes, the sandy-toned skin, the way their lips lifted at the corners—but most of the similarities stopped there. Dawn's dark-brown hair was tousled, her chunky sweater carefree, her personality both those things combined.

Lila was, well, Lila.

"The dress wasn't *that* bad. I thought you looked sweet. Like a cupcake with frosting and sprinkles and fairy wings on top." Dawn grinned. "By the way, what's Prince Charming's name again? Buick Buick? Porsche Porsche?"

Lila sighed. It was never a good idea to tell her sister anything related to men. She had a tendency to make mayhem out of molehills. "His name is Ford Ford, and he's going to be here with Emily any minute.

I'm serious about this, Dawn. I need to look prim and untouchable."

And, she didn't need to add, like a woman who'd never even heard the word *waltz* before.

Dawn tugged the bottom of Lila's beige jacket and brushed off her shoulders, even though there hadn't been any time for the suit to gather dust in the five minutes since Lila had pulled it from the deepest recesses of her closet. If she remembered correctly, she'd bought the thing to wear to her college admissions interview. She'd gotten into her first choice school with it, but she'd vowed that nothing short of an appearance in criminal court would get her to wear the sartorial monstrosity again.

Criminal court or a day spent in a handsome man's company, apparently. In Lila's world, they were basically the same thing.

"I haven't seen you this nervous since that time you got caught stealing chalk from the principal's office. Relax. I'm sure no one even noticed what you were wearing."

Lila grimaced. On the contrary, she'd never been such an eyesore in her life. Everyone knew she wasn't a woman who sparkled. Ford Ford needed to see her in her natural element, that was all. Then he wouldn't laugh at her with those dancing blue eyes. Then he wouldn't reduce her to an incoherent, blubbering, mortified mess.

"Just pretend I'm the most dignified person you know, okay?" Lila glanced at the clock on her bedside table. "Oh dear. They'll be here any minute. What time is Sophie getting in?"

"She's not. She's working on-site with that peanut allergy terrier all week."

"Drat." Lila had been looking forward to their youngest sister joining them for the day. If anyone was like a princess, it was Sophie. Cute, petite, friendly-to-a-fault Sophie was exactly what this situation called for. "I was hoping she could be here to help with Emily. She's good with kids. Kids love her."

"Kids love cotton candy and fart jokes. They're not complicated."

That bit of advice didn't help nearly as much as it should have. Lila couldn't remember the last time she'd touched cotton candy, let alone eaten it, and the only joke she knew was the one about the chicken and the road. And even then, she didn't think she told it right.

A knock sounded on the front door. Before she could help herself, Lila shot out a hand and grabbed Dawn by the wrist. "You won't leave me alone with them, will you? Promise you won't leave me alone with them."

Dawn laughed and made an X over her chest with her free hand. "Are you kidding? I'm dying to see what it is about this man that has you so flustered. At this point, wild elephants couldn't keep me away."

🐾🐾🐾

"Your sister took off in an awful hurry." Ford stood back and watched as the woman dashed out of the living room with her phone pressed to her ear. "I hope it wasn't bad news."

"I do. I hope it was terrible news. I hope it was news so bleak she won't be able to lift her head from her pillow for a week."

He turned back to Lila with his eyebrows raised, struggling to suppress a smile. No woman had ever uttered an oath with so much vehemence—and with such a strangely charming schoolmarmish air.

"Uh-oh. You two don't get along?"

The schoolmarm frown turned into a scowl. "Not anymore. The traitor."

"Daddy does that, too." Emily popped her thumb out of her mouth. It had been in there all morning, a sure sign that his daughter wasn't feeling nearly as secure about the day ahead as he'd hoped. A new face was always intimidating for her—a new house doubly so. He'd been half afraid that Emily would take one look at the Vasquez domicile and refuse to cross the threshold, but she'd taken in the quaint spinster furnishings with something akin to pleasure.

It wasn't a castle, she'd announced, but it was the next best thing. Ford was inclined to agree.

"He does what?" Lila asked.

"Pretends to answer the phone when he doesn't want to talk to people. How come that lady didn't want to talk? Doesn't she like kids?"

Lila blinked. "I don't know. I never asked her."

"Don't *you* like kids?"

"I don't know. You're the first one I've ever really met."

Ford tensed, prepared for his daughter's face to crumple in on itself and for the emotional retreat that usually followed interludes of this kind. The amount of rejection his daughter faced on a daily basis was staggering; even the kindest gestures had the potential to cut her down.

But Lila's matter-of-fact response only caused her to giggle. "You're funny. Do I get to pick a puppy now?"

Lila cast a helpless look in Ford's direction, making

him wish he had a pen and paper on hand. It was impossible to describe that look in words, but he could have captured it in a sketch easily enough. When she'd answered the door, he'd been surprised to find that the soft, floaty princess from the night of the ball had been replaced by a woman in what had to be the ugliest suit known to mankind. Ford was no connoisseur of female clothing—at least, not unless there was a rainbow unicorn emblazoned somewhere on it—but even he knew that something his mother might have worn in the eighties was hardly suitable for a statuesque woman with the most luminous eyes he'd ever seen.

Strangely enough, the outfit didn't make her less attractive. If anything, it drew him to her even more. He liked incongruities. He liked knowing there were several different layers to peel off this woman.

And, no, that wasn't a sexual innuendo. At least... not entirely.

"Don't look at me." He laughed and stepped back. "I'm new at all this. I was given an address and an order to place myself at your disposal. I'm not ashamed to admit how appealing I found the idea."

Her lips pursed. "Listen, Mr. Ford."

"Ford."

"That's what I said. Mr. Ford."

"You can drop the 'mister.' Or the Ford, but that might start to sound strange after a while. I suppose you could also call me Daddy, which is what Emily prefers, but—"

"Ford!" The schoolmarm pulled up to her full height. "I hardly think that's an appropriate request, given the circumstances." As if just realizing that there was a child standing at her knee watching the exchange with rapt attention, Lila drew in a sharp breath. "I'm sorry, Emily."

Without so much as a sign of wariness or hesitation, his daughter asked, "What for?"

It was wrong of him to take so much delight in the wash of expressions that moved over Lila's stern face, but he couldn't resist. She hadn't been joking when she'd said Emily was one of the first kids she'd ever met. He'd never known anyone so obviously far out of her depth.

"Circumnavigation," he said.

She blinked at him, those glorious eyes flashing. "What?"

"Perpetuity."

"Are you feeling okay?"

"Antidisestablishmentarianism."

She cast a quick look around. "Uh…"

"She's six years old. Words with more than four syllables and double entendres tend to pass below the radar. I promise you're safe with me."

"Are you telling jokes again, Daddy?" Emily said. Without waiting for an answer, she pulled Lila's hand into her own. "He *always* tells jokes to ladies. They think he's super funny."

Lila cast him an arch look, although her face remained pointed at Emily's. "They do, do they?"

"He doesn't tell jokes to Principal Brown, though."

"That's probably for the best."

"Or Mrs. Bates. She lives next door."

"A model of restraint."

"Or Grandma Louise."

Lila's lips twitched in what he suspected was the beginning of a smile. She vanquished it, though, causing a tiny indentation to appear at the corner of her mouth. *A dimple*. The princess-schoolmarm had a dimple—a tiny crack in an otherwise uncrackable exterior.

"How old is your principal, Emily?" she asked.

Ford straightened. He could guess where this was going, and it wouldn't end well for him. "Oh, well, that's not really—"

"Ninety? A hundred? I don't know. She has gray hairs—lots of 'em."

"So he doesn't tell jokes to older ladies?" Lila asked.

"Nope." His little traitor shook her head gravely. "Or ladies with husbands."

There was no way to save himself now. Emily, that sweet little soul of discretion, a child who couldn't look most adults in the face, let alone divulge his greatest sins to them, had betrayed all.

"Oh, look at that. My phone's ringing." He made a show of grabbing his cell phone out of his back pocket and holding it to his ear. "Yes, hello? It's an emergency? You don't say. What terrible timing. I guess I'll have to drop everything and come running."

Emily, well versed in his tactics, giggled obligingly. The sound was followed by a low, throaty chuckle that almost caused him to drop the phone.

That laugh, composed of equal parts phone-sex operator and chain-smoking screen goddess, was the final seal in a devastating turn of events.

This whole thing should have been a gift from heaven—in fact, it *was* a gift from heaven—this opportunity to match Emily with a service dog hand-selected and trained specifically for her. Pendred syndrome, the inner-ear disorder she'd been born with, not only impacted her balance and thyroid, but it also placed her in the moderate-to-severe hearing loss range. Cochlear implants helped quite a bit, as did lip reading and the occasional use of sign language, but there was a limit to what science could do for her.

Ford had done his best to teach his daughter to navigate a world where sound wasn't always a reliable source of information, but his best had a tendency to fall short of its goal. Emily was bright, hilarious, and everything he had in this world. She was also terrified of anything even a little bit outside her comfort zone.

So, yes. A service dog was the ideal next step in helping her build her confidence. That was why he'd been prepared for six weeks of hard work. He was ready for the late nights of puppy training and cleanup. He'd even been willing to don a suit and tie and smile at the appropriate benefactors who made all this possible.

But no one had told him about Lila Vasquez.

Not about how gracefully she moved or how perfectly she'd be able to match his steps in the waltz. Not that she was a woman of perfect proportions, the slender line of her waist leading to enticing curves above and below. *Definitely* not that the sound of her laughter would cause him to wish, for the first time in his life, that he had more to offer a woman than a charming smile and the ability to braid the shit out of a little girl's hair.

His equilibrium was offset enough that he committed to the lie, taking his fake phone call into the next room. He paused at the threshold to what looked like a bathroom, waiting to see what Lila would do next.

"Where are the puppies?" Emily asked.

"In the kennel attached to the back of the house. Do you want to meet them?"

Even though his back was to the pair, he could practically feel Emily's jaw drop. "*All* of them?"

"You can *meet* all of them, but you can't take all of them home. Other people need them, too, which means you can only choose one."

As before, there was no need for him to watch to gauge Emily's reaction. Nothing in the world would delight his daughter more than to be thrown into a pit of puppies and told to pick whichever one she wanted. It was like the world's largest candy store and theme park wrapped into one.

Which was why he tucked the phone away with a sinking heart.

Lila's obvious lack of experience with children might have been amusing to start out with, but she clearly didn't know how attached a six-year-old could become within the space of a few minutes. He liked dogs, he really did, but if Emily got her heart set on something like a greyhound or a Saint Bernard, which required more care than he had time to give, he was going to have to pull out his full bad-cop routine.

And he didn't mean that in the fun way.

"Actually, before we go in, I was hoping we could—"

"Oh, is your phone call done?" Lila asked with one eyebrow carefully arched. "I wouldn't want to interrupt something important."

"Crisis averted," he said, refusing to take the bait. "One crisis, at least. But before we create another one, we should probably lay a few ground rules."

"Ground rules? About what?"

Off the top of his head, he could think of at least three, but none of them had anything to do with his daughter or puppies. On the contrary, they were founded solely in his body's unexpected reaction to Lila's laugh.

I will not picture this woman naked.

I will not picture this woman naked and in my bed.

I will not picture this woman naked and in my bed and making those phone-sex operator noises.

Those were three very good rules, and he planned to stick to them at every turn. Starting…soon. Very soon.

"Our house isn't large," he said, his voice only slightly strangled. He couldn't help it—he was still caught up on that first rule. Lila's beige suit might not be flattering, but there was something about the boxy simplicity that enhanced every long limb and packed curve contained inside it. "So the dog needs to be on the small side."

"Oh, *dog* ground rules."

"And my schedule is a flexible one, but I can be up against some pretty tight deadlines, so a puppy that's going to require three-hour walks every day is a definite no."

"Mr. Ford—"

He sighed and ran a hand through his hair. If she was going to insist on calling him Mr. Ford for the next six weeks, he was going to have a seriously difficult time with that whole not-picturing-her-naked thing. Formality might work in putting some men off, but that air of authority was only making things worse.

"Ford," he said again, corralling his thoughts into a semblance of order. "Just Ford. And I don't mean to tell you how to do your job, but Emily can be—"

Stubborn wasn't right. Nor was *difficult*, though both those words occasionally applied. *Complicated* was more like it. The poor kid had only one parent, and not a very good one at that. She had regular appointments with audiologists, endocrinologists, and every other -ologist under the sun. She'd undergone her first surgery at age three and, since her condition was a degenerative one, probably had a lifetime more of them to look forward to.

She was a tough little bird, yes, but there was a limit to what he was willing to make her endure. A broken heart over a puppy she couldn't have was that limit.

"She's fast?" Lila suggested with another of those wonderful laughs. She nodded her head toward the back of the house, where Emily had made a beeline for the back door. His daughter was in a phase where the only kind of shoes she'd wear were soft-soled ballet flats that made about as much sound as a whisper on the wind. It was impossible to hear her coming—or going.

And she was going, no doubt about that. She'd known what was about to happen and decided to take matters into her own hands.

"Emily, you can't—" he called, but it was too late. Emily had already disappeared through the back door, slamming it gleefully behind her.

"They won't hurt her," Lila said as she began what seemed like the slowest possible walk in that direction. Slow *and* sultry, he noted, as though the only way to reduce her speed was to move her hips like a pendulum in slow motion. He could only assume she was doing it to torture him. Well, either that or to give Emily time alone with the puppies. "They're all exceptionally well behaved."

"It's not the puppies I'm afraid of," he admitted. "It's what's going to happen when she picks the biggest, slobberiest one you have, and I have no choice but to drag her away. You obviously have no idea what it's like to be the fun sponge."

Although it seemed impossible, her walk slowed down even more. *Tick, tock*. Back and forth. The steady beat of her body was mocking him.

"The fun sponge?" she echoed.

"One who sucks all the joy out of life. The void of happiness. The black hole of delight."

This time she stopped. Actually *stopped* mere inches from the door. Turning to face him, she asked, "You think you're a fun sponge?"

"Ask anyone," he said with a mock sigh. "I'm the biggest fun sponge on the block."

"And you think *I'm* not?"

The incredulity on her face almost had him laughing out loud. "Well, I don't know you very well, obviously, but based on what I've seen so far, I'd have to say no."

"Me?"

"Other than your weird dislike of white teeth, sure." He shrugged and shoved one of his hands in his pocket. It was dangerous to bring up the night of the ball, but he had no other choice. *She* might have been able to set her kindness toward Emily aside like it was nothing, but he'd been reeling ever since. "Think about it—your job is literally to play with puppies every single day. You went to a stuffy black-and-white-tie ball in a sparkling pink dress and pulled it off with panache. You make Emily laugh. Come to think of it, you make *me* laugh. That all sounds pretty fun to me."

Lila opened her mouth and closed it again, looking at him as though he'd arrived from a distant star.

Before she could reply, the door swung open again and Emily's head peeped through the opening, an expression of such rapture on her face that Ford knew he was done for. He hadn't seen his daughter light up like that in a long time.

Great. They were getting a Saint Bernard. They were probably getting *two* Saint Bernards, the pair of them conjoined at the massive, hairy hip.

"It's Christmas," she breathed. "Daddy, come see! It's Christmas."

He cast one last forlorn look at Lila before following his daughter into the dog kennel. This was going to be a long, painful slog of daily three-hour walks and buckets of dog slobber, but for Emily, he'd endure much worse.

His first thought as he moved through the door was that it was unlike any dog kennel he'd ever seen before. Instead of crates, each animal was held in a half-walled pen that allowed them to run and jump and sniff happily at the creature next door. It was also, as his daughter suggested, a lot like Christmas. There weren't any decorations up or anything like that—there was still a good month to go before the holiday hit—but half of the dozen or so puppies inside were adorned with giant red bows around their necks.

"Look!" Emily cried, as if his eyes weren't already open and drinking in the various puppies around him. "Presents. For *me*!"

"Emily, moppet, they aren't all for you—" he began, but he was cut short by Lila's low laugh.

"Yes, actually. They are." She brushed past him and

squatted down to Emily's level. It was the sort of thing that was going to be the death of him—not only was it a kind thing to do to make a little girl feel more comfortable, but it made it easier for Emily to understand her. "Emily, all the puppies with red bows are ones you can choose from. I picked them out specifically for you. They're the ones who are best at hearing the important sounds you might sometimes miss. They're not too big to follow you around school, but they *are* big enough to help catch you when you get dizzy sometimes. And most importantly, they love kids."

In other words, she'd done her research—and done it well. This woman he'd met only once had somehow anticipated every one of his fears and staved them off at the outset. He relaxed and crossed his arms, watching the pair of them interact. Apparently, he'd underestimated the princess.

"Any one of them will be a perfect fit for you." Lila added, "But—and this is the most important thing—you have to play with each and every one of them."

"I do?"

"Absolutely. This is going to be your dog for years and years, so you need to be sure you're going to be best friends first."

Emily's eyes widened, the weight of the decision heavy on her shoulders. "Okay," she said and lifted her finger. "I want that one."

"You want to play with him first? Sure. Let's get him out, and—"

"No, I don't want to play. I want him. I pick that one."

Ford had to struggle to keep his lips from twitching.

"Right. So, there's a special yard out back where you can introduce yourself. Then, when you're done with him, we can bring him in and we'll get another one out."

"No, thank you." Emily was nothing but polite as she turned down each and every one of Lila's suggestions. "I want the floofy one with the curly ears."

"Um." Lila cast a helpless look up at Ford. "Am I not explaining this correctly?"

"Oh, you're doing just fine. Better than most, in fact. But I warned you how it would be."

"His name is Jeeves," Emily announced.

"Actually, his name is—"

"Jeeves von Hinklebottom."

"I'm not sure—"

"Jeeves von Hinklebottom the Third."

Although Lila didn't look convinced, the floofy puppy with the curly ears seemed to accept his name with dignified grace. Then again, that could have just been how he always looked. There was something about his shaggy face—a perfect blend of black and white—and dark, piercing eyes that made him appear preternaturally wise. Especially when all he did was sit down and lift his head in a majestic nod.

That was a Jeeves von Hinklebottom the Third if Ford had ever met one.

With a laugh, he decided to come to Lila's rescue. It seemed the least he could do after she was so careful to set up a selection process that his daughter quashed in thirty seconds flat. "Jeeves looks absolutely perfect to me. What is he? A poodle of some kind?"

"Half poodle and half cocker spaniel, actually. He's what's known as a cockapoo. They're perfect for kids and perfect as hearing service dogs, but I wasn't kidding about the whole meet-and-greet process. She really should try to get to know them all first."

"I don't doubt it," Ford agreed. He held out a hand to help hoist Lila to her feet. He liked the way her palm felt, smooth and strong against his. "But as much as you might know dogs, I know kids—or *this* kid, anyway. She knows what she wants. Once she makes a decision, it's made, and woe to the man, woman, or child who gets in her way. It's a bit of a family failing, to be honest."

He had yet to release Lila's hand. Before he could second-guess himself, he tugged, drawing her closer. He didn't embrace her or touch any part of her except the hand she'd offered, but it didn't matter. The space between them was its own physical entity—a hot, pulsating thing he could almost reach out and touch. The enticing jut of her chest stopped mere inches away from his own, her chin tilted so that their eyes were level.

"We know a good thing when we see it," he added, his voice low.

Lila's lower lip fell, her soft pink mouth open just enough for an enterprising man to take advantage. Unfortunately, Ford's enterprising days were long behind him. All he had now were awkward, semi-inappropriate jokes to prop himself up.

"Jeeves peeves. Hinklebottom pinklebottom." Emily started laughing and dancing around the kennel, winding herself through their legs like a snake. "Daddy, did you hear me? I said 'pinklebottom.'"

"Yes, moppet. I heard." He heaved a sigh and released Lila's hand. The moment was lost—and with it, all chance he had of being the least bit suave. Once upon a time, he'd had suavity. Heaps of it, in fact. But it had long since been buried under stale Cheerios and lost sippy cup lids. "There's a whole alphabet for you to torture this poor animal with. What a treat for us all. Well, Lila? Is there something I'm supposed to sign? I can tell you right now the only way you're parting that child from that puppy is with a crowbar."

"What? Um. Yes." She blinked at him, still open-mouthed, still enticing as all hell. Not that it mattered. She managed to wrangle herself back into the school-marm zone within seconds. "There are a few things to fill out and go over before you take him home. I'll grab your schedule and your first day instructions so we can get started. You and Emily can stay here with Cooper—I mean, um, Jeeves."

"Von Hinklebottom," Ford supplied.

"I'm not saying that part."

"The Third."

"Or that."

"Uh-oh." He tsked, unable to help himself. Granted, it would have been so much better to be the suave man in a tuxedo, to take the princess into his arms and plant a masterful kiss on her lips, but he could only work with what he was given. "Sounds like someone is turning into a fun sponge."

She stiffened as if she hadn't been arguing *for* that not ten minutes ago. "I beg your pardon."

"The void of happiness."

"I'm no such thing."

"The black hole of delight." He waited only until she opened her mouth to retaliate before bestowing a liberal wink. "Don't worry. Holes of delight happen to be one of my specialties."

With a gasp and a blush, Lila turned on her heel and stalked out. He watched her go with a combination of admiration and regret. Admiration, because there was no doubt in his mind that Lila Vasquez was a woman worth getting to know. Regret, because knowing women—in the literal sense, in the Biblical sense, in any sense that mattered—was something he'd done without since the day his ex-wife had left, determined that *one* of them, at least, should make something of their life.

She'd done it, too, her professional accolades gathering by the dozen. It made his own accomplishments look paltry by comparison. Ford Ford might be able to make the young, unmarried ladies laugh, but that was only because he wasn't in a place to offer them anything else.

And that, unfortunately, was his *real* specialty these days.

chapter
3

"Knock, knock!"

No sooner had Ford pulled his trusty, if ancient, minivan into his driveway than a singsong voice hailed him from behind a snow berm. The problem with winters in Spokane wasn't the cold weather or the heavy snowfall, both of which he liked, but the fact that those giant mounds of plowed snow were the perfect hiding places. Not only did they conceal little girls who had a love of snowball fights while he was trying to unload groceries, but they also made it impossible for him to see women like Helen Griswold until they were practically on top of him.

"It's freezing out here!" She laughed as she knocked again—this time with her glove-covered knuckles on the driver's-side window. She also made a liberal rolling motion with her hand.

"Don't do it, Daddy," Emily warned from the back seat. "Me'nember what happened last time?"

Alas, he me'nembered. He me'nembered all too well. It had taken two hours and a promise to attend her annual Christmas block party to get rid of Helen. Unfortunately, one of them had to be the adult in this car.

That adult was him. It was *always* him.

"Don't be rude, Emily," he said with a severity he was far from feeling. Complying with Helen's request to open the window, he turned and put on his blandest smile. "Hello, Helen. You're looking positively radiant today. Or maybe that's just the frostbite settling onto your cheeks."

She blinked her hazel eyes, which were, in fact, looking quite nice. Snowflakes had caught in the lashes and were sparkling in the midday sun. When matched with the rosy glow of her ice-kissed cheekbones and the knit cap pulled down around her ears, she was an unquestionably attractive woman.

She was also an unquestionably nosy one.

"Oh, you," she said with a titter and a flash of teeth that Ford had to admit were a little too white for his tastes. Maybe Lila was onto something with that whole gleaming-enamel thing. There was something unsettling about it. "Always such a jokester. I haven't been out here long. I saw you pull up the street and dashed right out. Is Emily with you?"

Without waiting for an answer, she leaned forward and popped her head in the window. "Oh, there you are, love," she said, raising her voice to a near-shout and painfully enunciating each syllable. "And how are you today?"

"Daddy," Emily said by way of answer. "Jeeves has to pee."

"Good afternoon, Em-ee-lee," Helen repeated, louder this time.

"He's gonna pee on my new tights."

Helen pulled her head back out again, her hair tickling

against his cheek as she went. "Poor little thing," she murmured. "Rough day?"

Ford bit back a sigh and turned to his daughter, making a quick hand sign for her to be polite and say hello. Emily complied, but sullenly, not the least bit pleased at finding herself in the wrong. Technically, she wasn't—the last time he'd lectured her on her behavior toward their neighbor, he'd stressed the importance of saying something nice or not saying anything at all—but he hadn't expected her to take him quite so literally.

Not that he could blame her for it. No matter how much time Helen spent with them or how many times he tried to explain it, she always seemed to think a loud voice and slow speech were all that were necessary to overcome Emily's challenges.

"Did you have a doctor's appointment this morning?" Helen persisted as she stepped back to allow him out of the car. "We missed you at drop-off."

"Oh, our errand today was much better than a doctor's visit," Ford said, careful to keep his tone light. He had to. It was the part of the game they played, the persona he'd cultivated after years of living in a neighborhood like this one.

It contained mostly women—mostly single—and a nicer and more supportive group of people he had yet to meet. Since the day he'd moved in, women like Helen Griswold and Maddie Thomas and Danica DeWinter had gone above and beyond to help him figure out this whole single-parent thing. Most of them had children in Emily's kindergarten class, and most of them were kind, knowledgeable, genuinely interesting human beings who'd helped him out of a tight corner more times than he cared to admit.

Therein lay the problem. He *liked* them. He appreciated them. But there were times when all he wanted to do was unload his daughter and her new puppy without being interrogated about it. The women were invested in everything, from his childcare to his (lack of a) dating life. He'd once tried making up a girlfriend in Canada in the hope that it would buy him some space, but all that had done was launch a series of questions about maple syrup and universal health care that he was sure he'd failed at the outset.

"Daddy!" came a shout from inside the minivan. "He's peeing. I told you."

Helen lifted her brow at him.

"He's peeing," Ford apologized. "She told me. I should know better than to doubt a lady's word."

Without waiting for her to say more, Ford ducked his head and bolted around the van to extricate his daughter and the wriggling puppy, who was making quick work of turning the upholstery into his own private bathroom.

Lila had warned him that Jeeves might take a few days to settle into his new home and new routine, but she hadn't mentioned that the animal had little bladder control. Gently lifting the puppy and aiming his pink belly away from the van, Ford had to stand there, looking like a cherub in a stone fountain, until Jeeves had finally reached empty.

"He's not used to such refined company," he said when Helen came around to join them, a look of inquiry on her face. "His best friend was a mongrel, his last girlfriend a cur."

"His last girlfriend…?"

"You can't hold him like that." Emily hopped down from the van and held her arms out for her puppy. "Princess Lila said to be gentle. You're not being gentle."

Considering the streak of yellow snow leading from his formerly more-or-less clean van, he felt he was being extraordinarily gentle, but he complied with his daughter's request all the same. To be fair, Jeeves *was* a cute little thing, his curls flopping into his eyes and alternate patches of black and white all over his warm, chubby body. He was even cuter once Emily got hold of him. Ford had no idea whether all the puppies at Lila's kennel were this well behaved or if Emily had some kind of sixth sense, but Jeeves had taken to his daughter as quickly as she'd taken to him. As soon as the cockapoo—a name Ford found almost as ridiculous as his own—was clasped in her puffy-coated arms, he hefted a sigh of pleasure and rested his little head on her shoulder.

Only try to separate us now, that little head seemed to say—and in a British accent, too. Unlike him, Jeeves von Hinklebottom the Third had been aptly named.

"Oh, how sweet!" Helen cooed. "You got a pet. Isn't he the most precious, sweetest little—"

Emily stiffened. "Jeeves von Hinklebottom the Third is *not* a pet," she informed their neighbor in the exact same tone Lila had used with her. The stern, serious look was also identical. They both wore it too well for Ford's peace of mind. "He has a very 'portant job to do. You can't touch him."

"Well, really. That's not very nice."

"No, it's not. Her delivery could use some work."

Apparently, Emily disagreed. With a pert toss of her head, she added, "He is a servistus animal. No one can pet him but me and Daddy and Princess Lila."

"Is there a reason she keeps referencing Star Wars?"

Ford had to laugh. Helen Griswold was the divorced mother of two very imaginative, very rambunctious boys who believed the entire world began and ended in a galaxy far, far away.

"It's Princess *Lila*, and she's the dog trainer," he explained. He also started hoisting supplies out of the back of his van, even though he had no idea where he was going to put them all. For such a small animal, Jeeves had an awful lot of baggage. People had sailed on the *Titanic* with less. "Jeeves here is Emily's new hearing service animal. Or he will be, after six weeks of intensive training with Washington's finest dog expert."

Helen wrinkled her nose. "Washington's finest dog expert is a member of the royalty?"

"Oh, yes." There was no doubt in Ford's mind about that. A more commanding, regal woman he had yet to meet. And expensive. Even though he wasn't paying for the puppy or the training, thanks to Lila's generosity and a grant from the Auditory Guild, he'd looked up Puppy Promise's usual rates. If he worked very hard and donated an internal organ or two, he *might* have been able to save up enough by the time Emily was ready for college. "We were lucky to get her. But most of the early training has to take place at home, so Emily will be out of school until after the holidays. That's why we weren't at drop-off this morning."

Emily had tired of their company by this time, so

she wandered off across the yard with her puppy in her arms, pointing out to him the various items worthy of note. As these included such fascinating subjects as the mailbox—don't pee on that—the birdhouse—don't pee on that—and her tire swing—definitely don't pee on that—Ford let her make the grand tour without him.

He'd hoped that the explanation would signal the end of the conversation, but Helen placed her hand on his arm and adopted a low, confidential tone. "Won't it be tough for you, having her home all day?" she asked. The question was a lot like her—kindly meant, but far too intrusive for Ford's peace of mind. "What about your work? Your free time? Your social life?"

Ford kept his mouth clamped shut, even though he could have enlightened Helen about any of those subjects. His work as an instruction manual illustrator, done mostly hunched over his drafting desk in the kitchen, would have to be fit in around puppy training sessions. His free time had been a long-running and not very funny joke for years. And as for a social life, well, you could hardly miss something you didn't have.

But none of those mattered. "Any time I get to spend with Emily is time well spent," he said in a sharp voice he barely recognized.

The effect of his words was both immediate and regrettable. Helen flushed, her already-pink cheeks swelling with red, a hurt expression pulling at the corners of her mouth.

"I'm sorry," he said, instantly contrite. "That came out wrong. I only meant that it's taken care of. I worked out a full schedule ahead of time."

Helen accepted his apology with good grace, but the

damage was already done. "I was only trying to help," she said in a small, downcast voice.

"I know. And I appreciate it."

"I worry about you two, that's all."

"We'd be lost without you," he agreed. "Dropped in the middle of nowhere without a map."

"If we can't count on each other, who do we have?"

"Siri, mostly," he confessed. "And she's not nearly as sparkling a conversationalist as I'd like. I asked her on a date last night, but she told me her lack of a corporeal form would only get in the way."

The last of Helen's dejection fled, and she laughed. Ford had the benefit of knowing that her usual good humor was restored, but he bit back a sigh anyway. There were times when he regretted his tendency to resort to heavy-handed flirtation as a way to handle any social interaction with the opposite sex. What had started as an easy way to maintain emotional distance in the wake of his divorce had become a habit so ingrained that he didn't know how else to act anymore.

It worked with Helen just fine, obviously, and a reputation for playful irreverence ensured that he never sat alone at school functions. Still. It would have been nice to be a *little* bit less like the village fool.

With someone like Lila, for example.

"Alexa, now, she's a little more receptive to my allure," he joked as he finished unloading the van. "So far, she's got me strictly in friendzone territory, but I think I'm making headway. We cooked an Alfredo sauce last night that was to die for."

Helen laughed. She also pulled out her keys so she could unlock the front door for him while his hands were full. It was a small gesture but a thoughtful one, and typical of the women on this street. They carpooled and arranged playdates. They shared house keys for emergency lockouts. They babysat during last-minute appointments and always, always had children's aspirin on hand.

They were, to put it simply, a godsend. He'd never have been able to do any of this without them.

They were wonderful. And so very exhausting.

"Oh, you," she said playfully. "Don't you take anything seriously?"

"Not if I can possibly help it. Haven't you heard? I'm an unreliable rogue."

"I like a good rogue," she said with a grin.

He winked. "You only say that because I haven't called you to help me hide any bodies yet."

The banter had its intended effect, which was to send Helen on her way without any major rift in their relationship. She'd continue to believe him an incorrigible flirt, yes, but that was how the game was played. Since it was the same treatment he afforded *all* the single females of his acquaintance, she wouldn't lose any sleep over him.

He waited only until her retreating form moved down the driveway before sagging against the doorframe. One of these days, he was going to import a *real* girlfriend from Canada and save himself a lot of trouble.

"Are you done making Ms. Helen laugh now?" Emily asked, picking up on the cue at once. "Jeeves is getting cold."

"Yes, moppet," he said and sighed. That child was far too astute for her own good. *And mine.* "You two head on inside. We've got a lot of work to do getting that little guy settled in before Princess Lila comes tomorrow."

At the mention of her dog trainer, Emily perked up. "Do you think she'll wear her dress this time?"

Ford pictured the boxy suit Lila had worn today, as far removed from a princess as a person could possibly get, and laughed. "Maybe we'll call her later and ask," he said, deriving a considerable amount of amusement from imagining that conversation. "It never hurts to try."

chapter
4

Lila stared at her wardrobe with a mounting sense of frustration.

Here she was, a thirty-one-year-old college-educated woman and owner of a successful business. She drove a Prius. She spoke two languages. She had a sound retirement plan.

"Then why, oh, why, is it so hard to pick a stupid outfit?" she muttered.

She didn't have to supply an answer. She already knew full well what was bothering her, and it definitely *wasn't* a man with a ridiculous name and the best laugh she'd heard in her life.

The phone rang from the living room, saving her from the danger of dwelling on that laugh. The landline was their business number, which meant that one of her sisters would be sure to pick up the call. Sophie didn't live in the house anymore, having moved out to live with her boyfriend in Deer Park, but she usually came by for a few hours every morning to do basic training with the puppies. Dawn could be counted on to act as secretary, too, since she rarely left the house before noon.

"Sure thing, Ms. Askari. I'll put her on right away."

Sophie's head popped through the door, a smile on her lips as she took in the sight of Lila standing in front of her closet clad only in her underwear. The smile was no real surprise. Dawn would have told their youngest sister all about yesterday's beige suit. *And* about how she'd defected the moment she caught sight of Ford, leaving Lila at his debonair mercy.

Lila was sure they'd had a good laugh about it at her expense, too. They usually did.

"Lila, there's a woman from the Auditory Guild on line two."

Her sister spoke with a grave voice and professional mien that was largely faked. There was no line two on their phone. There was barely a line one, but when you were trying to impress an organization the size of the Auditory Guild, you improvised.

"Thank you, Soph." She took the phone and tried shutting the door behind her, but that didn't work. Sophie slipped through the crack and started rummaging through the closet, nothing but virtue on her sweet, heart-shaped face.

The traitor. Sophie was just as bad as Dawn—no, she was worse, because at least Dawn owned up to her sneaky, manipulative ways. Sophie was like one of those fluffy, adorable baby owls that blinked innocently before swooping down and murdering entire meerkat colonies. She was a fighter, that one. She'd had to be, since most of her childhood had been spent battling leukemia.

All the sisters' roles in life had been defined by that illness—of those years spent living in a hospital, of never knowing if Sophie's next breath would be her last.

It was in everything they said and did. Sophie looked fragile, yes, but she was forged of steel. On the surface, Dawn offered nothing but saucy indifference, but her heart was as soft and mushy as a bowl of oatmeal. And Lila, well...

Lila got things done. One of them had to, and as the eldest, the task had naturally fallen to her.

"Hello, Anya?" Lila tucked the handset against her chin. "I wasn't expecting to hear from you so soon. Is everything okay?"

"Everything is marvelous, darling. Absolutely marvelous." Anya's voice was breathy and fluttering, more suited for an East Coast society dame than the director of a nonprofit the size of the Auditory Guild, but Lila wasn't fooled. Anya could rip someone apart faster than Sophie and her meerkats. "Listen, I had a chance to talk with Mr. Ford last night, and I want you to know that I'm very pleased with how you're handling things so far."

"Oh. Um." Lila blinked and looked at Sophie, who was holding up some kind of yellow sundress that was laughable for this time of year. Lila shook her head and tried to focus on the call. "I'm glad he likes the puppy Emily picked out. She went with the cockapoo, which was one of my top choices. He's smart and sweet and just the right size for a child."

"Oh, yes. The cockapoo. Of course."

There was a pause that Lila knew from experience presaged a piece of news she wasn't going to like. She'd only known Anya Askari for a little over a year, but with that woman, a few months was all it took. Even before she'd run the Guild, Anya had been a fierce advocate for hearing services, a role she'd risen to after her two young children had been diagnosed with auditory processing disorders. If you wanted to do any kind of work in the field—and Lila did—Anya was there to make sure you did it correctly.

Lila respected the hell out of the woman. She was also terrified of her.

"To be honest, I'm less concerned about the animal and more concerned about you," Anya said, not mincing words. "You know I think the world of the personalized approach you and your sisters take, and I'm thrilled to think that this donation of yours could lead to future cases between us."

She wasn't the only one. Lila knew all too well that this case with Emily Ford was a trial run, a test to see if Puppy Promise lived up to the Auditory Guild's high standards. If they—if *she*—did, there was every possibility that the Guild would subsidize future charitable contracts.

"But?" Lila prompted.

"Well." Anya hesitated again. "The truth is, I was rather hoping you'd have Sophie or Dawn handle the juvenile cases."

As if to prove the wisdom of such a decree, Sophie held up a horrible lime-green bridesmaid dress that Lila had worn to a friend's wedding years ago before dissolving into silent giggles.

"Unfortunately, they're both in the middle of other training right now," Lila said with a glare at her giddy sister. Suddenly realizing the direction this conversation was headed, she stiffened and held the phone more precisely against her ear. "Wait—are you asking me to step down from the Emily Ford case?"

"Well, no," Anya said. "Not anymore. I *did* have my doubts about you, especially after meeting with Emily's medical team, but that was before."

"Before?" Lila echoed.

"Oh, yes. I had a long chat with Mr. Ford, and he couldn't sing your praises highly enough. And that princess ball gown... I have to say, darling, I didn't think you had it in you. It was *enchanting*. I wanted to tell you at the party, but you always seemed to be off hiding in a corner somewhere."

Lila couldn't help a flame of mortification from washing over her. Hiding in corners was precisely what she *had* done. "Oh, yes. Well..."

"Clearly, you understand children better than I thought. I wanted to apologize for doubting you and to let you know that I'm already lining up several other parents who might be interested in a consultation. I won't include you on our list of approved providers until this case with Emily is complete, but you're on the right track." She paused again, this time with a laugh lurking in the subtext. "Did you *really* put Christmas bows on all the puppies?"

Lila felt an inexplicable need to apologize. "I had some red ribbon left over from our groundbreaking ceremony a few years ago. It seemed like a good idea at the time."

"Mr. Ford was delighted by it. And by *you*, I need hardly add."

She didn't want to ask. It was unprofessional. It made her sound desperate.

She asked anyway. "What exactly did he say?"

"That he likes you. That he trusts you. That he

couldn't be happier with the way things are turning out."
Anya let the laugh go, but the soft breathlessness of it
was cut short. "Don't let him down, Lila. He's counting
on you. We all are."

Lila barely had time for these heavy words to settle
before Anya hung up. It was followed by Sophie flounc-
ing forward with a somber black dress Lila had only
worn to funerals.

"Since you don't like any of my other choices, how
about this?" she asked. She held it up to her frame and
grimaced at the overflow of the hem at her feet. Sophie
was a good six inches shorter than her two sisters, something that had always been a source of annoyance to her.
"Hmm. Maybe not. What was that about, by the way?"

Lila took the dress and tossed it onto her bed, which
was showing signs of becoming the untidy heap so often
visible in Dawn's room. "Anya wanted me to know what
a good job I'm doing so far."

Sophie perked up, her eyes widening in delight. "Oh,
Lil—congratulations. That's fantastic news."

"No, it's not." Lila groaned as she surveyed what
remained of her closet. The boxy suits and funereal
dresses that would keep Ford at bay were no good. Any
princess-like confections were out, too, since she was
going to be doing a lot of crawling around with a puppy
today.

Judging by Anya's call—and the implications behind
it—she needed something approachable. Something
soft. Something so wholly unlike her it was laughable.
She had no other choice. People were counting on her.
People were *always* counting on her.

"Why did we ever think it was a good idea to put me

in the same room as a child?" she asked. It was a rhetorical question, so she didn't bother waiting for an answer. "This is your fault, you know. Yours and Dawn's. If you hadn't wrangled me into that piece of pink fluff, none of this would have happened. Everyone would know me for what I am and adjust their expectations accordingly."

Sophie blinked at her, not the least bit intimidated by the criticism. "And what are you?" she asked.

Lila heaved a heavy sigh. That answer was easy.

"I'm the fun sponge."

🐾🐾🐾

Ford Ford's house wasn't at all what Lila had been expecting. Meeting a well-groomed man in a tuxedo—even one with a young daughter—had a way of creating the illusion of secret agents, sleek chrome-filled bachelor pads, and vintage sports cars.

As Lila double-checked the address and pulled up to a tiny brick house, she realized she couldn't have been further from the truth. All the houses on this street were boxy and small—less than a thousand square feet apiece—and almost every yard had some variation of a snowman built in it, with discarded carrots and scarves littering the scene. Christmas decorations were already up in abundance, many of the SUVs and family cars bearing fuzzy antlers and red-felt noses on their front bumpers—including Ford's.

"A minivan?" she said as she pulled open her car door and stepped out. "He drives a reindeer minivan?"

"He has to, unfortunately. He's in charge of car pool one week every month."

Lila held back a small shriek of surprise.

Ford appeared next to the large snow pile that must have been hiding him. "For a while there, I tried cramming the lot of them in my two-door sedan, but it didn't work. For some reason, kids get mad when you make them ride in the trunk." He grinned and drew closer. "Well, that's not true. The kids loved it. Their mothers, however…"

Lila remembered, almost too late, to breathe. The mortification of having been caught disparaging Ford's car was paltry compared to the sensation she felt at seeing him in nothing but a pair of red-and-black buffalo-check pajama pants. He had on boots and a coat thrown hastily over the top, not to mention a small puppy clutched to his bare chest, but he had to be freezing. It was all of twenty-five degrees out here, the windows on every parked car frosted over and clouds of her breath coming out in short, panting puffs.

"We don't have a fenced yard," he apologized as he curled the puppy more protectively against his chest. "And it takes at least half an hour to get Emily layered up to go outside, so that makes me the king of potty breaks. Come on in. Have you had coffee?"

Lila strove to find her tongue, but it was cleaved to the top of her mouth. She'd known that Ford in a tuxedo was attractive, all those folds of dark cloth molded to a body that knew what it was about. Even yesterday at the kennel, in jeans and a sweater, he'd looked a fine figure of a man, his shoulders broad and his stance powerful.

But this? Bare-chested? In the cold? All those firmly etched lines flexing with his every breath?

"I haven't had any either," he said. "Although I *have* fed and watered this little beast, so I figure I'm not doing too bad overall. Oh, *h-e-l-l*. Quick. Let's get inside before—"

"Ford! Ford, you've got to be kidding. You're going to catch your death of cold like that."

Lila turned to find herself being accosted by a pretty brunette in a puffy parka that went down to her knees. She held a steaming mug of coffee in each hand, which she extended toward the pair of them. It took Lila a moment to process that not only was Ford being offered a hot beverage, but she was, too.

"Here. I'll take that little darling so you can hold your cup. Jeeves, you said his name was? Oh—or am I still not supposed to touch him?" This question was directed at Lila, who found herself at a continued loss for words.

She didn't know what it was about these people that threw her so far off-balance, but they did. She was normally able to carry herself well in any situation. All it took was a little authority, a little dignity, and—

"I won't pet him, see? Just cradle him like this. He's awfully sweet." The woman buried her nose in the puppy's neck and inhaled. It was the exact same thing Lila did whenever presented with a four-legged bundle of joy, so she relaxed a little. "That's my special brew you're holding. It has a bit of spice to keep things warm on a morning like this one. I thought you two could use it. My name's Helen, by the way. You must be Princess Lila."

All attempts at relaxation fled, some of the special brew sloshing over the edge of Lila's mug as she reared back. "Oh, I'm not really a—"

Ford coughed heavily and cast a knowing look back over his shoulder. Emily stood in the doorway to the house, a long purple nightgown brushing the tops of her bare feet. It was an ideal opportunity for Lila to assert her position as a woman of good sense, a dog trainer who *one time* wore a pink dress to a party, but Anya's praise still hung heavily around her neck.

"I'm not really supposed to talk about my lineage," she said, resigned to her fate. If getting the Auditory Guild's seal of approval meant wearing crowns and carrying fairy dust in her pockets, then so be it. Dawn and Sophie were more suited to the post, obviously, but they didn't have a monopoly on benevolence.

She could do cheery. She could do light. She was even wearing some kind of gold-threaded sweater to prove it. It was the only thing she and Sophie could find that screamed *princess pizzazz.*

"It's a secret because of matters of immediate political importance," she added. "Like, um…" She scanned her memory for the most child-friendly diplomatic issues plaguing the world, but nothing seemed to fit. Chemical warfare reserves seemed a touch dark, as did systemic and concentrated genocide. And she was no expert, but she was pretty sure no kid wanted to hear about capital-gains taxes.

Ford seemed to note her struggle, his lips hovering over a grin. "The evil prince trying to take over her throne," he supplied.

Ah, yes. Evil princes. How could she have forgotten that one?

"He's my brother," Lila lied, thinking fast. "My twin brother."

Ford winked. "Her *evil* twin brother."

"Oh dear," Helen murmured sympathetically. "How terrible for your whole country."

Lila was impressed by the way Helen took it all in stride. She must have kids of her own. Apparently, a fertile imagination was one of those things they handed out at the hospital after a baby was born, like maternal instincts and those cute knit caps in alternating shades of pink and blue.

Lila took a sip of the coffee, surprised to find it as delicious as promised, with a hint of cinnamon and cayenne to spice the blood. However, Helen was giving no signs of leaving, which made Lila suspect that it wasn't really *her* she'd come over to caffeinate. She'd probably peeked out the window and seen Ford without a shirt. It was enough to get any hot-blooded woman's morning routine going.

Emily had disappeared from the doorway, so Lila took that as her cue to follow suit. "I'll take Jeeves in and start setting up the training." She reached for the puppy, that warm bundle of fur so easygoing that he took being handed from one person to another in stride. "Thank you for the coffee."

"No, wait." Ford stilled her with a hand on her arm. "I'll come with you. I'd like to watch how you do things."

"I can see I'm only in the way," Helen said, cheerfully unconcerned with being given the brush-off. "But before you go, Ford, I wanted to see if you're free this weekend. I hate to ask on such short notice, but I need a plus-one for a holiday party my work is throwing. I already have a sitter lined up for the boys, so you'd be more than welcome to leave Emily with them."

Now Lila *definitely* wished she'd escaped while she had the chance. She might have made another attempt, but Ford was still clinging to her forearm, his grip strangely firm.

"That's a tempting offer, but Lila will be keeping me pretty busy for the next few weeks."

She opened her mouth to protest. Hard work and diligence were important to ensure a successful placement, yes, but even she wasn't so unyielding that she required her clients to give up their entire weekends. Before she could utter so much as a syllable to that effect, Ford's clasp on her tightened even more.

"Isn't that right, Princess Lila?"

Well able to take a hint when it was being imprinted on her skin, she forced a smile. "Oh, yes. Weekdays, weekends, nights... A dog trainer's work is never done."

Helen frowned. "Really? Nights?"

"She's *very* diligent. It's her royal blood."

"But on a Saturday evening?"

Ford looked at Lila with a note of such appeal in his eyes that she found herself nodding along. She'd always thought she was impervious to that kind of pleading—puppies were notoriously good at it, the wretches—but something about it coming from a fully grown man knocked her sideways.

"I'm afraid so," she said. And since the lies seemed to be stacking up around her, she decided to add a bit of truthfulness. With a self-conscious pat on Jeeves's head, she added, "I'm kind of a stickler about things like that. About everything, really."

Ford's grip on her relaxed. "And you know how obedient I am, Helen." He winked. "Especially when the commands come from a woman like this one."

Lila wasn't sure she cared to hear what he meant

by that—if it was her stern demeanor or her apparent inability to work with children that made her so intimidating—but she should have known better than to trust a word out of his mouth.

Helen certainly didn't. "Oh, please. Getting you to do anything you don't want to is like trying to take one of my kids to the dentist." She beamed at Lila. "From the way they carry on, you'd think I was dragging them to their deaths. Well, either that or the hairdresser."

"They're not wrong about the hairdresser," Ford interjected. "I still remember that unfortunate episode you had with the bowl cuts."

A laugh escaped Lila before she could prevent it. Nothing about the conversation was in any way out of the ordinary—at least, not considering who Lila was having this conversation with. It didn't seem to matter to either Helen or Ford that they were discussing haircuts while Lila had a cockapoo held in one hand and a cup of coffee in the other—or that it was below freezing while they did it.

But at the sound of Lila's laughter, the other woman glanced back and forth between them, her lips parted in a sudden smile. "Oh, I see," she said with a knowing nod.

"See what?" Lila asked with a quick look over her shoulder.

When she turned back, it was to find Helen pointing first at Ford and then Lila, her smile spreading. "You should have mentioned something earlier," she said. "I wouldn't have barged in on you like this if I'd known."

Known what? Lila assumed Ford was just as mystified as she was, but his expression had relaxed into a devastating grin—a grin that was pointed directly at her. She was still reeling from it when he spoke again.

"Am I that obvious?" Ford asked, shaking his head with a mock sigh. "I was hoping to keep the news quiet for a little longer, but it's impossible now. You found me out."

"Well, really," Helen breathed. "I had no idea."

"Neither did I," Ford admitted. "But there's no use trying to hide what's staring us all in the face, is there? I hadn't spent five minutes in Lila's company before I realized my life would never be the same."

That last bit was directed at Lila. Her shock at hearing the declaration on Ford's tongue—how easily it tripped off, how natural it sounded—was swallowed in a squeal of delight. And not her own. Despite the fact that Lila was holding both a puppy and a mug of hot coffee, Helen showed every intention of pulling her into a wintry hug.

Acting on instinct, Lila backed away, but all that did was force her against Ford's chest. She had no idea how she could feel the heat of him through her thick wool peacoat, but she could have sworn that the temperature of all the places where their bodies touched jumped a good twenty degrees. Although he was no longer holding her arm, his stance made it impossible for her to flee.

Helen had to settle for a smile that seemed genuine, despite the fact that she'd just been turned down for a date. "Ford, you devil. Leading us all on like that. Maddie and Danica are going to be devastated."

"Alas, that's always been my curse." Ford clucked his tongue and sighed. "Leaving a trail of broken hearts wherever I go. I warned you how it was from the start."

"Well, I'm delighted to finally meet you, Lila, and can only apologize for monopolizing so much of your time." Helen laughed and shook her head, curls bouncing playfully around her shoulders. "I should have known something was up the moment I saw you two together. It was the royal blood that threw me off. We'd always been told you were from Canada."

"Canada?" Lila echoed, so far out of her depth that she was finding it difficult to come up for air.

"Well, I could hardly tell you her real country of origin, could I?" Ford asked. "What with the succession in so much danger and all." He still stood at her back, so close that his breath was a warm whisper against her neck. Lila hadn't worn a scarf that morning, but she firmly resolved to do so tomorrow. There was something caressingly intimate about his lips so close to her skin.

Touching but not touching. Laughing but not laughing.

Helen made the motion of a zipper over her lips. "I won't tell a soul. And bring those coffee cups back whenever, you two. I'm never in a hurry to do dishes."

Lila didn't dare breathe until Helen had walked to the end of the drive, darted a quick look down either side of the street, and dashed into a cozy-looking house situated diagonally to Ford's. Lila didn't move for a good thirty seconds after that, either, busy as she was trying to come up with something rational to say.

"It's a lovely view of the neighborhood, but would you mind too much if we went inside now?" Ford's voice was still far too close for her peace of mind. "I don't know about you, but I'm freezing my *t-i-t-s* off out here."

Lila's body gave another one of those involuntary twitches. She blamed it on the fact that he'd spelled the word out, making her fear that Emily was standing mere feet away and had overheard everything. But when she whirled around, it was to find the pair of them alone in the yard and Ford's tits very much on display.

If you could call them that, anyway. There was nothing soft or bouncing about his wall of a chest and clearly defined pec muscles.

"Yes, well. That's not my fault," she said. She wished she sounded more in control of herself, but it was a wonder that her voice worked at all. "I remembered to cover mine up before I left the house."

"I noticed. That was probably wise of you, under the circumstances." He nodded and took a sip of his coffee, but there was a lurking twinkle in his eye she didn't quite trust. "The royal circumstances, of course. A princess should be modest and decorous in all things."

"That woman doesn't actually believe I'm a princess, right?"

"Probably not. Helen's no fool."

"Or that I'm from Canada?"

"I'd say there's a fifty percent chance. There's something very northern about your air."

This last one was the most difficult to get out, but it needed to be said. "And she doesn't really think you're…in love with me?"

"Oh, that one was all her." Ford hunched one shoulder in the same half-shrug from the night of the ball. Turning on his heel, he led the way up the sidewalk, pausing only to cast a sheepish glance over his shoulder. "She could tell the moment she saw us together."

"Ford…"

"*T-i-t-s*," he said and pointed at his chest. "I wasn't kidding about them. A few more minutes out here, and I'm going to start developing hypothermia."

Hypothermia was the least of Lila's worries. Flushed with a combination of embarrassment, confusion, and— most of all—a pleasurable warmth that had more to do with Ford's bare chest than she cared to admit, Lila was in much more danger of melting through the snow.

Not that she allowed any of it to show. Even with her scant knowledge of princesses, she knew that at least one of them lived in a remote ice castle up on a hill. Of all the royal personas she might adopt for her own, that seemed the most apt for a woman like her.

Especially when faced with a man like *him*.

chapter
5

S o, the primary goal is for this little guy to become your second pair of ears." Lila sat cross-legged in front of Emily, talking to the child in a low, calm tone that was making it difficult for Ford to concentrate on his work. "Any sound that you think is important, we'll also teach Jeeves is important. That way, if you miss it for whatever reason—because you're doing your homework or watching cartoons or just not having a good day—he can remind you."

Emily nodded solemnly, her eyes wide as she sat at attention next to her puppy and absorbed the importance of what Lila was telling her. Ford was *trying* not to interfere and had turned his chair away from the three of them in hopes that he could focus on the coffee-maker manual he was drawing, but it was difficult.

And not just because there was a gorgeous woman on his living room floor in a golden sweater with her hair swept up in an elaborate crown of braids. The fact that she'd made a genuine effort to look regal was enough to cement her in his heart forever. That she spoke to his daughter as if she were a miniature adult, capable of making her own decisions, was going to be the end of him.

"I'll start. One of the sounds I think is super important is a smoke alarm. Have you heard one of those before?"

Emily giggled. "Only when Daddy burns the toast."

"I like a nice char on my bread," he called over his shoulder. "Crispy and full of flavor."

Lila ignored him. Ever since that morning's encounter with Helen, she'd been doing that a lot—she and Emily both. With the kind of determination rarely seen in a child three times her age, Emily had thrown herself wholeheartedly into the puppy training.

She's just like her mother. And, come to think of it, like Lila.

"Now it's your turn," Lila said. "What sounds are important to you?"

Ford turned back to his drafting desk, determined to concentrate on illustrating the best water reservoir in the history of coffee makers, but it was no use. Emily and Lila were having way more fun than him.

"I like it when the roosters crow at Grandma Louise's house. She has *eight* chickens."

"That's an excellent sound," Lila agreed.

"Are you sure about that?" Ford asked. "Emily failed to mention that of the eight chickens, seven of them are roosters. When they really get going, they're like a choir of sopranos with their throats cut. And usually well before dawn."

"Roosters are kind of like alarm clocks, aren't they?" Lila persisted, still ignoring him. "We can put alarm clocks on our list. That's a good one. Oh! And how about when a car is driving down the road? There are a lot of different traffic sounds we can teach Jeeves."

"Including the ice-cream truck?" Emily asked, getting into the spirit of things.

"*Especially* the ice-cream truck." Lila's pen tapped against the pad of paper in a thoughtful pause. "Let's see, what else… The doorbell, maybe? For when your friends come over to play?"

Ford whipped around and shook his head, but it was no use. Lila wasn't looking at him and therefore couldn't see the warning he was trying to send her way.

"No, thank you."

"You don't have a doorbell? That's okay. Knocking works, too. Jeeves is really smart. We can teach him that they mean the same thing."

"No."

"Well, maybe we could just add it in case—"

"No, no, no, no, NO!" Emily's vehemence grew with each repetition.

"Are you not allowed to answer the door?" *Now* Lila gave him her attention, her head swiveling toward his. "We don't have to teach her to open it—only to know that there's someone there. In case you're in the shower or something."

Ford tried to make the quick motion of a knife across his throat, but Emily's face had already started to crumple in on itself, all of her placid happiness coming to a crushing halt. At the sight of it, Ford's heart started to do the same, clenching with a familiar sensation of frustration and helplessness.

"This is a stupid game," Emily announced. Her thumb went automatically to her mouth, her other hand clutching Jeeves around the neck. The puppy took it like the true gentleman his name suggested, determined to absorb his lady's suffering no matter the cost. "I don't want to play anymore."

Lila looked as though she wanted to protest, but Ford just nodded. "Jeeves could probably use a break. Why don't you take him to your room for a few minutes?"

Emily gave a resolute sniffle, but there was little she could do to prevent the tears from gathering in her eyes. She held her head high as she marched through the living room, her puppy on floppy legs as he trailed in her wake.

"What did I say?" Lila asked as soon as Emily had slammed the bedroom door behind her. The house was so small that the action caused the pictures to rattle on the walls, but Ford wouldn't punish her for it. A slammed door was preferable to the withdrawn silence that so often took over. "Do you guys have a rule about guests that I should know about?"

Ford sighed and scrubbed a hand over his jaw, momentarily forgetting that he had a tendency to get ink all over his fingers while he sketched. "No, there's no rule. In fact, teaching Jeeves to recognize a knock on the door should probably go to the top of the list. In case you didn't notice, neighbors around here have a tendency to drop by at all hours and on the flimsiest of excuses."

At the mention of Helen and those empty coffee cups waiting to be returned, Lila's entire body stilled. "I'm sure it's none of my business," she said.

"Are you?" He sighed. "I'm not. Not after I let Helen walk away without setting the record straight."

Color mounted in her cheeks, but not by so much as a flutter of an eyelash did she show any other signs of discomposure. Which was probably for the best, now that he thought about it. At least *one* of them needed to have some dignity around here, and it obviously wasn't going to be him.

It never was. For as long as Ford could remember, he'd been lacking all those skills that would set him apart as a man of the world. He wasn't particularly driven. He had few ambitions outside of Emily's well-being. And he hadn't had a relationship—not a *real* one, anyway—in years.

It was why he was so good at the Helens of the world. The women in his life looked at him and saw not the shitty ex-husbands who'd left them to raise their children on their own, and not a man who had the potential to break their hearts, but someone who made them laugh. Someone safe. A *game*.

In other words, he was Ford Ford: charming and fun, flirtatious and harmless, great to have at parties.

And never, under any circumstances, to be taken seriously.

"I was hoping it would be a few weeks before we got to this point, but we might as well have the truth out now." He held out a hand to help Lila to her feet, but she only stared at his palm as though it might bite her. Since there seemed nothing else to do, he settled on the floor next to her instead.

He took up much more space than Emily did, which meant that by the time he found a comfortable spot between the coffee table and the wooden castle pushed up against one wall, his long legs extended in front of him, Lila was practically ensconced in his lap.

She didn't shift, though. Not away from him, but not closer to him, either. He was starting to realize that the stillness of her bearing, the careful way she both spoke and moved, was as much a part of her as those dark, penetrating eyes.

He rested his head back on the seat of the couch and sighed. It was a nice change, this restful way of hers. A man could get used to it. Especially one as exhausted as him. Taking care of a puppy in the middle of the night was almost as much work as having an infant.

"You have a smudge of ink on your face," she said by way of breaking the silence.

He grunted a noncommittal reply. He *always* had ink on his face. Either that or finger paint or mashed potatoes or, for reasons he'd never been able to fathom, nail polish. No matter how hard he tried to keep it on Emily's fingers and toes, it invariably ended up all over his person. Usually the carpet, too.

He was nothing if not classy.

Lila grew silent again, once more lulling him into a feeling of peacefulness. He tried to gather his thoughts, to marshal them into the easiest way to make Lila understand the unique position that he and Emily found themselves in, but they seemed a hazy, faraway thing. Just for a few minutes, he wanted to bask in the quiet, to enjoy the light scent of Lila's peach perfume and the warmth of the heater kicking on behind them.

And bask in it, he did. Ripe peaches and soft, supple skin were the last two things he remembered before he drifted off to sleep.

🐾🐾🐾

Lila was having a difficult time deciding which was worse: being so uptight that Anya Askari feared she'd make small children cry, or being so boring that a man fell asleep within seconds of sitting down beside her.

"He could at least have had the decency to drool," she muttered as she tiptoed down the hall to the closed door she assumed belonged to Emily. The yellow heart stickers plastered all over the bottom half were a good indication she was on the right track. "But, no. He looks just as good sleeping as he does awake."

It was his long, dark lashes that did it, curving against his cheekbone like a delicate fall of black lace. Eyelashes that beautiful were so unfair on a man, especially when combined with those clear blue eyes and cheekbones like the metal frame of a skyscraper. No woman stood a chance.

Not Lila or, apparently, coffee-cup Helen.

Since they hadn't had time to work on door alerts yet, she decided to head right in, turning the knob with a gentle snick. The girl didn't look up right away, which Lila took to mean she hadn't heard her come in, but Jeeves already knew his role and went to nudge Emily's hand. His little black nose sought purchase against her palm and remained that way until Emily noticed and glanced up.

"Hey, Emily," Lila said with what she hoped was a casual air. Turning her attention to the diligent cocka-poo, she added, "Good boy, Jeeves. Good alert."

Her pockets were always full of treats for a training session, so she handed one wordlessly to Emily. Like Jeeves, the girl was already learning her job well. She repeated Lila's praise and held her hand out for the puppy to take the reward.

The lick on her palm made Emily giggle. That, in

turn, lifted about eighty tons of weight off Lila's shoulders. She didn't know why the sight of that girl's huge tear-filled eyes had caused such a pang, but they had. Especially since she was pretty sure it was something she'd said that had put them there.

"Your dad is taking a nap," she said quietly, careful to face Emily so the girl could see her lips.

"I hate naps," Emily supplied.

"Me too. They're such a waste, aren't they? When there are so many other things to do?"

Emily nodded, still too sober for Lila's peace of mind. Admittedly, her knowledge of children was small, but they were supposed to be exuberant, hyper little things, weren't they? Like untrained puppies, bouncing from one room to the next.

She remembered that Sophie and Dawn had always been that way. Technically, she was only two years older than Dawn and four more than Soph, but she'd always felt more mature than her age. Even as kids, her sisters had been the ones to chatter and play and make up games that lasted for hours at a time. All while Lila had watched, set apart, wondering what it was about her that turned every party into a wake.

"Can you braid my hair like yours?" Emily asked suddenly. "Like a royal crown?"

More pleased than she cared to admit that Emily noticed her concession to the princess persona, Lila jumped at the chance. "Of course." She dropped the two fingers of her right hand over two fingers of her left—the ASL sign for *sit*—and patted the space between her legs. She wasn't very well-educated in sign language, but considering how much Emily lit up to see her make the attempt, she resolved to improve her studies.

Emily obliged with the request, settling onto her knees and holding herself perfectly still in front of Lila. Turning around, she said, "Daddy makes me sit like this. No wriggles. No talking. Else he messes up."

"Can your dad braid?" Lila asked, impressed. Her own father could barely manage a ponytail holder without snapping his fingers off. With three daughters and a wife who excelled at hair duties, there'd never been any need for him to learn.

"Not like you," Emily confessed as she turned back around. Whatever uneasiness had been left between them fled in that moment. Lila had no idea if it was the mention of Ford that had done it, or if the mere act of running her fingers through the girl's corn-silk hair was the cause, but Emily's guard dropped. "Ms. Helen and Ms. Maddie taught him how. Ms. Helen only gots boys, but Ms. Maddie has a little girl like me."

"Oh?" Lila murmured. She doubted Emily could hear her, seated as they were, so she didn't press the issue.

As it turned out, there was no need. Emily pressed it for her. "Her name is June. She knows all about bugs and how to jump off swings so you get super high. She doesn't want to be my friend."

Lila had no idea what to make of this, so she focused on the intricate twists of Emily's hair instead. Her cochlear implants made some of the side bits a little tricky, but Lila had done her sisters' hair so many times that she was something of an expert.

"Byron and Neil don't want to be my friend, either. Nobody does."

This time, Lila was moved enough to voice a protest, but she stopped herself short. Ford might have found her company so unstimulating that he fell asleep rather than explain Emily's outburst, but the little girl seemed to have no such qualms. She was explaining plenty.

"They have to play with me a'cos their moms make them, but it's not the same as having a real friend." For the first time, Emily showed a tendency to squirm, twisting until she was looking up at Lila. "Do you have real friends?"

Lila was startled enough by the question that she grabbed a rubber band and twisted it around Emily's hair to hold her place. Emily didn't seem to mind that it took Lila so long to gather her thoughts. She sat patiently with Jeeves in her lap, an expectant look in her eyes.

"Well, I have two sisters," Lila eventually confessed.

"And the evil prince brother?"

"Er, yes," she fibbed, remembering her cover story. "Him too. But my sisters aren't evil. They're very nice, actually."

"Like you?"

That startled her even more. "Much nicer," she said. "We work on training puppies together, so we spend a lot of time in one another's company. But as for friends, *real* friends, the kind of friends I'm not related to, no. I don't have many."

Emily sighed wistfully. "Don't you want some?"

That was the most startling question of all. It had never occurred to Lila to question the number of friends she had in her life. She had acquaintances aplenty— work colleagues and old college study buddies, as well as the rare handful of ex-boyfriends she *wasn't* ashamed to own up to. What they didn't provide in terms of social stimulation, her sisters did. Rarely a day went by without the three of them sharing dinner or drinks or, as was more often the case, a barrage of invasive questions and general lack of privacy.

For some reason, Lila felt that didn't count. She loved Sophie and Dawn so much it hurt sometimes, her whole world wrapped up in everything they said and did. But if they'd met as strangers, she doubted either of them would have wanted anything to do with her. They were both so much fun, so alive, so unafraid to put themselves out there.

So unlike me.

"I do want some, actually," Lila admitted. "How about you?"

Emily nodded solemnly.

"Is that why you don't want to teach Jeeves about the door? Because no one comes by to play?"

Emily nodded again, her lower lip quivering. Lila had never seen anything so tragic. What was the matter with the kids on this street that they'd reduce this poor, lonely creature to tears? She had half a mind to storm over to Helen's house and chuck those coffee cups at the door, demanding answers. But although that might be something Dawn would do—in fact, she was pretty sure her sister had thrown a tire iron at a man's house—Lila was a model of decorum. She always had been.

She was not, however, heartless.

"I know that you and I haven't known each other long, but maybe I could be your friend?" she offered. "I'm not very fun, and I don't know any jokes, but—"

"Daddy!" Emily sprang to her feet before Lila could

finish her tentative offer. From the way Ford leaned against the doorframe, his legs casually crossed at the ankle and an unreadable expression on his face, she had a feeling he'd been there a while. "Princess Lila is doing my hair in a crown like hers."

"I see that. It's very fetching on you both."

"And she's going to be my friend. My *real* friend."

"Is she?" That unreadable expression melted into a smile. It was a good smile, all devastating attraction and lopsided charm. Lila felt her heart stutter at the sight. "I'm glad. That means it'll be much easier for me to make her mine."

Lila knew, from a semantic standpoint, that Ford was speaking of friendship. Having his daughter and her dog trainer on friendly terms meant that it would be that much easier for he and the dog trainer to be on friendly terms. That was all.

But the phrasing, that *make her mine*, was doing strange things to her equilibrium. She wasn't the sort of woman who cared to belong to anyone—male, female, or anywhere in between—but for a brief flicker, she felt as though she might be willing to make an exception. To belong to Ford, to matter to him, seemed like an experience worth having.

"Emily, there's a peanut-butter sandwich in the kitchen with your name written all over it," he said, unaware that the world had just tilted on its axis. "And there's a bowl of puppy chow for Jeeves. Make sure you don't get them mixed up. I tasted the kibble, and it's terrible. I don't recommend it."

Emily giggled. "I know. I ate one yesterday. It tastes like worms."

Finding nothing odd in that pronouncement, Ford straightened and watched his daughter trot out of the room, Jeeves obligingly at her heels. Lila got to her feet and made a motion to follow them to the relative safety of the kitchen, but Ford blocked the door, his wide shoulders almost filling the gap.

"You fell asleep," she accused. It wasn't the most pressing issue on her mind, but it seemed the safest.

"I know. I haven't done that in ages. Thank you."

"Oh." She blinked, once again caught unaware. Ford had the disconcerting ability to say the last thing she expected, and with such nonchalance that it threw her seriously off-kilter. "Um. You're welcome?"

He grinned. The ink smudge had been wiped from his face, but that smile was just as effective in making him appear boyishly charming. "You should have warned me that having a puppy is as bad as having an infant. Jeeves howls."

"He does not."

"Like a werewolf under the light of a full moon."

Lila stiffened. It was one thing for Ford to mock her, but to mock her highly trained puppy was another thing altogether. "I beg your pardon. Jeeves has never howled a day in his life. Did you feed him?"

"Of course."

"Water him?"

"He was practically attached to a hose."

"Take him outside to go to the bathroom?"

"Every hour on the hour." Ford shifted from one foot to the other, his blue eyes twinkling. "I think he did it because he missed you. To be honest, I felt a little like howling myself."

That was taking things too far—even for a man Lila was coming to realize was unable to open his mouth without nonsense spouting out. "You did no such thing," she protested. "You don't even know me. I could be a horrible person. I might troll people on the internet or fail to use my turn signal at a busy intersection."

He laughed, the sound deep and rich and devastating to her sense of balance. "If you think not using a turn signal is the worst thing a human being can do, I'm pretty sure we're going to get along fine. Besides, you didn't out me to Helen this morning, and you just offered to be my daughter's friend. The way I see it, that makes you damn near perfect."

She didn't take that as a compliment. She couldn't. Perfect was an insult that had been leveled on her far too many times in her life already. It came mostly from men, and mostly with the intention of making her feel about two inches tall.

Patrick Yarmouth had been the most recent transgressor—and the most painful. *I can't keep up with your goddamned perfection*, he'd said in the same tone he might have used with a serial killer. *Are you even human under all that?*

She hadn't bothered to ask him what "all that" was supposed to be. Her clothes? Her hair? Her *skin*? There were enough lizard-people conspiracy theorists out there that she wasn't sure she cared to hear the answer.

"I'm not perfect," she said stiffly. "And I have half a mind to march over to Helen's house right now and tell her that I've never been to Canada."

He laughed, but it carried a rueful tinge this time. He also lost some of his swagger, his shoulders coming down a fraction. "Please don't do that. I know it was wrong of me to encourage her to think we're dating, but you have no idea what a favor you'd be doing me if you'd pretend to be madly and desperately in love with me. Oh, and jealous in the bargain. Like, the kind of jealous that ends in televisions and baseball bats thrown onto the front lawn."

Lila tried to keep her stiff upper lip, but it was difficult. Mostly because no one would believe it if she started tossing televisions onto front lawns. Not only was it a terrible waste of resources, but all that broken glass would be devastating to puppy toes. She'd end up spending hours crawling over the yard with tweezers in hand.

"Couldn't you have just told her you're not interested in going to her work party?"

"Theoretically? Yes." He sighed. "But it's not what you think. My relationship with Helen is...unique."

"Unique like your relationship with Maddie and Danica?" she guessed.

His eyes flashed with a quick glimmer of humor. "You caught that part, huh? I know how it looks. It *sounds* even worse."

"Try me."

He stole a peek behind him, probably to ensure that Emily wasn't anywhere near, and dropped his voice. "You heard most of it already," he said. Lila had to step closer to hear him, even though proximity to this man was the last thing she needed. There was something about him that was so...*easy*. Easy to like, easy to trust.

Easy to fall for.

"Emily has never been great at making friends."

He sighed. "I don't know why. I used to think it was because of the implants and the speech classes she has to go to, but there's more to it than that. She's… Quiet. Reserved."

Lila nodded. Quiet and reserved were two qualities she was intimately acquainted with.

"So much of her life has been spent being poked and stared at by strangers, dragged from one specialist to the next. She's taken every bit of it in stride, but that's a lot to ask of such a little kid. Add a parent who has no idea what he's doing most of the time, and this is what you get. A six-year-old with the weight of the world on her shoulders."

That was another thing Lila could readily understand. Take an already level-headed child and throw her into a routine of doctors and adult responsibilities, and the results were understandably quiet. Reserved. *Cold*.

"I owe Helen so much," he added candidly. "Helen and Maddie and Danica and pretty much every other parent within a five-block radius. Some days, they're the only way I'm able to get from start to finish. Other days, well…"

"Well?" Lila prompted.

He shrugged his shoulder and offered her a rueful grin. "There's just so many of them." With a laugh, he added, "It was wrong of me to use you like that, and I really am sorry about putting you in that position, but you saw how quick she was to give us some time alone, how easily she dropped her plans for this weekend. She almost never does that. As strange as it sounds, this is the first time in years that I've been able to *breathe*."

If Lila had thought that being physically close to

this man was a bad idea, it was nothing compared to the effect his confession was having on her. His flirtation startled her, his playfulness unsettled her, his charm knocked the air from her chest. Honesty, however, was turning out to be the worst of the lot. In that moment, his handsome face so earnest—so *pleading*—he could have asked her for anything, and she'd have given it to him.

Partially to preclude this catastrophe from taking place and partially because he seemed to expect a response, she nodded once. "Okay."

He shifted, his posture again resuming its strong, wide stance. "Okay, what?"

"Okay, I understand. Okay, I forgive you."

"That's it?" His voice dropped into a note of suspicion. "What's the catch?"

"You are, obviously."

He tilted his head in a question, one brow raised. The arch of that brow was so cool, so debonair, it forced a laugh out of her. This man had no idea what kind of effect he had on women. He probably had no idea how dangerous it was for him to saunter around in the cold without a shirt on, either. Or even *with* one on. He wouldn't be standing there in a skintight thermal and faded jeans, his feet in fuzzy red socks, if he did.

"You don't think it's a little bit weird that every unattached mom in your life is on the prowl?" she asked.

For the first time since she'd met Ford, he looked more flustered than she felt, the tips of his ears glowing adorably pink. He glanced away. "They're not on the prowl. It's just a game we play. It's not easy, meeting people when you have children."

She almost snorted. "Helen's cute. She could swipe

right and have plenty of men lining up to introduce themselves."

"It's not like that. Our kids go to the same school."

"Oh, is that what people find attractive? Proximity and shared bake-sale duties? No wonder I'm still single. I've been going about this all wrong." She shook her head, amazed that such a seemingly intelligent man could be so dense. "Ford, you're a single dad. You're gainfully employed. You have the face of a Skarsgård and the body of a Hemsworth. And from everything I've been able to glean, you'll flirt with anything that has a pulse."

The pink had yet to die down from his ears, but he regained some of his composure. It was accompanied by a mischievous smile she didn't trust. "I didn't quite catch that bit about the Hemsworths," he said.

Lila opted for the high road. "I don't know what you're talking about."

"Or the bit with the Skarsgårds."

"You're missing the point." She leveled him with a careful stare, her breathing only slightly hitched. The look he was giving her was so eager, so *hungry* that it was no wonder he had all of the women in this neighborhood at his feet. "Most men go through life without sending every female they meet into a flutter."

"But every woman doesn't go into a flutter," he pointed out. "You didn't."

She opened her mouth and closed it again, unwilling to make the error of speaking her thoughts aloud. She could have enlightened him on a number of things, including her indifferent feelings toward him, but she didn't. Mostly because her feelings were anything but indifferent. Like Helen and Maddie and Danica and

Lord knew who else, she'd taken one look at him in that tuxedo and counted herself a goner.

Unfortunately—or fortunately, as was more likely the case—she had a job to do. And she'd do it, too, no matter how much his blue eyes twinkled.

"Helen will figure the truth out eventually," she said.

"I know." He hunched his shoulders in an apology, but she wasn't buying it. Not when the gesture was accompanied by a sneaky glance at her from under his lashes. "But would it be the worst thing in the world to play it out a little? You'll be here until New Year's anyway, so it's not like you'd have to go out of your way to spend time with me. Plus, I can pretend you dumped me over the holidays, which means I can hide behind a broken heart for at least six months. I could eke it out a year if you really demolish it. Would you be willing to cheat on me, do you think?"

She just stared at him.

"It's too bad I don't have any brothers, because then you could have an affair with one of them. Or sisters, come to think of it. I suppose I could always kill you off, but…"

"Ford, you wouldn't!" Lila was unable to tell if it was laughter or anger that caused the waver in her voice, but she was balancing precariously between the two. "What about Emily?"

He blinked. "What about her?"

"Um…you don't think it might affect her?"

"Not really, no. She's a smart kid. She'll understand—especially if it means we can have a few free days in the meantime. Helen's a nice woman, and she does her best to try to understand Emily, but she always ends up making her feel small." He feigned a thoughtful look. "The poor child might object to murdering you, though, so that endgame is out."

"I'm *not* having an affair."

"You're an old-fashioned woman, I see. Loyal to the core. That must be what I love about you."

There were so many things wrong with this conversation, not the least of which was the fact that they were holding it inside a child's pink, fluff-filled bedroom— *his* child's pink, fluff-filled bedroom. "I hardly think we've known each other long enough for you to start throwing around the l-word," she said primly.

He laughed. "That shows what you know. All that stuff I told Helen out in the yard was the truth. I was yours the moment I first saw you, ranting about dental hygiene in a giant pink ball gown."

She wouldn't fall for it. She wouldn't fall for *him*.

"If you knew anything about me, you wouldn't call me old-fashioned," she said. "Monogamous, maybe, but not old-fashioned."

The appreciative gleam deepened. "I like the sound of that. Elaborate, if you please. Are we talking about your political views or your *s-e-x-u-a-l* ones?"

It was ridiculous that a grown man spelling out the word *sexual* should have so much power over her, but there it was. Had he just thrown the word out there, trying to get under her skin with his teasing flirtation, she'd have immediately stopped him in his tracks. But she doubted he was even aware he did it. Spelling out naughty words, protecting his daughter even when she was on the other side of the house, came as naturally to him as breathing.

"My views are none of your business," she replied somewhat breathlessly. "Use your imagination."

"Are you sure that's a good idea?" he asked. "My imagination can be quite...fertile."

Taking one step forward, he drew so close they were within kissing distance. All Lila had to do was lift her chin up a few inches, and their lips would be touching.

She didn't do it, though. Neither did he. It was as good a reminder as any that the game they were playing was just that—a *game*. His words, not hers.

"I'm not going to lie for you," Lila said. A game had rules and boundaries—two things she happened to excel at. "Just so you know. I can't stop you from telling those women anything you want, but if anyone asks me a direct question, I'm going to answer it truthfully."

He didn't seem dismayed by this. "Noted," he said with a nod. "Loyal, monogamous, and honest. I clearly have great taste."

"And I'd appreciate it if you kept things strictly professional between us. As strange as it may seem to you, I'm here to do a job."

"A great work ethic, too. My heart can't take much more."

She gave in to the urge to laugh and immediately wished she hadn't. Laughter carried with it a soft chuff of breath, which met his in a warm swirl mere inches from her lips. It wasn't a very big leap from mingled breath to mingled mouths, to tongues entangled and—

"Ahem."

Lila blinked, startled to still find herself in Emily's bedroom—and to be leaning this close to Ford. She didn't dare move, though. To do so would be to admit that she was aware of him, of how intimate the moment had become. "Um. What?"

She felt rather than heard him chuckle. "I asked if I could make one last request of you. I know I have no right to, not after everything you're already doing for me and Emily, but it's not a big one, I promise."

In that moment, with Ford's long, lean body not quite touching her, her knee-jerk reaction was to deny him anything and everything. She'd only been here one day, and she was already throwing common sense out the window.

She, Lila Vasquez, famed for her level head and propriety.

She, Lila Vasquez, the fortress no man had yet penetrated. Psychologically speaking, that was.

She, Lila Vasquez—

"Sure," she said, unwilling to indulge in further remonstrance. What was the point? She could make a fifty-page list of all the reasons she should run screaming from this room, but lists hadn't been doing her a whole lot of favors lately. Sophie didn't make lists. Dawn didn't make lists. And look how much better people liked them. "What do you want?"

"Oh, lots of things," Ford said, his voice rumbling with laughter. "But for now, I'm only hoping you'll teach me how to braid Emily's hair like that."

chapter
6

Uh, Lila? Did you fall down a well or something?"

Lila slid into her favorite booth at her favorite restaurant, where she and her sisters had dinner at least three times a week, with her head held high. "I'm fine, thank you."

Dawn and Sophie shared what they thought was a secret look. It was a thing they'd been doing for at least two decades, a sort of half side-eye that didn't require them to move their heads. As was usually the case, Lila did them the honor of pretending not to notice. Their hearts—and their pride—would break to know how obvious they were.

"Is it windy outside?" Sophie asked with another one of those looks at Dawn.

"A little." Lila hung her purse from the hook supplied under the table and started arranging her silverware in front of her. "The weather report says we should be getting a pretty big snowstorm later. Have you already ordered?"

It was too much to hope that her sisters would take the hint and find something else—*anything else*—to discuss. Skipping the clandestine look this time, Dawn nudged Sophie on the shoulder. "You ask her. She never yells at you."

"This is Lila we're talking about. She never yells at anyone. She just uses that icy voice and changes the subject."

"My voice is not icy," she protested. "And I can't change a subject that neither of you has the nerve to broach outright."

"It's just that we've never seen you look so…askew."

Lila stifled a laugh. *Askew* was putting it mildly. That was a term used to describe a slight upheaval, a delicate shift from the norm. Her hair looked as though someone had dipped it in one of those cotton-candy machines and set it on high.

"If you must know, I ended today's training lesson with some client-building rapport." Lila hid her face behind a menu, even though she knew it by heart. None of the Vasquez sisters were the least adept at cooking, which meant they'd been coming to the Maple Street Grill for so many years that she could have recited its offerings in her sleep. "I think I'll have the salmon tonight. With a nice chardonnay."

Her tactful attempt at retreat failed. Before she could feign an interest in the wine list, Dawn plucked the menu out of Lila's hand and sat on it. Sophie waved away the waitress who was hovering nearby and leaned across the table, her chin propped on her hands. "Define 'client-building rapport,'" she ordered. "And don't leave anything out. It must be good. I've never seen you turn that shade of red before."

"That's because you haven't seen Ford Ford," Dawn said knowingly.

There was no mirror handy, but Lila was pretty sure her shade of red deepened. "How do you know I wasn't building rapport with Emily?"

"Because *I've* seen Ford Ford. Spill. Did he ravish you? I bet he did." Dawn sighed. "I haven't been ravished in forever. I'm starting to fear I've forgotten how."

Sophie, who was being ravished on the regular by her large, incredibly rugged firefighter boyfriend, waved Dawn off. "You've had enough ravishing to last a lifetime. It's Lila's turn now. Seriously, Lil—it does look as though you spent the better part of the afternoon wrestling in the sheets. What happened to that beautiful crown of braids you had this morning?"

Lila saw no other option than to tell them the truth. Mustering her most respectable air, she said, "Mr. Ford asked me to teach him how to re-create that particular style. Apparently, Emily is fond of elaborate braids."

Neither the mister in front of Ford's name nor the fact that she really *had* used an icy voice this time caused either of her sisters to so much as blink.

"He braided your hair?"

"He touched your head?"

"He threaded his large, nimble fingers through your supple strands?"

"And more to the point, you let him?"

Lila was having a difficult time determining which of her sisters was worse, but she was leaning toward Dawn and her *supple strands*.

"Emily wanted to watch, so it made more sense for me to be the model," she said crisply. *Crisp* was the only way she could speak for fear her voice might crack otherwise. There was nothing extraordinary about building client rapport—all three of them knew that and practiced it as much as possible. When you spent six full weeks with someone, working days and nights, learning the intricacies of their routines so you could fit a puppy in seamlessly, there was a certain amount of intimacy involved.

There was, however, everything extraordinary about sitting at Ford's fuzzy-red-stockinged feet while he ran his fingers over her scalp. In Lila's experience, that level of intimacy existed somewhere been second and third base, a shortstop detour before things started to get hot and heavy. Especially since Dawn was right—Ford's fingers had been both large and nimble. She wasn't a hundred percent sure what he did for a living, but she knew it involved drawing of some sort. The strength of his of hands had proved it. He'd twisted and turned and looped her hair with a kind of dexterity that made her flustered to remember even now.

"I'd always considered myself something of a wizard at this," he'd said, laughing, after the first failed attempt. "I see now that I've met my master. Do you mind if we try again?"

She had minded. She'd minded a lot.

But of course she couldn't say so. It was out of the question to admit that the sensation of his hands working through her long, thick hair led inexorably to ideas about all the other things he might be capable of doing with them. That would only give power to this idea that she was attracted to him, that the same flirtatious routine he pulled on every woman under the age of fifty was capable of knocking her knees together until they were nothing but gelatin.

"This is the third attempt, if it makes you feel any better," Lila said. "You should have seen what I looked like after the first one."

Her sisters would have probably kept going in this vein, demanding answers and details and in-depth descriptions of the calluses on every one of Ford's fingers, but they were interrupted by a flash of unmistakable blinding white from the restaurant doors.

Well, it would be more accurate to say that they were interrupted by the man attached to that preternatural flash, but the idea held fast. Lila's heart, however, did not. It plummeted to the pit of her stomach, holding her in place.

"My, my, isn't this a pleasant surprise." The man approached their table and bestowed his dazzling smile equally on all the Vasquez sisters. "It's not often that I'm lucky enough to find the three of you together. My ship must have finally come in."

Lila sat perfectly still, striving to think of a way to slide her entire body under the table without anyone being the wiser. It wasn't the most elegant way to go about things, but her only other option was to fake a fire and run screaming out the emergency exit doors.

She was debating the merits of just such an approach when a white knight came to her rescue. *Two* of them, actually. Her sisters might be pushy and interfering and giddily romantic, but they were also unquestionably on her side.

"What do you want, Patrick?" Dawn asked without bothering to hide her grimace.

His eyes opened in mild surprise. "To see your sister, of course. I happened to be walking past and —"

Dawn had never been one to swallow lies. "Oh, please. You know we eat here several times a week. What are the chances our waitress will confirm that you've been by every day in hope of coincidentally running across us?"

"Intelligent as well as beautiful." Patrick put his hand over his heart. "Why did I ever think I stood a chance?"

"Because the only thing bigger than your pride is your ego." Sophie scooted to the far end of her booth seat to preclude him sitting down next to her. "Can we help you with something?"

Love for her two siblings went a long way in lifting Lila's spirits. Even though they didn't know all the details of her relationship with Patrick, they were all too aware that things hadn't ended well between them.

As if he, too, was remembering the discord of their last parting, Patrick reached out and touched one of the locks of hair that had slipped out of Ford's inexpert braid.

"Hey, Lil," he said, his voice low with familiarity. "I like this new look. It suits you."

No, it didn't. She looked ridiculous, as her sisters had already pointed out, but there hadn't been time to fix it before she'd rushed over here to meet them. Punctuality was more important than aesthetics, no matter how much it pained her to present anything but her pristine best.

Ford had pointed it out, too, laughing apologetically as she'd beaten a hasty retreat. "You came to us looking like a princess and are leaving looking like something the puppy choked up," he'd said, and then had smiled so warmly that it had been impossible to take offense.

Besides, taking offense was right up there with

admitting how much she'd enjoyed the sensation of his fingers running through her hair. She felt nothing for Ford except cool, professional disinterest, dammit, and no one could accuse her otherwise.

Patrick Yarmouth, however…

"You could have just called like a normal human being," she said. She started to rise out of her seat, hoping to take this conversation outside, but it didn't work. Either because he assumed she was moving over to make way for him or—even more likely—because he'd never been great at taking a hint, he lowered himself onto the red vinyl seat next to her.

In addition to a dazzling smile, Patrick had a number of attributes that made him look like a model in a toothpaste ad. Most of those attributes had to do with his being shaped exactly like a square. His jaw was square, his eyes were square, his shoulders were square, and even his hair, which gleamed a burnished auburn under the lights of the restaurant, had a distinctly cube-like shape. It wasn't a bad thing, all those clean-cut angles and solid masculinity, but Lila found that she preferred a sharply chiseled pair of cheekbones and a touch of gray at the temples.

"Well, girls," he drawled, emphasizing a term he *knew* Lila hated, "I hear congratulations are in order."

Lila knew better than to ask him to elaborate. So did Sophie and Dawn, but of course that didn't stop Patrick from barreling right ahead.

"A little birdie told me you're making great progress on the Auditory Guild contract," he said. "Good for you. It's just the thing to put Puppy Promise on the map, and it couldn't have happened to a better organization."

To the untrained ear, Patrick sounded sincere. He looked sincere, too, what with all those teeth flashing around the table. It was part of his charm, that ability to distract and awe, a brilliantly plumed peacock performing his mating dance to everyone close enough to revel in it.

Lila's ear, however, was anything but untrained. Five months of dating this man had taught her a thing or two about reading between the molars.

"Thanks, Patrick," she said. And because she knew the lines by heart, she added, "We couldn't have done it without you."

He turned to look at her, a queer light in his eyes. "You think so?"

She knew so. As much as it pained her to admit it—and the pain, it loomed large—Patrick had been the one to introduce her to Anya in the first place. He was also the one who'd encouraged them to donate a service animal, who'd showed them the benefits of allying Puppy Promise with an organization as large and influential as the Auditory Guild. As an otolaryngologist, Patrick had plenty of clout in the hearing services field. As an attractive man in his early forties—well educated, well spoken, and well-to-do—he also had plenty of clout with Lila.

Or so she'd thought.

"You know how instrumental you were in getting us that contract," Lila said, since it was no more than the truth. "And if the only thing you've come here to do is make me feel guilty about it, then you're wasting your time. I *know* how much we're in your debt."

Some of Patrick's brilliant wattage dimmed. "I'm not

here to make you feel guilty, Lil. I only wanted to tell you that you have my full support."

He said it the way he said most things—a magnanimous man making a magnanimous gesture—causing all of her hackles to rise. But then he added, "I'm also here to apologize."

"*Apologize*?" All three Vasquez sisters turned his way with a shared look of incredulity.

He chuckled, though his attention remained riveted on Lila. "I know. It shocked me, too. But I'm man enough to admit when I'm wrong, and I was wrong about you. I'm sorry, Lila."

Lila couldn't have felt more dazed if the chef had come by and knocked her across the head with a cast-iron frying pan. Once upon a time, in the manner of all fairy tales, she'd thought her happily ever after was within reach. For four months and thirty days, she and Patrick had been an unstoppable force, sharing long philosophical discussions over eggs Benedict. They'd done all the things respectable couples were supposed to do: brunches and lunches and working side by side to complete the Sunday *Times* crossword puzzle every week.

And they'd done it, too—that was the thing that bothered her the most. Lila had been doing that blasted crossword puzzle for the majority of her adult life, but she'd never managed to finish Sunday's by herself. But Patrick and his esoteric knowledge of historic military campaigns and Latin root words had done the trick. What she couldn't figure out on her own, he'd supplied with that beaming smile and some hastily scrawled penmanship. Honestly, it was enough to drive a woman out of her mind with desire.

It had been enough to push Lila that direction, anyway.

Until, of course, the fourth month and thirty-first day. *That* was when he'd pulled the plug without a hint of warning. *That* was when he'd blamed her for driving him to it.

Because she was too perfect. Too demanding. Too reserved. Too cold.

In other words, she was a lizard person. Cut her up and measure her out, and she'd be the perfect handbag— with or without the matching shoes.

"You're sorry?" she echoed, blinking at him.

"Yes." His hand shot out and covered hers, his grip heavy. "I only meant the best when I warned Anya that you weren't ideally suited to working with kids."

"Oh, hell no—" Dawn made a motion to get up out of her seat, but Lila stilled her with one raised, shaking hand. It suddenly seemed *very* important that Patrick be allowed to finish.

He continued, unabated and unabashed. "Of course, that was before I heard about the way you wooed Emily Ford by dressing up as a princess."

Lila didn't bother correcting him. At this point, she was almost willing to pretend that had been her intention all along, provided everyone stopped talking about it. Instead, she took a moment to gather her thoughts. She knew that was one of the things Patrick disliked about her—the way she was slow to speak and careful to act— but it was better than releasing the hysteria building up in her chest.

"I'm not sure I understand," she eventually said. "You told Anya Askari that I shouldn't be around children?"

He winced apologetically. "Not in so many words, no. But the subject of service dogs came up when we were discussing Emily's case a few weeks ago, and I felt it prudent to mention that you aren't exactly an… affectionate woman."

Lila's hand clenched under his as Anya's words rang loud in her ears. *I did have my doubts about you, especially after meeting with Emily's medical team. The truth is, I was rather hoping you'd have Sophie or Dawn handle the juvenile cases.*

"That was you? You're on Emily's medical team? You're one of her doctors?" The full weight of his confession sank in. "You tried to get this job taken away from me?"

"Come on, Lil," he said softly. "It's not like you can deny it. All that warm, fuzzy stuff is hardly your style."

Unlike the last time he'd leveled that insult at her, he spoke without malice or rancor, his smile striking that perfect balance between condescension and kindness. Seeing it—how calm he was, how sincere—Lila felt as though she'd been sucker punched from inside her rib cage.

Technically, everything he said was true. She wasn't warm or fuzzy. She wasn't the soft, maternal type. She was the last woman anyone would turn to for a comforting embrace.

But that didn't mean she didn't have feelings. It didn't mean she couldn't *love*.

Her sisters must have realized how close she was to losing it, because they intervened before she could make the mistake of saying any of this out loud.

"Oh, would you look at the time?" Sophie said with

an obvious look at her wrist. "If we don't hurry, we're going to be late." As she wasn't wearing a watch, not even Patrick Yarmouth at his most obtuse could fail to pick up the meaning.

"So late, so late, for a terribly important date," Dawn added. The rhyme was playful, but her voice was not. "We won't keep you any longer, Patrick. Thanks ever so much for stopping by."

Patrick opened his mouth as if to argue but wisely closed it again. No man on earth was strong enough to fight that pair when they went into full protective mode. Lila watched, somewhat dazed, as her sisters slid out of the booth and strong-armed Patrick to his feet. She knew she should say something—apologize back to him or fly up in her own defense or even ask never to see his face again, thank you very much—but she was having a difficult time processing it all.

In the end, the only words she could muster were ones she had to borrow from someone else. "Wait, Patrick. Before you go…"

Her sisters each had one of Patrick's arms in their own as they propelled him toward the door. At the sound of her voice, all three of them halted and looked back.

"I just want to know one thing. Do you gargle with bleach, or do you use that new charcoal toothpaste everyone is going on about?"

Patrick's heavy—and square—eyebrows snapped together. "What?"

"Your teeth," she said and made a gesture in the general direction of his mouth. "A friend of mine wants to know. What do you do to make them so bright?"

"You can't gargle with bleach, Lila," he said in his

best doctor voice. "The soft tissue damage alone would be unthinkable."

He sounded so earnest, so concerned about the state of her oral health, that Lila actually found it in her to laugh. It sounded brittle and felt tight, but it was a laugh all the same. *Sheesh*. She might be not be warm and fuzzy, but at least she knew a joke when she heard one.

"I'll keep everything you say in mind, Dr. Yarmouth," she said and ignored the clenching in her chest. Some of the things he'd said had been real doozies. "As always, your wisdom knows no bounds."

chapter 7

L ila strolled through the front door at exactly eight o'clock in the morning, her arms laden with bags of all shapes and sizes. "We'll start with tea, I think," she said as she set them down.

"Good morning to you, too." Ford rubbed his eyes, wishing he had a fraction of her energy. Jeeves might not actually howl at night, but there was no denying that the advent of the puppy into his household was seriously disrupting his regular sleep cycle. "I was planning on starting with a fifth of bourbon, but to each his own."

Lila stared at him for only a second before accepting this remark. "As long as you drink it from a teacup, I don't care what vices you indulge in. Where's Emily?"

Ford found it difficult to reply to the question. Not because he was exhausted, although he was. And not because indulging in various vices with Lila Vasquez was *exactly* how he'd like to start his day, either. No, it was because Lila was shrugging herself out of her wool coat and hanging it carefully on the coatrack by the door.

Against all reason and weather reports, which

promised yet another snowstorm before nightfall, she seemed to be wearing a bright yellow sundress. It fit tightly across the bodice, suspended by two of the flimsiest straps he'd ever seen, and flared improbably wide at the skirt. It took him a few slow, careful blinks before he realized that there were some kind of ruffled petticoats puffing the dress up to reveal much more of Lila's long, sleek legs than he ever thought to see in his lifetime. To top it all off, her hair was pulled back in yet another twist and coil of braids, this time offset with a crown of flowers woven into the strands.

"Um, did I miss the invitation to the local Renaissance fair?" Ford asked. "I wish you'd said something earlier. I have an elven sword I'm always looking for an excuse to roll out."

Lila ignored him with her usual bland efficiency. "Is Emily still sleeping?"

She didn't wait for an answer. Instead, she smoothed her skirts and looked about the room, her eyes narrowed as she appraised its contents. "That's good. It'll give me a chance to set everything up."

"Actually, she's been up since about four o'clock this morning. She and Jeeves have been working out the intricacies of all the different rooster crows at Grandma Louise's house." *That* finally got Lila's attention. She swiveled toward him, her lips slightly parted. "I'm not sure how accurate the training has been, but you'll be pleased to know that the pair of them seem to have the volume part down just fine."

"Oh, Ford." Lila's hands flew to her mouth, but not before her smoky laugh managed to escape. If he'd thought the power of that laugh while she was dressed in a boxy beige suit was bad, it was nothing compared to the effect it was having on him now. "Did you get any sleep at all last night?"

"Not really, no," he admitted, but stopped himself from making the mistake of telling her that it was a low-voiced dog trainer who had been responsible for most of his restlessness. "But I used my time wisely, if that makes you feel better. I watched no fewer than twenty-seven YouTube videos on how to make the perfect princess braid. I'm thinking of opening a shop. Can I poke around in yours?"

Her hands moved to her head, curling protectively around the flowers. "No, you can't poke—" As if remembering something, she snapped her mouth shut and drew a deep breath before starting again, this time with painstaking formality. "Of course, Mr. Ford. Anything you'd like."

He made a gentle tsking sound, his tone matching her own. "You might want to be careful with those kinds of promises, Ms. Vasquez."

Her mouth formed a prim line. "If it will help Emily and Jeeves with their training, then you can do whatever you want to my hair."

"Whatever I want? You obviously underestimate my ingenuity."

"Oh, I rate your ingenuity just fine. Your sincerity, however, is highly suspect."

He chuckled. Lila obviously still took him for some kind of loose screw, incapable of uttering a truthful word. If she had any idea how much he meant what he said—of how much he longed to unwind her braids and bury himself in her hair, her scent, her body...*well*.

Maybe it was a good thing, after all. There was such a thing as coming on too strong.

"Since you haven't dressed yet, can I suggest you put on something a little more formal than usual?" she said. "A bow tie, if you have it. Otherwise, a nice shirt and slacks will do the trick."

"A bow tie?" he echoed. He cast a look down at himself, aware that today, as yesterday, he was sadly unprepared for the arrival of a gorgeous, well-put-together woman in his home. He had on the same worn-out pajama pants from the day before, his torso bare and his feet in a pair of the fuzzy socks Emily proudly bestowed on him for every holiday.

He wasn't always such a sad sack of a man, and could, if given enough warning, put together an altogether presentable appearance. But he had a puppy, dammit. And a kid. And a bed that, no matter how many times he tossed and turned and thumped the pillows, never got close to the comfort he'd felt at having Lila seated at his knee while she talked him through the steps of braiding her hair.

"A bow tie is out of the question, I'm afraid," he admitted. "The tuxedo, too. I probably should have warned you that it was a rental. Owning one is a bit beyond my reach."

"No bow tie?"

He shook his head.

"No tuxedo?"

He spread his hands in a gesture of futility. Although he knew Lila didn't take him the least bit seriously, he was grateful for the opportunity to clear the air. She already knew, on some level, that his financial situation

was precarious enough that it didn't allow him to purchase a service dog without the help of the Auditory
Guild. If that hadn't convinced her that he was a man
of simple means, then one look at his house and the
trusty—and now pee-soaked—minivan would have
given her a clue. Single parenthood and hefty medical
bills were no joke in this neighborhood.

It was a sobering thing, admitting his penury out
loud. Or rather, it was until Lila spoke again.

"Yet you have an elven sword at the ready?"

His crack of laughter brought Jeeves trotting into the
living room, Emily not far in his wake.

"What is it, Daddy?" Emily asked, her eyes wide with
curiosity. They remained that way until she saw Lila
standing there with her hands on her hips, betraying by
not so much as a flash of that dimple that she'd bested
him at his own game. "Oh, it's Princess Lila. She's
making *you* laugh this time."

"Yes, moppet," he said as he dropped a kiss on his
daughter's hairline. Once again, that sapient, all-seeing
child had managed to sum up the situation in a few disconcerting seconds. "I imagine Princess Lila is always
making the young, unmarried gentlemen laugh."

At that, a look of pain swept across Lila's dark gaze.
It was a brief flicker and nothing more, gone so fast
he might have missed it. But he *hadn't* missed it, and
he didn't care for the way it snagged and caught in his
chest.

Before he could do any probing into its cause,
however, Lila turned to Emily. She waited until she
had Emily's full attention before speaking, but it was
obvious she had something serious to impart. "We're

going to have a very important tea party today, so I
need you to go to your room and put on your prettiest
dress," she said.

"A tea party?" Emily breathed. "For real?"

"For absolute real," Lila replied. "I brought an
obscene number of cakes and cookies with me, so I hope
you're hungry. And, um, that your dad doesn't mind if I
pump you full of sugar first thing in the morning."

"Why not? I can always sleep when I'm dead."

"There are treats for Jeeves, too," Lila said with a
casual disregard for Ford's state of well-being.

At the sound of his name, the cockapoo's ears perked.
He was a restful little creature almost all of the time,
patient in ways that seemed unnatural to Ford, but he
was never quite able to subdue his ears. They drooped
when he was sad, twitched when he was playful, and
flopped the rest of the time.

Emily clasped her hands in front of her. "And it's all
for me? Just for me?"

"Well, you're the guest of honor," Lila said with a
nod, "but I've invited a few others to join us."

Just like that, a shutter came down over Emily's eyes.
"What kind of others?"

Abort. Change course. Back oh-so-slowly away.

It was sound advice. He'd tried throwing parties for
Emily in the past—birthday parties and summer parties and, yes, even tea parties—but they rarely ended
well. Each time, the RSVPs flew in and lifted Ford's
hopes accordingly. They rarely stayed that way for long.
It only took a few arrivals and even fewer minutes to
realize that the children were there under strong parental compulsion. When she was younger, Emily hadn't

noticed as much, but school had taught her a lot more than the basics of the alphabet. Social training started early these days.

But in this, as in all things, he'd underestimated Lila.

"I can't tell you, I'm afraid. It would jeopardize their safety."

Although Emily's thumb was still snaking a treacherous path toward her mouth, she allowed herself to be distracted. "Whose safety?"

Lila cast a careful look around the living room as if expecting villains to emerge from the dusty corners. "I can't say more without risking everything. But you should definitely put something fancy on. They'll be expecting it."

There was nothing more for her to say. Emily took Lila at her somber, regal word, her eyes wide with the importance of the task laid before her. Without another word of protest—and with her thumb now firmly at her side—Emily lifted her chin and went to her room.

Jeeves followed, of course, but not before he lifted his ears in an almost exact imitation of the tilt of Emily's head.

"Um, I hate to critique a plan you've clearly put some thought into, but nothing short of the Queen of England on that doorstep will do now," Ford said. "You realize that, right?"

"You really don't have anything nicer than pajama pants?" she asked by way of answer. Her eyes flicked over his bare torso. "Not even a matching shirt?"

He might have felt embarrassed to be caught in such a state of bare-chested déshabillé if not for the way her gaze lingered a shade too long. It was the same way his own eyes kept trailing back to the tight bodice of her dress, enjoying the way each breath swelled both fabric and skin.

"Alas, my wardrobe is the product of my existence," he said. "There's no need for finery when I rarely leave the house."

"Surely you must go out sometimes," she persisted. "What do you wear on dates?"

"Nothing."

A flush of color washed over her, by now a familiar sight. Ford was coming to realize that it was the only sign Lila ever gave that she was the least bit flustered. She held herself prim and polite in almost all situations, but not even she could control the movement of blood through her veins.

"I don't go on dates, that is," he supplied with a grin. "I'm not in the habit of sauntering around in the nude."

"You could have fooled me."

That response, almost as much as the blush, told Ford that she wasn't as indifferent as she wanted him to think. It was a much-needed boost to his ego, which had been showing signs of deflation lately. Back in the day, he'd been just as vain as the next relatively good-looking young man with the whole world before him, and he'd done what he could with it.

Unfortunately, it was difficult to puff up with self-importance while doing things like making peanut-butter sandwiches and buying toilet paper in bulk. And, if the email that had crossed his desk last night was any indication, when there was a good chance his employer was no longer going to offer flexible options in working from home.

Hello, Lila. I'm borderline unemployed and unable to

cough up a tuxedo to wear to my daughter's tea party.
There's dog hair on my pants, and I may or may not
have remembered to brush my teeth this morning. Have
I swept you off your feet yet?

Yeah, his game was definitely lacking these days. If
he had to resort to flexing what few muscles he had to
get this woman's attention, then he'd do it. Pride, like
suavity, was one of those things he'd long since dis-
posed of.

"Your notes told me to turn the temperature up in the
house," he pointed out. "To help Jeeves acclimate. It's
not my fault I had to strip down. I'm very sensitive to
the heat."

Lila lifted her chin, her tone just as lofty as her posture. "What you wear in your own house is of no concern to me." Then, bringing her chin down a fraction,
"And what do you mean, you don't go on dates?"

"Exactly that. Dinner, movies, making out in the
back seat of my sweet minivan—it's all off the table. I
haven't been on a date since, oh, let's see…"

He let his voice trail off and tapped his chin as if
thinking. In truth, there was no need for him to hesitate.
He could have rattled off the exact day and time of his
last date. It had involved a very pregnant wife, a bucket
of fried chicken, and a blood oath that under no circumstances would he forget that she wanted every painkiller
made available to women pushing human beings out of
their bodies.

It had been a good date, all things considered. He
liked fried chicken.

"Since just before Emily was born," he eventually
said.

Lila stared at him. There was no malice in that stare, but there was plenty of incredulity.

"I've been busy," he protested. "And you saw what happened with Helen. Can you imagine what would happen if I took anyone out, even for a casual meal?"

"No dates at all?"

"Nary a one."

"Not even for coffee?"

"Not even for one of those chocolate-covered espresso beans."

Lila swept another one of those appraising gazes over him, this time not lingering on his exposed parts so much as absorbing the whole. He did his best to appear disinterested, but he feared he might have puffed his chest out a little.

"If it makes you feel any better, I do sometimes buy myself roses on Valentine's Day," he said. "But I usually wait until the day after so I can get half off. The nice perk about doing this sort of thing alone is that no one cares if the flowers are a little wilted."

Ford had no idea what caused Lila's eyes to widen and her color to pick up even more, but one thing he knew for sure—this wasn't the good kind of blushing. A low humming sound built up in the back of her throat, and she extended a hand toward him before allowing it to fall again.

"Oh, *s-h-i-t*," she said. "I'm so sorry, Ford. I wasn't thinking."

He cocked an eyebrow at her, struggling to suppress a smile as she spelled out the obscenity. It had taken him three years and a lot of slipups to get the habit down. Lila was a fast learner. "What did you just say?"

"It didn't even occur to me to ask about Emily's mother." Her color picked up even more. Another minute or two of this, and she was going to be as bright as the flowers in her hair. "Or maybe you don't want me to ask. That's okay, too. It's none of my business. Forget I said anything."

A fair request, especially considering that she'd grabbed the wrong end of the stick with both hands, but Ford couldn't help himself. He rarely could.

"Alas, my heart is frozen," he said with a palm held to his chest. "So are the rest of my parts. I only need the right woman to bring them back to life again."

"Well. Um." Her gaze fixed somewhere above his right shoulder. He was pretty sure the only thing back there was a sketch he'd made of Emily when she was a toddler, but it appeared to absorb Lila's whole interest. "I'm sure you'll find her someday."

It was on the tip of his tongue to tell her that he'd already found her. She was the smart, fierce, levelheaded brunette standing in his living room incongruously wearing a puffy princess dress, planning tea parties with mystery guests, and blushing like a virgin bride.

But of course he didn't. That wasn't the Ford Ford way. Women like Lila Vasquez didn't look at him and expect earnest declarations of affection. He was good for a flirtation, ideal for a laugh. He used to be decent in the sack, too, but he doubted he'd be up to anyone's standards these days.

Least of all a woman like her.

"It's just me, all alone in my castle," he said with a mournful note that wasn't entirely faked.

"You have Emily."

"There's no one to hold me at night."

"I've always found I get better sleep that way."

He ignored the remark, which was offered with a growing note of skepticism. "No one to kiss. No one to cuddle." He caught Lila's eye. "No one to *f-u-c-k*."

"Ford!" Lila reared up to her full height, but not wholly with indignation. There was laughter in that gaze; he was sure of it.

"What?" he asked with bland innocence. "You started spelling things out first."

"Yes, but only because I thought you were mourning the loss of your wife."

"Oh, I make it a point never to mourn Janine," he said. "She ran off to the North Pole to escape me. I know when to take a hint."

"The North Pole?" Lila echoed blankly. "You mean—"

"That I'm not pining for the lost love of my life?" He gave in to the urge to grin this time, but only because Lila was developing another one of those deep blushes. "No, I'm not. Or, rather, I wasn't until a few days ago. Now it's nothing but gnashing teeth and painful longing everywhere I turn."

"I'm sure I don't know what you mean."

"Are you, Lila?" He drew closer, unable to keep his distance any longer. *She* might be able to pretend to ignore the pull of attraction between them, but he didn't have a fraction of her strength. "Are you absolutely sure?"

"You're being highly *i-n-a-p-p-r-o-p-r-i-a-t-e* right now," she said. Her whole body was stiff, but she didn't back away. If anything, she leaned closer, drawn inexorably toward him, too.

"That one's probably safe enough to say out loud. What would really be inappropriate, however, is if I were to tell you just how much I'd like to kiss you. Or cuddle you. Or, if you're up for it, to *f-u—*"

She leaped forward with a suddenness that made him hope, for a fraction of a second, that she was going to stop his words with a kiss. She didn't, opting instead to press her palm over his mouth. As this required her to stand so close that her breasts jutted against his chest, her face mere inches from his, it seemed like the next best thing.

"Your daughter is right down the hall," she hissed.

Yes, and most likely pulling every dress she owned out of the closet to weigh the pros and cons of each one. Until one of them went in there and demanded that she make a decision or risk missing out on the tea party altogether, there would be no parting her from the exigencies of her wardrobe. Lila's hand was still over his mouth, however, so he couldn't offer her any of these assurances.

"You're incorrigible. Honestly, if you can't learn to control yourself, I'm going to have to…" Lila's voice trailed off, her brow furrowed as she sought an ideal torture. Since there was little she could to do hurt him, short of handing the training over to one of her sisters and escaping from his life forever, he wasn't too alarmed.

He was, however, highly intrigued when a look of cunning took over. It was evident in the slight narrowing of her eyes, the irrepressible dimple forming at the corner of her mouth.

"You know what?" she said as she dropped her hand from his mouth. "I think you might be on to something."

"I am?" he asked before correcting himself with a cough. "I mean, I am. Of course. Always on top of things, that's the Ford Ford way. And by on top, I mean—"

"I know what you mean. I'm not an idiot. You mean your body moving over mine. You mean the two of us entangled in your sheets." Her laughter this time was gentle but somehow all the more powerful because of it. No low-throated laugh, this. It was an intimate sound, a private one. One he could feel rumbling through his entire body. "Okay. Let's do it."

"Do…what?"

"*It*," she said. "The horizontal mambo. The slap and tickle. The rusty moose."

He was fully on board with her suggestions until she reached the last one. Subduing a sudden choke of laughter, he asked, "The rusty moose? That's not a real thing."

"Sure it is." She blinked up at him. Although he suspected she was only toying with him, calling his bluff in hopes of scaring him away, she said this part with perfect solemnity. "Anything can be a euphemism for *s-e-x* if you say it right."

"Um, I don't think so. There are some pretty freaky words out there."

She trailed her fingers up the line of his bare arm. Even though he knew she didn't mean it, he couldn't help but respond. God, it felt good to do this again—to flirt in earnest, to banter with a woman in hopes that it would lead to something more, instead of just using it as a shield.

"Come on, Ford," she murmured softly. "Wouldn't you like to give me a taste of the ol' rusty moose?"

Yes. She was obviously onto something here. He'd give her a rusty anything if she kept looking at him like that.

"Or maybe we could slip outside for some pickle juice," she cooed.

Absolutely. Pickle juice. Pickle juice sounded amazing.

Those trailing fingers moved to his chest, where her palm lay flat against the rapidly increasing *thump-thump* of his chest. "Oh, Ford, I love it when you climb the broken ladder."

He should put a stop to this, he knew. There were too many phrases in the English language for her to throw out in that sultry voice of hers, too many ways for her to ruin inanimate objects for him forever.

"The hairy knuckle," she whispered, allowing a soft sound to escape her throat. "A lipstick smear. *Tater tots.*"

"No, Lila," he said with a groan. Was it his imagination, or was the room starting to grow blurry around the edges? "Not tater tots."

"Ta-ter. Tots." She was careful to enunciate each syllable, her lips exaggerating the shape of the word. "Hot, salty wedges of potato."

Okay, he took it back. He took it all back. Where this woman and that voice were concerned, anything could be a euphemism for sex. In fact, if he didn't do something about it, everything *would* be a euphemism for sex.

"Well?" she asked, still arch. Her hand remained on his chest, her lips parted as they reached up toward his. "What about it?"

"What about what?" he asked. At least, he thought he asked it. His mouth was so dry, all his blood coursing southward, that he wasn't entirely sure he was still breathing.

"You and me, of course. Kissing. Cuddling. *F-u-c-k-i-n-g*."

Her mouth was so close that he could almost taste her. He knew exactly what he'd find if he gave in to the urge. The light mint of her toothpaste, the soft pink gloss that gave her lips a delicate sheen, the warmth of her mouth giving way underneath his... It was almost more than a man could be expected to bear.

But bear it he did. He was already so far out of his depth with this woman, so much at a loss every time she walked in the door. He'd prove to her that he was more than just the neighborhood flirt—that he could, when it mattered, control himself.

He *could*.

"What's the matter, Ford?" she asked archly. "Having a change of heart?"

Nope. Not even a little bit. If it weren't for his daughter in the next room, if he wasn't so determined to show Lila that he was capable of restraint, this woman would see firsthand how he intended to repay her for defiling tater tots forever.

Her scent drew him even closer, swirling his head and making him forget that he was standing in his living room in his pajamas. There were just two people, standing face-to-face, attraction pulsating between them.

Fortunately—or not—a blast of cold air from a poorly sealed doorframe jerked him back to a realization of his surroundings. It also stopped him before he made the mistake of cupping the back of her neck and pulling her in for a slow, deep kiss.

Lila misinterpreted his move, a wry smile twisting her lips.

"See?" she said, looking much more in command of herself than he felt. "You don't really want me. You just can't help yourself. I'm female, I have a functioning nervous system, and I'm not as old as either Emily's grandmother or her principal. I don't think you know *how* to act any other way. Can we move on now?"

"That's not it—" he began, his arm shooting out to catch her about the waist. He might have managed it, too, but she stepped out of his reach, her professional mien back in place.

"It should take me about half an hour to get the tea party set up, which will give you time to shower and dress. The first guest will be arriving around ten, so we want to make sure Jeeves is ready before that."

"Jeeves?" The blood hadn't returned fully to Ford's brain yet, his pulse still thumping madly to keep up, which made it difficult for him to follow along. "What about Jeeves?"

She waved a hand around the living room, not stopping until she reached the pile of her bags. "Puppy training? Doorbells? The whole reason I'm here?"

"Oh. Right. That." Understanding finally took hold, and with it, any chance Ford had of making it out of this thing with his heart intact. He stared at her. "Wait. Is *that* why you're setting up this whole thing? The dress, the cookies, the secret guests—it's to practice having people at the door without upsetting Emily?"

"I thought it might be fun." The blush crept back over her face. "I'm not experienced with kids, I know, and I'm not a particularly...*warm* woman, but the one advantage I do have in this world is my sisters. They'll make up for anything I'm lacking, I promise. Just give me a chance."

This last part was offered in a whoosh of entreaty, as if Lila was making a deep, dark confession about a crime she'd once committed. Or, at the very least, an admission about what she proposed to do with those tater tots.

"Are you kidding?" he asked, blinking down at her. "You're fantastic with Emily."

Her cheeks were still suffused with color, her discomfort clear, but he couldn't understand why. True, she treated Emily more like an adult than a child, but that was part of what made her—what made all of this—so incredible. Lila didn't pander to his daughter, didn't belittle her by assuming she wasn't capable of doing anything she set her mind to.

"That's nice of you to say, but—"

"But nothing." He spoke more forcefully than he intended. Lila's eyes widened, and her hand halted in midair, but she didn't move. He didn't want to draw close again—there was still too much energy thrumming between them to make *that* a wise choice—but he did soften his voice as he added, "Your sisters are always welcome here, of course, but Emily and I don't need them. Not when we have you."

Lila opened her mouth and closed it again, teetering on the edge of response. Ford held himself perfectly still in hope that she'd decide to share whatever was on her mind, but to no avail.

"You're only saying that because you haven't seen them at work before," she said with an airiness that didn't match her eyes. "Believe me when I say that a tea party with my sisters is something neither you nor Emily will soon forget."

❦❦❦

"Ho. Ly. Crap."

Lila didn't turn from her position at the kitchen counter, where she stood chopping up strawberries in a belated attempt to not go down in history as the dog trainer who sent a child into sugar shock.

"Ho. Ly. C—"

"Soph, you know they can probably hear you, right?"

Her sister snaked a pair of arms around Lila's waist and bestowed a kiss on her cheek. The gesture was an affectionate one, but it was also calculated to place Sophie's mouth right next to Lila's ear. Quieter this time, but still with that breathy squeal underscoring her voice, she said, "Ho. Ly. Crap."

Lila sighed. There was no way she was going to be able to live this one down now. Her sisters had seen Ford Ford in a tight, blue button-down shirt. They'd watched him hitch his even tighter slacks as he poured his daughter tea and discussed the merits of tulle versus satin for daywear. They'd been the recipients of his heavy-handed flirtation and long, fluttering eyelashes.

Life, as she knew it, was over.

"I love him. I want to marry him. I want to bear eighteen of his children and grow old watching him drink tea with every last one of them."

Lila was forced into a chuckle. "I think your bodyguard out there might have something to say about that."

"Who? Harrison?" Sophie waved off the love of her

life with a laugh. "I'm sure he won't mind. From the look of it, he's halfway in love himself."

Lila peeked behind her, even though there was no need. She'd committed the tableau to memory—in fact, she doubted she'd ever be able to get it out of her head after this. Harrison, Sophie's oversize fireman boyfriend, was dressed all in black and standing intimidatingly by the door. He refused by so much as a smile to show that he was enjoying himself in his self-imposed role as bodyguard to the Vasquez royal line, but he obviously was. He'd even demanded that Bubbles, his service Pomeranian, be given a share of the tea.

Her sisters had gone all out, too. Sophie wore a crown on her head and ruby-red slippers on her feet. Dawn was in the lime-green bridesmaid dress for reasons that Lila was sure were meant to cause her acute embarrassment.

And in the middle of them all sat Emily. As soon as she'd realized that her guests were ringing the doorbell one by one, each arrival timed to give Jeeves a chance to go through the training steps necessary for door alerts, she'd thrown herself wholeheartedly into her role as hostess/dog trainer.

In other words, Lila's plan had been a success. She was getting through to the client, training a puppy, doing the work that needed to be done. And if she just happened to be the least fluffy woman in the room while it happened?

Well, so be it. Someone had to cut the strawberries and make sure the training stayed on track.

"Dawn wasn't kidding," Sophie added with a not-so-discreet look over her own shoulder. "That man is next-level kinds of gorgeous. And funny, too. How is he still single?"

"From what I understand of the matter, it's by choice. He has plenty of opportunity, but he isn't interested in most of the women he meets." Lila spoke with what she hoped was quelling sternness.

It wasn't.

"Oh, so he's exactly like you."

Lila turned to face her sister, still with the knife in one hand. She probably looked deranged, holding out a weapon with strawberry-stained hands, but that seemed about right. She *felt* deranged. At some point in the last week, her life had gone from a quietly predictable routine of her own making to complete and utter chaos.

And like the quietly predictable woman she was, she seemed to be the only one who noticed it. Everyone else was out there having the time of their lives.

"He's not the least bit like me. He's just dedicated to his daughter, that's all. He has enough going on in his life. He doesn't have time to bother with romance."

"Bullshit," Sophie said cheerfully. Without the least qualm, she plucked the knife out of Lila's hand and took over the fruit-cutting task. "She's a cute kid, I'll give you that, but no thirtysomething man who looks like that one is going to take a vow of celibacy unless he has a good reason. Longing for the wife, maybe?"

"No, I don't think it's that. He was able to crack jokes about her living at the North Pole, so I think they must have parted on amicable terms."

Sophie's brow lifted in a perfect arch. "So you *have* talked about it?"

Dammit. Lila could have kicked herself for being so

obvious. For an ice princess, she was doing a terrible job of hiding herself away. "It came up in the regular course of conversation, that's all."

"Sure it did. I mean, I usually wait until the second week of training until I plumb the depths of my clients' previous relationships, but you've always been much more efficient than me."

"It's the truth!" Lila dumped the fruit onto a platter and did her best to hide her suddenly flaming face. Okay, so her interactions with Ford had a tendency to strain the bounds of propriety, but it wasn't as if she had any other choice. Dealing with a man like that one required all the ingenuity she had. He crushed formality with his ready smile and put her into a flutter with no more than a word. In fact, the only thing that seemed to work at all was treating him to the same cavalier flirtation he was inclined to show her.

And, you know, every other woman he met.

Lila had just wiped her hands on her apron when the doorbell sounded once again. It alarmed no one except her. Although the steady stream of guests to the door was the whole point of this exercise, she hadn't invited anyone else to attend.

Jeeves performed his part to perfection as everyone went about the normal business of enjoying high tea. As soon as he heard the sound of an arrival, his curly black ears pricked up and his little body went rigid, just like a butler preparing to answer the door. Since he was never far from Emily, he was able to dash to her side and press his nose against her hand in a matter of seconds. Emily performed her part, too, looking to her father for permission before following Jeeves to the door.

"*More* company?" she squealed, remembering to thank Jeeves for his good work before using both hands to turn the knob. "Hello, and welcome to my—"

Her voice cut out the moment the door swung open to reveal the newest addition to the party. "Hello, Em-ee-lee!" Helen spoke in an overly loud, overenunciated voice. "How nice to see you again. And looking so grown up in that dress. I hope I'm not interrupting."

Only Lila was looking at Ford as his neighbor descended upon them, so only Lila noticed the flicker of weary resignation that crossed his expression before being replaced with a beaming smile. It was as good an indication as any that the face he showed to the world wasn't representative of his true feelings.

He was a nice man, obviously, and cared enough not to let anyone see just how wearisome he found their company, but it would serve her well to remember it. *A smile doesn't mean he likes you. A laugh doesn't mean he cares.*

"Oh," Emily said, her shoulders falling. "It's Ms. Helen."

Ford did a much better job of greeting the newcomer. "Hey, Helen. You're just in time. We're about to start spinning plates to work off all this sugar. Apparently, Princess Dawn here is something of an expert."

Princess Dawn dipped into an elegant curtsy. "I spent six months traveling with a circus once. You should see what I can do with flaming swords." She paused and frowned. "Actually, you shouldn't. I'm a little out of practice. There's a good chance I'd light the curtains on fire."

Once again, it spoke volumes about Helen's

personality that none of these greetings—not the dismay on Emily's face or the flaming circus stories, which had the misfortune of being true—caused her the slightest hesitation. "Oh, really? You should come practice at my house. All my belongings are made of fireproof materials. Boys, you know."

None of the Vasquez sisters *did* know, since they'd grown up in a brother-free zone, but Lila could appreciate the wisdom of such a precaution.

"Anyway, I didn't mean to interrupt." Helen held out a small white envelope. "I only wanted to drop this off for Princess Lila. It's an invitation to my annual Christmas Eve block party. Seeing as how you're one of us now, I thought you might want to join in on the fun. It's pirate-themed this year, but I'm sure your usual attire will work just fine. No need to go all out."

Lila stood in the space between the kitchen and the living room, her feet frozen and her head in a whirl. *One of us? Pirate-themed?* She might have remained in place indefinitely, but Sophie lifted the plate from her hands and gave her a nudge.

"'No need to go all out' means that she's hired professional actors, and nothing short of our arrival under billowing sails will do," Ford said as though all of this were perfectly ordinary. Because who didn't invite virtual strangers to their weirdly themed holiday parties? "I've already rented a parrot and taught him every swear word I know."

Helen released a trill of laughter. "Oh, Ford. As if you would." She pressed the envelope into Lila's hand. "Don't bother to bring anything. Just the pleasure of your company will be enough."

"Um, I'm not sure if I'll be free—"

"These must be your sisters," Helen said as though Lila hadn't spoken. She took in the room's inhabitants without blinking. "I can always tell. My, you're an attractive bunch. Is this a celebration of some sort?"

"A training exercise, actually," Lila said, grateful for the distraction Helen's question provided. *Work.* She was here to work. It would do them all a world of good to remember that. "We're teaching Jeeves about doorbells."

Helen's hands flew to her mouth. "Oh dear. Did I ruin everything, coming when I did?"

"Not at all," Ford said politely. "In fact, we're in your debt. You gave us an opportunity for extra training. Why don't you stay and have some cake?"

Helen seemed to hesitate, glancing anxiously from face to face before finally settling on Lila's. "I don't know. This looks like a family gathering. I wouldn't want to intrude."

Lila was in no position to offer hospitality in a house that wasn't her own, but something about Helen's expression gave her pause. The poor woman looked so eager, so lonely, so desperate to be included. Lila smiled and nodded her agreement before she could second-guess herself. "Dawn's plate spinning is worth sticking around for," she said. "And we're mostly done, anyway. I'm just cleaning up and getting ready for our afternoon training."

It was all the invitation Helen needed. With the wide smile back on her face, she started unwinding her scarf and shrugging herself out of her coat. "Well, if you're sure I won't be in the way…"

The only person who seemed dismayed at the addition to their party was Emily, but the prospect of flying plates meant that even she was inclined to accept Helen with good grace. Especially once she started helping move the living room furniture out of the way to make room for the spectacle.

"I didn't really rent a parrot," Ford whispered as he drew Lila aside. No part of him touched her, and there was nothing particularly intimate about the way he leaned in, but she felt a shiver move through her all the same. "A costume, however, has been acquired. I'm going as s-l-u-t-t-y Blackbeard, in case you want to get one to match."

Oh, for heaven's sake. "You won't say s-l-u-t-t-y, but you'll dress up that way? And what's the counterpart to that, anyway? Anne Bonny?"

"S-l-u-t-t-y Anne Bonny," he corrected her.

She stopped her laugh just in time. "Sure. That's what I'll wear. I'll be the toast of the neighborhood, all t-i-t-s and a-s-s. The mothers at the party will be delighted."

"I don't know about the mothers, but I'd sure as h-e-l-l like to see it. Or them, I guess I should say. I'm partial to both."

She was sure he was. Her tits and ass, however, were going to remain covered for the duration of this training. Yes, she was making efforts to soften her appearance and her approach, to show Patrick and Anya that she was just as capable of handling young clients as her sisters, but she drew the line at actual nudity.

Even if the idea of nudity and Ford Ford was appealing in the extreme.

"Now would be a really good opportunity to tell Helen the truth about us," she said, tamping down any and all images of this man without any clothes on. She'd seen enough of his chest to last her a lifetime, thank you very much.

"I thought you were only going to do that if she asked you a direct question," Ford said with a self-conscious start.

"Yes, well. That was before she started coming by with invitations to parties."

He heaved a sigh. It was a playful sigh, as usual, but Lila couldn't help thinking there was some meaning behind it. When he spoke, however, it was with nothing but irreverence. "I still think it'd be nicer if you could find it in your heart not to dump me until Christmas, but feel free to disillusion her. I'm going to watch the plate spinning. *You* might be accustomed to having circus freaks for siblings, but I'm new to all this family intrigue. Does she throw knives, too? I've always wanted to try that."

Lila knew there would be nothing but nonsense out of Ford now. "Not to my knowledge, but I'm sure she'd be willing to give it a try if you asked nicely. Maybe you could volunteer to be her first target."

"There's no need. My heart has already been pierced by a glorious Vasquez sister. Want to guess which one?"

She couldn't resist. "Sophie's a sweetheart, but I doubt Harrison will give her up to you easily. And in terms of sheer physical prowess, the man has you beat. You'll be better off with Dawn and her knives."

Ford turned his head toward Harrison, who was, in fact, looking rather large and intimidating today. He looked large and intimidating most of the time, except when his gaze landed on either Sophie or Bubbles. Then it was all teddy bear, all of the time.

"Oh dear. Is *that* your type?" There was no regret
or envy in Ford's voice—only that laugh. *Always that
laugh.* "It'll take me a few years to bulk up, and I can't
promise that my biceps will ever get that big, but if
that's what you find attractive… Emily, honey? Will
you bring me the carton of eggs? I'm going to need to
get started right away."

Emily wasn't looking at her father, so she didn't
catch what he said, but she was so used to his ways that
she merely giggled when he moved his fingers down
in the sign of a cracking egg. Lila was grateful for the
sound of the girl's bubbling laughter, since it covered up
her own. She was equally grateful for Helen, who came
forward to offer her help in washing dishes.

"I might be a party crasher, but I'm a party crasher
with two perfectly good hands," she said.

Lila was just desperate enough to get away from Ford
that she agreed. "That'd be great, thanks. My sisters
have things well under control in here. Plus, this will
give us a chance to have a little chat. There are a few
things you and I need to get straight."

She cast an obvious look at Ford as she said this last
bit. It was only fair that she give him advance warning
of her intentions. Which was a mistake for a lot of reasons, but none of them as pressing as the fact that Ford
Ford wasn't a man who played fair.

"She's going to whisk you away and tell you that she
doesn't love me," he said with a sad shake of his head.
"Apparently, she prefers men with more meat on their
bones. I'm only just hearing about it now."

"Ford!" Lila cried.

"It's okay. Lucky for you, I prefer a woman who

throws me an occasional curveball. Hey, Harrison—you have a minute? I have a few questions about your exercise regimen. Do *all* the men on your wildfire team look like you when they get started, or are some of them spindly nobodies like me? It's for science."

As he loped off in Harrison's direction with every appearance of chatting about protein powder, bench presses, and firefighter lifestyles, Lila could only watch him go. Matters weren't helped any when Helen wound her arm through Lila's and led her toward the kitchen with a confidential air. "I don't know how you do it, Princess Lila," she said. "Walking and talking and working like a normal person. If Ford said half of those things to me, I'd be melted in a puddle at his feet."

Yes, well. Perhaps that would be for the best. Then Ford might slip and have to be taken to the emergency room. Not even *he* could make one of those flapping blue hospital gowns look good.

She kept these reflections to herself, especially since the image of his bare backside was causing a sudden fluttering low in her belly. "You can just call me Lila," she said instead.

"I know, but the princess part seems to make Emily happy." Helen's smile faltered. "It's the least I can do. The poor little thing doesn't like me very much. She never has."

Lila could tell. She also had a strong suspicion as to why. The sentiment had its roots in those two words: *poor* and *little*. Oh, she was no child expert, obviously, but she'd spent enough time in the pediatric cancer ward when Sophie was young to realize that pity was the last thing any child with a serious health condition wanted to be given. Sympathy was theirs for the taking whenever they wanted it; being treated just like any other normal kid, however, was something to be cherished.

She was still trying to work out how to tactfully convey this to a woman she barely knew when Helen interrupted with a bright "So, how long have you two known each other, you and Ford?"

Lila could have kissed her for making this so easy. Busying herself with the tap, she said, "I met him for the first time in my life last Saturday."

Helen's brows dashed up as she handed Lila a plate. "Last Saturday? Oh my. I had no idea."

"Why would you?" Lila asked congenially. She thought but didn't add, *When Ford has done his best to give the exact opposite impression?* "The company I run with my sisters is contracted through the Auditory Guild to provide Emily with a service puppy and training through the end of the year. Given how closely we work with our families, we like to focus on building easy rapport."

"In that short a time, though?" Helen asked. The disbelief in her tone was evident even over the sound of the running water. "You must work quickly."

On the contrary, Lila was incredibly slow. Slow to think and slow to act, careful never to step anywhere the ground might be unstable. And it was unstable here, that was for sure. She turned off the tap and gave Helen her full attention.

"It was a tough job for us to get in the first place, and there are some fairly high stakes involved if we want to keep it," she said carefully. "And we do want to keep it, very much. So you can understand why the relationship between me and Ford is strictly a professional one."

"Ohhh," Helen breathed. She followed it up with a grin and a wink. "Right. Strictly professional. *Now* I understand."

Lila fought an inward groan. Unless she was mistaken, Helen understood very little.

"My sisters will tell you the same thing," she protested with a glance at the pair of them in the living room. They might find this whole situation hilarious, but like her, they wouldn't lie if asked a direct question. "Until last week, I'd never even heard of Ford Ford, let alone—"

Directly behind them, the phone rang. Lila would never presume to answer the telephone in someone else's house, but Helen had no such qualms. Drying her hands on a dish towel, she reached for the handset and held it to her ear. "You've reached the Ford residence. This is Helen speaking. How may I help you?"

She placed her hand over the mouthpiece and said in a low voice, "It's okay. I work part-time as a receptionist in a dental office. I'm used to this." She paused as a low male voice sounded on the other end of the phone. Lila couldn't make out all the details of what was being said, but it was only a few seconds before Helen's brows went up and an amused smile flickered across her face. "Yes, just a moment, please."

She held the handset out to Lila. "It's for you."

"For me?" Lila echoed.

"Last Saturday, huh?" Helen laughed and tapped the side of her nose. "Don't worry. Your secret's safe with me."

Lila held the handset between two fingers, dangling it as if it contained a curse. Which, for all she knew, it did. The only two people in the world who would feasibly call her at a client's house were spinning plates in the next room. In fact, they were also the only two people in the world who knew she was here right now. *So, who—?*

"Hello?" she asked, holding the phone tentatively to her ear.

"Oh, hey, Lil. I thought I might find you there."

"*Patrick?*"

"I hope you don't mind me calling like this," he said. Without waiting to hear that she did, in fact, mind, he went on. "I know you always turn your cell phone off during client visits."

It was true, and for a perfectly good reason—because it was highly unprofessional to take personal calls while in someone else's home. Then again, it was just as unprofessional for her sister to be throwing tea plates all over a client's living room. And for her to be harboring highly suspect feelings for a man she barely knew. Every ethical and personal boundary she'd ever put up was crumbling to pieces around her.

"I'd rather you didn't, but there's not much I can do about it now, can I? What do you want?"

"To apologize. You didn't let me finish at the restaurant."

That almost caused her to drop the phone. Drawing a deep breath, Lila gripped the handset more tightly and did her best to look calm. Helen's attention was focused on the dishes, but she kept sneaking sideways glances at her.

"Okay, Dr. Yarmouth," she said in hopes that the other woman would hear the word *doctor* and realize this was no social call. "You may proceed."

Patrick chuckled. "Gee, thanks. Only you could turn an apology into a funeral."

Well, obviously. Turning perfectly ordinary situations into gloom and doom was exactly what he'd accused her of before. If Patrick's idea of an apology was to call her up at a client's house and remind her, however, she had no intention of lingering long enough to hear it. "Could we move this along, please? Puppies don't train themselves."

"Did I hear you say 'Dr. Yarmouth'?" Ford's voice sounded from directly behind her, causing her to jump.

If she'd been paying attention, she'd have noticed that Helen had given up on dish duty to make way for Ford's approach. In the ordinary way of things, she *would* have been paying attention, since focusing on details was the way she liked to work. But her ex-boyfriend calling her at a client's house while she wore a yellow sundress in the middle of winter was hardly ordinary.

"Yes," she said, suddenly seeing a way out. "Helen must have been mistaken. It's for you."

Although she heard a murmur of protest coming from Patrick's end of the phone, she held the handset out until Ford took it. Patrick would just have to come up with a believable lie—or, failing that, pretend he dialed the wrong number. That would teach him to call her during working hours.

She smiled blandly at Helen, hoping that would end the intrigue, but she'd underestimated the amount of romanticism in the other woman's soul. As Ford took the phone, Helen bumped Lila with her hip, a knowing gleam in her eyes.

"One of these days, you're going to have to tell me the *real* story of how you two met."

"I already did," Lila protested.

She might as well have not spoken for all the attention Helen paid her. "I warn you—I'm awfully persistent when I like someone. I won't rest until you're sitting in my kitchen with a glass of rosé in hand. I'll kidnap you if I have to. Don't think I won't."

Lila looked inadvertently to Ford. She was sure he'd share her amusement at Helen's willingness to hold people hostage in the name of friendliness, but he was holding the phone to his ear with a strange look on his face. She had no idea what Patrick was telling him, but it couldn't be good. That look was strangely bleak, in no way suited for the handsome, laughing man he was most of the time.

"Oh God." Lila's mind went directly to all the potentially devastating news a child's otolaryngologist might be forced to impart over the phone. She waited only until Ford hung up before pouncing. "What did he say? Not anything bad? Not…Emily?"

Ford shook his head, still somewhat dazed, though the smile had returned to his expression. It was his usual grin, equal parts charming and disarming, but for the first time, it didn't quite reach his eyes. Those orbs still held their usual blue brilliance, but they were distant. One might almost say *cold*.

But that wasn't right. Lila was the cold one. Ford was everything attractive and happy and warm.

"Emily's okay," he said. "Emily's fine."

"Then…?" It wasn't Lila's business, she knew, but she couldn't help herself. What on earth had Patrick been telling this man to bring such a shadow to his face?

"He was just checking in." Ford smiled again, and this time, it seemed more genuine. "He's good people, Patrick Yarmouth. But there's no need for me to tell you that, is there?"

The question was a rhetorical one. With a cheerfulness that Lila couldn't decide was faked or not, Ford wrested both Helen and her away from the kitchen, vowing that no one was allowed to wash dishes in his house without his assistance.

"I've worked really hard to teach Emily that it's standard for a sink to be overflowing with dirty dishes," he explained, laughing. "I'd hate for you two to reverse my six years of painstaking training."

"Oh, Ford." Helen giggled and took the arm he offered her. "I don't know how you put up with him, Lila. Does he ever mean any of the things he says?"

She should have said something to put him in his place, to reinforce the boundaries that must, of necessity, exist between them. But Ford was watching her with an oddly keen expression. It was almost as though her answer carried weight—like she might actually possess the power to hurt him.

The feeling was unsettling, which was why Lila summoned up the brightest smile she had. "Not to my knowledge, no," she said and even managed a laugh. "But even an incorrigible flirt is right twice a day."

chapter

8

"G iles! You're just the man to help me out." Ford pushed his chair from his drafting desk to his computer desk. As both were crammed in one corner of his kitchen, it wasn't much of a journey. "I'm going to email you a link, and I need you to tell me exactly what you think about what you see."

"Hello to you, too," Giles replied.

His project manager was long accustomed to these kinds of conversations, so he accepted the request with no other comment. He had to. This was what happened when a man spent the majority of his time either with a child or staring at sketches of kitchen appliances by himself. Any overture of adult conversation was grasped at gratefully—especially when it came after Emily was tucked in for the night.

"Be perfectly objective," Ford said. "What's the first thing you notice?"

"Um…" Giles paused. "Are you sure you sent me the correct thing?"

"Are you looking at a picture of a ridiculously good-looking man in a surgical cap?"

"Yes."

"Then it's the right one." Ford infused his voice with a flippancy he was far from feeling. "One a scale of one to ten, how bright would you say his teeth are?"

"Have you been drinking? I can call back tomorrow morning."

"They're weirdly white, right?"

Giles paused again. Although they were separated by about three hundred miles, Ford could practically see the other man's brow furrowing. The pair of them had been roommates in college, so he'd seen that furrowed brow plenty of times before. It was probably why they were separated by so much more than distance now. While Giles had almost always been found bent over a textbook, Ford had been out enjoying the extracurriculars offered at one of the nation's top party colleges.

"It's a nice smile," Giles hedged.

"Come on, man. Indulge me. This is a matter of life and death."

"Everything is a matter of life and death with you," Giles said, but he heaved a sigh and gave in. "It does seem a little unnatural, to be honest. I feel like I'm looking into a spotlight."

Ford slapped his hand on the desk. "*Ha!* I knew it. I believe we've found our mystery heartbreaker."

"That's a strange thing to be excited about."

Oh, Ford wasn't excited about his findings. On the contrary, there had been a weight lodged in his chest ever since the tea party had broken up. The tea party itself had been fine—better than fine, actually, if you counted things in terms of Emily's happiness and Jeeves's training success. Which, Ford admonished himself, *he did*. But there was no mistaking the subdued manner that had taken over Lila after that phone call.

That phone call with Dr. Patrick Yarmouth, the eminent otolaryngologist who'd been seeing Emily since she was three years old.

That phone call with Dr. Patrick Yarmouth, a man one small step removed from a god.

That phone call with Dr. Patrick Yarmouth, who looked like he gargled with bleach and regularly caused self-controlled women to go on emotional tirades.

"How much do you think a guy like that earns in a year?" Ford asked.

"More than you," Giles said. "And me. Combined, probably. Which, if you'll let me get a word in edgewise, is what I've called to talk to you about. You got my email?"

Ford switched the computer off with a stomach that matched the heaviness of his heart. "To answer your earlier question about whether or not I've been drinking, the answer is no. Do I need to be for this conversation?"

"We're not firing you."

That statement wasn't as comforting as it should have been, if only because of the unspoken word at the end of it: *but*.

"In fact, this could be the exact step your career needs," Giles continued. Ford could envision the other man gesturing with his hands as he followed the script that had been placed in front of him. Giles was a hell of a project manager, but he'd never been great at the personal side of things. Not once, in all the time they'd worked together, had he ever asked about Emily. As far as that man was concerned, children existed in a separate universe where nannies and boarding schools materialized out of thin air. "The truth is, Ford, we're consolidating the art department."

"'Consolidating' sounds like a fancy word for layoffs."

"Well…"

Ford bit back a groan. This had to be the worst timing known to mankind—and he didn't just mean that for his own sake. There were at least a dozen contract artists in situations like his. Working from home, struggling to raise families and pay the bills, facing down a Christmas holiday in a few short weeks… "Give it to me straight. How long do I have?"

"Forever, if you want."

Ford stilled. "I'm not sure I follow. Are you proposing to me?"

"We're reducing the department, not closing it altogether. The powers that be have decided they can get a lot more productivity out of three or four artists working on-site than with the current setup. And I agree." Giles paused again, but with a kind of smug triumph this time. "I pulled some strings. It seemed the least I could do, considering our history together. Starting the first of the year, it's nine to six, Monday through Friday, full benefits and a tidy retirement package."

"And by on-site, you mean…?"

"Seattle, naturally. It's a dream job, Ford, and in one of the most vibrant cities in the world. And it's only across the state, so it's not like you'd have to move far. There's literally nothing holding you back."

Sure, if by *literally nothing* he meant a home and a child, a familiar routine of doctors, a cost of living that didn't include avocados at twelve bucks a pop. "I don't suppose you offer day-care services and flexible parent hours in there, do you?"

"Of course not. You know most of our team is male."

Ford didn't point out the obvious. There was no need. Even if Giles could be brought to understand that children were created from the combined efforts of both men and women, he'd never admit that a job might come secondary to family.

"There's not much of a bump in pay, I'll admit, but you'll love working with a team again. Client dinners, trips overseas… I just got back from one of our factories in Mexico. I'm still working off the effects of all that tequila. You used to love Mexico. And tequila, if I remember correctly."

Of course he had. Everyone under the age of twenty-five loved tequila. It was one of the rules of being a millennial, right up there with twelve-dollar avocados. But "You know I have a daughter, right?" he said. "My whirlwind tequila days are over."

"Just think about it, Ford, that's all I'm asking. I can give you until Christmas Eve to decide, but then I've got to start sending these pink slips out."

"Rolling out the jolly old Krampus right on schedule this year, are we?"

"What's that? You have a cramp? Are you sure you're not drinking?"

Ford sighed. Giles never did have much of an imagination. Or a sense of humor, now that Ford thought about it. "Never mind. It's not important. Thanks for letting me know in advance and for, uh, pulling those strings."

Giles paused. "There is a zoo here, you know. And

one of those museums where the kids can touch all the exhibits. Emma would like that."

Ford didn't bother correcting him—either about Emily's name or on the fact that an occasional visit to the zoo was hardly compensation for a forty-five-hour workweek with an hour-long commute thrown on top. There was no need. The decision had obviously already been made. All Ford had to do was take it.

"Thanks, Giles. I'll be in touch."

He hung up the phone and returned to his drafting desk, even though it wasn't of much help. Instead of the coffee makers he was contracted to finish by next week, he'd spent the past hour sketching various images of Lila in a whirling, twirling yellow sundress.

"I bet *she* knows who Krampus is," he muttered as he picked up his pen again. Not once had he been forced to explain any of his jokes to her, never had she struggled to keep up with his rambling asides. She met him stride for stride, with no signs of feeling winded. "I bet she could defeat him, too. With puppies. And tea. And fancy braided whips."

Even though he knew he should focus on drawing the best coffee maker in the history of coffee makers, he pushed his illustrations aside. Why bother? He could hardly get *more* laid off than he already was, and this was a much more enjoyable way to blow off some steam.

Which was why, with a square-jawed, white-toothed vision of Santa's evil doppelgänger beginning to take shape in his imagination, he set about putting a whip in Lila's hand and letting her free to do her worst.

chapter 9

"Hey there, Lil. Rough day of training?"

Lila didn't bother opening her eyes. To let in vision and light would be to ruin the tranquility of her happy place. She breathed deeply and spread her arms instead.

"One...two...three...*four*?" Dawn's voice was laughing but sympathetic. "Oh dear. I haven't seen you take a four-puppy time-out in a long time. Not since—"

"—since Patrick dumped me for being the coldest, least interesting woman on the planet," Lila supplied for her. She gave in and opened one eye. It was promptly licked by an exuberant pink tongue. "I know. I would have gone for five this time, but Pip is having some tummy troubles over the new puppy chow. I wasn't going to risk it."

As if sensing that more playtime was indeed vital to her happiness, the twin golden retrievers began a rollicking game of tug-of-war with the bottom of her shirt. She didn't mind. It was her turn for kennel cleaning, which meant she was wearing a ratty pair of jeans and a plaid shirt that had seen its best days about a decade ago.

The other two puppies—one a fluffy white Akita

with the coldest nose known to mankind and the other a chocolate Lab whose tongue had now found its way to her ear—continued their own playful assault. The Akita was a snuggler through and through; the Lab preferred to gnaw on the long strands of her hair. Lila breathed deeply and basked in it all. Lying on the floor of the kennel covered in warm bellies and wayward puppy kisses might not be the most obvious way to go about handling stress, but she had yet to discover a better method. As long experience had taught her, the puppies would snuffle and climb on top of one another and generally make pests of themselves until they all came crashing down into an exhausted puppy heap—with her at the bottom. For the first time in two weeks, she actually felt calm.

Until Dawn spoke.

"Well, you might want to package one of those honeys up to go, because I have bad news."

Lila groaned but didn't move. There was no bad news in the happy place. The happy place was fur tickling her nose. The happy place was tails wagging against her neck. The happy place was—

"Mom's here."

"Dawn, you wretch." Both of Lila's eyes were open now. She gently lifted two of the puppies away and sat up to glare at her younger sister. "I sent you over there so I wouldn't have to talk to her."

"I know, but she insisted. You know how she gets whenever one us shows the least interest in procreating. I think she's already ordered a layette."

"What are you talking about? I'm not interested in procreating. All I wanted was for you to pick up my old diary."

Dawn laughed and held up her hands. "Don't shoot the messenger. I told her you needed it for a work project, but once she started opening those boxes of our childhood crap, there was no stopping her. She'd like a March wedding, ideally. Apparently, you can get great discounts that time of year."

Lila groaned and started wrangling the puppies. It took some doing, since they'd discovered a piece of fluff and were doing their best to bring its life to an untimely end, but she eventually got her hands on the two golden retrievers. She held them up to her sister. "Good God. What did you say to set her off?"

"Nothing, I swear!" Dawn paused as she took the wriggling, golden-haired bundles and lowered them to their shared cubby in the corner. A thoughtful purse twisted her lips. "I mean, I mentioned that the diary was for a young client you're trying to understand better. And of course she wanted to know about Emily's parents, so I mentioned Ford. That's it, I swear. The rest was all her. There's no derailing that train once it pulls away from the station."

Lila wasn't buying it. "You sneaked a picture of him, didn't you?"

Dawn busied herself making sure the puppies had water.

"When?" Lila demanded as she lifted the remaining two animals and placed them back in their beds. "At the tea party? Did he see you do it? Oh my God. Is that why he kept looking at me all weird for the rest of the week?"

"It was Sophie's idea," Dawn protested. "And no, he didn't see me. I'm very discreet. He was probably looking at you weird because you wore a different crown to work every day."

"I wore those for Emily."

"*Sure* you did. You know, I've encountered many a strange fetish in my lifetime, but this princess fixation of Ford's takes things to a whole new level. Did I tell you that I was looking up royalty-themed lingerie the other day? There's this one where you literally shove a string of pearls up your—"

Lila was saved from having to hear where the pearls were supposed to go by the appearance of Alice Vasquez. The family matriarch—and a woman for whom the ravages of time hadn't bothered to stop by—stood in the doorway to the kennel with a photo album clutched to her chest. As usual, her light-brown hair was impeccably framed around her face, her long legs encased in a white pantsuit.

"There you are, my love," she said.

"Mom!" Lila tugged her shirt into place and did her best *not* to look as though she'd spent the last half hour crawling on the floor with various canines. It was important to put forward the most serene front possible; her mother was even worse than her sisters when it came to sniffing out romantic troubles. "You didn't have to come over. I only wanted that old diary I used to keep."

"Oh, don't worry. I brought it." Her mother tapped the photo album. "But I thought you might also like to take this to your young man and his little girl. Kids love looking at old pictures."

Lila turned to glare at her sister.

"I never said he was your young man," Dawn protested, laughing. "In fact, I distinctly remember telling her that you've given up on dating until the entire male population evolves and catches up to you."

"Such a sweet name, Emily." Their mother sighed.

"Well, you must have told her something, because she has that look in her eyes. Mom, please stop fluttering your eyelashes like that. I'm not going to show two perfect strangers the pictures you have of me and Dawn and Sophie naked in the bathtub."

"I knew an Emily once. Emily Lusitano. Your father and I used to play bridge with her parents. The last I heard, she has three children. Can you believe that? *Three*. And she's not even thirty yet."

"You've broken her," Lila accused her sister. "Nothing but a grandchild will appease her now, and I refuse to be the one to give it to her."

"Of course, Ford is a fine name, too, though I can't imagine what made his parents give it to him twice. Were they hippies, do you think?"

Dawn bit on a quivering lower lip as she finished securing the puppies. "Strange, isn't it? There's no explaining the tortures parents will put their children through. Well, Lil—should we draw lots for it? The short straw takes Ford Ford to husband?"

"You can have him," Lila offered, but there was no denying the tight squeeze in her chest as she did. It was silly to feel proprietary over a man who had literal hordes of women immolating themselves at his feet, but there was no help for it. Her feelings were proprietary. They were also inappropriate and only growing the more time she spent in his company. The best she could hope for was to push them as far down as they could go. "Mom, I don't know what kind of stories Dawn has been telling you, but I promise there's nothing between me and Ford."

Her mom's smile drooped. "Nothing?"

"Not a single spark," she lied.

"Oh dear. Then why were you lying on the floor surrounded by puppies? You haven't done that since you broke up with—"

Lila groaned and pinched the bridge of her nose. The problem with loving and overly involved relatives was that they had a tendency to be, well, loving and overly involved. No wonder so many princesses allowed themselves to be locked inside towers. It was probably the only peace they got.

"Let's just go look at that photo album, shall we?" she said, latching desperately onto the only escape she could find. "I'll open a bottle of wine, and you can tell me all about your friends' grandchildren and how lonely you're getting in your old age."

Her mother allowed herself to be led away, but not before she landed a parting shot. "That shows how much you know, love. I might be a silly and emotional old woman, but it's never been *my* loneliness I worry about."

❖ ❖ ❖

"Here you are, trying to eat the Fourth of July fireworks. And here you are, sliding down that horrible winding staircase we had in our first house. I only managed to save you from breaking every bone in your body by putting a vacuum cleaner at the bottom. You were terrified of that vacuum cleaner." Her mom flipped the page of the photo album and chuckled deeply. "Oh! And this is when you tried riding your tricycle off the back deck. To this day, I have no idea what you thought was going to happen."

"Mom!" Lila pulled the album across the table and stabbed a finger at the picture in question. "I had a tricycle on the edge of a precipice, and you stopped long enough to grab the camera?"

"Well, we didn't think you'd actually go through with it. You were a wild little thing, but you weren't *stupid*."

Lila peered closer at the muted colors of the pictures, which had been taken and printed in the days before digital photography. "You're sure that's me?"

"Well, of course I'm sure. I know you don't have much experience with kids, but I promise that parents can generally tell them apart." She glanced up and took a deep pull from her glass of wine. Dawn had opted to do some extra puppy training rather than face their mother in a mood as wistful as this one, so it was just the pair of them drinking the whole bottle. It had been having a mellowing effect on them both, so there was nothing but mild interest in her mother's eyes as she asked, "Did you find what you were looking for in that journal?"

Lila placed her finger on the page she'd been reading and shook her head. "Not really, no. I was hoping it would offer insight into the depths of a young girl's heart and soul, but it's mostly lists of things. Look—this one is called 'Ten Lies Dawn Told Today.' *Number one: Said she ate all her peas but then put them on Sophie's plate when Mom wasn't looking*." She chuckled. "Poor Soph. She always hated peas."

"You *all* hated peas." Her mom tilted her head thoughtfully. "You know, you might be putting too much thought into this. Kids aren't complicated. They mostly just want—"

Lila sighed. "I know. Fart jokes and cotton candy."

"Well, I was going to say someone to love and understand them, but I suppose yours works, too." Her mom put out a hand to take the diary, pausing for a moment to flip through the pages. "This is awfully dry stuff, dear. How old were you when you kept this?"

"I don't know. Ten? Eleven? It was before Sophie was diagnosed. I remember that much, so we can't blame my lack of imagination on that."

Her mother's glance was sharp. Unlike her daughters, who all shared the same dark eyes, hers were an ethereal gray that could turn steely in a matter of seconds. "You don't have a lack of imagination."

"Um." Lila pointed at the page that had fallen open. "'Ten Times the Mailman Was Late.' *Number one: May 3, 1998. Number two: May 4, 1998.* This is literally a list of ten days in a row."

Her mom chuckled. "I expect you were just being funny. You've always had a good sense of humor."

Lila stared at her. No one, with the exception of Ford and Emily, had ever accused her of being funny before.

"Look," her mom added, oblivious to Lila's incredulity. "This one is 'Ten Reasons I Like Puppies More Than My Sisters.' You can't pretend that wasn't a joke. No one loves those two more than you."

"Sure, I do *now*," Lila protested. "Although I might still prefer puppies to them, to be honest. Dogs are much less likely to spill the details of my love life to my mother."

Her mom looked as though she'd have enjoyed

nothing more than to delve into the deep psychological meaning behind this remark—especially since the name Ford Ford hadn't crossed their lips even once—but she kept her comments to herself.

On that subject, at least.

"Balderdash." She snapped the diary shut and handed it back to Lila. "Since the moment Dawn was born, you've been their champion and savior. We were a little worried, your father and I, that you were going to teach them to cycle through the air and eat smoke bombs, but you settled down the moment we brought Dawn home. I've never seen anything like it."

"Like what?"

Her mother blinked and took another sip of her wine. "Your transformation. I'm not sure how or why it happened, but you took one look at Dawn's scrunched pink face and became everything a big sister should be. Responsible, wise, caring... It was as though you knew, instinctively, that she was yours to protect."

"I was wise? When I was two?"

"The perfect little mother," her mom agreed, blandly disregarding her sarcasm. "And a good thing, too. I sometimes wonder what would have happened if we'd left you an only child. You probably would've become a stuntwoman."

"Me?"

Her mother nodded.

"A stuntwoman?"

She nodded again.

"On purpose?"

This time, her nod was accompanied by a laugh. "Either that, or you'd have broken your neck before you came of age. The only thing this diary is missing is 'Ten Times Lila Gave Her Poor Mother a Heart Attack.'"

Lila stared for a long moment, unsure what she was supposed to do with this picture her mother was painting. Of all the Vasquez sisters, she was the last one anyone would accuse of flying in the face of convention, of taking risks and accepting the outcome. No step in her life had been taken without careful deliberation—and, yes, list making—ahead of time. Going to college to get her animal behavior degree, opening a puppy-training business with her sisters, even buying the house they lived in together—all of it had been weighed and reweighed, the cons stacked up against the pros until a decision could be safely and responsibly made.

"Patrick, too," she said aloud.

"What's that, love?" her mother asked.

She didn't dare repeat herself, and not just because her dating life was at the top of the list of Ten Things You Should Never Discuss with Your Mother. Until that exact moment, she'd never realized just how much of her head—and how little of her heart—had been invested in her relationship with Patrick.

Although she hadn't gone so far as to make an actual list before agreeing to go out with him, she could recall doing a little light stalking before their first date. She'd known where he went to school (University of Washington), where he'd done his residency (Seattle Children's Hospital), the Zillow value of his condo (upward of three hundred grand), and the date he'd earned his scuba license (July 2015). Even if she *had* been on the fence about him, that shining list of accolades would have tipped her firmly over onto his side.

And why wouldn't it? On paper, Patrick Yarmouth was everything she wanted out of a partner. In the flesh, however…

"Mom, can I keep this?" She curled her arm protectively around the photo album. "I'd like to take a better look at it."

"Of course. You can even show it to that nice young man and his daughter."

"Mom…"

"I said *that* nice young man, not *your* nice young man. See? I'm learning." Her mom paused, a wistful expression curling her lips. "Dawn did show me a picture of him, though, and it seems an awful waste for you not to make at least a little push in that direction."

"Mom!"

"What? I'm middle-aged, not dead. And one of you had better start having children soon, or there's no telling what kind of trouble I'll get up to. You're not the only one with a streak of daredevilry, you know."

Even though the cover was closed, Lila glanced down at the photo album, those images of her much-younger self burned into her memory. No one had ever accused her of daredevilry. No one had accused her of much of anything, unless you counted Patrick and Anya fearing she'd lure children into her gingerbread house and eat them.

Except, of course, for Ford. For reasons she couldn't work out just yet, he'd taken one look at her and decided that she—*she*—was the fun Vasquez. It was almost enough to inspire the creation of a whole new list. In fact, as soon as her mom left, that was exactly what she planned to do.

Ten Signs Lila Vasquez Might Not Be a Lizard Person After All.

Number one: His name is Ford Ford.

chapter

10

I had the pleasure of my first kiss underneath these very bleachers."

Ford shifted the long, coconut-scented strand of Lila's hair from one hand to the other, making sure he twisted this time before he wove it underneath the braid.

"Of course, calling it a pleasure might be a bit of a stretch. Lord knows I enjoyed myself, but poor Katie Barnes probably tells a different story. See, I thought you were supposed to dart your tongue in and out, like a turtle poking his head out of his shell." He sighed and worked down another row of Lila's hair. How one person could have such shiny, unbroken strands was beyond him. It was like running his fingers through a waterfall. "Come to think of it, I used to think that was how you were supposed to do a lot of things where the fairer sex was concerned. It's probably Tallulah Grey who deserves my *real* apology."

Lila held herself motionless, her torso barely moving—even to breathe. She'd done this the last time he braided her hair, too, only relaxing whenever he happened to touch the soft patch of skin behind her right ear.

"Tallulah Grey," he added helpfully, "was the girl who gave me the pleasure of my first—"

"I can guess the rest, thank you," Lila said primly. Then, with a note of suspicion in her voice, "Doesn't this school only go up to the fifth grade?"

"Yes."

She paused. "Don't kids go to fifth grade when they're ten years old?"

"Ten or eleven, thereabouts," he confirmed. "But I was a grade ahead, so I must have been about nine."

For the first time since they'd seated themselves near the middle of the bleachers, Lila twisted to peer up at him. All of her hair slid out of his grip as she did, the ten minutes of painstaking braiding gone in a flash.

Ford didn't mind. He liked the way she looked like this, her long, dark hair breaking softly over her shoulders and curling enticingly around the mounds of her breasts. Her sequin-covered pink tank top was already distracting when viewed head-on, and this additional bit of elevation was nothing short of dazzling. She obviously had no idea just how much cleavage he could see from his position one bench above her.

He wasn't about to enlighten her, though. She'd never let him keep braiding her hair if he did, and he was so close to finally figuring out that last damn twist.

"You had your first kiss at age nine?" she demanded. And then, instead of reprimanding him as he expected, "How old was poor Katie Barnes?"

"Oh, twelve, at the very least," he said, delighted to find that Lila wasn't following the script. He was rapidly coming to learn that she almost never did. "She didn't go here. She was the principal's daughter. I've always aimed for women who are out of my league."

Lila's only response to this was a slight narrowing of her eyes and a harrumph as she sat back in place. For braiding ease, he had his legs parted enough to allow her to settle between them. She wasn't *leaning* on him, per se, but the space between his legs and her back was so close he could feel the heat emanating off her.

And sense the gentle in-and-out movements of her breath.

And smell the delicate scent of her peach soap, which mixed with her coconut hair to make him dream of exotic cocktails on a beach somewhere.

He'd long ago forgotten all the details of that kiss under the bleachers with Katie, but he felt sure that if he repeated the performance right now with Lila Vasquez, he'd carry the memory of it to his grave. He wouldn't bother with any of that in-and-out business, either. A kiss with a woman like this would require every ounce of finesse he had.

He blamed the thought of her mouth opening under his for the way he swept her hair up off her neck, allowing his fingers to graze that magical spot behind her ear. Although she didn't go so far as to purr, she did release a low, throaty sound that he doubted she was aware of. She also arched just enough to grant him better access.

Taking shameful advantage of that, too, he grazed his thumb across the delicately throbbing pulse on the side of her neck. She relaxed a fraction, her shoulders down and her breath coming easily, before he set to work on the braid again.

"I'll get it this time, I swear," he said, his voice only

slightly strained. Although Lila was losing some of her stiffness, his own, er, stiffness, was only increasing the longer they sat here. He could hardly be blamed for it. It was these damnable bleachers and all those memories of his burgeoning sexuality.

And her. There was no denying that part. He'd spent many a long hour in these seats with dozens of single, attractive school moms and felt no more than the mildest stirrings of interest.

Since it seemed prudent to keep the conversation going or risk burying his face in Lila's hair and inhaling like a psychopath, he added, "They must be finishing up the tour soon."

Lila, sharing none of his weird and inappropriate sexual longings, glanced casually at her watch. "They have another half hour before school starts, so we're fine on time. It was great of your principal to take the pair of them around so early in the day. Jeeves will feel much more at home if he gets to sniff it all out before there are hordes of kids clamoring around."

It was on the tip of Ford's tongue to argue. What was great about this scenario wasn't that the school administrators were willing to accommodate his daughter—they'd been doing that since the day she'd started at this school, going above and beyond to ensure her success. What floored him was the fact that Emily had accepted the mantle of responsibility Lila had thrust upon her shoulders with no more than a blink.

"School is where you spend most of your time, so it's very important that Jeeves feels comfortable here," Lila had said, once again crouched at Emily's level, once again speaking to her as though Emily was a miniature adult able to tackle the problems of the world. "It's also important that he learns to take his orders from you and not me. Do you remember them all?"

Emily had. *Sit* and *stay*. *Come* and *heel*. *Drop* and *good boy*.

It had been on the tip of Ford's tongue to tell Lila that he, too, needed the occasional *good boy* to keep his spirits up, but he hadn't dared while Principal Brown had been standing there. Lila intrigued him, but Principal Brown was much more likely to inspire feelings of terror. The woman was a sixty-year-old former drill sergeant who wasn't afraid to tell parents exactly how horrific their precious darlings acted when freed from the parental yoke. He was sure she'd be equally up to the task of telling him she'd never seen a man make such a fool of himself before.

He didn't need to be told that. He *knew*. But he'd been playing the role for so long, he'd forgotten how else to act.

"Show him around, let him smell everything and anything he wants, and make sure he feels comfortable," Lila had said. "We'll sit here in the gym until you're finished."

The braiding, strangely enough, had been her idea as a way to spend their time. He'd hardly been able to believe his luck. Having an attractive woman between his legs wasn't the most appropriate way to spend a morning in an elementary school gym, but he'd never been one to pass up a gift handed to him on a soft, supple platter.

"I can't figure out why this is so hard for me," he said as he set to work once more. "French, I can do.

Fishtail is no problem. I can even do that one where Emily has to tip her head upside down and I work from the bottom."

"Emily told me that Ms. Maddie taught you how to braid," Lila said.

He twisted and inhaled the scent of coconuts. "She did."

"And Ms. Helen."

He tucked and dreamed of a tropical paradise with her in it. "Her too."

Lila paused. "I've been thinking about taking Helen up on that offer to attend her Christmas Eve party."

His mild "Oh?" didn't capture a fraction of the interest that spiked through him. As tantalizing as this conversation was starting to become, he was too busy trying to turn the last strand at the exact right angle. He'd master this blasted braid if it was the last thing he did.

"I know I shouldn't, since it's best to keep our social interactions to a minimum, but she's been so nice to me. It seems rude to refuse."

His murmur was even more noncommittal the second time around.

"And it might give me a chance to clear the air. Thanks to you, my conversation with her at the tea party was useless. Not only does she still think we're a couple, but she also believes we're hiding our relationship for the sake of professionalism."

"There!" He snapped the rubber band into place and released his hold on Lila's hair. The coil of princess braids was decidedly lopsided, and there was one strand on the side threatening to come loose to frame her face, but he didn't care. He'd never seen such a masterpiece before—and he wasn't just talking about his handiwork. How such a woman could contrive to look this good at eight o'clock in the morning, with crooked hair and sleepy eyes, he had no idea.

It probably had something to do with the slightly bewildered air about her, the way she pulled her lower lip between her teeth in an unconscious gesture that betrayed her discomfort with the situation. Like the tell-tale blush and sensitive spot on the side of her neck, it was one of the few signs Lila ever gave that she was in anything but full control of herself.

It was a small leap from there to picturing all the other ways she might let herself go. That smile. That laugh. That phone-sex operator voice. All it took was a little imagination and a slow, careful lick of her lips to set his pulse thumping.

"I've done it," he announced, since it seemed there should be some kind of ceremony to commemorate his success. Also, because it suddenly seemed very important to do *something* with his mouth. "I'm a braid master. A hair connoisseur. A magician of—"

"Oh, crap." Lila shot to her feet, almost toppling him over in the process. "Quick. We have to hide."

"We have to hide?" he echoed, but his blood was still too thick, moving sluggishly through his veins. It wasn't until she yanked him by the hand and practically pulled him over the side of the bleachers that he realized what they were fleeing from.

Or, rather, *who*.

"Well, fiddle. They're not here." Helen's voice echoed through the empty gym, followed not long thereafter by the *clip-clop* of her heavily booted feet. "Principal Brown was sure this was where I could find them."

A pair of determined hands propelled him from the relative safety of the side of the bleachers to the woodwork maze underneath. "Ford, you have to *move*. She'll never believe me about our relationship if she catches us like this."

He opened his mouth to point out that there was little chance of Helen believing her anyway, but he closed it almost as quickly again. Lila was right behind him, her body soft and warm where it pressed against his.

And urgent. There was no mistaking the urgency.

"I thought you said you were some kind of expert at this," she muttered. Her lips were close to his ear, the whisper of her breath causing a shiver to work through him. "Or has it been so long you don't remember how it's done?"

In the rational part of his brain, an admittedly small portion that seemed to be growing smaller by the second, he knew what Lila meant. She was talking about his expertise in finding his way under the rafters to the most secluded spot in the center of the bleachers—to the place where they couldn't be seen or heard by Helen. His less rational parts, however, could only focus on one throbbing syllable.

Sex.

It had been a long time since he'd enjoyed that particular activity, and he was sure there had been one or two improvements since he'd last partaken, but he remembered just fine. In fact, remembering was pretty much *all* he'd done.

Well, that and imagining. Picturing. Longing. Hefting his own—

"Oh, for the love of Pete, would you move already? What's Helen going to think if she finds us under here?"

Thanks to all that picturing and longing and hefting, he had the answer ready. Several of them, actually.

"That we slipped down to enjoy an early-morning quickie," he said, his voice low. "That we can't keep our hands off each other. That I've decided to recover my reputation and prove to Katie Barnes and Tallulah Grey that I've learned a thing or two about what to do with my tongue. Who and where was your first kiss?"

They'd reached the center of the bleachers by now, the pair of them surrounded by dust and wadded-up papers and a lone basketball shoe with the laces removed. Of Helen there was no sight—or sound—but Ford wasn't about to point that out. Not when he and Lila were wedged between the rafters, their bodies pressed so closely he could feel the in-and-out movement of her breath.

"My first kiss?" she echoed. "You want to know about that *now*?"

It was either that or stand here agonizing over every inch of Lila's body sliding against his. He needed something to distract himself, and flirtatious banter was the only thing he was good at.

"Why not? It's only fair. I told you all about mine." He feigned a thoughtful pause. "I hope yours was a frog prince instead of some creep you've never met taking liberties while you slept. Those stories always leave me feeling unsettled. Who writes that stuff, anyway?"

"I don't kiss frogs!"

"Then it *was* the creep you've never met." He sighed. "That's it. Tell me his name, and I'll go slay him, dragon-style. I can't promise I'll be any good at it, but—"

"Would you be serious for five seconds?" Lila hissed as she glanced around. "I'm trying to see where Helen's gone."

It didn't take Ford the full five seconds. He lifted a finger and pointed it straight up.

Lila froze as she took stock of the booted feet ten feet above their heads. "What's she doing?" she asked. Her voice was barely more than a whisper.

Partially to keep his voice down and partially because he couldn't resist the warm lull of Lila's proximity, Ford brought his lips to her right ear before replying. "Waiting for us, I presume. I should've warned you before you took flight that she has the patience of a rock. She can outlast anything and anyone. When the world comes to an end, the only remains of humanity will be Twinkies, cockroaches, and Helen Griswold. It seems like a fairly good representation, if you ask me. Cockroaches I could do without, and Helen can be a bit of a trial sometimes, but I adore Twinkies."

"Oh, please. The only thing you adore is putting me in highly uncomfortable situations."

"You lured me down here, not the other way around," he pointed out. "But now that you've managed to get me where you want me, what do you plan to do? Are you going to tell me about that frog prince after all?"

"My first kiss was *not* a frog prince."

"Hmm." He feigned thoughtfulness. "Captain of the football team? Head of the cheerleading squad? The emo kid who kept checking out the library's only copy of *Catcher in the Rye*? No, I have it! Debate team champion, right?"

That last one felt uncomfortably accurate. Of all the hearts a young Lila Vasquez must have been able to capture, a brilliant, successful, driven one seemed like the best fit. The guy probably went on to earn six figures and drive a Ferrari, often wondering what happened to the bright, gorgeous girl who'd shared his first kiss.

There'd probably been none of that turtle-darting, either, the bastard.

"Well?" Ford prompted. The answer to this question suddenly seemed more important than he cared to admit.

"If you must know, my first kiss was an English major named Peter Darracot. He smelled like patchouli, and I couldn't get that dratted smell out of my hair for a full week afterward." As if to prove it, she tossed her head. Ford's braid held, but that didn't stop him from imagining all the delightful scents and sensations that were contained within that long, dark bounty.

"Patchouli Peter Darracot. I like the sound of that. Very tweedy. Did he read you some of his handwritten poetry first?" A thought occurred to him, and he paused. "Wait—he was an English major? In *college*? *D-a-m-n*. Here you are, trying to make me feel bad for hitting up the principal's daughter, when all along, you were luring young men into borderline indecency."

"I beg your pardon. I was of age."

"And by *of age*, you mean…what? Fifteen? Sixteen? As the father of a girl, I feel like this is information I should know."

"I mean the usual definition, obviously. The *legal* definition."

The words were out before he could stop them. "You were eighteen years old before you had your first kiss? What the *h-e-l-l* was wrong with the boys you went to school with?"

Lila shifted from one foot to another, her gaze fixed on a point somewhere over his left shoulder. "They didn't much care for me, I'm afraid. Most of the kids I went to school with found me somewhat...cold."

Well, they obviously hadn't stood this close to her underneath the bleachers, because cold was the last thing Ford felt. Even without Lila's body emanating heat next to his, he was overwhelmed with a burning desire to pull her into his arms. There was nothing cool about the things he wanted to do to her, either. In fact, he was starting to overheat just thinking about it.

"Were you a late bloomer?" he suggested with only a slight hitch in the back of his throat.

"No, Ford." Her gaze snapped over to meet his once again. Although her eyes remained as meltingly delicious as ever, they held a painful reserve. It was as if a shutter had been drawn, some of her internal light dimmed. "I mean that I've always put people off, even when I was young. No one kissed me because no one wanted to. All the boys I went to school with wanted to be around nice girls. Sweet girls. Warm girls. Not...a lizard person."

It was wrong to laugh, he knew. Clearly, Lila had been running with the wrong crowd, because he couldn't think of anyone nicer or sweeter or warmer than her. The things she'd done for him and Emily in a short space of time were overwhelming in both number and variety. She'd pretended to be a princess and danced a waltz with a perfect stranger for no reason other than to please a little girl. She'd donated a service dog and her time so Emily could feel more supported every day of her life. She wore a pink sequined tank top to keep up the royal pretense, her hair in a lumpy braid she'd painstakingly walked him through until he got it right. Hell, she was even hiding under the bleachers because he'd let Helen believe they were a couple for his own selfish ends.

At this point, he would have been well served if she stormed away and asked never to see him again. It was what any rational woman would have done under the same circumstances. Yet here she was, her body mere inches from his, talking to him about lizard people.

"Can you, um, enlighten me as to what, exactly, a lizard person is?" he ventured. "Are we talking about cute little geckos or, like, full-on Gila monsters?"

"It's not funny."

"I'm partial to those blue-tailed ones that dart around here in summer, but it always freaks Emily out when their tails fall off."

"I'm serious, Ford."

"About being a lizard person?" He shrugged. "That works for me. Just please keep your tail on whenever Emily is around. I can't be held responsible for what might happen otherwise. The last time we saw a lizard lose that part of its anatomy, she made us hold a funeral for the tail in the backyard. I shudder to think what will happen if it gets accidentally unearthed."

It would forever baffle him how he missed all the incoming signs. Maybe it was that he was so much out of practice that he'd lost the ability to sense a woman's interest. Perhaps it was the fact that he was suddenly picturing Princess Lila and her braided whip transforming into a lizard to bring down the likes of Krampus and all other foes in her path. Whatever the reason, her lips were pressed against his before he knew what was happening.

For the first ten seconds or so, that was all right with him. Being caught so far off guard was a novel experience—and a delightful one. His back hit one of the wooden beams, Lila pressing intimately against him as her mouth sought purchase with his.

This is no cold lizard woman, he thought as he sagged and parted his lips to let her in. There was little else he could do when there were so many soft, round parts touching him. Especially not when the rest of his senses were in such a whirl of contradictions. Her scent was still enticingly fruity, which made him think she'd taste the same way, but nothing could have been further from the truth. Her mouth was a little minty and a little sweet, a whole lot warm.

It was the heat that undid him the most. He didn't know how or why, but everywhere she touched him left a lingering scorch that burned through to his blood. He should have kissed her back, allowed his tongue to war with hers and give as good as he got, but he didn't. He just stood there and let her have her wicked way with him.

It was a little mortifying, to be honest. The first time he'd kissed a girl under these bleachers, he'd been terrified and wholly out of his depth. He'd also enjoyed the hell out of himself. In fact, he'd resolved, in those heady, glorious hours afterward, that he'd do his utmost to ensure that every kiss thereafter was just as magical for his partner as it was for him.

Yet here he was, standing still, terrified and wholly out of his depth.

Damn, but that woman knew how to *kiss*. He was starting to get the impression there wasn't anything she couldn't do.

"Oh my God." She pulled away just as suddenly as she'd kissed him, the back of her hand pressed to her mouth as if in horror. "I shouldn't have done that. I'm so sorry."

Her eyes were wide and her color flushed, both of which Ford found immensely attractive, if only because they proved his theory. When Lila lost control, it was a glorious thing for all those lucky enough to be involved. He wanted to tell her exactly that—that there was nothing to be sorry *for*, that she was welcome to attack him under the bleachers any time she wanted—but his tongue clove oddly to the roof of his mouth.

"Please forget this ever happened," she added. "It was so unprofessional of me, so inappropriate, so—"

Just as he was finally able to unstick his tongue and start making human sounds again, Emily and her entourage returned to the gymnasium. From the multiple voices filling the cavernous space—including the youthful pipings of Helen's sons—he was guessing the entourage had undergone an expansion.

"And then Princess Dawn dropped three plates—*bam*, *bam*, *bam*! But they didn't break, 'cause Daddy made her use the plastitics ones."

"The *plastic* ones," came the gruff correction from Principal Brown.

"That too," Emily said proudly. "Want me to show you how to do it?"

Ford assumed the answer was a negative, since no projectiles started flying through the air. Not that he could blame Principal Brown for declining the honor. Even from his limited vantage point, he could see that in addition to Byron and Neil, who were trailing behind Jeeves, there looked to be two more adults added to the party.

Lila noticed them, too. She clutched at his hand with an urgency that made him laugh. "Don't you dare say a word," she said in a low-toned murmur. "No one can know we're down here."

"We can hardly hide forever," he pointed out. Rather reasonably, he thought. As enticing as the idea of Lila holding his hand in a confined space was, they would eventually have to eat. And pee. That basketball shoe might hold a little overflow, but...

"We can at least hide until they leave," Lila hissed. "Why, oh why do I let you goad me into these things?"

"Is that what I did? I had no idea I was so persuasive. Was it the kissing or the hiding that I drove you to with my enticing ways?"

"Neither one. Both. Oh, what does it matter?" As if just noticing that their hands were entwined, she released her grip. She also glared at him as though *he* was the one doing the hand-holding. "You know, you could at least pretend to be enjoying yourself a little less."

"I could, but I've never been very good at pretending. Everything I say and do is the honest truth."

Even her snort of indignation carried a hint of elegance.

"When you come to know me better, you'll realize

I'm serious. I'm always serious. Like our illustrious founding father, I cannot tell a lie."

"George Washington was a slave owner and a misogynist."

"Yes, but at least he was *honest* about it."

Since the crowd had gathered closer, a stomp of her foot on top of his was the only retort Lila could make without giving their location away.

"That's strange. I don't see your father or Ms. Vasquez anywhere," came Principal Brown's voice from just to the right of their hidey-hole. "Did you notice them leaving the gymnasium, Ms. Griswold?"

"Nope," Helen said cheerfully. She leapt up from her perch and bounded down the bleachers, shaking the rickety wooden structure around them. "It's just been me in here the whole time. I see you've managed to gather my children around you. I'm sorry if they got in your way. Hello. I don't believe we've met before, have we?"

One of the adults replied to Helen's chatter in a soft, breathy voice Ford recognized almost immediately. "No, we haven't, although this isn't my first site visit here. I'm Anya Askari. I work with some of Emily's service providers."

The name must have also registered with Lila, because she stopped breathing altogether.

"And I'm one of those providers" came a male voice. Ford recognized that one, too, and it caused his own lungs to seize up. "Patrick. Patrick Yarmouth. It's nice to meet you."

Ford couldn't help stealing a look at Lila to see how she was reacting to this news. He had no way of knowing for sure that this was the man with the teeth, but one look at her rigidity, and he had a feeling he was on the right track. The feeling wasn't a good one.

What on earth did Yarmouth do to her?

Ford didn't have to voice the question aloud. He was no expert in relationships, as his failed marriage indicated, but he could tell a broken heart when he was looking at one. His own heart gave a creak in empathy. Patrick Yarmouth had obviously worked a number on this woman.

Given Lila's reaction to Patrick and Anya, Ford was prepared to retreat even further under the bleachers and stay there for eternity, basketball shoe urinals notwithstanding. Which was why he was so surprised when Lila reached down and slipped the sparkling pink shoe from her foot before tossing it to him.

He caught both the shoe and her meaning in an instant.

"I found it!" he called in a voice that was too loud to be mistaken. "It must have gotten wedged between two of the seats as it fell."

"Oh, thank goodness," Lila replied, her own voice projecting. "My sister would have never forgiven me if I lost this. It's her favorite."

"Our very own Cinderella story," he joked as they emerged from underneath the bleachers. The entire party was surprised to see them—with the sole exception of Jeeves. The cockapoo, dressed in a stately red vest that he wore as though it were a suit of armor, looked up at them as though he'd known they were there the whole time.

Ford caught his daughter's eye and winked. "You'll appreciate this, moppet. I almost had to go scouring over the entire school to find Princess Lila's glass slipper. I'm her Prince Charming."

"Daddy," Emily admonished. "You're not a prince. You're all dirty."

"Am I?" He glanced down to find that he was covered with grime from his sojourn under the bleachers. All that kissing must have raised quite a lot of dust. "Well, it wasn't an easy shoe to find. And why would it be? The best princesses require a little extra effort. Hello, Principal Brown. How did the tour go? And Dr. Yarmouth. What are you doing here?"

He thought he'd done a fairly decent job of showing surprise, but Helen laughed and lifted a hand to his lips. With a maternal gesture he'd seen repeated countless times on Byron and Neil, she wiped at his mouth with the pad of her thumb. Even in his slightly startled daze, he noticed the pink lipstick that came away.

Thanks to her quick thinking, however, they were the only ones.

"Sorry," she apologized with a wink. "There was a cobweb right there. I was afraid you might have swallowed a spider. Isn't it strange how I could have been sitting here all along and never heard you two down there?"

"Very strange," he agreed, unable to suppress a quick glance in Lila's direction.

By this time, she'd finished putting the shoe back on her foot. The pink flush in her cheeks could have been explained by the way her head was ducked down, but Ford wasn't going to lay any odds on it. She was mortified, plain and simple. Helen had heard every last bit of their interaction. Or she'd at least caught the juicy part, which was all that mattered.

Lila, however, was able to get control of herself fairly easily. With a fake, bright smile that did nothing to bring out the dimple on the side of her mouth, she turned to Patrick and Anya.

"I didn't know you had a site visit scheduled today. I wish you'd have said something earlier. I'm rather…" She lifted a hand to her head in a gesture that was as feeble as it was futile. Not only was she just as dirty as him, but her hair had gotten worse with time and no one had bothered to wipe the lipstick from the side of *her* mouth. "It's been a bit of a morning."

"I like your shirt, Lil," Patrick said, ignoring the bulk of this commentary. He spoke with a familiarity that was as easy as it was unsettling. "Is it new?"

She glanced down at her shirt, doing a good impression of a woman who wasn't horrified to find that her clothes were just as disheveled as the rest of her. "Of course not," she said. "I always dress like this, remember? My mother, *the queen*, thinks it's important to look the part whenever I'm in public."

As if in solidarity, Emily reached up and slipped her hand into Lila's. Lila gave only a slight start before smiling down at her. The dimple was clearly visible this time.

"I think you look beautiful," Emily said.

Lila lifted her free hand to her chin and dropped it again in the sign for *thank you*. "You look beautiful, too," she said.

Still holding hands, they confronted the rest of the gathered assembly. Helen had managed to get a grip on her two squirming sons, but she was staring at Patrick Yarmouth with a dazed expression on her face. It was all that was needed to confirm Ford's suspicion that a broad-shouldered, white-toothed doctor was exactly the sort of man who could bowl over every woman in his path. In all her years of flirting with him, Helen had never looked at him quite like that.

"Are you here to see how Jeeves is doing so far?" Lila inquired, her voice polite but tense. "As you can see, he's an absolute gentleman. Emily and I can walk you through his progress, but it's only been—"

"Oh, it's nothing so formal as that," Anya responded. "I had a meeting at the school this morning and thought I'd check in while I was here, that's all. Things are going well, I take it?"

"Couldn't be better."

Anya turned to Ford as if for confirmation. Since he wasn't sure what else was expected of him, he flipped a quick thumbs-up.

"Actually, it's my fault Anya's here," Patrick said, his attention fixed on Lila's sparkling pink tank top. As Ford himself had spent an unholy amount of time staring at it, he shouldn't have felt annoyed.

But annoyed he undoubtedly was.

"You wouldn't let me apologize before, but I need to get this out," Patrick added. "I'm sorry for underestimating you, Lila, and for jeopardizing your position within the Guild. I should never have doubted your capabilities, and it was wrong of me to intercede based on my personal relationship with you. I had no business interfering outside my role as Emily's doctor."

This speech naturally held no interest for Emily, who wasn't looking at him—or either of Helen's boys, who were showing a tendency to squirm even more—but the adults all stood transfixed. Helen was still staring at Patrick, Patrick was staring at Lila, and Principal Brown and Anya Askari shared a knowing look that made Ford feel as though he had no place at the grown-up table.

"Okay," Lila said.

"Okay?" Patrick echoed with a pause that indicated he was expecting more.

"Yes, thank you. Apology accepted."

"But—" Patrick opened his mouth and closed it again. For the first time since Ford had known the man, he looked less than his usual assured self, his eyes fixed anxiously on Lila's profile.

Me too, buddy, Ford thought with an inward sigh. *Me too*.

"Well, now that everything's all cleared up, we should get going." Anya was a small woman, her voice lightly fluting and her smile warm, but no one dared contradict her. "We've taken up too much of your time with this business already, Lila. We'll let you get back to work."

With the ease of long practice, she signed her appreciation to Emily for introducing her to Jeeves and for taking her around the school. She took a more verbal departure from the rest of them, whisking Principal Brown off with a request that she see her out.

Ford wasn't too far behind. Even though he longed for nothing more than to wrap an arm around Lila's waist and haul her bodily away from Patrick Yarmouth, he thought they could use a moment.

He wasn't alone in that regard. Helen grabbed both her boys by their shirt collars and pointed them toward the cafeteria. "My nose tells me they're serving cinnamon rolls for breakfast this morning," she said with an unprecedented show of tact. "What say we throw my diet out the window and gorge ourselves? I bet I can eat two, if I put my mind to it. Ford?"

"I'll raise you one and add a fruit cup," he instantly replied.

Neil and Byron agreed to this plan with a shout and a scramble toward the door. Ford had to repeat the offer to Emily, who showed a decided preference to stay in Lila's company. She stood watching the backs of the retreating boys with her usual wariness wherever kids her age were concerned.

"Jeeves can't eat cinnamon rolls," she said by way of explanation.

"Very true," Ford agreed with a glance down at the puppy. Jeeves still sat at attention, but the mention of food had caused those mobile ears to start roving. "But I imagine he'll enjoy the smells. Look at how his ears are twitching already."

Emily looked as though she wanted to protest, but she nodded and followed them out of the gym. It was a strange procession, and a somewhat subdued one, but Ford was determined to see it through.

And if the thought of leaving Lila and Patrick alone so close to those enticing, dark, dusty bleachers wrenched his heart a little? Well, too bad. There were cinnamon rolls waiting for him in the cafeteria.

Three of them, actually. And a fruit cup. What a roaring, riveting life he led.

❧ ❧ ❧

"Patrick Yarmouth and I used to date."

Ford made a scrambling motion at his drafting desk, dropping his pen and hastily covering the papers he was sketching. "Oh. Uh. Really?"

Lila drew a deep breath and forced herself to get through this. Painful though the conversation was going to be, it had to be done. Patrick and his stupid ill-timed gallantry had forced her hand. "In the spirit of full disclosure, I thought you should know. I had no idea that he was one of Emily's doctors when I took the job, and to be perfectly honest, I wouldn't have let that stand in my way even if I had. We broke up a while ago."

"Is that why he called the house during the tea party?" Ford asked.

"Yes." Lila hesitated, unsure how much detail was necessary to clear the air. With any other client, she'd have maintained as stiff and professional a front as possible. With a client she'd ruthlessly kissed underneath the elementary school bleachers, stiff professionalism seemed a little silly.

Considering how much she wanted to kiss Ford again, it was a lot silly.

"He's a bit of *d-i-c-k*, to be honest," she confessed. "He always was. The problem is, he's only just realized it."

A shout of laughter started to escape Ford's lips, but he clamped it down before it got too far. Emily and Jeeves had just settled down for a nap, and he didn't want to wake them. Emily had taken to clutching the puppy next to her like a teddy bear while she slept, and Jeeves, with only a slight sigh for the trials that beset him, let her.

"Why do men do that?" Lila asked. "Take forever to admit they're wrong, and then, when they finally do, fall into an *o-r-g-y* of apologizing that only serves to make everyone feel worse?"

Ford's lips twitched. "If Dr. Yarmouth's *o-r-g-i-e-s* make you feel bad, I don't think he's doing them right."

She eyed him with misgiving. "Is this where you tell me that you had your first *o-r-g-y* in the back of a school bus at age fourteen? Spare me the details, please. I've had enough of your depravity to last me a lifetime."

"I don't think I could ever have enough of *your* depravity" was his glib response. "And for your information, no, I didn't hold *s-e-x* parties in the back of school buses. I did feel up Greta Lawrence once, though."

This conversation was one Lila knew she should stop in its tracks. Not only did she suspect Ford was making up the bulk of his youthful escapades in an attempt to shock her, but so far, his youthful escapades had a tendency to lead to adult ones.

She opened her mouth anyway. "You seem to have met an awful lot of obliging young women during your formative years."

"I know, right?" He flashed her a devastating grin. "There's something about me that brings out the wanton in even the most well-bred girls. *You* know how it is. Is it my devilish charm, do you think?"

Yes, she did. It was his devilish charm and his easy smile and the way he had of making everything seem like a game. To a woman who wasn't used to playing anything—except the occasional bout of Scrabble—it was a heady experience. "I already apologized for kissing you under the bleachers," she said stiffly.

"True, but I haven't apologized yet for not kissing you back. In my defense, you caught me off guard. I'll do better next time, I promise." He tilted his head in a considering way. "I can, you know."

She didn't bother responding. There was little doubt in her mind that Ford Ford could perform any number of tasks that would make her forget who—and what and where—she was.

The real question was, could she?

According to her mother's impeccably kept photo album, the answer was a resounding yes. Once upon a time, she'd been the kind of person who was daring and fearless and *bold*. Someone who did what she wanted, took what was offered, and flew on the edge. Lila couldn't remember that girl, but she felt a profound urge to make her acquaintance.

Hello, Lila. I took care of us the best way I knew how, but I don't think it's working anymore. Please, will you take over for a while?

"Hey," Ford said, his voice softer than she could remember it being before. "I know I talk a big game, but if you want me to forget it ever happened, I will. Word of a gentleman. It was never my intention to make you uncomfortable."

Lila paused, too absorbed in her own thoughts to pick up on his meaning right away. By the time she realized he was giving her an opportunity to return to the Lila she'd always been—the Lila she'd always known— she'd already reached a decision.

"Will you go out with me?" she asked. The words rushed out in a tumble of breath and embarrassment, but she didn't regret them.

Ford didn't help matters any when his only response was to blink and say, somewhat blankly, "Out? As in… to your car?"

"No. Out as in a date. Dinner, movies, making out in the back seat of your sweet minivan…" She flushed as she repeated the exact conversation they'd had the day of the tea party. "I know you said you don't do that sort of thing anymore, but we really should put up some kind of professional boundaries while we're working. I was hoping that by meeting outside of puppy training—"

"Yes."

"I didn't finish."

"*H-e-l-l* yes."

"Please don't feel like you have to agree."

"*F-u-c-k* yes."

She bit down on a giggle. She couldn't remember the last time she'd actually giggled, but she liked the way it felt, like champagne tickling her nose. "I was thinking next weekend might work, but is it difficult for you to find a sitter for Emily? Especially considering how she feels about strangers?"

Ford rubbed his hand along his jaw, his ink-stained fingers leaving a smear like a question mark. "I could always ask Helen, but she's going to want to know what we're doing. It might shock her to hear my intentions toward you."

Lila ignored this, assuming it was designed merely to get a reaction out of her. "I'm going to make a suggestion, but I want you to know that you're in no way honor bound to take me up on it," she said.

"Is it a lewd suggestion? Because if so, I'm in."

She was forced to laugh. "Oh, it's definitely not lewd. It involves my mother."

"The queen?"

A more apt term had never been applied to anyone. "The very one. Sophie was sick when she was younger—as in *really* sick, and for years—so she's great at making kids feel comfortable. And she's, uh, already heard about you two, so it won't come as a surprise if I ask her to help out."

There was no mistaking the knowing gleam that sparked Ford's eye. "She's heard about me and Emily?"

"Yes."

"From your own mouth?"

She shifted from one foot to the other, even though fidgeting was something she normally strove to keep to a minimum. It was the knowing gleam in his eye that did it. She had to do *something* to release the pressure building up between her legs, or there was no telling what other unseemly actions she'd be driven to perform.

"We're a close family. We talk about a lot of things—including men who do their best to make me regret I ever heard the words *Ford* and *Ford* in tandem."

"Poor Lila." He got to his feet. "And you think this suggestion contains no lewdness whatsoever?"

She jumped out of his reach before he'd managed to get his hands halfway up. In fact, she couldn't say for sure that she saw them coming—it was more as though she sensed them, knew even before Ford did that he'd be unable to resist the invitation such a confession would offer.

"Not while I'm on the clock, please," she said. She

strove to keep a firm note in her voice, but the plea wavered on her lips. "You saw that display put on by Patrick and Anya at the school. I do need to at least pretend that I'm qualified to train your daughter's puppy."

Ford narrowed his eyes, although it did little to quell their glowing warmth. "So, what you're saying is, I can't *touch* you while you're here in an official capacity?"

She shook her head. "No."

He leaned nearer, the scent of him a combination of ink and coffee and the peanut-butter sandwich he'd had for lunch. It was somehow the most alluring thing she'd ever smelled. "But I can get as close as I want as long as there's no physical contact?"

She closed her eyes in hope that would pull some of her whirling senses back to order.

"I can put my lips right here next to your ear, but as long as I don't let my mouth drop that last tantalizing inch, we're in the clear?"

"Ford…" Her voice came out strangled, but it was the best she could do under the circumstances. She wanted so much to wind her arms around his neck, to pull him into an embrace that would show him just how much she wanted to wind the rest of her body around him, too.

Right here. Right now. With his daughter napping just down the hallway and her entire professional future in the air.

Oh dear. This must be what it feels like to eat the Fourth of July fireworks.

"I guess I can make this work," Ford murmured, his lips still a heartbeat away from the sensitive spot on the side of her neck. "I'll follow your rules and wait for you to take me out in the grand style, but only if you're still

willing to let me practice those braids in the meantime.
I want to learn that Renaissance fair one next."

The thought of sitting at this man's feet while he
slipped his fingers up and down her scalp caused an
anticipatory shiver to work through her. The smart thing
to do would be to tell him to practice on his daughter
or even to purchase one of those creepy plastic heads
they used in beauty schools, but of course she suggested
neither of these things. Common sense, like her resolve,
was fleeing fast.

"That braid's an awfully complicated one," she
warned.

"I like complicated things." His laughter rumbled
through them both. "And people, in case you haven't
noticed."

Oh, she'd noticed. For reasons that weren't quite
clear to her besotted brain and lust-fueled body, Ford
Ford liked her. *Her*, Lila Vasquez, who made most
men's blood run cold. *Her*, Lila Vasquez, who knew as
much about children and happiness as she did quantum
physics.

"It could take hours of practice," she added.

"I'm willing to put in the time." Inhaling deeply, Ford
finally wrested himself back to a normal standing position. Her sudden wash of relief at the separation disappeared when she caught sight of the mischievous smile
that hinted he was about to say something outrageous.

She wasn't disappointed.

"In fact, I'm willing to put almost anything anywhere
you want it," he added with a wink. "Remember that for
our date and plan accordingly. There will be no mercy
for either of us otherwise."

❦ ❦ ❦

"Lila! Princess Lila!"

Lila stood at the end of Ford's driveway, jumping only slightly at the sight of a parka-bundled woman running across the street toward her.

"Oh, good. I was afraid I wouldn't catch you before you left for the day." Helen didn't wait for a response before grabbing her by both hands and giving them a squeeze. "Are you and Ford going out tonight, or did you have other plans?"

"Actually, I was going to—"

"Whatever it is, reschedule. I just cracked that bottle of rosé and will drink every drop of it myself unless you come over and share it with me."

"Rosé?" Lila echoed blankly.

"A nice one, too," Helen promised. With a somewhat embarrassed look, she added, "I know I threatened to ask all kinds of nosy questions about you and Ford if you came over, but I didn't really mean it. I come on strong sometimes, but that's only because I have to. Most days, it's just me alone in that house with Byron and Neil. I love them to death, I really do, but if I didn't coerce other adults into keeping me company from time to time, I'd be drinking that wine by the case. So you'll come?"

"That's really sweet of you, thanks, but—" Lila stopped herself before she finished the sentence. The polite refusal had sprung automatically to her lips, her customary approach to overtures of friendship like this one. There was plenty of work to be done back at home—puppies to train and paperwork to fill out. She might even go crazy and run a vacuum cleaner over the floors. In fact, that was exactly what she did most evenings. Even though the puppies weren't allowed in the house, their hair seemed to follow everywhere she went.

She tamped down the images of all that fur breeding in dark corners and put on a smile instead. Cleaning and hard work were the hallmarks of Lila Vasquez, dog trainer and general stick-in-the-mud. That image no longer fit. Now she was Lila Vasquez, adventurous seductress and breaker of conventions.

One, moreover, who had asked Ford Ford out on a date and been gleefully accepted. Ordinary life held no allure for her anymore.

"You know what?" She pulled out her phone and sent Dawn a quick message asking her to run home and feed the puppies. "That sounds perfect, actually. Thank you."

The beaming smile that Helen bestowed on her was more than enough to convince Lila that she'd made the right choice. She might not have much in common with this woman—a busybody of a single mother who made no attempt to hide her feelings from the world—but she liked her all the same.

"Oh, famous!" Helen clasped her gloved hands together. "You have no idea how much I need this."

On the contrary, Lila was starting to develop a very good idea of how much Helen—and how much she—needed this. Wine. Companionship. *A friend.*

"And I meant what I said about promising not to ask anything you don't like," Helen said as she led her across the street. "The moment I cross a line, just say the word. I don't take offense easily. I'm a difficult woman to ruffle."

That much became apparent the moment Lila followed her through her front door. The house was almost an exact replica of Ford's, the small living room-kitchen combo offset by a cramped hallway that led to two bedrooms and a single bathroom. It also bore the same kind of busy, homey cheer inevitable when small children lived in close proximity to their parents.

All resemblances, however, ended there.

"En garde!" One of the boys lunged at them from the arm of the couch, a foam sword in his hand and a band of fabric with eyehole cutouts around his head. Lila wasn't sure, but she thought this one was Byron.

"None shall pass!" the other one added. He was also carrying a sword, but his attire ranged more on the side of caped crusader than pirate. "Walk the plank, ye ugly scabbards."

"I don't think you've officially met my monsters yet," Helen said, taking the scene in without a blink. "Byron and Neil. Boys, this is Ms. Lila. You saw her at school this morning. She's the princess helping to train Emily's new puppy."

Lila was torn between feeling grateful that Helen tactfully avoided any mention of her relationship to Ford and a strong urge to laugh. As soon as the word *princess* entered the equation, both boys shied off with strong expressions of horror.

"Retreat!" cried the piratical one. "Blow the man down!"

"Gross," said the other. As he also paused thoughtfully

to add, "I like that puppy, though," Lila didn't take too much offense.

"You can see why I had to make my Christmas party pirate-themed." Helen sighed as she watched them scamper toward the bedrooms. "Every year, I have visions of an elegant soiree with gold-dipped candles and a champagne fountain. Every year, I get voted down. Take my advice, and don't run your family like a democracy. Last year we did dinosaurs."

It was just as well that Lila couldn't think of any response to this, because Helen moved to the kitchen with a gesture for her to follow. A pair of stools sat pushed up against the counter, which held a tray of fresh-baked cookies and the bottle of wine already uncorked.

"Took a lot for granted, didn't I?" Helen set two unbreakable silicone wineglasses in front of them and poured generously. "If you said no, I was going to resort to bribery. My chocolate-chip cookies are amazing. Try one."

Lila didn't have to be asked twice. Since she and her sisters had inherited their inability to cook from both parents, home-baked goods were a rarity. If she'd had any doubts left that Helen was a delight of a human being, one bite into that doughy cookie was enough to convince her forever.

"See?" Helen laughed and started crumbling one into pieces in front of her. "They always say the way to a man's heart is through his stomach, but I find it works just as well with women. Better, actually, because it's rare that someone cooks for *us*."

"You didn't have to make cookies to get me over here," Lila said, somewhat guiltily reflecting that had the invitation come a few weeks ago, nothing would have prevailed upon her to accept.

"I know. But I wanted to. I like baking." Helen smiled, but it was offset by the anxious way she kept poking at her crumbs. "I also sort of wanted to, um, ask you a favor."

"A favor?"

The color of Helen's cheeks deepened into a pink flush that brought a relief of freckles across the bridge of her nose. "I wouldn't normally take advantage like this, but I figure we can skip straight to the good stuff since you're dating Ford."

Lila opened her mouth to deny this claim—as she had so many times before—but stopped herself short. Technically, she *was* dating Ford now. Or close enough to it to count, anyway.

"Of course," she said and settled more comfortably onto the stool. She also took another cookie. "If it's within my power, I'd be glad to help out."

"I'd be careful making promises like that around here. For all you know, I'm going to ask you take the boys for a weekend." At Lila's stricken look, Helen laughed. Feathery lines extended outward from her warm, hazel eyes. "Don't worry—I wait at least two months before I start begging for those kinds of favors. You're safe for now. This one is about that man we met at the kids' school this morning. Dr. Yarmouth, I think his name was?"

"Patrick?" Lila asked with more violence than was warranted by the situation. She couldn't help herself; just hearing his name set off a knee-jerk, negative reaction. "What about him?"

"Well…" Helen picked up the cookie crumbling in earnest. "He's awfully good-looking, isn't he?"

Lila paused to consider the question. "He's not *un*attractive," she was forced to admit. "I mean, all his parts are there—and in the correct proportions. The problem is, he knows it."

She'd never really thought about it before, but that summed up most of her issues with Patrick Yarmouth. There was no doubt in him, no self-deprecation, no ability to admit his flaws and laugh at them. When he had occasion to wear a tuxedo, he didn't ruefully liken himself to a penguin and wish himself back home in flannel pajamas. Instead, he sauntered about, one hundred percent aware of the impression he made and eager for others to know it, too.

She was about to elaborate on this subject—and at voluble length—when she caught sight of Helen's face and stopped.

"Oh," she breathed. "Ohh. You mean he's *awfully good-looking*."

Helen didn't dare meet her eyes. "And a doctor, right? One of Emily's?"

"A very good one," Lila agreed. "Well-off. Not only is he a top specialist in his field, but he comes from money."

"That's not what I meant," Helen said quickly. "I only wanted to know if he's, you know, smart. Stable. Dependable. That sort of thing."

"Oh, he's definitely all those," Lila said. "He's good at crossword puzzles, too."

"Is he?" Helen asked.

"Phenomenal. Do you want me to set you two up?"

Helen's eyes flew up to meet hers. "Could you?" She blushed deeper and added, "What I mean is, do you know him well enough to set something up, or would it be awkward? I wouldn't want to put you out."

There was no way it wouldn't be awkward, setting her ex-boyfriend up with the neighbor of a man she was kind of seeing, but Lila wasn't about to say as much out loud. For one, the wine was already having a strong effect on her, making her feel rosy and warm and as though nothing in the world could touch her. For another, she was struck by the strong feeling that these two would get along incredibly well.

Amazingly well, actually. If you asked someone to mold a human being as far removed from Lila Vasquez as possible, Helen Griswold would be the answer. She was petite and friendly, outgoing and warm. She answered phones and baked cookies and would probably idolize the ground Patrick walked on. In fact, Lila had a strong suspicion she already did.

"I can, and if you want me to, I absolutely will." She hesitated. "I should probably warn you, though, that he and I used to date."

"I thought so," Helen said. She spoke with wistful matter-of-factness. "You two looked great together. You're both so elegant."

Elegance was all well and good, but it obviously hadn't brought either of them much in the way of happiness. Lila said as much out loud. "Don't take it so hard. *Everyone* looks elegant when they stand next to Patrick. He's like a little black dress."

Helen sighed and held a hand to her chest. "He is, isn't he?"

Lila hadn't meant it as a compliment. She'd meant that he was functional and bland, suitable to bring out for any social occasion, but not very exciting for all that. Of course, she didn't dare say so in the face of such swooning admiration. Reaching down into her bag instead, she extracted the notepad and pen she always carried. She might be turning over a new leaf and all, but some habits died hard.

"Okay," she said in a businesslike tone, the pen poised above the paper. "Do you want me to make this an official blind date, or would you rather casually run into him somewhere without him knowing it's a setup?"

Helen's eyes widened. "Can you do that?"

"Of course I can. And I vote that we should, since we can make sure you're all dolled up and looking your best beforehand. He'll think you roll out of bed every morning looking like a million bucks." She considered before adding, "Which, to be honest, you probably do. I have no idea how you're old enough to have two kids Byron and Neil's age."

It was the right thing to say to put the other woman at ease. Helen stammered and tittered and buried herself in her wineglass before finally reaching a decision. "You know what? Let's do it your way. I've always hated the awkwardness of both parties knowing it's a setup. And this way, you can be there, too. Just in case I need you to take the edge off."

"Consider it done." Lila paused before jotting down all the places they could reasonably run into Patrick without it seeming too obvious. He kept to a fairly rigid schedule, which meant it would be easy to accost him at the gym or outside his office, but neither of those appealed to Lila's burgeoning sense of the romantic. Spandex-packed, sweating bodies might appeal to some men, but not Patrick Yarmouth. The medical professional in him liked cleanliness too much. He also had a tendency to eschew hanging out at places like coffee shops and bars, since he saw these as a waste of time.

Then again, it was also a waste of time to hang around a diner and an elementary school for the sake of an apology, but he seemed to be doing plenty of that lately.

"What is it?" Helen asked quickly. "Why do you keep writing things down and then crossing them off?"

Lila tapped the pen against her teeth, thinking. "I was just wondering if it might be best if I ask him to meet me somewhere—for dinner, maybe, or even to come over to my house to pick something up. Oh! I like that one. Then we can arrange it so you just happen to be there, too. What could be more natural?"

"You wouldn't mind?" Helen asked.

"Of course not," Lila said. In fact, the more she thought about this plan, the better she liked it. With any luck, Helen would distract Patrick from whatever guilt was driving him to self-flagellate all over her. *And good riddance*. "That way, you can bring the boys along. They can help me out in the puppy kennel so you won't have to worry about a babysitter."

"You'd do that?" A loud crash sounded from the direction of the boys' room, followed by a muffled howl. Helen made no move to go to her sons' aid, instead stifling a sigh and giving Lila a wary look. "Are you sure? They're an awful handful. Especially—"

Lila clutched the pen between her fingers, bracing herself for the inevitable. *Especially for a woman like you. Especially for someone with no affection or sincerity or love for her fellow humans.*

But Helen surprised her. "Especially when you've already done so much. Emily's wrong. You're not a princess. You're my fairy freaking godmother."

That description pleased Lila almost more than the third chocolate chip cookie Helen slid onto her plate.

"If that's the case, we also need to decide on what you're going to wear." Lila got her pen ready again. "Now. What do you have in your closet that sparkles?"

chapter
11

Lila was quick to close her internet tab when Dawn walked into the office, but not quick enough.

"Ooh, are we going on an ice-fishing trip?" She wrapped her arms around Lila's neck and dropped a kiss on her cheek. "I mean, dead fish are gross, and the last thing I want to do is sit in a wooden hut on a frozen lake for hours on end, but you know me—I'll try anything once. Twice, if there's alcohol or an attractive man involved."

"Don't worry. I'm not taking you ice fishing." Since the damage had already been done, Lila clicked open the tab again. The Inland Ice Fishing Adventures website wasn't very modern-looking, but it did promise a frosty good time.

"Then who's the lucky girl?" Dawn pulled up an ottoman and parked herself on top of it. "Or would it be more accurate to call him a 'lucky guy'?"

Lila turned to her with a finger outstretched. "Don't."

"I didn't say anything!"

"You didn't have to. I can feel you thinking it."

Dawn pulled the mouse from under Lila's fingertips and began scrolling through the page. "Fish-cleaning facilities on-site? Taxidermy and mounting options available?" She shuddered. "That sounds like a living nightmare, not something you pay three hundred bucks for. Does Ford fish?"

Lila gave up on trying to pretend this was anything but what it so clearly was. Dropping her forehead to the desk, she said, "Yes. No. I don't know."

"Hmm. Have you noticed any fishing supplies in his house?"

"Uh, no?"

"Does he tell boring, long-winded stories about the catch that got away?"

"Dawn, you know he doesn't!"

Dawn closed the tab with a flourish. "Then he doesn't fish. People who kill things for fun are like people doing a juice cleanse. Five minutes into the conversation, and they'll make sure you know."

Lila picked her head up from the desk, but only because the edge was cutting into her skin. Also because trying to hide anything from Dawn was fruitless. She'd dig and prod and crack jokes until every last secret was extracted.

"I'm trying to find a good winter date activity for the two of us," Lila admitted, hoping she didn't sound nearly as pathetic as she felt. "This website I found said to try ice fishing."

"Did they also tell you to do a juice cleanse? Lil, you've got to stop believing everything you read on the internet." She turned Lila's chair until they were sitting with their knees bumping. Lila's knees were encased in a pair of sensible gray slacks; Dawn's had ripped-open holes with just the right amount of artistic disintegration.

"What happened to the good old-fashioned dinner and a movie? Or, you know, dinner and sex?"

Lila felt herself coloring up, but she forced herself to meet her sister's frank gaze. "I wanted to plan something fun."

"Well, I don't know about you, but I find sex pretty fun. I haven't talked with Ford very much yet, but I'm guessing he agrees with me." She made a show of reaching for the landline. "I can call him right now and ask, if you want."

Lila made a mad dash to prevent her sister from putting that threat into action. She was the kind of person who totally would—and not feel an ounce of regret or embarrassment afterward. "Please don't," she said, her hand over Dawn's on the receiver. "I'm trying to show him that I'm experienced at fun, no-strings-attached dating, not some sort of freakish schoolmarm who never gets out."

Dawn's lips pursed in the way that usually preceded a piece of worldly wisdom that Lila neither wanted nor needed to hear. "To be fair, you're *not* experienced at fun, no-strings-attached dating."

Well, obviously. That was the whole problem. She'd asked Ford out on a wave of bravery and had ridden that crest all the way from Helen's house. But now that she was here, surrounded by the familiar file cabinets and sticky notes lining the walls, she had no idea what she was doing. When she was with Ford, being the funny, lively woman of the world he seemed to think her was easy.

On her own, however, she was nothing more than what she'd always been—a neurotic mess who couldn't even come up with creative winter date ideas without Google's help. It would be laughable if it wasn't so depressing.

"Can I ask you something?" she asked before Dawn could follow up with any more of her less-than-helpful insights. "Something serious?"

Dawn let both her hand and her playful attitude fall at once. It was one of the things Lila loved most about her—how quickly she could move from frivolity to frankness and back again. Like most of the things Dawn said and did, the frivolity was mostly for show. No one felt things as deeply as her sister did.

"Absolutely." Dawn made the motion of an X over her chest. "Consider this a judgment-free zone for the next twenty minutes."

Lila hesitated, trying to determine how best to put her question. It wasn't, as Dawn probably assumed, about possible date venues. She needed help in that department—obviously—but she'd find something eventually. Diligence and determination could go a long way.

"If you were to meet me on the street or in a café somewhere—not as my sister, but as a complete and total stranger—do you think we'd be friends?" Lila was aware of how rushed the question came out, so she slowed down and tried again. "What I mean is, if we hadn't been born into the same family, do you think you'd want anything to do with me? Socially speaking?"

Dawn didn't respond right away, staring at her in a wide-eyed, meltingly compassionate way instead. Lila did her best not to squirm under that stare, which she knew was meant to discompose her. That was Dawn's other way of eliciting secrets—rampant kindness.

"Damn," she said. "Patrick really got into your head, didn't he?"

There was only one way to answer that—with a nod.

"And Ford?"

There was only one way to answer that, too. Lila nodded again.

She waited while Dawn drummed her fingernails on the desk, thinking. "I don't know, to be honest," her sister eventually said. "I mean, we don't share a lot of interests—outside of the puppies, that is—and you definitely wouldn't have come across me in an ice-fishing shack somewhere."

Lila's lips lifted in a slight smile. "You're never going to let that drop, are you?"

"Then again, I don't have much in common with Sophie, either. Not if we look strictly at facts. She likes to knit and hang out with old ladies, and she's even started playing in the Deer Park bowling league. She's pretty good at it, actually. It's weird."

"But if you met her, you'd want to get to know her, wouldn't you?" Lila persisted. "Someone who knits and hangs out with old ladies and goes bowling is interesting."

Dawn blinked at her. "Yes, but so is someone who has a master's degree in animal behavior and lies under piles of puppies when she's stressed and would willingly take a man ice fishing if she thought he might enjoy it."

"He won't enjoy it."

"And thank God for that," Dawn said, laughing warmly. "I supported you throughout that whole dating-Patrick thing, and I'd do it again a thousand times over, but I don't know how well I'd do if you took up with a fisherman. Every sister has her limits."

The light words were meant to reassure her, Lila knew, but they only made her feel worse. Dawn would support her if she dated *ten* fishermen, but that was because she was her sister. She had to. It was one of those rules that Lila was so fond of.

"He really did a number on me," Lila admitted. It was the first time she'd ever spoken the words out loud, and they felt stiff on her tongue. "Patrick, I mean. No matter what I do, I can't seem to shake this idea that he's right—that I'm cold and reserved and unable to let my guard down with anyone."

She should have known that Dawn wouldn't accept a statement like that without a fight. Her sister leaned close and gave a lock of Lila's hair a tug. "But your guard is down with Ford, Lil. I've seen it with my own two eyes. When you're with him, you're like an entirely different person. Not"—she said firmly—"a better one or a worse one, but a different one. One I like and love just as much as the one I liked and loved before."

Lila's vision swam with sudden tears. That was the entire problem in a nutshell. When she was with Ford, she *felt* like an entirely different person. He made her laugh and sparked life in parts of her that she hadn't known existed. And then she came home, and those parts were still open—raw and exposed and unlikely to close ever again.

He'd done that to her. He'd done that to her, and she'd *let* him.

"I really like him, Dawn," she said, her voice barely above a whisper.

"I know you do, Lil."

"And I really like Emily and Helen and maybe even Principal Brown, too."

Even though Dawn had no idea who that last one was, she nodded and extended her arms to pull Lila into a hug. Lila went willingly, taking comfort from her sister's strong, capable, judgment-free clasp.

"You'll find the perfect date idea, I'm sure," Dawn soothed, the wavy strands of her hair tickling Lila's cheek. "And if you don't, you can always fall back on my dinner-and-sex plan. It's not very innovative, I'll admit, but it does the trick almost every time."

Lila laughed, the sound of it muffled by her sister's shoulder. Trust Dawn to restore her humor just when it was needed most.

"To be honest, sister dearest, I'm surprised you bother with dinner," she said.

Dawn responded with a laugh of her own. "To be honest, sister dearest, I rarely do."

❈❈❈

"What are you drawing?"

The sound of Lila's voice had Ford scrambling to hide the pages he'd been scribbling on. They weren't, as he'd so optimistically planned for the day, the remaining figures for his coffee-maker project. The idea of Lila the Lizard Queen had taken hold of his imagination in a big way. He was having a difficult time working on anything else.

Not so difficult was the decision to hide any and all evidence of it from Lila's view. Acting mostly on pan-icked instinct, he swept a frantic arm over his drafting desk, scattering papers all over the linoleum floor. Luckily, the only ones that fluttered sketch side up were of coffee makers. And a quick likeness of Jeeves that he'd done while the puppy had twitched his way through a dream last night. Though not his best work, at least the drawing wasn't one of the many images of Lila with a tail and a knife strapped to one shapely thigh.

"I thought you and Emily were outside working on traffic sounds today," he accused.

"Did you do this?" Lila asked by way of answer. She held the picture of Jeeves between two fingers. "Ford— this is good. As in, *really* good."

"Oh, uh. Thanks." He took the picture and started stacking up the rogue pages, just barely hiding a dangerous one before she drew close enough to see it. There were a lot of ridiculous parts of himself he was willing to show Lila, but his sketches of her weren't one of them. "I get bored with coffee makers, so I like to mix it up. You don't want to know how many pictures of Emily I have tucked away. Or Judge Judy, for that matter. It's borderline obscene."

"Judge Judy?" she echoed.

He shrugged. "I like to draw from real life, and since it's rare that I leave the house, Judy and I have grown close. She's a fascinating subject. She has a very expressive face."

Lila stared at him. He was afraid she was going to comment on the depressing state of a man whose primary point of contact with the outside world was a televised small claims court, but he should have known better than to doubt her.

"We live in the golden age of streamed television, yet you spend your days watching *Judge Judy*?" she asked.

"Well, not *all* my days. Sometimes I branch out into *Law & Order* reruns. I've got quite a Sam Waterston collection in one of these files."

"Really? That's the best you can do?"

Judge Judy wasn't the only one with an expressive face. The lift of Lila's brow perfectly captured her current mood—one of playfulness and of disbelief. It was a mood she often displayed in his presence these days. The playfulness he could—and did—appreciate, but he wished she wasn't quite so disbelieving where he was concerned. Yes, it sounded ridiculous that a grown man would keep a running marathon of daytime television on in the background, but he liked the noise. It helped him concentrate.

"Judy is one of my oldest and dearest friends, I'll have you know," he replied. "She keeps me entertained without distracting me from my work. I used to watch *Game of Thrones*, but I kept getting sucked into the story. Well, that and all the *b-o-o-b-s*."

She choked on a laugh. "How industrious of you."

"It's not my fault. I'm very partial to *b-o-o-b-s*. Yours, for example, are quite lovely."

As if realizing for the first time that she did, indeed, possess such attributes, Lila crossed her arms over her chest and glared at him.

"Speaking of, what time are you officially off this evening?" he asked. "I was thinking we should get some practice in before our big date. I had the minivan detailed and everything."

"Oh, no you don't." She crossed her arms harder, which only served to cup her breasts and thrust them enticingly upward. Since she was wearing a fairly modest sweater, Ford couldn't see much beyond the gentle swell of her upper cleavage, but that was more than enough. "I'm leaving in an hour, and no amount of persuasion on your part will lure me into your van."

"What about candy?"

"No."

"Drugs?"

"Absolutely not."

He paused to consider his options. "Not even a promise to appreciate your *b-o-o-b-s* to the fullest?"

"Especially not that." Lila uncrossed her arms and stood staring down at him, her expression serious. So was her next remark. "Ford, you're a really talented artist. I had no idea."

"It's a living," he replied with a shrug. Then, because Lila was still watching him in that unsmiling way, he added lightly, "You should see what happens when I get an assignment for toasters. You wouldn't believe what I can do with a coil filament and a brand new number two pencil."

By not so much as a blink did Lila betray that she'd heard him. "I don't know much about the art world beyond what I see in the occasional gallery, but it seems like an awful waste to spend your life drawing coffee makers."

"Are you forgetting about Judy? I thought about sending in one of her portraits to see if she'd like to commission a painting, but my lawyer keeps throwing around words like *stalker* and *restraining order*." He heaved a mock sigh. "Don't tell him I said so, but lawyers are the real fun sponges of the world."

"Is that what you studied at school?" she persisted. "Art?"

Ford wasn't sure what it was about her direct gaze and level voice that he found so unsettling, but it was a struggle to answer in his usual style. "Yes, alas. I wish I could go back and tell my younger self to take up medicine or engineering or anything that commands a halfway decent wage, but I was determined to be the next Will Eisner." At her questioning look, he added, "He's a famous graphic novel artist. *The* most famous one, actually."

"Oh."

That remark was a pretty standard response whenever he started talking about his pet hobby, so he prepared to change the subject with a smile and a return to the tantalizing topic of his minivan and how quickly he could get Lila into it.

Lila had other plans. "Soph used to read a lot of those," she said. "In the hospital, I mean. She didn't always have the energy to finish full-length books, so the shorter format worked well for her. She used to complain that all the girls had stupid parts, though. Nothing but *t-i-t-s* and *a-s-s*, if you know what I mean."

"Oh, I know what you mean. Why do you think I was so interested in them as a kid?"

Her gaze remained disconcertingly direct. "I imagine it was because you had an artist's eye, even back then. Or was it the superhero trope you were drawn to? There's just enough chivalry in you that I could see it going either way."

"It did go either way, to be honest," he said, doing just that—being honest. As in *really* honest; not just telling the truth, but allowing himself to speak from the heart. It felt surprisingly good. "At first, it was the superheroes. My dad cut out when I was really young, so Mom raised me on her own. The comics were a kind of escape. Nothing cures boredom like epic battles of good versus evil. She worked a lot."

"Grandma Louise?" Lila guessed.

"The one and only. She's retired now, but she lives out near Pullman with her countless feathered friends, so we don't get to see her as much as we'd like." He made a vague gesture over his desk. It was especially untidy now that he'd made a mad dash to hide all his secret Lila drawings, but there was no denying that it never looked very orderly. "It's one of the main reasons I lead such a fascinating life drawing coffee makers. After Janine left, I promised myself that I'd be around for Emily, even if it meant cutting back on the finer things in life."

He shifted his attention to the window overlooking the backyard, so he missed Lila's expression. Which was probably for the best, since he wasn't sure he cared to see her reaction. His own feelings on this subject were so mixed—those promises he'd made himself shifting under the stifling weight of the job offer. He had yet to make any kind of decision, but the clock was definitely ticking.

"The drawing side came later," he added as soon as he was able to wrench his attention away from Jeeves and Emily and back to the conversation at hand. "I didn't start appreciating the artistry of graphic novels until I was a little older. It might have been right after that kiss with Katie Barnes, actually. She sparked both my sexual and artistic awakening. It was probably the *t-i-t-s* that accounts for it. I spent years after that perfecting the art of the areola."

Lila put a hand down on his desk, her palm lying flat against the picture of Jeeves. She didn't make physical contact, but there was barely the breadth of a pencil between them. "Don't do that," she said.

He stared down at where their hands didn't touch. "Don't do what?"

"Make it into something *s-e-x-u-a-l*. Make it into a joke." Her voice softened and her pinkie twitched, but by no other signs did she betray her feelings. "You take amazing care of her. I know you worry about how withdrawn she can be, but she's a good kid. A *happy* kid."

He didn't dare tell her what he was thinking—that it was the advent of Lila and Jeeves into their lives that had truly transformed Emily. A few weeks ago, she'd been a good kid, no doubt about it. But happy? He wasn't so sure. He'd never gotten around to explaining to Lila how he'd come to be separated from Emily the night of the ball, but it hadn't been an accident. His daughter had taken one look at that room full of polished strangers and hightailed it for the nearest exit.

And who could have blamed her? The overwhelming press of people, her inability to distinguish the sounds of so many voices rising up at once... It was enough to overset anyone, let alone a little girl who wasn't used to moving too far out of her comfort zone. The only safe place she'd seen had been a woman standing proud and tall in a pink gown—a princess, a queen, a woman so confident in herself that she could have been stark naked and no one would have questioned her right to do exactly as she damn well chose.

Every minute that Emily spent in Lila's company, she seemed to be absorbing some of that confidence. Gone was the little girl who refused to look strangers in the eye; no longer did she rear back from situations that might present a challenge. And instead of her thumb working toward her mouth, as it always had in moments of stress, it moved to her puppy's soft, curly head instead.

Jeeves was changing her. *Lila* was changing her.

They're changing me, too. In what was rapidly becoming a habit whenever Lila was around, he felt himself torn between the man he'd always been and the man he wanted to be. All those flirtatious games he played, the steps he took to ensure that no one— including himself—was allowed to get too close, were starting to feel all too real.

"You're a great dad," Lila added softly. "There aren't a lot of guys out there who could have pulled off half the things you've done for her." A wry smile twisted her mouth. "Or made it look so good."

His pulse gave an involuntary leap. "I thought we weren't going to make this into something *s-e-x-u-a-l*."

"I guess your bad habits must be brushing off on me." Her fingers skimmed over the top of his before pulling away. His own instinct was to take those fingers of hers and press them against his lips, his heart, his *cock*, so his bad habits couldn't have had that much of an effect on her. "I hate to ask it of you when you're already hurting for sleep, but could you set a couple of alarm clocks for tonight? We don't want Jeeves to get complacent at night, so it'll be good for him to be caught off his usual guard. Maybe just after midnight and around three?"

Ford heaved a sigh that was only partially faked. He didn't mind the extra work with regards to the puppy—at this point, he considered Lila nothing short of a dog whisperer and would do literally anything she asked where Jeeves was concerned—but the fact that she slipped so easily back into working mode was sobering. Not even the prospect of their date beckoning in the distance had the power to sway her.

"Sure thing, boss lady," he said. As he caught sight of Emily bounding toward the door with a snow-covered cockapoo at her side, he added in a quick undertone, "But if I fall asleep in your lap tomorrow, you have no one to blame but yourself."

chapter
12

Lila wasn't sure what woke her.

She sat up, her sheet clutched to her chest as she made a quick survey of her surroundings. The house wasn't on fire, no nighttime intruder was creeping in through her window, and no puppies seemed to be howling from the kennel. In fact, if it weren't for her heart pounding like a bass drum in her chest, she might have thought this was nothing but a dream.

Her phone buzzed from the side table, clattering against the wood-grain surface. That sound caused both her body and her heart to jump once again, reinforcing the idea that she was very much awake—and probably would be for hours.

"What the—" she muttered as she scrambled to grab the phone and peer at the screen. "Who's calling me in the dead of night?"

The call wasn't, as she'd at first feared, from her parents. She didn't recognize the number, but as she glanced at the clock to find that the time read exactly 12:15, she had a good idea who might be at the other end.

"Hello, Ford," she said, ignoring the thump of her

heart, which beat more from anticipation than fright this time. "Did the first nighttime alarm go well?"

"It worked like a charm, as I'm sure you already know. Jeeves woke up. He woke Emily up. She woke me up. I, unfortunately, seem to be the only one who didn't immediately fall back asleep."

Lila smiled into the handset, but she kept her voice coolly polite as she responded, "And you felt it incumbent upon yourself to make sure I suffered along with you?"

"Yes, *d-a-m-m-i-t*. If I'm going to have to lie here until the next alarm, staring at the ceiling and wishing you were in this bed with me, then the least you can do is talk to me in your phone-sex-operator voice."

She was so startled she almost dropped her cell phone. She clutched it in suddenly shaking fingers, her knees sliding up under the sheets to rest against her chest. "I'm sorry—what did you just say?"

"You heard me," he growled. His voice was rough with what she assumed was sleepiness. "You can start by telling me what you're wearing."

"You can't just call me up in the middle of the night and demand to be told a story," she countered, though without much heat. Being awakened by a grumpy man who wanted to hear about her monogrammed pajama set was a new experience for her, but it wasn't an unpleasant one. "*You* tell me what *you're* wearing."

"Flannel pants," he said curtly. "The same ones you've seen me in twelve thousand times already."

She clutched her knees more tightly against her chest. She might not be the most imaginative woman in the world, but she could clearly picture Ford at that exact moment. He was in those weirdly attractive black-and-red-checked pants, his chest bare, his hair tousled. With any luck, he'd have the rough growth of his beard already coming in, his blue eyes darker than usual with desire.

Unable to help herself, she emitted a small sigh.

"I do have other pajamas," he added somewhat defensively. "But these are comfortable, and they keep me warm when I have to go outside five times a night."

"Jeeves shouldn't need to go out that much. Are you sure you're not overwatering him?"

He growled once again. "I didn't call to talk to you about that *d-a-m-n* dog. What are you wearing?"

She extended her legs out in front of her and examined the pink floral shorts and matching top. There was no way to describe them with anything but terms like prim, proper, and prudish, so she changed the subject. "My mom says she's free to babysit on Saturday, if that works for you. I thought we might go—"

"Lila Vasquez, I swear on everything I know and love, if you don't tell me about the wisps of satin and lace currently adorning that gorgeous body of yours, I'm going to drive over there and examine them for myself."

She chuckled and sank into her pillows, unable to prevent a pool of longing from spreading warmly down her belly. Wisps of satin and lace would have been a much better choice in this situation, but there was no way she could have guessed that her night would end up like this. Men didn't normally call her and demand to be aroused by nothing more than the sound of her voice.

At least, they didn't used to. Clearly, her life had been a sheltered one up until now.

"You're kind of a grouch in the middle of the night,"

she accused. "Is my voice really like a phone-sex opera-tor's? I always thought those jobs were given to sixty-year-old chain smokers."

"That is *not* the image I want in my head right now, thank you very much."

"Well, it's the image you're getting, so stop com-plaining. She can be a bosomy chain smoker, if that helps."

His low laugh did nothing to abate the spike of plea-sure that was working its way up from her belly toward the rest of her body—particularly her own bosomy areas. She'd been acutely aware of those parts for days, of pleasure and anticipation tingling in every nerve.

"If that's all you're going to give me, I'll take it," he said. "You could recite the alphabet to me, and I'd be hard by the time you reached *F*. Tell me all about this chain smoker. What's *she* wearing?"

"Leather pants," Lila said promptly. She wouldn't normally play along with such a ridiculous demand, but these particular ridiculous demands were doing strange things to her insides. She needed the distraction. "They're a relic of her youth. She used to be part of a motorcycle gang."

His growl this time contained less grumbling and more interest. "I like where this is heading. Proceed."

"Um…let me see." She paused a moment. Storytelling was yet another in a long line of skills she'd never had an opportunity to practice, but there was a first time for everything. *A lot* of first times, actually, considering her recent track record. "Her father was a powerful gang leader who kept a close watch on her. He had to, of course. Because of the bosoms."

"Tell me about them."

"About her bosoms? Or did you want to hear about mine?"

"Well, I'd prefer to discuss the state of yours, but I'm not picky."

"Am I allowed to use bad words, or should I spell them out?"

He laughed. Like the growl, it was an *interested* laugh, with a strangled restraint to it that made her feel as though her limbs were liquid. It was a powerful thing, to reduce a man to such guttural noises using no more than her words.

"I'd prefer you use the real deal," he said. "The dirtier the better."

"Well, I don't know very many dirty words for boobs, so don't get your hopes up. Let's see... I know tits and knockers, hooters and melons. Uh, fun bags? Or how about love pillows? My love pillows are all soft and squishy. Well, except for my nipples. Those are growing awfully tight."

"Oh my God. I'm not going to last very long if you start describing your nipples. Go on with your story. What happened to this ridiculously overdeveloped motorcycle heiress of yours?"

Lila tried to marshal her thoughts in a more appropriate direction, but she was having a difficult time with anything but the physical demands of her body.

So far, Ford had said nothing extraordinarily provocative, but that didn't seem to make a difference. Just knowing he was on the other end of the line—enjoying her, *laughing* with her—made her feel like she was sneaking around under the bleachers with him again. She squirmed more deeply into her sheets, the pressure between her thighs growing stronger with each movement.

"She fell in love, as all overdeveloped motorcycle gang heiresses do, with a rival gang's equally over-developed son. Do you want me to tell you what *he's* wearing?"

"Unless he's in a thong, no. And now that you mention it, I'm pretty sure this is the plot to *Romeo and Juliet*. Is this normally how you do this?"

"How I normally do this?" She cast a look down at herself, somewhat surprised to find that she was still in her prim pajamas, her limbs twisted up in the crisp white sheets she changed every three days like clock-work. Those things were the same as they always were, predictable and boring. *She* was the only thing that had changed. As was usually the case where this man was concerned, she was forging new territory here—sexually charged territory where she laughed and played and threw all discretion to the wind. "I don't know. I've never had phone sex before. Don't most people do it via video chat these days?"

"Woman, if you had any idea what kind of agonies I'm in just listening to your voice, you wouldn't suggest such a thing. I don't think my heart can take it." He paused. "Have you really never done this before?"

She squirmed again, this time uncomfortably. How could she admit to this man that her sex life, though not lacking in opportunity, had never been what one would call adventurous? She'd done it in beds and on couches, on the floor and the kitchen counter, but that was about the extent of her experimentation. She'd never even sent someone a nude. She'd tried once, but she couldn't seem to get the angles to work to her satisfaction.

"To be honest, it hasn't come up," she said.

"Never?"

"Not really, no. I've only had the ordinary kind of sex." She hesitated briefly before adding, "Probably because I've only had the ordinary kind of partners."

He paused again, long enough this time to cause her some alarm. It went against her nature to lie about her experiences, but maybe she should have played a *little* coy. She didn't want Ford to think she was boring.

"In that case, I'm about to rock your world. Are you ready?"

"Ready for what?" she asked, somewhat bewildered. Was there a protocol that no one had told her about? Was this another one of those life lessons that everyone else seemed to be born knowing?

Oh dear. Why, oh why, hadn't it occurred to her to ask Dawn what to expect when hooking up with a gorgeous, flirtatious man of the world? Her more experienced sister would have been able to prep her accordingly. Or at least provide ample warning.

"Your leather-clad grandmother has nothing on me, I'm afraid. Is your right hand free? Yes? Good. Slip it down your stomach until you get to the top of your panties."

"What makes you think I'm wearing any?" she asked, her voice only partially strangled.

A low, strangled sound escaped his throat. "You're such a liar. You've done this a million times before, haven't you? You wouldn't ask such a dangerous question otherwise."

"I'm a fairly intelligent woman. I can guess that nudity appeals to your imagination."

"*You* appeal to my imagination, Lila. You could be encased in a bubble made of explosive plastics, and I'd still rip through it with my goddamned teeth to get a taste of you."

It was the first time he'd ever sworn—*really* sworn, the word coming out without a trip or a hesitation, no sound of a spelled-out letter anywhere. She might, under any other circumstances, have been able to hold her own against him, but that loss of control—that tiny slip from a doting father to an uncontrolled, passionate man—was her undoing.

"Oh," she said, unable to come up with a better retort.

"You're damn right, *oh*," he said. "Now slide your hand over the top of your panties. No going inside until I tell you. All you can do is run your fingers over the top of the fabric. Are you doing that?"

She wasn't, but it seemed rude not to comply. More importantly, she *wanted* to comply. Like kissing him under the bleachers, like breaking all the rules to ask him on a date, she was giving up and giving in.

And, oh, how good it felt.

"Yes." She gasped as she trailed her hand down her own body. It felt strangely foreign to her, the dips and swells she knew so well suddenly taking on new shapes. "I'm doing what you say."

"Good girl. As a reward, you can cup your mound and slide a finger between your legs."

She complied with both of these requests, all too happy to give herself over to the task of doing exactly as he said, exactly when he said it. She'd never thought it was in her nature to be submissive, but there was something exhilarating about letting him dictate her pleasure from halfway across town. For once in her life, no one was counting on her to carry the moment, no one expected her to do anything but enjoy herself.

And enjoying herself was precisely what she planned to do.

She closed her eyes and snuggled deeper into her pillows. "Okay," she said, closing her eyes and giving herself over to the moment. "Now what?"

It occurred to her—if fleetingly—that she had yet to offer him any instruction in return. "Wait—should I also be telling you what to do with your hand?"

"My hand is busy enough right now," he said in a low-toned reply. "I'd tell you exactly what I'm doing and how vigorously I'm doing it, but I'm trying not to shame myself over here. What do you feel?"

What did she *feel*? That seemed like a silly question. She felt excited. She felt alive. She felt each press of her fingertips against her clit like a jolt of electricity.

"Um" was all she could manage. The rest was a kind of moan and whimper wrapped up in one.

"Good," he said gruffly. "Now slip a finger—just one, mind you—into your pussy. Do you feel how slick it is, how wet you are for me?"

"Mmm-hmm," she said with another one of those moan-whimpers. It was all she could manage as she encountered the slippery, swollen lobes. "Can I—?"

"Yes," he said. "Touch yourself. Rub yourself. Imagine it's me over there with you, spreading your legs wide and fingering you until you scream."

She did all those things. She touched and rubbed and

pictured Ford in the bed with her, making sexy demands and using all the profanity he could muster in the heat of the moment. Which, for the record, was quite a bit. She lost track after the third *fuck*, but this man apparently had no qualms about swearing when the situation called for it.

"I'm starting to think I'm on the phone with a stranger," she gasped after a particularly detailed outburst. "Are you sure I shouldn't be telling you what to do? To take some of the edge off?"

"There's only one way to take the edge off," he said. "I thought you'd have realized that by now."

Oh, she'd realized it. She'd realized it the moment she'd made contact with her own body. The pair of them had spent *weeks* tiptoeing around this—well, Lila had tiptoed; Ford had barreled in with his usual laugh and a smile. She had no idea what it was about her that seemed to incite this man to such fiery passion, but she liked it.

She liked *him*.

"Then do it," she said, no longer surprised at her own daring. Admitting how much she liked this man—and how he made her feel—was only the first step. She had the feeling that once that barrier came down, there would be no stopping her.

Or him.

"I want you to finish yourself off," she said. "Don't hold back. Don't slow down. Keep running your hand up and down your cock until you forget your own name."

"I have a name?" he asked in a strangled voice.

She chuckled. It had been her intention to keep going, to detail exactly how close she was to setting her whole body alight, when he interrupted her.

"That laugh…" Ford groaned. "*Fuck*, Lila. I could spend the rest of my life coming on the sound of that laugh alone."

It wasn't the most erotic thing he'd said to her during their phone call, and it wasn't even close to the most graphic. In fact, a laugh seemed like the most innocent thing that either of them had shared for the past ten minutes. But there was something so honest—so raw—about the way he spoke that Lila gasped and felt herself giving in. She wanted to prolong this moment, to show the kind of resolve that would delay her orgasm as long as possible, but it was no use.

As Ford's breath caught and pried loose again, finally giving over to release, her own body shook in shuddering waves against her hand. It was no use trying to fight it—or him. She had no choice but to give over to everything but Ford Ford and the pleasure he wrought wherever he went.

She lay against the ruffled pillows, sated and panting, the phone still pressed against her ear as her breathing resumed a normal pattern. His did, too, the pair of them not talking but sharing a strangely connected moment all the same.

"I didn't know phone sex could be like that," she said, the first to break the silence. She felt oddly shy, but it seemed as though one of them should make the attempt at speech.

"Like what?" Ford's own voice was lazy and, she hated to admit it, a little smug. Considering what he'd just made her do, she decided his pride was justified.

She also knew that she should answer him, but she was having a difficult time deciding on the right word to describe the experience. It had been more fun than she'd expected—funnier, too, the same way everything with Ford was. But although the laughter had surprised her, it hadn't taken her breath away nearly as much as the intimacy.

"Good," she eventually said. It was an inadequate way to describe the experience they'd just shared, but it was also accurate. She felt *good*.

"I know," he agreed. "Me either."

She sat up with a start, and all her blankets fell away. So did the feeling of peace that had been settling over her. "Wait a minute—I thought you said you'd done this before. You jerk. You set yourself up as some kind of pro, getting all sexy and telling me what to do. I should have known better than to believe a word out of your mouth."

"I only meant that it was good for me, too—great, in fact." He paused, the mood oddly heavy. "I wouldn't lie to you, Lila. I never have."

"Yeah, right. And I'm a sixty-something chain smoker with a rack like a Vegas showgirl."

Another interminable silence followed. She was half afraid that she'd said something to ruin the call, that Ford was genuinely insulted by her remarks, but he eventually released a low laugh. "Please don't start up with her again. I'm begging you. I don't think my body can take it."

"You might have to. There are over two hours until the next alarm goes off. We're going to have to do *something* to pass the time."

"You could always recite the alphabet."

She sank back into the pillows. The dangerous

moment—that feeling of contentment slipping away from her—had passed. She was more grateful about it than she cared to admit. She wasn't ready to end this call, wasn't prepared to tell Ford goodbye.

"I can do you one better," she promised and settled in for a long chat. "Ready? 'Two households, alike in dignity, in fair Verona, where we lay our scene…'"

chapter 13

I don't understand. I thought you were giving me until Christmas Eve to decide."

Ford stood at the kitchen window, watching as Lila and Emily worked on leash training with Jeeves. They were ostensibly teaching the puppy where to stand to provide care and balance of his charge while out for a walk, but they seemed to be spending most of their time laughing and chasing snowballs. Well, Emily chased snowballs. Jeeves was far too intent on his training to allow himself to be distracted. Not even the red-and-green-plaid bow tie that Lila had brought to decorate the puppy had done anything to decrease his dignity. There was a job to be done, and nothing would prevent him from doing it.

Although Jeeves seemed to have accepted this state of affairs readily enough, Ford was finding it much more difficult. Lila had a way of making work seem like a pleasure, and pleasure feel like ecstasy. Even a late-night phone call with her had somehow become the most satisfying sexual experience of his adult life.

"Oh, you still have a few weeks. This call is about bribery, plain and simple. And it took some doing, so you'd better be grateful." Giles spoke with the proud assurance of a man who wasn't currently besieged with longing for a woman who was literally untouchable. "Three days in, two days out. That's the best I can offer. And you can set the days yourself to fit around Emma's schedule."

Ford had to wrest his attention away from the backyard. As much as he wanted to be out there with them, he was determined to spend the rest of the day chained to his drafting desk. Despite his best intentions, he hadn't drawn a single damn coffee maker in days. Whip-yielding, Krampus-slaying lizard Lila, however, was taking shape quite nicely.

"I'm sorry. You said three in, two out?" he asked.

"That's it," Giles agreed. "You could spend Monday through Wednesday at the office and then make the last two days your home office ones. Or you could switch it up so you're doing Monday, Wednesday, and Friday here, and then filling in the other two remotely. The boys upstairs don't love the idea, but they do love me, so they're willing to relax a little. What do you say?"

"Uh." Ford blinked, his eyes losing focus as the importance of what Giles was saying finally sank in. "You're offering me flex hours? If I come to Seattle?"

"It's what all the competitive firms are doing these days. I asked around. There's even a government kick-back or two come tax time. Apparently, it's better for the environment if you let your employees do a day or two at home." Giles laughed. "That's how I sold it, anyway."

Ford was more touched by this gesture than he could say. Giles still didn't know Emily's name, and he doubted his friend would want much to do with his daughter if they did end up moving across the state, but there was no denying that he was making an effort. There was also no denying that the offer was a tempting one. A full benefits package was no small matter where Emily was concerned, and two days a week at home were better than none.

Or, you know, *all* of the days at home, which was his only other alternative. He could always fill in the unemployment gaps with freelancing work, but there was no guarantee to that sort of life. No stability. That might fit the devil-may-care character he'd been playing for so long, but that role was starting to pall.

Emily deserved more than that. *He* deserved more.

"That's really great, Giles. I mean it."

"Why does it sound like there's a *but* hovering in the air?"

A rueful grin lifted Ford's lips. "Because there is. Not the one you're thinking of, though. It's just that I can't decide on anything without discussing the idea with Emily first."

"Isn't she like…a baby?"

He chuckled. Poor Giles. Someday, he'd get married and have kids of his own, and Ford was going to fling every last one of these comments back at him. "Not quite. She's six, which means she's old enough to understand what a move like that would entail. She should get to have a say in the matter. *H-e-l-l*, I should probably run it by Janine, too."

"Janine?" Giles echoed. "Jesus. I haven't thought about her in years. How's she doing these days? Still studying ice cores in the great white north?"

"Oh yeah. You know how she was back in college.

She won't stop until there's a Nobel Prize under her belt. She has a video chat with Emily coming up for the holidays, so I can run it by her then. I doubt she'll care one way or the other, but I'd like to keep her in the loop. It's a big change."

He hesitated, his gaze flicking to where his daughter and Lila sat tossing snowballs for Jeeves to fetch. Lila made a comment that caused Emily to dissolve into laughter, the pair of them rolling around in the snow in their mirth. It struck him that he'd never seen such a beautiful, more inspiring scene before, and his fingers twitched to pick up his pen and switch to the Lila versus Krampus pages. A sidekick—that was what the lizard queen needed. A scrappy little peasant girl, not very popular with the villagers, perhaps, but with the heart of a warrior. And a valiant pet cockapoo by her side, clad—naturally—in a suit of armor.

Other than that slight waver of his hand, however, he didn't reach for the pen. That was what stability meant, right? Working when he'd rather be playing? Putting his financial future in front of his present happiness?

It's what men like Patrick Yarmouth do, anyway.

"Well, tell Janine I said hello, and call me as soon as you have a better idea about your plans, will you?" Giles asked. "And if you'd like me to start looking around at rentals, let me know. I can line up some housing prospects close by to cut down on your commute times."

"Thanks, Giles. I know I don't sound very grateful, but I appreciate what you're doing."

He hung up the phone with an oddly heavy heart for a man who'd just received a job offer that had the potential to change his life for the better. Giles was going above and beyond for him. He was giving him time and opportunity to make a decision. Unfortunately, Ford had no idea what he wanted to do.

No—he did know, and therein lay the problem. What he wanted was to pull on his boots and join Lila and Emily outside. What he wanted was to consign every *g-o-d-d-a-m-n* coffee-maker illustration he'd ever drawn to flames. What he wanted was to discuss this prospect with a girlfriend, a partner, a *wife*.

I'm just so tired of doing this alone.

And there was the bald truth of it. He *was* tired— not because he'd been up all night with Lila, and not because of Jeeves, but because for the first time since his divorce, he could see a different future for himself. One in which laughter, not loneliness, made up the bulk of his days. One in which Lila's level head and calm good sense balanced his own downfalls.

That was the one thing about single parenthood that no one had told him ahead of time—the deep, dark secret of it all. From the day Emily had become his sole responsibility, he'd stopped seeing women in terms of sexual partners and started seeing them in terms of life partners instead. In fact, he was attracted to Lila's strength and competence just as much as her beauty. But what kind of a compliment was that?

Your financial stability rocks my world. I love your work-life balance. Damn, but you look good in that cloak of adulthood.

He could hardly say any of that out loud, especially when his own future was still so murky. He didn't know where he'd be in two months, let alone two years, and even if he worked his ass off the entire time, he'd never be good enough for a woman like Lila. In fact, the only thing he knew for sure was that there would be no finding his way back from her.

Not even if he went all the way to Seattle to do it. Not even if he spent the rest of his life trying.

❧❧❧

"I swear to *G-o-d*, if I have to look at one more coffeemaker, I'm going to start putting tails on the filter baskets and eyeballs in the power switches." Ford tossed his pen down in disgust and rubbed a weary hand over his eyes.

Despite his determination to be a man of duty, he wasn't going to last another minute of being chained to his desk. A hard-working, dedicated businessman he decidedly was not, especially after a sleepless night. Poor Giles had no idea what he was getting himself into with that full-time job offer.

"Distract me with something," he begged the woman standing in the doorway to the kitchen. "Anything."

"Why do I get the feeling that's a loaded question?" she asked.

He swiveled his chair to face her. Although Lila had theoretically had *her* night's sleep disturbed, too, no sign of it showed anywhere on her person. To look at her, with her loosely flowing braid over one shoulder and an enormous flower pinned to the front of her blouse, she was getting ready to attend church or PTA or anywhere else people congregated with the most honorable of intentions.

"Because you have a highly suspicious mind," he countered, but couldn't help a yawn from escaping and ruining the moment. "Maybe it's the cost of having sold your soul to the devil. How else can you stand there, looking like that, after what you did to me last night?"

"What *I* did to you?" she asked blankly. Her bemusement didn't last long. With a narrowing of her eyes and a suspicious tone, she added, "Why? How do I look?"

There were a dozen different ways he could have answered that question, most of them based on the fact that all she had to do was walk in a room to make him feel as though the sun had finally come out from behind a cloud. She was bright and brilliant and beautiful, and he could feel her presence even if he wasn't looking directly at her.

He could hardly say any of that out loud, however. *You look like the sun after a long, cold blizzard, like the rainbow after a storm. Your air of quiet dignity makes me long to throw you over my shoulder and perform any manner of undignified acts in the back of my minivan.* Ford was no stranger to making a fool of himself, but even he drew the line there.

"You look perfect," he decided.

She pushed herself off the doorway, her spine straightening into a lightning rod of stiffness. "I beg your pardon?" There was a dangerous note in her voice, as though daring him to repeat such a claim.

So he did.

"I could throw you into a wind tunnel with three feral cats, and you'd emerge looking exactly like that," he added with a mock sigh. "I hope the devil gave you a good bargain, because it's wasted on me. Not even a feral cat attack could make you any less beautiful in my eyes. Well? What's next on the puppy agenda?"

Lila pursed her lips and watched him for a few seconds, as if deciding whether or not to let his comment pass by. She wanted to engage, he knew, but she wouldn't. Not during working hours.

He was right. With a glance down at her slim gold watch, she said, "Actually, if it's not too much trouble with your schedule, I was hoping we could take an outing this afternoon."

"An outing?" Ford echoed.

"Yes. It's when you change out of your pajama pants and leave the house in the middle of the day. People do it all the time. Some of them even like it."

He glanced down at himself with a suppressed laugh. He was, in fact, wearing the infamous pajama pants once again, but that had been an act of pure mischief. He'd done laundry and dressed like a dignified man that morning, but the second those worn, checkered pants had come out of the dryer, he couldn't resist putting them on again.

It had been worth it, too, to see the way Lila's gaze strayed to his bottom half and stayed there, her lower lip caught in her teeth as she recalled their activities.

"I happen to be rather fond of these pants," he said. "I like the way they fit, all hot and tight and—"

"Ford!" Lila glared at him, but her lips wobbled in a clear attempt to suppress a smile. "I'm on the clock, if you'll recall."

"Oh, I recall. Believe me when I say that it's very, very hard for me to think of anything else." He heaved another sigh—this one with less mockery—and tried to gather his thoughts. Fatherhood. Puppies. *Work*. "Well? What did you have in mind?"

"Anything in a public setting. We need to get Jeeves used to behaving himself out in the world."

Ford lifted a brow. "And you think I'm going to be a help with that? I don't know if you've noticed, but behaving myself in public isn't one of my strong points. In fact, behaving myself in any capacity is becoming an almost impossible chore."

The color mounted in Lila's cheeks, but she maintained a dignified stance, her gaze pinpointed just above his right shoulder. That seemed to be one of her favorite spots whenever she was trying not to let him get the better of her. "The mall is crowded enough this time of year to work as a good training ground. Is there any holiday shopping you need to do?"

"Well, I *do* need a cutlass for my Blackbeard costume," he suggested. "And unless you've been busy on your own, I'm guessing *s-l-u-t-t-y* Anne Bonny could still use some work. I have a few ideas. Several of them, actually. Want to hear what they are?"

The pink suffusion didn't abate any. "I never said that's what I'm wearing."

"I know, but a man can dream, can't he?"

Emily appeared in the doorway, Jeeves obediently at her heels. Already, the puppy had almost doubled in size, the soft swell of his baby belly slimming down to a more manageable pudge. There was some sort of lesson in there about how fast children and puppies grew up, how fleeting was youth and how wasted on the young, but Ford ignored it. There was time enough to regret the yoke of responsibility. Today, he just wanted to enjoy some time with Lila and Emily.

And he'd do it, too, dammit. *Sorry, Giles.*

"Well, moppet?" he asked as soon as Emily's gaze caught his. "What do you say to going to the mall and helping Princess Lila pick out her costume for Helen's party? We can get a few more things for yours while we're at it."

"Can we?" Emily clasped her hands and gazed up at Lila with wide, adoring eyes. He could have kissed his daughter for bestowing that particular look, all innocence and entreaty. He doubted Lila would be able to resist it. *He* certainly couldn't. "Dress-up will be so much more fun with a friend. I never did it with a friend a'fore."

Lila's expression melted. "Of course we can, Emily. In fact, we can start right now with Jeeves. Do you still have that special vest he's supposed to wear when you go out together?"

Emily nodded and dashed off to acquire the service animal harness, leaving the two of them alone in the kitchen once again. Ford lost no time in leaping to his feet and drawing close to Lila. The rules might state that they couldn't touch, but he could still lean in, basking in the heat and scent of her.

"You know they teach spelling in kindergarten, right?" Lila asked. She didn't move closer, but she didn't pull away, either. And was it his imagination, or was there a strangled quality to her voice? "I looked it up. One of these days, she's going to figure out what you're actually saying."

"You smell like strawberries today," he said, inhaling deeply. "Yesterday, it was pineapples, and before that, it was peaches. Do you shower with a fruit basket?"

"Either that, or she's going to ask Principal Brown what the words mean. Is that what you want? A parent-teacher conference about why Emily's spelling test is covered with obscenities?"

"You don't taste like fruit, though, which is weird," was his response. He brought his face closer to the slope of her shoulder, which was visible above the slightly offset neckline of her white, fluffy sweater. Strands of her hair tickled his nose. "At least, your mouth doesn't. I have the wildest hope that your skin tells a different story. Does it?"

Lila held herself perfectly immobile, but the whisper of his breath over her neck caused a line of goose bumps to form. That, combined with the sudden hitch in her breath, almost had him tossing all his promises and resolve out the nearest window.

"I don't make it a habit to lick myself," she said.

"I intend to," he murmured, dropping his mouth so close to her shoulder that he could feel the soft, downy hairs of her skin tickling his lips. "And I plan to leave no part of you untouched or untasted."

A low, soft moan escaped from Lila, but it was interrupted by the skitter of puppy claws on linoleum. Ford glanced down to find that Jeeves was wearing his vest inside out and upside down, which was as good a segue as any. It was impossible to continue thoughts of seduction with a half-dressed puppy and an excited child underfoot, so Ford pushed those wayward sentiments down as far as they could go.

Which, considering he caught sight of Lila sneaking a lick on her wrist when she thought he wasn't looking, wasn't very far.

❀ ❀ ❀

"You know, Helen *did* say I could just wear my usual princess gear." Lila crossed her arms over her chest— partially because the gesture suited her current mood, and partially because she feared her boobs were going to pop out the top of the corset otherwise. A ruffled white blouse ostensibly provided a modest touch to the pirate costume, but as it left her shoulders bare and only just skimmed the upper swell of her cleavage, she wasn't sure this was the sort of thing one was supposed to wear around children. "I could always roll out the sparkling pink ball gown again."

It said a lot about her current state of discomfort that she'd willingly consider the bubble-gum monstrosity, but neither Ford nor Emily picked up on the subtext. Either that, or they didn't care. With Ford, she was only willing to wager a fifty-fifty chance.

"Come on, Princess Lila." A small hand popped through the side of the curtain. "I want to see."

"Yeah, Princess Lila," Ford echoed. "I thought we were playing dress-up together."

The laughing underscore to Ford's voice was her undoing. He knew very well that Emily's idea of dress-up and his idea of dress-up were two different things. As was almost always the case where this man was concerned, however, his words were laced with entendre.

Entendre and a challenge. He didn't think she'd actu- ally go through with it.

Fine. She might not be the phone-sex champion of

the year, but that didn't mean she wasn't without her strengths. She'd show him that she wasn't so easily subdued. Hoisting her ankle-length maroon skirt, she pushed aside the curtain and stepped carefully out. Carefully was the only way she *could* step. The time of year meant that there weren't any Halloween stores open, so they'd had to settle for a store that specialized in cosplay and pop-culture gear. The result was a pirate costume that was both deplorably anachronistic and highly inefficient. There was no way she'd be hoisting any sails or loading any cannons in a faux-leather corset and boots with three-inch heels.

"I wouldn't last five minutes onboard a pirate ship in this," she complained as she examined herself in the panel of mirrors. "I'd fall overboard with the first strong gale and then sink slowly to my doom."

She glanced over her shoulder to see if her companions shared her opinion. Although Jeeves tilted his head in judgmental inquiry, neither of the Fords seemed the least bothered by her lack of historical accuracy. Ford, because he was staring at her with openmouthed hunger that sent her heart racing, and Emily, because her eyes grew wide with delight.

"Daddy," Emily breathed. "It's 'xactly like your pictures."

Lila was so caught up in Ford's glinting blue gaze— which seemed to have zeroed in on all the parts where her corset pinched and pushed—that she didn't catch Emily's meaning right away.

"She just needs her big, long rope," Emily added. "The one that kills all the bad guys."

"Rope?" Lila echoed blankly. "I don't think that's

how pirates killed people. They mostly used swords. And poor hygiene, most likely."

"Oh, um. Emily—" Ford stopped and glanced anxiously around the dressing room, which was more like a storage closet in the back of the store than anything else. To Lila's well-trained eye, he looked an awful lot like a man desperately searching for the nearest exit. "You don't know what you're talking about."

"O' course I do, Daddy," Emily blinked up at her father. "It's the pictures you were drawing yesterday. The ones with Princess Lila and the monster."

"The monster?" Lila asked. She dropped her skirts and turned to stare back at Ford. She didn't linger on his bosomy parts, focusing instead on the pink-tipped ears that were a dead giveaway he was hiding something. "Pictures?"

"They're real good, Princess Lila," Emily said. "He drawed me, too, but I don't have a rope. I only have Jeeves. I wasn't a'sposed to see the pictures, but I did."

"She's confused, obviously," Ford said, putting up his hands in a gesture of belated innocence. "Your beauty has staggered her beyond comprehension. She may never recover."

Emily wasn't looking at her father and didn't hear him. "There's a big monster, too," she confided to Lila. "In a Santa hat. He has lots of teeth."

"Would you look at that?" Ford reached for his back pocket. "What terrible timing. My phone's ringing. I'd better—"

"Oh, no you don't." Lila dived for the phone and had it in her hand before he managed to pull it up to his ear.

"I'm not falling for that one again. You'd better put this somewhere safe, Emily."

Emily giggled and took the phone, tucking it carefully into one of Jeeves's service vest pockets, but a grave expression settled over her not too long after. "You're not mad, Princess Lila, are you?"

"Mad?" She shook her head, surprised to find that of all the possible emotions she might be feeling right now, anger wasn't even remotely close. She felt ridiculous in this pirate costume, there was no doubt about that. She felt besotted by the admiration shining so clearly in Ford's eyes. She also felt a profound curiosity to see these pictures of his.

And happy. Happy most of all. Like Emily, Lila had never played dress-up with friends before, but she could see the appeal. She might look silly in this getup, but Emily and Ford seemed to be enjoying themselves, and that was enough for her. More than enough, actually. Sometime in the past few weeks, their joy had become synonymous with her own.

"Of course I'm not mad," Lila said, speaking primarily to Emily. Despite the danger of making any sudden movements in an outfit as precarious as this one, she squatted down to the girl's level. "I'm mostly curious. How long has your dad been working on these pictures?"

"Forever," Emily said. "It's a whole book."

"Does he stop working whenever you walk into the room?"

She nodded.

"Does he try to hide his pages so you can't see what he's drawing?"

She nodded again.

"So that's it," Lila said, remembering Ford's repeated attempts to hide his work from her. She'd assumed he didn't like an audience while he sketched, but that had been her first mistake. Ford wasn't lacking in modesty—he was a rogue, through and through. She should have known he was doing something devious and inappropriate. She rose to a standing position and pointed at him. "You have some serious explaining to do, young man. And I want to see this book."

"It's not really a book," he admitted, the pink tips of his ears flaming anew. "It's just doodles."

"Then I want to see these doodles. I'm deeply interested in doodles. Especially ones that feature me dressed up like a pirate."

"Technically, you're not a pirate in them."

She cast a look down at her ridiculous outfit and blanched. "A tavern wench?"

Ford's laugh was mostly silent, but there was no mistaking the quirk of his lips. "Don't worry. I didn't take things quite that far. You can see for yourself, if you want. I'll show them to you as soon as we get home."

Lila halted at the sound of that word—*home*. Naturally, he was talking about his own home, that cute little house where he and Emily created so many happy memories together, but she couldn't help envisioning what it might look like if it were her home, too. There'd be no space for her, of course, and she'd be an intruder in a world that wasn't hers, but she felt a pang all the same.

I want that. The mess and the chaos, the joy and the noise. And above all else, the life.

Her sisters had those things—had been born with

them, radiating warmth and light everywhere they went. Helen had those things, too. In fact, Lila was starting to realize that Patrick hadn't been wrong when he'd broken up with her. Who could blame him for wanting more than a block of ice? *She* certainly did.

Ford must have misread her sudden stillness, because he reached for her. It broke their agreement for him to grab her hand like that, to press his palm against hers and give it a squeeze, but she couldn't find it in her to care.

"They don't show anything bad," he promised. "It's just a little side project I've been working on. For fun. To blow off steam. In case you couldn't tell, there's been a lot of that building up lately."

Oh, she could tell. Her own reservoirs had become downright scorching.

"You look pretty in the pictures," Emily added, blithely uninterested in the adult half of the conversation. "And in that costume. Please will you get it?"

It had been Lila's intention to dress modestly for the party, conceding to the pirate theme with a boat-neck shirt or by cutting a pair of pants into ragged edges at the knee, but the Fords were an oddly compelling pair. Once upon a time, she'd been a woman of resolve and dignity, a woman who'd dressed with all the neatness and propriety expected of someone her age.

Once upon a time, she'd also been stiff and unyielding, her heart and body untouched by anything real.

"Of course I will," she said. "If you approve of it, then that's all I need to hear."

Emily squealed her excitement. This unprecedented action startled Jeeves, who pricked his ears and began

looking around for the cause of his mistress's distress.
Lila could almost sense his dismay at having missed
something potentially important; he knew it was his job
to interpret the sounds of the outside world. The mall
Santa and the gaggles of children waiting in line to
see him hadn't upset him. The elf with jangling shoes
working at the food court had been a mere nothing. But
Emily's burst of enthusiasm had him all in a twitter.

It took a full five minutes of careful training before
both the puppy and his human were capable of standing
at attention again. Lila could only be grateful for the
distraction, as it relieved her of the burden of witnessing
Ford's reaction to her capitulation.

He'd be triumphant, she knew. He'd also be staring at
her corset again, making it almost impossible for her to
withstand the intensity of his gaze. Helen obviously had
no idea what she was getting into with this pirate theme
for her Christmas party.

Lila glanced up to catch Ford staring—not at her
chest this time, but at the tight binding of her waist—and
was unable to stop a flush from stealing over every inch
of skin she had exposed.

Then again, maybe Helen was a genius in disguise.

🐾🐾🐾

"They're just a rough sketch." Ford stood at his desk
with a clutch of papers held between his hands. From
where she and Emily stood, Lila could only make out a
few black-and-white scribbles in a vaguely humanlike
shape. "I haven't made any touch-ups or refinements."

"Noted."

"And you're much more difficult to capture than

Judge Judy. She's all grimaces and smiles, but your tendency is to hide your emotions as best you can."

"They're rough, and your subject is an expressionless monster. Got it."

Ford didn't, as she'd hoped, hand over the sketches. He stared at her instead, his continued abeyance making her nervous. She shifted from one foot to another in anticipation.

"See that?" he said, pointing a finger at her.

"What?" she asked and cast a quick glance around her.

"When you moved just now. You've been standing perfectly still for like five minutes waiting for me to get these out. That tiny shuffle of your feet is the only indication you've given that you're the least bit interested in me or my pictures."

The only indication? She goggled at him. There was the most ridiculous pirate costume in the world in a shopping bag by the door, and she had every intention of wearing it in public for no reason other than the way he looked at her when she had it on. She'd spent all day in a state of squirming discomfort, doing her best not to acknowledge that she could feel Ford's eyes on her every movement. Her mouth was dry, her palms were sweaty, and her lungs constricted every time he drew near.

And he thought that one small shift was her sole sign of interest?

"I'm only warning you so you realize how much intense study had to go into these pictures. Hours of it, in fact. So if there's anything you don't think I got right—"

"Oh, give me the dratted things already." She reached

out and plucked them from his hands before he could stop her. However, she really *wasn't* an expressionless monster, so she paused before glancing at them. "And for the record, Ford, I'm interested. In both you and your pictures. Does that help?"

The smile that broke across his face could have shattered glass. In a way, that was exactly what it did, cracking anything that might have remained of the ice around her heart.

"Yes," he said. "That helps."

"Can I see them, too?" Emily jumped up on her tiptoes and tugged at Lila's hand. As much as Lila enjoyed the little girl's company, she felt oddly reluctant to share this moment with anyone. No one had ever drawn her before—at least, not to her knowledge, and not in an outfit that sounded as though it was one small nip-slip away from a serious wardrobe malfunction. But both she and the demands of her body were coming to realize that when a child was involved, certain sacrifices had to be made. Sex took place over the phone in the dead of night, and she couldn't bury herself away in a hole and pore over every detail of Ford's sketches by herself.

She dropped to the kitchen stool and patted the one next to her, waiting until Emily was settled before spreading the papers out before her. There were quite a few of them—over a dozen in all—each page progressing through what looked an awful lot like an actual story line. One Ford had put thought and time into. *Care*, even.

The first few pages were simple, but she was able to follow along. In them, a cartoon version of Lila, dressed like a pirate princess, sat in a beautiful garden like an ornamental statue. She might have been insulted at the idea that she was a decoration to be admired if it weren't for the quick story-line progression. A huge, beast-like creature with several rows of teeth emerged from behind a bush shaped like a candy cane, at which point Lila transitioned from a stately pirate princess to a pirate princess with a lizard-like tail and a forked tongue. Lizard Lila lost no time in extracting a braided whip that was coiled underneath her skirt and lashing at the toothed beast with it.

The beast, with a laceration forming on his cheek, howled his dismay, but he wasn't beaten. Before Lizard Lila could lash at him again, he grabbed some kind of wrapped package from the middle of a stone fountain and ran off with it.

There wasn't any text to accompany the pictures, so she couldn't say for sure what was happening, but it looked as though Lizard Lila then began a quest to retrieve the package from the beast. About five pages in, a small street urchin with Emily's cochlear implants and an armor-clad cockapoo that was every inch the image of Jeeves joined the fight. Urchin Emily was a scrappy little thing, too. She even staved off a few evil-looking Christmas elves with only the dog to aid her.

Emily noted the likeness with glee. "There's me!" she cried, clapping her hands and running her finger over every inch of the image. "I told you. I'm getting the bad guys, too. Look, Lila. We're getting the bad guys together!"

"So we are," Lila murmured, restraining a similar impulse to trace the lines of her own figure. She kept her hands clasped tightly in her lap instead, struggling to work through the feelings evoked by the images Ford had rendered of her.

She could feel him hovering in the background—not anxious, but obviously hoping for some kind of response.

"Well?" he asked. "How did I do? It's a pretty good likeness, wouldn't you say? I hope you don't mind that I brazenly stole your lizard idea. Once it was in my head, it was impossible to rout out again."

She had no idea what to say. The woman looked like her; that was for sure. She had the same wide mouth and large facial features, her eyebrows slanted at the exact angle of her own. The body was similar, too, insofar as a cartoon lizard woman could be said to resemble an actual human being. But there was something else...

"See that?" Ford leaned close, hovering at her back. He dipped his head so it was level with her own, smelling faintly of aftershave. "That's how you look when Jeeves doesn't follow your order the first time around, and you haven't yet decided whether it's your fault or his. That one right there is the exact way you stand when you're trying not to let your emotions show. And *that's* the way your lips twitch whenever you don't want to admit that I'm hilarious."

She turned her head just enough to gaze up at him, her senses swirling in confusion. Ford wasn't talking about her likeness in terms of nasal structures and bust-to-waist ratios. He meant things like her mannerisms and habits. He was setting out to capture her *personality*.

"Does that mean this is how I look when I'm fighting evil?" she asked. She pointed at a particularly badass version of Lizard Lila flying through the air with one leg out in a fierce and painfully high kick.

His laughter shook them both. "Well, I had to use some artistic license for that one. But, yes, that's how I imagine you look when you're fighting evil. It's a Krampus, actually. He's trying to steal Christmas, but you and Emily and Jeeves are determined to stop him. You'll do it, too, if I ever get to the end."

"You will."

He hesitated for a moment before she felt him shrug. "Maybe. Like I said before, I was only drawing them for fun. It's not very…useful work."

She began neatly stacking the pages before handing them to Emily to browse at her leisure. "It might not be useful work, but it's good. It's *great*, actually. You could probably sell this to someone. You're talented."

He seemed strangely reluctant to accept this. "I'm all right. And it seems to make Emily happy, which is what really matters."

If the smile on the little girl's face as she flipped through was anything to go by, it *did* make Emily happy. It also made Lila happy and Ford happy and, she was guessing, would provide infinite amusement to her sisters and Harrison. Even Patrick might wring out a smile at seeing her portrayed in such a state of reptilian disarray.

"What do you call it?" she asked. "The title of the book, I mean?"

"*Doodles by Ford*, installment number three thousand and fifteen. The Christmas Krampus edition."

She looked a question at him, surprised to find that his ears were tipped with red again. He gave a one-shouldered shrug, his eyes not quite meeting her own. "It should look great next to installment three thousand and fourteen, although that one has a lot more areolas in it. Not yours, in case you're worried."

She placed her hand over his and refused to move it away until his eyes met hers. She needed him to see how much she loved these pictures, to realize how grateful she was for the portrayal. Ford had capitalized on her biggest fears and turned her into the literal personification of her cold, reptilian ways, and she couldn't be more delighted about it. He'd turned her not into a woman who kept everyone at arm's length, but a princess, a superhero, a force of good in the world. He'd assumed that being a lizard person was something to cherish and admire—something to be proud of, in fact.

And for the first time in her life, she *was*.

"You're doing it again," she said and didn't wait for him to ask what. "Telling a joke. Making the lady laugh instead of saying what you're really thinking. Have you ever tried to sell any of the comics you've drawn?"

He slid his hand out from under hers. "That's not really the point of them."

"But you have a gift for drawing and a gift for making people laugh," she said. "It seems like an awful waste to spend it all on coffee makers."

"Don't tell that to the coffee makers," he quipped.

Frustration took shape in the pit of her stomach, a hot rock lodged in place. From the moment she'd met this man, she'd been thrown off-kilter by how easy he made everything look. He laughed and teased, joked and played. He treated life like one big game—and it was a game he was clearly winning, if the way people reacted to him was any indication. They loved him. All of them—the Anyas and Patricks of the world, the Helens and the Maddies and the Danicas. Her sisters were in raptures, and she'd even seen that scary Principal Brown crack a smile in his presence.

But he *hated* those coffee makers, sighed every time he pulled himself away from Emily and put his pen to paper. The only time she'd ever seen him look unhappy was when he was sitting at his desk with his head bent to his work.

"I'm serious, Ford," she said. "Even if nothing comes of it, you have to put yourself out there. You have to *try*. Don't you want more out of life than this?"

She punctuated the *this* with a swift glance at his drafting desk, where the scattered pages of his coffee maker project lay in wait. He followed the line of her gaze, though his took a more circuitous route to include the rest of the kitchen, which bore all the untidy hallmarks of regular home-cooked meals. Without losing any of the strain in his mouth or in his eyes, he opened his mouth to reply…

But was beaten to the punch by Emily, who tilted her head in consideration and asked, "Daddy, what's an areola?"

Lila's hands flew to her mouth in a gurgle of laughter, which she was unable to suppress in time. Ford, too, couldn't seem to help but recognize the futility of holding this kind of conversation while Emily was in the room. Even though she probably hadn't heard enough to make real sense of what they said, she caught the occasional word.

Swooping down to scoop her in his arms, Ford said,

"It's an atmospheric phenomenon, moppet. The areola borealis, when the nighttime sky turns green. You can usually only see it in Alaska during the winter."

"Oh," Emily said, accepting this deflection at face value. "Okay. That sounds neat."

"It *is* neat," he agreed. "And later, we'll look at some pictures of it online. But right now, you need to go wash your face and hands so you can help me make dinner."

Emily agreed to this plan with her usual good humor, taking herself off with Jeeves following placidly behind.

"That's going to make for an interesting science project someday," Lila murmured as she watched them go. "Maybe you should have spelled that one out."

"Perhaps," Ford agreed. The constrained note in his voice was still there, but he didn't acknowledge it. For whatever reason, the subject of his work was one he wasn't willing to broach—not even in jest. "But I, for one, would much rather watch the night sky light up with areolas than a few paltry green swirls. I don't know if you remember, but I'm rather partial to—"

"I remember," she said quickly. She also examined him closely, wondering how far she could push the subject. In the end, she decided she'd already taken all the ground she was going to get. "I'm also starting to wonder if there's any part of the female form you're *not* partial to."

"None that I've found yet," he said and winked. "But you know me. I'm always willing to take a deeper look."

chapter
14

We're going to the symphony. We're visiting art galleries and sipping overpriced white wine. Oh, I've got it! You're taking me to the fanciest store in the city and buying me a new dress. I'll be like Pretty Woman, except you won't have to pay me for *s-e-x* later."

Ford cast a sidelong look at Lila. She'd caught her lower lip between her teeth, but she didn't look up from the phone in her lap.

"I like to make the first one free to get the ladies hooked," he explained. "Then I ratchet up the price accordingly."

That didn't get her to take the bait, either. "Turn right at the next intersection," she instructed him. "Parking should be in the big lot on the right. And for the record, I don't think that's a very good way to run your gigolo business. Why would the cow pay for milk after the fact?"

"The cow isn't the one paying for the milk. The cow is the one providing it." He clucked his tongue and shook his head. "And here I thought you were supposed to be the smart one."

That got her to glance up, her gaze sharp. "I never said that."

"No, you didn't," he agreed cheerfully as he pulled his minivan into the last of a row of cars. "But that doesn't make it any less true."

She had no response to this, which was just as well since they'd arrived at their mystery destination. He had no idea where they were or why, but he didn't care. The fact that he was on an actual date with Lila was enough.

It wasn't just any date, either. He'd had to lift nary a finger to make it happen. Apparently, Lila took her role as invitee very seriously. From dropping Emily off at her mom's house to planning the evening from start to finish, she'd handled everything on her own. All Ford had to do was doll himself up and wait to be whisked away for an evening of romantic bliss.

It was a new experience for him—and a delightful one. Lila was wooing him. Lila was wooing him hard.

He, too, was hard just thinking about it.

Although that wasn't really fair. He'd been in the same state of agonized anticipation for days. No number of cold showers or hot showers or short, frantic showers with his cock in his hand had helped. Nor had Lila's constant presence in his home. How she managed to sit with his daughter and Jeeves, cool and collected as she went through the steps of puppy training, was a mystery.

"Here. We're going to need this." Lila reached into the pocket of the white wool coat she wore and handed him a flask. "It's like fifteen degrees outside. It's straight bourbon, in case you're wondering."

"You remembered," he said as he accepted the flask and took a long pull. "My vice of choice."

It wasn't the cheap stuff, either. The woodsy-sweet

taste coated his tongue and throat, the warm burn making him feel almost giddy.

"I have my occasional value," she admitted. "Remembering things in painstaking detail doesn't make me a very endearing person, but it does make me a useful one."

He opened his mouth to argue, to tell her that her value lay primarily in her ability to make him feel relaxed and happy and like a hot-blooded man again, but he didn't have a chance to get the words out before she pulled a white knit cap over her head and secured her gloves onto her hands.

Lila was a stunning woman almost all the time, her poise and grace so ingrained that he doubted she was aware of them, but there was something about the way that cap framed her face that almost undid him. She looked absurdly youthful, her cheeks flushed from the bourbon and the cold and—he hoped—the company.

Unable to help himself, he leaned across the console and dropped a kiss onto her slightly parted lips. Surprise rendered her delightfully malleable, her mouth giving way to his for a full ten seconds before she realized what was happening and kissed him back. That was delightful, too, but for entirely different reasons—most of which had to do with the fact that she wasn't about to let him have his wicked way with her without giving him his own back again. In fact, that was a thing she'd done since the day they'd first met. He could, on occasion, catch her off guard, but it rarely lasted for long.

She proved it by deepening the kiss. The assault of her tongue and the warm press of her mouth against his invoked every sense he had—taste and smell and glorious touch. She even released a soft moan into his mouth that made his head whir with possibilities.

And then she ended it as quickly as it began.

"Let's skip the date," he said before he'd even managed to open his eyes again. "I don't care if we're flying to the Eiffel Tower on a private jet run entirely on champagne. Let's stay in this van and make out instead."

She didn't move. "You don't want to see what I have planned?"

He'd opened his eyes by this time, but the parking lot lighting was dim, and what little vision he did have was obscured by the stars dazzling his vision. *Actual g-o-d-d-a-m-n stars*.

"Nothing you have planned can be any better than just being here with you," he said with perfect honesty.

"Not even a snow maze?"

Some of the stars flitted away. "A snow maze?"

She sat back in her seat and gazed out the window, making it impossible for him to read her expression. "Yes. It sounds silly, I know, but I read about it online and couldn't resist. This church built it entirely of snow and ice, and if you find the middle, there's an ice tower you can climb. It's supposed to be… Um, I thought it might be…" She paused and drew a deep breath. "Well, *fun*."

"Fun?" he echoed.

Her laugh came out in a chuff of self-conscious air. "I know. It's not my normal scene, obviously, but I didn't think you'd want to do any of those art galleries and symphonies and things. Do you hate it?"

For what must have been the first time in Ford's life, he was at a loss for words. Not because he hated the idea of a snow maze—in fact, getting lost inside icy tunnels with only Lila for company sounded like his idea of heaven—but because of how far it was from her normal activities. As much as *he* might enjoy running around in below-zero temperatures and slipping around on sheets of ice, she was accustomed to much more sophistication.

Sophistication that he had never particularly enjoyed. Sophistication that he couldn't really afford in the first place. Sophistication that was much more suited to a well-bred doctor than an illustrator whose primary food groups were peanut butter sandwiches and stale fruit snacks.

"It's perfect," he said. And thought, but didn't add, *for a man like me*.

She hesitated as if not sure whether to take him at his word, but he reached out and squeezed her gloved hand. He might not be able to offer Lila much in the way of refinement, but he had four glorious hours of freedom, a flask full of bourbon, and the most beautiful woman in the world as his date.

If he couldn't pull together a good time out of that, then he wasn't worthy of the name Ford Ford.

Then again, when it came to such a ridiculous combination of syllables as that, who was?

🐾 🐾 🐾

"Ha! I told you we already came this way." Ford pointed at the red X marked near the bottom of the snow wall. "Drink up."

Lila peered closer at the X, unsure whether it was her shade of lipstick that had marked it, or if there was another lost couple who'd taken to similar tactics. As much as she would have liked to blame this on someone else, that was definitely Velvet Kisses. At fifty bucks a tube for it, she doubted there was anyone else fool enough to waste it like this.

"Okay, fine." She straightened and held her hand out for the flask. "But I could have sworn that was the way out. I still think you cheated somehow."

There wasn't much bourbon left by this time, but Lila kicked back the remainder. She'd lost track of how much of it she'd consumed, but it didn't really matter. The warm glow that filled her had little to do with alcohol and a lot to do with the fact that she couldn't remember the last time she'd enjoyed herself this much.

"And now we really do have to find the exit, because we're out of liquid sustenance." She tipped the flask upside down to prove it. "From here on out, we have only our wits to guide us. Or, considering how much better you are at this than me, I should probably say *your* wits."

"Well, my wits and that little boy in the fox hat."

Lila swiveled to stare at her date. "What?"

Ford gave a laugh and a sheepish shrug of his shoulders. "He's been in and out of this *d-a-m-n* thing half a dozen times already, so it seemed like a safe bet. Besides, he'll trade tips for knock-knock jokes. How do you think we made it this far?"

"You mean we've been following the advice of a strange child for the past hour and a half?" Lila demanded.

"Knock-knock," was Ford's only reply.

Lila fought to suppress a smile. "I'm not answering that door."

"Interrupting sloth," he said, ignoring her.

"I don't see how you expect—"

Ford started to move slowly toward her, his arms outstretched and a ridiculous grin on his face. "Sloooooooooth," he said, drawing the word out as he continued his long, leisurely approach.

Lila couldn't help it—she laughed. She'd spent enough time in Emily's company lately that she'd heard any number of terrible jokes, including ones about interrupting cows and interrupting sheep and any other animal that could be counted on to provide a convenient punch line.

She stood perfectly still until Ford's sloth-like arms wrapped around her. The evening was chilly—almost unbearably so—but between scrambling through the maze and the bourbon and the laughter that never seemed to stop for longer than a few seconds at a time, Lila had never felt so warm.

"Two right turns, one left turn, and then we can scramble over that low wall to get out," Ford murmured. His mouth was pressed against the right side of her neck, his words a deep rumble in her ear. His breath smelled faintly oaky, which only added to the appeal of having him near. "Just say the word, my lady, and I'll whisk you away to safety."

"I don't bargain with cheaters."

He dropped a soft kiss on the curve of her neck, undismayed by her threats. "It's not cheating—it's self-preservation. I always have an exit strategy in mind."

Lila knew that to be the truth. Since the day she'd met Ford Ford, she'd been aware that he always had one foot out the door, his lighthearted raillery designed to keep anyone from getting too close. The way he'd joked about his ex-wife being at the North Pole and his actions over the comic book the other day proved it. Lila was allowed to flirt with him and maybe even sleep with him, but that was it. She couldn't touch any of the parts that mattered. He'd made it amply clear that his body was hers for the taking, but his heart?

She wanted to see it. She wanted to know it. She wanted to *hold* it, if only for a moment.

When she didn't respond right away, too busy trying to fight off the realization that she'd never be able to return to her cold, closed world after this, he added, "Well?"

"Well, what?"

"Do I whisk you to safety now, or do you want to go get lost in the snow maze with me again? I'm game either way. I've always wanted to be trapped in the cold with a beautiful woman. I know all about how we survive. The trick is to get naked."

It was ridiculous that the word *naked* should have such a profound effect on her, but her whole body flushed at the sound. She wasn't even all that against the idea of stripping down right here and now, which should have made her ashamed of herself. They were next to a church, for crying out loud, surrounded by children and families. And yet she was the horny teenager she'd never had a chance to be, the giddy girl she'd never allowed to come out of her shell.

"I think there's a little bit more to it than that," she said, striving to match her tone to his. "A sleeping bag, for starters. Otherwise, I'm pretty sure you're just hastening death."

His hold around her waist tightened, one hand creeping inexorably toward her ass. "There's one of those tinfoil blankets in the back of my minivan," he murmured. "Will that do?"

"A tinfoil blanket?"

"Yeah. And a first aid kit and jumper cables and enough protein bars to last at least three days. You're not the only one who's good at preparation, you know. I'm known on my block as Mr. Safety."

"Mr. Safety?" she echoed again. She wished she could come up with something more articulate, but it was difficult when he was squeezing the breath out of her like an anaconda.

"That was my nickname in college, too, now that I think about it." His head dipped low, his lips brushing against the side of her neck in a soft whisper of a kiss. "Except it wasn't protein bars I carried around in bulk back then."

She laughed, a sound that quickly turned to a gasp when the hand that had been moving downward finally found something it wanted to hold on to. He'd somehow bypassed her roundest parts, his fingers clenching instead against the spot where her upper thigh met the bottom of her ass. It was a sensitive spot rendered all the more so because he seemed to have no qualms about what he was doing or why he was doing it. In fact, if she hitched her leg just a little, his hand was actually between her legs, his fingers pressing against—

"Excuse us." A stern, elderly voice sounded behind them, causing Lila to jump. "Honestly, Paul. If I'd have known this maze was just going to be a place for teenagers to make out, I never would have let you talk me into it. You ought to be ashamed of yourselves, both of you."

Lila buried her face in Ford's neck, torn between mortification and laughter—not to mention a thrill of delight at being mistaken for someone half her age.

"We're sorry, ma'am," Ford said, doing a decent job of sounding contrite. "We got carried away and forgot where we were."

"Do your parents have any idea where you are?"

"Well, no," he admitted. "Mine don't. Hers do, though, and they gave us their blessing."

"They did no such thing!" the woman protested.

At this, Lila couldn't help but pull her face from out of her comfortable, oak-scented hiding spot. "Actually, they did. Well, not my dad, but my mom. She told me that if I had a lick of common sense, I'd get myself in a compromising position and force this man to make an honest woman out of me."

Ford swiveled to stare at her, laughter and interest lighting his eyes. "Did she really?"

Unfortunately, yes, she had. She'd taken one look at Ford in the flesh and ranged herself on the side of Lila's sisters. "Stay out as late as you want, love," she'd whispered in between the introductions to Ford, Emily, and Jeeves. "Stay all weekend, if you have to. He's wonderful."

Wonderful, ha. He was a menace, plain and simple. He wouldn't be looking at her like that if he was anything else.

"We're sorry to have upset you," Lila said, doing her best to ignore Ford and that intense gaze. "We were just leaving anyway."

She grabbed Ford's hand and started dragging him away before he could demand a detailed explanation of what her mother had said. Two right turns, one left turn, and a scramble over the low wall later, they were freed from the icy pathways. It seemed the little boy in the fox hat knew what he was doing.

Partially to stave off the inevitable and partially because she was still feeling a little giddy, Lila said, "I can't tell you the last time someone took me for a teenager—not even when I *was* one. They used to let me into the wine bar next to my college campus when I was only nineteen, and they were notorious for checking IDs. They took one look at me and assumed I was a member of the faculty."

Ford lifted a hand to her cheek. He gave a gentle tug on a tendril of hair that had come loose from her cap, winding the lock around one gloved finger. "How scandalous. Did you take advantage and sneak bottles out to your friends?"

"No, of course not. I wouldn't even drink any when it was offered. I didn't like breaking the rules."

His lips parted in a silent laugh, but his mood was serious. At least, she *thought* it was serious. Although the maze had been fairly well lit, the church parking lot wasn't. Most of the illumination was provided from the moon overhead, its glow highlighting the chiseled angles of Ford's face and casting him in a heroic light.

"And now?" he asked.

"Oh, I always drink wine when it's offered now," she said lightly.

His fingers were still wound up in her hair, his hand cupping her cheek in a gesture of tenderness. Brushing his thumb over her lips, he lowered his voice and said, "Yes, but how do you feel about breaking the rules?"

Given her actions over the past few weeks, it seemed silly to answer that question. He had to know. He had to realize. She was doing all the things she'd never thought possible: dating a client, putting her emotional and physical desires before her work, risking everything—even her heart—for the sake of this man's touch.

She was forging new territory without a map, and most surprising of all, she was enjoying it.

"Do you remember where we parked?" she asked by way of answer.

"In the middle of a church parking lot, surrounded by dozens of other minivans," he said. "So you can stop purring at me like that, because I do have some decency left."

She held up her fingers in the approximation of an inch. "Exactly how much decency are we talking about? This much? This much? Or…" She expanded her suggestion until it required both hands. "*This* much?"

He yanked her hand into his own and gave it a tug, a low growl escaping his throat as he did. "I don't know why I ever thought you'd be a good influence. I'm onto you, Lila Vasquez. You might look like a princess and act like a schoolmarm, but you're going to be the death of me."

"I am?" she asked, delighted at the thought. She'd never been the death of anyone before. At least, not unless they were dying of boredom. "I'd apologize, but you're the one dragging me to your car, not the other way around."

He ignored the argument as they approached his van.

"Get in," he ordered. "And give me the address for the next part of this date of yours. But be warned—if it's not the nearest seedy motel, then I refuse to be answerable for my actions."

She gave a low chuckle and shook her head. A mad dash for a seedy motel was yet another in a long line of experiences she had never had before, but she drew the line somewhere outside a flashing neon vacancy sign. She wasn't *that* far gone. Bedbugs and staph infections were no joke.

"I asked you out, remember?" she said. "That means I get to call the shots."

"I remember," he grumbled as they both got into the van. "And it serves me right. If I'd had any initiative, I'd have done this my way from the start."

"What's your way?" she asked, sure she already knew the answer.

She did.

"Nudity," he said. "And lots of it."

🐾🐾🐾

"You want me to put it *where*?" Ford asked, staring at Lila.

"I know it looks hard, but I'll make it comfortable, I promise." Lila batted her eyes, beguiling him with a slow, careful smile. "I always entertain my gentleman callers this way."

Ford had his doubts on that score, but he wasn't in a position to cavil. He wasn't in a position to do much of anything, really, except follow Lila's every command. She could have ordered him to jump off the nearest cliff into a pit of spikes, and he'd have done it. Gladly, in fact, eager to discover what kind of ecstatic agonies awaited him at the bottom.

"Your wish is my command," he said and unfolded the blanket she'd provided for the purpose. It was fuzzy and pink, but did little to make the concrete floor of the dog kennel look more appealing. "But are you sure you wouldn't rather hit that seedy motel?"

"I'm sure." She hesitated, watching him put the finishing touches on the blanket, before adding, "You draw as a way of working through your issues, right? As a way to have fun and unwind? Well, this is what I do."

"You take naps on concrete floors?"

"Just lay down and close your eyes," she said. Almost as an afterthought, she added, "Please."

Ford didn't see what else there was for him to do but comply. He knew it had been a long time since he'd been on a formal date with a woman, but he couldn't imagine that things had changed this much in the eight or so years since he'd been a man about town. Then again, he'd never before been out with someone like Lila, so he wasn't in a position to judge. When a gorgeous woman told you to lay yourself out on a concrete slab like a body in the morgue, you did it.

"Okay, fine." He lowered himself to the floor and sprawled out according to her specifications. However, he couldn't resist crossing his arms over his chest before gently closing his eyes.

"Very funny," she muttered. "If you hate it, just say so and we can go to a strip club or something more your style."

He opened one eye and stared up at her. Even from

this vantage point—or, to be more accurate, *especially* from this vantage point—she was a vision to behold. Her hair flowed in loose waves around her shoulders, her eyes dark as they stared down at him. She seemed impossibly tall, her legs long enough to wind around him half a dozen times and tie him up in knots.

"I won't hate it," he promised. "As long as you're in the room with me, I doubt I could hate anything."

She stared at him for a moment, her eyes narrowing in a flash of disbelief. As usual, she seemed to find it impossible to believe that he might actually be telling the truth and to take him as anything more than a flirtatious fool. But he *was*, and he held her stare long enough for her to glean some measure of it. He wished there was some way for him to demonstrate his feelings—to show her that simply being with her filled some part of him he hadn't known was empty—but short of going down on one knee and begging her to give him a lifetime to prove it, he didn't know what he could do.

With a sigh, he settled back against the concrete and closed his eyes again. "Okay. Hit me with your worst. My body is ready."

A good minute passed before he was hit with anything. The temptation to open his eyes and sneak a peek was a strong one, but he resisted it. The soft whimpers of sleepy puppies and Lila's calming voice were intriguing him too much. He forced his limbs into stillness, his heartbeat into a normal pattern, as he waited for what she had to show him.

He must have done too good a job of it, because Lila spoke sharply. "Don't you dare fall asleep on me, Ford, or I'll never forgive you. I'm still recovering from the last time."

"It was a compliment!" he protested. "I don't let my guard down with just everyone, you know. Behind this charming, hilarious facade lurks the soul of a deeply vulnerable man."

"I do know," she said quietly. "In fact, I'm starting to wonder if you've let anyone meet him."

He didn't have a chance to reply as a warm, wriggling body landed on his stomach with a soft *whomp*. More taken by surprise than by pain, he released a gasp. It was swallowed by an excited bark at his feet and an exuberant tongue on the side of his face.

The tongue wasn't, as he'd hoped, Lila's. He could hardly protest, however, when he finally opened his eyes to find four puppies crawling over him, their noses snuffling against his neck and hair and hands as they sought to determine whether he was friend or foe.

Friend must have won out, because it wasn't long before he was being overtaken by small paws and even smaller tongues. Two of them were golden retrievers, he knew, and one of them seemed like some kind of Chihuahua, but his ability to discern between them didn't last long. They were too eager to snuffle into every nook and cranny of his head and neck, licking at him as though they hadn't seen a human in days. There was nothing the least bit suave about a grown man covered in puppies, but he found he didn't mind when Lila bent down and stretched herself on the concrete next to him. She released a soft breath, her head pillowed on her hands as she turned toward him.

"At the end of a long day, nothing beats a pile of

puppies," she said. "I've been doing this for as long as we've had the place. No matter what kind of day I've had, these little guys never fail to cheer me up."

One of his favorite things about Lila was how the woman she presented to the world and the woman she carried inside were such vastly different people. To see her, whether she was poised in a pink ball gown or trying to scare him away in a boxy beige suit, you'd think she'd never even touched a puppy, let alone rolled around with them on a regular basis. Yet here she was, basking in four-legged comfort.

"Is that how you got into this business?" he asked. "Your love of dogs?"

"Not exactly." One of the fluffier puppies—a white thing with a curled tail—wedged itself between them, its head buried in the soft curve of Lila's waist. She dropped a negligent hand and began stroking the animal's fur. "We couldn't have pets growing up because of Sophie's compromised immune system, so dogs were out. I'd see service animals around the hospital a lot, though. They always seemed so out of place to me—those flappy tongues and wet noses in such a sterile environment."

"The appeal of incongruity," he agreed. "I know it well."

"Do you?" she asked, latching on to his understanding with eagerness. She was obviously unaware that the incongruity he spoke of, the appeal he couldn't seem to shake, was *hers*. "Then I'm sure you understand what I mean."

"Tell me anyway," he urged. Lying on the floor with puppies wasn't exactly how he'd imagined this date would end, but he couldn't regret the direction they'd taken.

She hesitated but allowed herself to continue. "We—all of us, Sophie and Dawn and my parents and me—spent so much time in the hospital. For a few years, it felt more like home than our actual house did. We even celebrated a few of our Christmases on the ward. It was…hard on my parents."

He could imagine it. The agonies of uncertainty he'd suffered on Emily's behalf, the lengths he'd go to in order to ensure her safety—he sometimes wondered what it was that parents with perfectly healthy children found to worry about.

"My mom bore the brunt of it, unfortunately," Lila continued. "She never had much time for anything but looking after Sophie. And that was okay—don't get me wrong. I didn't begrudge a single minute of her time. I still don't. Soph needed her more than I did."

"But?" he prodded.

"But nothing," she said and rolled onto her back. If there had been a sky overhead instead of a drop ceiling, he'd have assumed she was gazing at the stars. "It was just that I always felt better after seeing a service dog trotting along the hospital halls next to its owner, going about its day like nothing was out of the ordinary. For those service dogs, nothing *was* out of the ordinary. They were happy just to be of use, to do their jobs. Nothing else mattered. That idea stuck with me long after Sophie went into remission and I went away to college. Terrible things happen and life is hard, but someone needs to keep trotting along and getting things done. Turns out, I'm really good at being that someone."

Ford couldn't decide if that was the best or the worst thing he'd ever heard, but he was leaning toward the latter. Terrible things *did* happen all the time, and life could be a real son of a bitch when it wanted to, but Lila deserved a lot more than being a service dog to someone else. In fact, it was impossible for him not to draw the parallels between her story and his own feelings for her. He'd already admitted to himself that he was drawn to her efficiency and levelheadedness, that he'd willingly hoist all his burdens onto her capable shoulders.

What the hell kind of man does that make me?

The Chihuahua-like puppy burrowed under his hand until he gave in and began running his fingers up and down her spine. "You could have become a doctor instead," he pointed out. "That would have been the more logical progression."

"I know. And I did half a year of premed before switching to animal behavior. I don't know why, but I always kept coming back to this. It might be those incongruities again. Puppies are the last thing anyone associates with me, but I like them. There's no judgment in them, no reserve. Everything they feel is right there on the surface." She smiled as the puppy under his fingertips proved her words to perfection. The animal wriggled onto her back, her tongue lolling—happy and heavy—out the side of her mouth. "Don't tell Sophie I said this, but she's exactly like Pip there. I've always envied that about her. She feels what she feels, and she just puts it out there for anyone to see."

"Sophie seemed nice," Ford said.

"Dawn's like that, too, now that I think about it. But I'd say she's driven more by her actions than her emotions. She does what she wants to do, and people can either take it or leave it. Most of the time, they take it."

"Don't forget Lila."

Lila stopped petting the fluffy white puppy. "What?"

"You're like that, too," he said.

"Me? No, I'm not."

He reached for her and intertwined his fingers through hers, pausing only to lift her hand to his lips for a gentle kiss. He knew he shouldn't let himself get drawn in like this, that it would be fairer to them both if he packed up his sorry life and let her get on with her own, but he couldn't. He wasn't that strong.

"I hate to break it to you, but you don't hold much back, either," he said. "Have you forgotten what happened the first time I ever saw you? You were telling my sobbing, brokenhearted daughter about how little she should trust a man's teeth."

Lila choked on a laugh. "That doesn't count. I got carried away in the moment. I was having a rough night."

"And *then* you went on to undress me with your eyes," he continued. "Oh, no. You can't deny it. You stripped me of that tuxedo in five seconds flat."

Her cheeks flamed with color. "I did no such thing," she said and went on to contradict herself two seconds later. "Besides, you can hardly blame me. You must know how you look in a tux. Every woman there must have been ogling you. It was unnatural."

At that, a flame of desire flickered in his gut. Ford didn't know or care what other women had been doing that night of the ball; he was only conscious that Lila had found something to admire.

"Unnatural, huh?"

"Don't look so smug. We've already been through this. You're an attractive man, Ford Ford. *Too* attractive for your own good." She paused and pursed her lips. "And mine, apparently. You never should have been able to win me over this easily."

That small flame roared up in an instant, working its way through his whole body before settling in his groin. His cock grew hot and heavy, as though a weight—the weight of a woman, perhaps—was bearing down on him. Lila's confession was exactly what he was talking about, exactly the point he was trying to make. She might not be as unguarded as either of her sisters, but there was something unnervingly honest about her all the same. She was unafraid to admit a flaw, unwilling to pretend to be something she wasn't.

That was something *he* envied about *her*. She was constantly surprising him by the things she said and did, but that was because she only said and did the things that were truly in her heart. Unlike the rest of them, who hid behind pleasantries and polite inanities and jokes that kept all the young, unmarried ladies from getting too close, Lila was one hundred percent herself, one hundred percent of the time. A man would always know where he stood with her.

"And *then* you lost no time in making me an indecent offer," he said. It was, he knew, another one of his jokes, but he didn't know how else to proceed. "And in taking shameless advantage of me underneath the elementary school bleachers."

"I did not!"

"Kissing me until I forgot that we were in a public place. Holding me captive while Helen Griswold kept watch above. Slipping your tongue into—"

"Ford, if you know what's good for you, you'll stop

right there." Her voice was half laughter, low and sultry. "I didn't bring you here so you could fling my indiscretions at me."

"Then why did you bring me?" he asked. The question came out strangled, almost as though he was buried under the weight of two dozen playful puppies instead of just one.

The feeling of gentle pressure didn't abate any when Lila said, "I don't know, really. You showed me your happy place, so I wanted to show you mine."

He didn't know what it was about that simple confession that broke down the last of his barriers, but everything he knew and felt came roaring to the surface all at once. He loved that Lila had brought him here. He loved that she'd taken the time to really think through their date. He loved how that careful thoughtfulness came through in everything she said and did.

He loved *her*, period.

"Lila, I—" he began. She stopped him by plucking the golden retriever from his chest and shifting her body closer to his.

"Until recently, building this place for me and my sisters was the best—and bravest—thing I'd ever done." The dimple appeared in the corner of her mouth. "But that, of course, was before I met *you*."

It was impossible after that for Ford to lie there and pretend he was going to escape this thing with his heart intact. Maybe, if he'd been a man of resolution, he could have walked away and saved himself a world of pain. Unfortunately, resolution was the one thing that had always failed him. Well, that and dignity—a thing that was rapidly disappearing as he found himself shifting several puppies out of the way to bring his lips to hers.

It was somehow fitting that this—his first kiss with Lila where both of them were horizontal, the length of her body pressed out against hers—was being conducted in a kennel with half a dozen pairs of watchful eyes on them. Not because Lila worked with puppies, but because every moment leading up to this one had been fraught with the same dangers. There was always something or someone in the way, forcing them to steal whatever moments they could where they could find them.

It wasn't suave or debonair, and Ford was pretty sure the tongue currently working its way into his ear wasn't Lila's, but this was what his life looked like. Stolen kisses and inelegant concrete floors and a frantic desire to be inside this woman in spite of it all.

"Does it seem strange to you that we're making out in the middle of a dog kennel when there's a perfectly good house a few feet away?" he asked as he moved from Lila's lips to her cheek, and from there to the curve of her neck. This was as much of her body as he'd been able to taste so far, and he was greedily determined to make a more thorough survey.

Preferably in a bed. A big one. With pillows and sheets and all the time in the world at his disposal.

"There's a blanket," she pointed out. She also arched her neck to give him better access to the soft patch of skin behind her ear. He was distracted enough by this— and by the coconut swirl of her hair enveloping him— that he almost forgot where they were.

Until, not unnaturally, he rolled onto his back and almost landed on one of the poor, wriggling creatures.

He laughed and nudged the puppy out of the way, careful to keep one hand on Lila's waist as he did. Her sweater had slipped up to reveal a warm and tantalizing expanse of skin along her midriff, and he wasn't about to give it up easily. "I don't know if you noticed, but there are also several pairs of eyes locked on us." He trailed his fingers along the curve of her waist, taking a slight detour around her belly button. It was an outie, small and coiled, which struck him as both adorable and some-how fitting. "I already admitted to you that I haven't done this in almost six years. The least you can do is let me bungle my way through without an audience."

Unable to resist much longer, he leaned down and pressed a kiss against her belly button. Nothing about her skin tasted the least bit fruity, and he almost lost himself at his delight in finding it so.

"Please," he said—*begged*, really. "I don't know how much longer I can go without you."

Lila gave a low moan of approval, but she managed to wrest herself up into a sitting position before he man-aged to do much more than slide his tongue along the soft slope of her stomach. "Five minutes," she gasped. "That's all I need."

It was on the tip of his tongue to tell her that he, on the other hand, required an eternity, but that wasn't what she meant. As usual, responsibility was at the forefront of her mind. She rose to her feet and began putting the puppies back in their kennels.

It should have dampened his ardor, this attention to detail, each animal requiring a treat and a compliment before Lila was ready to move on to the next one, but it didn't. If anything, watching her work only turned him on more. Each movement she made was elegant, every line of her body swaying gracefully to and fro. And she had no idea—that was thing that unsettled him most. She was unconscious of anything but her duty. She trotted along, doing what needed to be done, wholly unaware of the picture she presented as she did.

When the last animal was secured, Ford gave up on any pretense of holding himself back. He came up behind Lila and swept her into his arms. As in, literally swept her, scooping her up from the ground and hoisting her against his chest. She was no light burden, but she was a delightful one, all her rounded parts pressing against him in her squirming attempts to get free.

"Ford, what do you think you're doing?" she demanded.

"Your sister's boyfriend taught me this," he said as he tucked one arm under her ass and lifted her to his shoulder so that she was slung over it, caveman-style. "He knows all kinds of handy tricks about carrying women away from danger."

"You didn't ask him how to do this!" she cried, half laughing, half incredulous.

"Oh, yes I did." He secured his other arm around the back of her thighs and started moving toward the door. "You told me you were attracted to large, manly men. This seemed like the quickest way to get there."

"Ford!"

"I don't think I'll drop you," he promised. "But you should probably stop moving around *quite* that much."

She instantly stilled. "You're really going to carry me to the bedroom?"

"Every step of the way."

"Where you'll have your wicked way with me?"

"As wicked as I can possibly make it."

She hesitated. "Even though you haven't done this in almost six years?"

"*Especially* because I haven't done this in almost six years." Making a declaration while Lila's ass was inches from his face wasn't the most romantic way to go about this business, but Ford was nothing if not willing to play the game. "I've been waiting for the right woman to come along first. And *you*, Lila Vasquez, are that woman."

He had no way of knowing if it was his admission that caused her to grow silent, or if she was merely allowing him to focus his concentration on opening the door without dropping her to the floor, but she didn't move until he approached the hallway where the bedrooms were located.

"Should I kick them all open in my passionate attempts to find the right one, or will you direct me where I'm going?" he asked.

"Second door on the right," she replied. "And you can put me down now. You made your point."

No, he hadn't. How could he, when he didn't even know what his point was? To be sure, sex was one of his primary goals right now, as the rigid state of his cock was all too ready to attest, but there was more to it than that.

He liked having Lila in his arms. He liked knowing he could carry her away from her responsibilities, however temporarily. He liked feeling as though she was really and truly *his*.

Ford made it through the door easily enough, pleased

to find a king-size bed awaiting them on the other side. Lila gave a squeal as he tossed her onto the handmade quilt that covered it. He was interested enough in this room—Lila's private lair, the place where she went to sleep each night—to make a survey of his surroundings, but Lila's laugh stopped him short.

"No one has ever thrown me ruthlessly to the bed before, so I'd say your lack of practice isn't holding you back so far. What else have you got up your sleeves?"

He had no interest in lampshades or impressionist art after a comment like that. Especially not when his gaze dropped to where Lila lay, her body in a pose of relaxation and a laugh on her generous lips. He wanted to keep her like that—relaxed and happy, relaxed and *laughing*—so he allowed a slow smile to cross his lips. He also began rolling up his sleeves, carefully undoing the button on each cuff and revealing his forearms one fold of fabric at a time. He might have felt silly about it, except that Lila caught sight of what he was doing and pulled in a sharp breath. Her legs also fell open a few inches. Even though she was wearing jeans, the tantalizing vee at the juncture of her thighs and the promise of all that was contained between them caused his cock to twitch. It was all he could do after that to keep from giving up on his damned cuffs entirely and ripping his whole shirt from his body, Hulk-style.

"I didn't mean that literally," she said as he finished with his sleeves and strode closer to the bed. "Is this going to be one of those games where you have to do everything I say?"

He was on the verge of agreeing to this plan—one that appealed to both him and his body with rigid interest—when she added, "I've never played that game before. Or any games, really. At least, not any that take place in the bedroom."

"We can play anything you want," he said, his voice gruff. He circled his fingers around her ankle and gave it a gentle tug. Her whole body scooted down the bed toward him. "But first, I'm going to discover if any parts of you taste like that fruit basket."

She still had on all her many winter layers, which meant it was Ford's privilege to strip them off, one by one. Yellow wool socks came first, tugged away to reveal two rows of neatly polished toenails.

"Your toenail polish is perfect," he said, distracted by the pearly-pink color glinting up at him. He shifted his glance to Lila's face. "How do you keep it from getting all over your skin? Is there a trick I should know?"

If Lila found anything strange about this detour, she didn't let it show. "Is this another one of your princess braid obsessions?" She wriggled her toes out of his grasp. "Because I'm not sure I can add playing with my feet all day to our list of acceptable physical contact. I'm having a hard enough time as it is."

Ford glanced at her toes with renewed interest. He'd never had much of a foot fetish before, but with this woman, he was willing to make an effort. "Why?" he asked as he ran a finger along her foot's delicate arch. "Does this turn you on?"

"No!" she gasped and gave a convulsive twitch. When her foot missed his face by mere inches, she said, "I'm just very ticklish there. And if you use that against me either now or anytime in the future, I swear to everything—"

"I would never," he promised, a laugh rumbling through his chest. "But I find these physical weaknesses of yours to be highly intriguing. Are there any other sensitive areas I should know about?" He tugged on her ankle again, pushing the leg of her jeans up to expose as much skin as he could. Pressing a kiss against the curve of her calf, he paused long enough to ask, "There, maybe? There? Or how about...here?"

"That one's a little questionable," Lila gasped as he lingered a moment near the back of her knee. "Maybe you should just skip to the good parts."

"These *are* the good parts," he protested, but he gave in at least partway. Lila's jeans were starting to provide a serious impediment, so he gave her leg yet another tug. This time, he didn't stop until he'd managed to get her waist within reaching distance. He meant to make short work of the zipper and remove the pants altogether, but her sweater was askew enough to expose even more of her stomach.

This time, he gave all the way in to the urge to explore that undulating expanse. He started by pressing a kiss against her belly button, savoring the taste that greeted his tongue. She was salt and skin and the soft, downy fuzz that covered her belly.

"If this is what you're like when you're out of practice, I'm not sure I could handle you at your best," Lila said with a soft moan. He was working his way downward, but slowly, taking his time savoring each tantalizing inch. "Besides—it seems like I should be the one reintroducing you to how this all works. Are you sure you don't want to switch places?"

Oh, he was sure. One press of that woman's

well-formed mouth anywhere near his cock, and this interlude was going to be over before it even began. Already, each brush of her body against his erection was making him long to rip every shred of her clothing off and bury himself inside her.

"There's plenty of time for that," he said as he flicked the button of her jeans open. As this elicited a gasp of Lila's approval, he had no qualms about sliding the flat of his palm inside.

Ford had no way of knowing what kind of underwear she'd been wearing the night of their phone sex, but the panties she had on today were the merest scrap of lace. They dipped low on her belly, providing a tempting barrier. He was man enough to appreciate that they'd been worn for his benefit, in anticipation of being seen and appreciated to their fullest. Determined not to let her down, he paused and leaned down to kiss the white scalloped edge.

She gasped and buried her hands in his hair, her whole body giving a convulsive twitch as he continued his gentle assault. At least, it started out gently enough. Ford was determined to enjoy every second in this woman's bed, but as soon as he managed to tug her jeans down her hips, he lost his resolve. The lace covered just enough of her mons to qualify as underwear, but that was it. Everywhere else he looked and touched and tasted was gloriously bare—and even more gloriously bared to him. Soft with desire and pliable with need, Lila's legs fell open enough to allow him to slide between them.

Her hands were still buried in his hair, her grip on his scalp surprisingly firm. He was half afraid that she

was going to yank him away from his current delightful
vantage point, but all she did was use the leverage to
slide closer to the end of the bed.

"You don't taste like a fruit basket at all," he mused
as he finished tugging her jeans off the rest of the way.
From there, the only thing he could do was work his way
back up from the ankle again, this time unrestricted by
clothing. He paused for a few moments near her knees
and then up her thighs, pressing increasingly deeper
kisses the closer he drew to her center.

"I hope you're not disappointed." She released a low
moan and twisted her hands in his hair as he flicked
a tongue along the inner edge of her panties. "I'm no
princess, after all. Just an ordinary woman."

Nothing about Lila was ordinary, and Ford would
have been glad to expound on this topic at length. At
least, he would have if it weren't for the fact that she was
well within licking distance. He could have wasted time
with sweet nothings, telling her of all the ways she'd
brought joy and light to his life, but words seemed like
a wasteful use of his tongue.

So he answered her with a kiss. Not a soft, slow,
sensual one, but one that took shameless advantage of
her parted thighs and the fact that his head was buried
between them.

Ford had been looking forward to this for weeks,
anticipating the loss of Lila's control as one might await
the reveal of a masterpiece. He loved the idea of her
wriggling and squirming against his mouth, of tasting
the deepest parts of her and savoring the flavor of her on
his lips long after she came.

Somehow, in all those imaginings, he'd forgotten that

his own control was a thing of the past. He was unable to take his time, even more unable to enjoy the gasps and moans of Lila's pleasure. As soon as his tongue found her clit, he lost all sense of anything else.

He was still in her bedroom, he knew. He had one hand angling her hips up to keep her pressed against his mouth, the other stroking her inner thigh and all the silken softness it offered. He could smell her and taste her and *feel* her, but that was where he ended and she began.

Lila was everywhere. The rhythmic motion of her hips was the beat of his heart. The wet heat of her was the air he breathed. The slide of her skin under his fingertips was his entire fucking world.

And when she came—not gently or primly—but in an uncontrollable wave of ecstasy against his lips, he knew that his world would never be the same again.

As much as he would have loved to stay where he was forever, Ford eventually drew back, but not before planting one last kiss on her inner thigh. Lila found the power to speak long before he did, her low, sultry voice laughing even now.

"*Well*," she said with all the air of a satiated woman. "You don't seem too out of practice with that, either. I know you've been watching a lot of YouTube videos on braiding lately. Have you added cunnilingus ones to the mix?"

Ford shook his head and slid up the bed to join her, his hands skimming over thighs and hips and stomach as he did. Lila still had her sweater on, so he didn't stop until his palm lay against her rib cage, nestled against the band of her bra. This, too, he noted was lace.

This, too, he resolved to remove at the earliest possibility.

"*Are* there YouTube tutorials about cunnilingus?" he asked. He lifted her sweater and began examining the lace bra in earnest. It matched the panties perfectly, all delicate and white and barely sufficient to cover the areolas he'd heard so much about. "That seems like it might contradict the terms of their service. It's really just porn by that time."

"I wouldn't know," Lila said. "I expect that's more your area of expertise than mine."

Her tone was stiff enough that Ford stole a peek up at her face. She wasn't, as he'd feared, insulting him. In fact, he suspected that the strangled note in her voice came from the lower lip she had pulled between her teeth. This theory was confirmed when he grazed his fingers over the lip of her bra and came in contact with the peaked tip of her nipple.

"Well, I *have* been celibate for an awfully long time," he said. His own voice was becoming noticeably hoarse. His erection, which had maintained a hard, steady presence during his foray between Lila's legs, was now making more painful demands. "And there's only so much pleasure I can get out of Judge Judy."

"Ford!" Lila sat up with a gasp.

"*Artistic* pleasure," he said. He paused a moment to appreciate Lila's disheveled and mostly naked appearance. Her lace bra was more of a shelf than anything else, lifting and displaying her breasts in a way designed to drive a man mad. Unable to resist, he lifted a hand to one of those taut, temptingly lifted globes. Her skin was like silk, her moan like music, and he was powerless against both.

"Don't worry," he added, his voice tight. "You have nothing to be jealous of. Judy pales in comparison to you."

"I swear, if you mention that woman's name one more time…"

"You'll what?" he asked. He was much too taken up with the weighty delight of her breast in the palm of his hand to take her threat very seriously. He grazed his thumb over her nipple. "You've already made this a night I won't soon forget. Judy and I can take whatever punishment you have in mind."

Her punishment, as it turned out, was to laugh. It was the same sound that had struck him so forcibly the first time he'd heard it, so low and sultry, and he realized now why it had so much power over him. That was no titter, no giggle, no fleeting amusement at his antics. That laugh came from somewhere deep inside her, drawn from a place that he suspected few men trod.

"I can't stop you from doing or saying whatever you want," Lila said as she arched into his touch. "But I *was* promised that you'd kiss me and cuddle me. And, if I recall correctly, that we'd fu—"

He fell upon her then, refusing to let another word escape those laughing lips. He remembered very well the things he'd promised, although he had no idea which one of them he'd promised them to. Lila, yes, but also himself. Kissing her was heaven; cuddling her a delight.

And as for *fucking*, well…

"You're going to pay for that," he said as he lay her back against the bed, his own body drawn along the length of her. He still had most of his clothes on, which seemed like a damn oversight at this juncture. He wanted to be naked and inside her. He wanted to bury himself in her velvet heat and never let go.

Fortunately, Lila took on most of the burden of undressing him. She was damnably slow about it, though, taking her time with each button of his shirt, revealing his chest inch by inch. She did it with that dimple peeking out of the corner of her mouth, her hands lingering every time they brushed against his skin.

"Ah, there's my old friend," she said as she flicked the final button and watched as he shrugged himself out of the sleeves. Her hand lay flat against his abdomen, her palm scorching. "I'm surprised it took you so long to pull him out for our date. I've never known a man so much in love with his own chest."

He tried to respond in kind, but Lila's hand was snaking in a decidedly southward direction, her fingers so close to his cock that he was lucky to still be breathing.

"Sauntering around all the time without a shirt." She clucked her tongue and tugged at his fly. "Wandering the neighborhood half-naked. You should be ashamed of yourself."

"If you keep doing that, I promise I will be," he said.

The curve of her lips deepened into a smile that was equal parts wicked and breathtaking. "If I do what?" She gave his waistband a strong tug. "This?"

He groaned as she slipped a hand down the front of his jeans. A jolt worked through him at the contact of her palm against his erection. It was just a hand, he knew, the only thing that had been bringing him release for years. But Lila's sharp intake of breath and the way she sucked in her lower lip made all the difference.

"Six years, remember?" he asked hoarsely. "Be gentle with me. I'm more fragile than you realize."

"Don't worry, Ford," she replied. "I do realize it."

He had no idea how he was supposed to take that. He'd meant it as yet another joke, a way of introducing levity into a sexually fraught moment, but Lila wasn't laughing. In fact, there was a note of sobriety in her dark eyes that he found he didn't much care for. Determined to replace that look with something—anything—else, he kissed her.

It was a deep kiss and a long one. He still had the taste of her on his lips, but she didn't seem to care as she wound her arms around his neck and held him close. In fact, if the hitch of her leg around the back of his knees was any indication, there would be no escaping from her clutches any time soon.

Not that there was anywhere to go. Stretched out on top of Lila—her body rocking in waves under his, her hips pressing against his in need—was the only place he wanted to be.

"Condoms," she gasped as he transferred his kiss from her lips to that oh-so-predictable place on the side of her neck. She was practically purring by this time. That sound coiled in and around him, tightening his cock and thrumming in his veins. "In the bedside table. So many condoms."

"One should suffice for now, but I appreciate your preparedness." He leaned across and pulled open the drawer in question, a low whistle escaping his lips as soon as he saw the bounty contained within it. "And your optimism. Damn, woman. There's enough here to see us through the apocalypse—and back again."

A light suffusion of color crossed her face. As she was already flushed with pleasure, her nipples darkening in arousal and her breath coming in short, panting bursts, it made a delightful picture. "They're from my sister, I swear. I usually stock a normal human amount."

He grabbed the nearest foil package, which promised ribbed pleasure for them both. "Oh, I'm not complaining. There's no one I'd rather fuck during the apocalypse than you."

"Aw, that's weirdly sweet. There's no one I'd rather fuck during the apocalypse, either."

"Then that settles it." He lost no more time in ripping open the package and rolling the condom along his length. "When the end of times come, I'll fight fire and dragons and even Krampus to come find you. You bring the condoms."

"I think I'd better leave those up to you," she said and shifted her position so that he could more easily enter her. "I'm the one who fights Krampus, remember?"

Oh, he remembered. That story took up too much of his time—too much of his emotional energy—for it to be otherwise. As creator, he'd imbued Lizard Lila with any number of virtues and strengths and capabilities, but it was the real woman who provided the source material. There was nothing she couldn't do, no one she couldn't slay with one killing blow.

Including him.

"I'd fight fire and dragons and Krampus for you, too, Ford," she said. "I'd fight a lot more than that just to have you inside me right now."

There was nothing for him to do after that but comply. There was too much of her to do otherwise.

Not in terms of tits and ass, though there were plenty of both to keep him occupied for hours, but in the way she surrounded every part of him. Her room, her hair, her legs—everywhere he turned, there she was. The scent of her filled his nostrils, the taste of her lingered on his lips. Even the sounds of her pleasure, mingled with laughter, threatened to take him over. As he drew up her legs and finally penetrated her, there was also the vast, intoxicating heat of her pussy to contend with.

This last one proved to be his undoing. All those years he'd been without a woman were nothing compared to the few weeks he'd spent in Lila's company. Without Lila in his life, he could have gone for half a dozen more years alone, relying only on his imagination to satisfy his body's needs. But the moment she'd taken his daughter by the hand, he'd been awakened on every front.

He needed her. He wanted her. And for right now, he had her.

Ford had no way of knowing how long that moment lasted, which was probably for the best. As he buried himself between her legs, he lost all sense of time and place and self. All that mattered was that Lila never stopped moving. She was an ocean underneath him, a scorching field of lava. She mewled and moaned and thrashed and—just when he thought he couldn't last another second—screamed on a wave of ecstasy.

He let himself go at the same time, unable to last another second. It was like being pulled into a vortex, all the sensations of his orgasm swirling in and around them both.

The vortex was one he was happy to remain in for as

long as he could. So was Lila. With their legs entangled, he braced his arms around her and flipped her on her side. The result was that he nestled against her back, still trapped inside her, still lulled by the soft curves of her body.

"Well, *s-h-i-t*," he murmured into her neck. Her hair had formed a fan around them both, the long strands tickling his cheeks and nose.

"*S-h-i-t*, indeed," she responded. Her tone was followed by a laugh that robbed it of any formality.

He would have liked to say more—something about how all the waiting had been worth it, about how he'd never be able to look at a princess the same way again—but words were beyond him. For Ford, that was saying something. He *always* had a response, a joke never far from his lips.

But right here—right now—there was nothing he could do or say that would top the simple joy of having Lila in his arms.

Not that it mattered, anyway. As his heart resumed a normal pattern and the rush of blood left his ears, an unfamiliar sound filled the room. Well—it was unfamiliar to him. Lila recognized it in an instant.

She groaned and released another one of those low laughs. "Talk about terrible timing."

Ford had begun to trail his hand up and down the curve of her hip, but he stopped as soon as those words left her lips. "What is that?" he asked, his head cocked to listen better. "It almost sounds like…"

"Howling?" She slid out of his grasp, but not before turning and planting a kiss on his lips. It was long and slow and made Ford wish for nothing so much as to pull her into his arms again. And he would have, too, except she added, "That's because it is. Those little beasts."

He propped himself up on one elbow and watched as Lila lifted herself out of bed. Before he could do much more than suck in a sharp breath at her breathtaking nudity, she wrapped herself in a floral satin robe that fit her body like liquid. She was beautiful all of the time, but there was something about this relaxed state of semi-undress that undid him.

Life could be like this always. If only…

"Do you mean the puppies actually heard us all the way in here?" he demanded.

"So it would seem."

"I didn't know that was a thing. I've done a lot of kinky things in my life, but I've never made dogs howl before."

Her dimple appeared as her eyes met his. They were dark with meaning and light with amusement. It was an intoxicating combination. "Me either, but don't worry—it should only take a second to calm them. Then I'll be back for all that kissing and cuddling you promised me."

Kissing, yes. Cuddling, *yes*.

"And maybe, if you think you can manage it one more time," she added with her deep, tantalizing laugh, "to *f-u-c-k*."

chapter
15

Pure coincidence led to Emily's appointment with Dr. Yarmouth so soon after their last meeting.

In the general way of things, Emily's interactions with the medical community were few and far between. As a toddler, when the doctors had first started to show concern about her hearing and development, he and Emily had seen specialists by the dozen. Ford barely remembered those days—could only recall long hours in waiting rooms and the tense uncertainty about his daughter's future.

The first few months after they'd diagnosed her disorder had been just as busy, though much more hopeful. As unsettling as it had been to hear terms like *degenerative hearing loss* and *early surgical intervention*, it had been good knowing that her condition had a label—and a plan of action. Although Emily's hearing would only grow worse with time, and she had to be wary of things like head injuries for the rest of her life, there was nothing stopping her from leading the full, happy, active life of her choosing.

Visits to doctors now had a tendency to run more like social calls than anything else. Emily was well liked by

her care providers, which meant they plied her with
cookies and stickers after a quick checkup before they
sent her on her way.

Today was no exception. At Dr. Yarmouth's behest,
they'd come in that morning for an equipment check.
Emily sat in a chair with her legs swinging carelessly
over the tip of Jeeves's head, a lollipop in hand, as
Patrick and Ford discussed the latest in external auditory processors.

"I didn't want to say anything until it was official,
but Anya's been working with Emily's school to get
a Bluetooth microphone system set up," Patrick said.
He sat across from Ford at a huge mahogany desk that
looked as though it could double as a rescue boat, should
the need arise. "It's a great new tech that will stream her
teacher's voice straight to her processor. She'll be able
to hear instructions much more clearly, even if she's
sitting away from the front or working on a different
project at the time."

"Really?" Ford glanced quickly at his daughter. She
showed no interest in the conversation taking place, too
content with her treat and the red and white stripes of
her candy-cane tights to care. "I had no idea Anya was
doing that for us."

"Well, it's not for you, specifically," Patrick allowed.
He steepled his fingers and placed them in the middle
of the desk. His gaze was direct and made Ford feel
uncomfortably like a child being reprimanded in the
principal's office. He wasn't used to feeling this way in
the doctor's presence—had, in fact, thought him a pretty
decent guy.

Technically, Patrick still *was* a decent guy, but Lila

had called him a bit of a *d-i-c-k*, and Ford was prepared to take her word for it.

"Anya recently got a grant to convert the entire district," Patrick continued. "They're piloting the program in the schools where there are currently students who have compatible implants. We'll just need to upgrade Emily's external processor, and they'll be able to plug her in. It shouldn't take more than a few weeks to get the order placed."

He pushed a piece of paper across the desk along with a pen that Ford recognized at a glance as a Montblanc. He picked up the pen but could only weave it through his fingers like a quarter in a magician's trick.

"There won't be any additional cost to you," Patrick said as if sensing Ford's hesitation. "And if she doesn't care for it, you can always go back to the old processor. There's no rule that says she has to use it once the system is up and running."

"It's not that," Ford admitted, though in some small way, it was. Money was a consideration where these things were concerned. Money was *always* a consideration.

"I would have mentioned the pilot program when I saw you at the school, but Anya hadn't gotten the final approval yet. There was also the other small matter." For the first time since Ford and Emily had arrived, Patrick showed discomfort. He shifted in his chair and offered a rueful smile. "I don't know if Ms. Vasquez has said anything about our history together, but—"

"She told me," Ford interrupted with a quick glance at Emily. She didn't appear to be watching their mouths, but that wasn't always a guarantee—especially since the ambient noise in here was almost nonexistent.

"Ah, yes. She would. A stickler for the proprieties, that one. She always has been."

The way Patrick made the claim, as though his relationship with Lila had been forged at the dawn of time, made Ford's chest clench. Part of it was the natural jealousy of a man who had recently enjoyed the sensation of Lila moving underneath him. There had been nothing the least bit proper about the way she'd lost herself in the moment. It was an experience he was eager to repeat—and as often as their situation would allow.

There was more to that tight feeling, though. One glance around the office was enough to made Ford feel as if he was being pressed under a column of cement. The medical degrees lining the walls, the expensive models and books lining the shelves, even the kind, fatherly smile on the other man—who was probably five years older than him, at most—could have been hand-selected to set him at a disadvantage.

I can't compete with this. I wouldn't even know how to start. A woman like Lila needed a kingdom. She deserved a prince. The village idiot might amuse her for a little while, but a small cottage for three wasn't how that story was supposed to end.

"The truth is, I'm not entirely certain we'll still be here after the holidays," Ford said. He kept his voice low, since he hadn't yet broached the subject with Emily. "I've received a job offer that might require a relocation to Seattle. It wouldn't be fair to order new equipment for Emily if she won't be here to use it."

A look of mild surprise crossed Patrick's face. "Seattle?"

Ford winced at the volume in the doctor's voice, but

Emily was kicking her legs against the seat and didn't appear to notice. "Nothing is settled, so I haven't said anything yet. It's a good opportunity, though. At least, it is for me. I'm not sure about—"

Patrick picked up on his meaning almost at once. "We'd miss you, of course, but I'm highly confident in the team at Seattle Children's. I did my residency there. I promise we could make the transition as easy as possible on you both." He glanced at Jeeves, who was sitting with his little head resting on his paws, and smiled. "All three of you, actually. When will you know?"

"A week? A week and a half?" The clock was ticking, and he'd have to make a decision soon. He tapped the page. "When would you need this form?"

"Oh, it can wait until you have a final answer. There's no hurry. Take it home with you. Think it over." Patrick sat back in his chair, which creaked heavily under his weight. "Will you be completing the puppy training before you move?"

"Yeah. If I do end up accepting the job, it wouldn't start until the new year." Ford made a motion to stand. "Lila should be done with us by then."

"Oh, she will be," Patrick agreed, standing up along with him. "No doubt about that."

Ford glanced sharply at the other man. Patrick's expression was straight-faced, making it impossible for him to tell whether the vague threat carried within those words was the product of his imagination or not.

"She's very efficient. If she gave you a timeline, she'll stick to it, no matter how attached she might grow to you in the meantime." Patrick paused. "And Emily, of course."

Ford barely had time to offer his hand to Patrick and give his a perfunctory shake before the buzzing sound of the other man's phone on the desktop drew his attention.

"That'll be about tonight," Patrick murmured after one quick glance at the screen. "If you'll excuse me…"

He'd already pulled the phone to his ear and offered a brief, "Hang on a second, will you?" before turning to Ford and saying, in a friendly but dismissive tone, "Let me know as soon as you decide about Seattle. I can start getting the referrals going anytime."

There was nothing for Ford to do after that but to offer his daughter his hand and lead her back out to the waiting room. He was never more grateful for the friendly farewells of the office staff and the delighted exchanges as Emily showed off her service puppy to them. It gave him an opportunity to gather his own thoughts, though what he hoped to do with them once they were all in one place, he had no idea.

Ignore them? Bury them? Throw them into a fiery pit and watch the glorious way they burned?

That last one didn't seem too bad, especially with Patrick's words still ringing in his ears. *Lila should be done with us by then. She'll stick to a timeline.* The other man might not have meant them maliciously, but Ford was forced to concede their truth. What other choice did he have?

From the outset, Lila had only been offered on loan to them. She was a gift from the powers that be, a bright flash in their lives, a Christmas miracle that would end when the holiday decorations came down. As much as it might pain him to admit it, they'd never made any promises otherwise.

So, yes, the fiery pit seemed the best way to go. The flames wouldn't remain for long, and the world would probably seem barren and cold once they went out, but *d-a-m-n* it all to *h-e-l-l* and back—Ford would make sure he enjoyed the warmth while it lasted.

🐾 🐾 🐾

"I swear to everything that's sacred, Patrick, if you apologize to me one more time, I'm going to shove this mistletoe down your throat."

"Mistletoe?" he asked hopefully.

Lila was careful to whisk the plant well away from herself before Patrick got any ideas in his blockish head. As she also pulled the front door open to let him in, she hoped he wouldn't take too much offense. "It's not that kind of mistletoe," she warned.

"What other kind is there?"

"The kind I brew into a poison and force you to drink if I so much as hear the words 'I'm' and 'sorry' cross your lips in succession."

Patrick looked at her through narrowed eyes but allowed the threat to stand. And a good thing, too, because she meant every word. She liked Helen enough to set up this not-a-date for her sake, but she had enjoyed just about enough of Patrick's company to last her forever, thank you very much.

"Are your sisters at home?" he asked as Lila led him into the living room, where she was putting the finishing touches on the holiday decorations. With the exception of the Christmas tree, the halls were just about decked. Sophie and Dawn loved decorating the tree, as all good sisters must, but they always did their best to have plans during the rest of it. That, like so many other unenviable and laborious tasks, fell to Lila. She was the hen baking bread for someone else to enjoy, the ant doing all the work while grasshoppers danced about.

For once, she didn't mind the distinction. She might not be the wild and carefree woman of every man's dream, but Ford seemed to enjoy her company. In fact, if his eagerness to go down on her not just one more time, but *twice* the other night was any indication, he enjoyed it quite a bit.

The grasshoppers could have their dance. This ant was doing just fine the way she was.

"Nope. You're safe." She handed him the end of a garland and gestured for him to pin it above the doorway. "They won't attack you tonight."

He obligingly lifted the garland, but with a sidelong glance of suspicion. "You seem to be in an awfully good mood."

"That's because I *am* in a good mood," she replied. "And before you go looking at me like that, no, it's not because you're here."

"I know," he said, surprising her with a lopsided smile. It was the first time she'd seen him present anything but a perfectly symmetrical front. "It's Ford, isn't it?"

Her heartbeat picked up, but she feigned nothing but cool disinterest as she said, "I'm sure I don't know what you're talking about."

He stepped back to admire his handiwork. "Yes, you do. You're a lot of things, Lil, but stupid isn't one of them."

No, she wasn't, and neither was Patrick. It was what

had drawn her to him from the start, even if all that crossword-puzzle wisdom had started to pall after a while. Giving up the pretense, she allowed her lips to lift in a smile. "What gave me away?"

He took the question seriously, turning to her with an intent expression. "Well, for starters, you've never threatened to poison me before."

An inelegant snort of laughter escaped her. "Maybe not out loud, but believe me, Patrick, I've felt that way many, many times."

His grin answered hers. "I suppose I deserve that."

"Don't," she warned, her hand upflung to stave off what she knew was coming.

"No apologies, I promise," he said and continued his weirdly intent stare. "I was just going to say that he's good for you. I don't think I've ever seen you so… Well, *relaxed*."

She stopped Patrick before he went any further. Her state of relaxation was no longer his concern. "I didn't invite you over here to argue, so let's please talk about something else." She handed him a plastic box with the Christmas supplies and a request that he stack it in the corner. "In fact, I only wanted to see you so I could—"

The doorbell rang before she could finish her sentence, which was just as well, since it wasn't much of an ending. She'd searched through the entire house in hopes of finding something of his she could return, but to no avail. There wasn't so much as a toothbrush in the bathroom she could pretend to give back to him. Despite seeing each other for five months, he'd made no lasting imprint on either her home or her heart. The best she could come up with was a few questions about auditory disorders as it related to service dog training, but they sounded feeble even to her own ears.

"Are you expecting someone?" Patrick asked.

"I don't think so," she lied and moved to open the door. "Maybe it's just carolers."

As planned, Helen stood on the threshold, looking fit to slay any number of hearts. The other woman always looked adorably put together, but she'd outdone herself in a jersey dress over woolen tights with boots that reached just above her knee. She even wore a pair of those cute little boot ruffles to draw attention to her thighs. A little overdressed for just stopping by, perhaps, but Lila doubted Patrick would notice. He'd never been one to go in for heavy compliments when it came to female attire.

"So sorry I'm dropping in on you like this," Helen said, sticking to the script they'd decided on ahead of time. She lifted a bottle of wine with a red bow wrapped around it along with a plate of her cookies. "But I'm doing my holiday rounds and hoped you might be in. Oh, dear. It looks like you have company. Should I come back at a better time?"

Helen proved herself to be a much better liar than Lila would ever be. She couldn't help being impressed by the ease with which Helen got in the door without so much as a blush or moment of hesitation.

"It's no problem. This is just my friend Patrick. Patrick, this is Helen Griswold and her sons, Byron and Neil." For a brief, horrified moment, Lila was afraid she was going to forget which child was which, but she'd underestimated herself. Byron lived up to his namesake with a scowl and a look of distaste at all the frills and furbelows that filled the house. Neil, the younger of the two, was practically vibrating with excitement over the promised visit with canines.

"Where are the puppies?" Byron asked with a heavy note of suspicion. "Mom—you said there'd be puppies. You *promised*."

Helen coughed, a sound Lila took as her cue to act.

"Oh, did you want to see the animals?" she asked, feigning innocence. "I can take you back to meet them. In fact, they're in desperate need of attention. I've been working so much lately, I haven't had time to play with them nearly enough. All nine could use some love."

"*Nine?*" Neil echoed.

"No one has nine puppies," Byron said, still suspicious but visibly thawing.

"I do." She accepted Helen's coat before having two smaller, damp ones cast unceremoniously into her arms. "Um, I'll just put these away. Do you need—?"

"To teach these children some manners? Obviously. I'm so sorry… Patrick, is it? They aren't normally like this." Helen paused and released a trill of laughter. "Actually, they're *always* like this, but don't worry. Lila knows how to handle them."

"She does?" Patrick asked. Catching Lila's eye, he amended his statement, "I mean, she does. Of course. Can I, uh, help you with those—?"

"Cookies? Yes, please. You can even eat some, but the wine is supposed to be a gift. Not very imaginative, I know, but everyone loves alcohol." She turned to Byron and Neil with a firm look. "You can go with Princess Lila to see the puppies, but make sure you mind her, okay? It's not too late to cancel Christmas."

"Mom!" Byron cried.

"It's written in the rulebook." Helen shrugged. She looked up at Patrick through playful hazel eyes, and Lila had the benefit of seeing her ex-boyfriend blink as though dazzled. Either that, or he was dazed. Lila was pleased with both options. It would do this man a world of good to get knocked off his high horse for a change. "Isn't that so, Patrick? You have up until the day before to put in a request for a cancellation, don't you?"

"Er, yes. You just need twenty-four hours' notice, I believe."

"See?" Helen said triumphantly. "And Patrick is a doctor, so he knows what he's talking about."

That position held enough power over the boys to awe them into temporary silence. Sensing an opportunity, Lila smiled down at them. "Would you like to go see the puppies now? They're just through the door in the kitchen. That is, if you two don't mind…"

Helen had enough presence of mind to wait for Patrick to decide. It took him all of three seconds to come to the conclusion that eating cookies with Helen Griswold was about fifty times more appealing than hanging out with Lila in any capacity.

"Don't worry on my account," Patrick said. "I'm sure Helen and I can entertain ourselves for a few minutes."

Unable to suppress a smile, Lila turned away and motioned the boys to move in the direction of the kennel. She lingered just long enough to hear Helen ask Patrick how he felt about chocolate chips before following the boys out. Helen would know how to handle Patrick from here—much better than she'd ever done, at any rate.

They'd agreed that thirty minutes was ideal for a child-free introductory tête-à-tête, so Lila set the alarm on her phone to remind her when the time was up and surveyed the mountain of a task she'd undertaken. The puppies were easy enough, of course, all nine of them jumping and squirming with delight at the sight of newcomers into their domain. One snap of her dog-training clicker would have them in order within seconds.

The children, however, were another story. Byron stood a few yards ahead of her, appraising the animals with a keen eye and a plastic cutlass in one hand. It was on the tip of Lila's tongue to demand an explanation of how he'd managed to smuggle it past his mother when Neil started running up and down the main aisle at a speed that probably could have won him Olympic gold medals.

Sweet, reserved Emily was nothing compared to these boys. Maybe this wasn't such a good idea, after all.

"Puuupppppies!" Neil cried, his hands out to either side as he ran. His fingertips grazed ears and paws and, in the case of the golden retrievers in the corner, a pair of enthusiastic tongues. "So many puuupppppies!"

Byron showed every sign of following him with—one would assume—his cutlass outstretched, so Lila decided to start there.

"There are no weapons in the kennel, I'm afraid," she said with her palm outstretched. "All sharp objects must be left at the door."

Byron glanced first at his cutlass and then back at Lila, as if determining how far he could push it. That was when she noticed he also had leather-style pirate cuffs on each wrist and dark-ringed eyes that had been applied, one would hope, with his mother's eyeliner.

"Captain's orders," she said, making a stab. "This is my ship, and if you want to be onboard, you have to follow my rules."

With a sigh, Byron handed the cutlass over. She was about to thank him when he bent over and pulled a matching plastic knife from his sock. As this was accompanied by an *actual* butter knife from his pocket and a wadded-up ball of paper that may have been masquerading as a hand grenade, she was thrown somewhat off her guard.

However, she was coming to understand the rules. Emily lived in a world where princesses appeared out of nowhere to help her find her missing father. Byron and Neil lived in a world where the rules of the high seas applied to everyday situations.

They were strange creatures, children, but she could appreciate their commitment to a theme.

"Thank you," she said, looking around in vain for a place to store all her booty. In the end, she had to end up tucking most of it into her own pockets. The cutlass, however, was too large. That had to be tucked into her belt, imbuing her normal walk with a swagger.

That swagger lost her no credibility in the Griswold boys' eyes. With a stern look, she planted herself in front of Neil. He was forced to come to a stop before her.

"Yours too, if you please."

"I don't have any," he protested.

She made a quick scan of his small person and identified a lumpy bulge in the region of his solar plexus. "Under your shirt. Right above your belly."

The boys shared a wide-eyed look of wonder. "How did you know?" Neil demanded, but he lifted his small shirt to reveal yet another butter knife taped around his midsection with what looked like every Band-Aid that Helen must have owned. "Do you have X-ray vision?"

Remembering that half of his heart belonged to the world of caped crusaders rather than pirates, Lila shook her head. "Of course not. That would be preposterous. No one has X-ray vision." As she followed this up with a heavy wink, Neil took none of this amiss. He breathed a sigh of wonder and stood at her feet, awaiting her next order.

"Now that we have everything settled," she began, "you may each choose one puppy at a time. No, not to take home, so don't get too excited. It's just for this evening. They need playtime, and your job is to make sure they get it. There's a box of toys in that corner, which you're free to make use of, but you must be gentle. No tugging ears. No pulling tails. And no, um, biting?"

She tried to think of what other activities these two redoubtable children might come up with to torture her poor animals, but decided to stop there. No need to put ideas into their heads.

"There's only time for you to play with one or two of them, though, so choose carefully," she said. Byron took her at her word and started to walk up the center of the kennel, appraising each puppy in its turn. Neil, however, paused and glanced shyly up at her.

"Is this where Emily got Jeeves?" he asked.

"Yes."

"Did she get to pick any one she wanted?"

"For the most part, yes. Only she gets to keep hers forever."

He nodded. "I like Jeeves," he said and, with a somewhat defiant glance at the back of his brother's head, "I like Emily, too."

"So do I," Lila confessed. In fact, she was rapidly coming to love that little girl. It was difficult to imagine a time when she'd been terrified at the prospect of spending eight hours in her company. Or, she reflected ruefully, in her father's company. Despite their flaws and fears and—in Ford's case, at least—their flirtations, those two had won her over, heart and soul.

It had just taken a little time, that was all. Time and understanding and...

"You know what?" she asked, suddenly struck with inspiration. "Do you see that puppy in the third kennel down?"

She pointed at a fluffy tan-and-white collie. They'd only just bought her, earmarked for use as a seizure alert dog for an upcoming case. The animal had already shown extraordinary sensitivity—which was great from a training standpoint but meant that she exhibited nervous tendencies.

"That one?" Neil asked, following the line of her finger.

"Yep. She's my favorite, but don't tell anyone."

Neil looked doubtfully at the collie puppy, who was eyeing him with the same wariness. "She's all right, I guess. I like the one next to her."

Predictably, he indicated the boisterous Chihuahua with a tail like a whip. She was showy and enthusiastic

but had a tendency to lose interest in just about everything after ten minutes.

"Really?" Lila asked, allowing a note of incredulity
to creep into her voice. "Pip's good, too, I guess, but for
my money, Andromeda's worth ten of her. She's a little
wary of strangers, but she's stronger than every other dog
in here. She just hides it until it's needed. Hang on a sec,
will you? I think your brother has decided on the Akita."

She was careful not to glance over at Neil as she
got Byron settled in with the friendly ball of white fur
he'd chosen. Already, he seemed to have forgotten that
his weapons had been confiscated. He was far too busy
patting the puppy and dancing a bright red rope in front
of his eyes. Confident that Byron wouldn't tug, pull, or
bite the animal, Lila turned her attention back to Neil.
She sauntered slowly over, pretending not to notice that
he was poking into Andromeda's kennel with a tentative finger.

"Pip, I think you said you liked?" she said as she
made a big show of reaching for the Chihuahua.

"Who names all the puppies?" Neil asked. "Do *you*
get to pick them?"

"Sometimes, if they don't have names when they
come here. But I have to share with my sisters, so I don't
get to pick as often as I'd like."

"*Ugh*. Sharing."

She ignored this terse—if accurate—assessment of
life with siblings. "Andromeda was already named when
we got her. Why? Don't you think it fits?"

"No!" he said quickly. "I like it. I like her. She's
really smart, see?"

He showed off the dog's intelligence by making a face

like a chimpanzee puffing out its cheeks. Andromeda's ears perked, and she tilted her head in sudden attention. When Neil shifted into a grimace, the puppy jumped to her feet and drew closer.

"She doesn't like it when I make that face," he informed her.

"That's because it's her job to know when you're not feeling well. She can read all kinds of cues—including expressions. It's because she's so serious. She watches and listens and learns, absorbing everything around her. She's going to be a very special service dog someday, but I can see why she might not appeal to an active little boy like you."

Neil's eyes slid over to the Chihuahua. "No..." he agreed doubtfully. "But maybe I could play with her anyway? Just for a few minutes?"

Lila had to fight an urge to shout in triumph. She hadn't been sure her plan would work, but Neil was proving to harbor a soft, sentimental inner core. He was his mother's son, that was for sure, and Lila couldn't think of a better compliment to give anyone.

"Absolutely," she said. "I bet she'd love that. Not many people offer to play with her, which is why it's all the more special when she finally makes a friend."

Neil's glance at her was sharp, making her fear that she'd been a little too heavy-handed in trying to draw the parallels between Andromeda and Emily, but he let it pass. He also jumped wholeheartedly into the next twenty minutes of playtime. In that short time, he discovered that collies were extremely tolerant of children, but also that in the animal's eyes, he was little more than a sheep.

"She won't let me leave, Princess Lila!" Neil laughed as he tried to get around the puppy to reach the other side of the kennel. "Lookit! If I go to this side, she follows me. And then if I go to that side, she comes back. I'm trapped."

"She's herding you, I'm afraid," Lila said. "I warned you how it would be. Once a special animal like this one decides she likes you, you're friends for life. She'll follow you anywhere."

Byron had given up on the Akita by this time, much more interested in his brother's puppy than his own. Lila was about to suggest they grab their coats and head outside for some more rambunctious fun when the alarm on her phone started chiming.

"Oh, *s-h-i-t*." She made a fumbling attempt to turn the sound off before the boys noticed and asked her questions, but there was no need. As much as she was learning about children, she still had a long way to go.

"Princess Lila, you spelled 'shit.'"

"Um. What? No. No, of course I didn't."

"You did. *S-h-i-t* is shit. I know that one."

Neil nodded in perfect solemnity. "And *d-a-m-n* is damn."

"Yeah. We're not allowed to say those words. Especially not *f-u-c-k*, which is—"

"We can all spell that word just fine, Byron, thank you." Helen appeared in the kennel in time to save Lila from her fate. At first, she was fearful that the other woman was going to be upset at finding her children swearing like pirates in addition to looking like them, but there was no mistaking that smile.

It was the smile of a woman who had spent a pleasant

half hour in a handsome man's company. It was the smile of a woman who'd been struck hard by Cupid's arrow and planned to do nothing to stop the bleeding.

Lila knew that because it was the same smile she'd been wearing for weeks.

"You two have taken up more than enough of Princess Lila's evening, I'm sure. It's high time we headed home and got you ready for bed. Everyone is having baths tonight." Helen gestured for her kids to join her back in the house. Instead of complying, the pair showed signs of mutiny.

"But Mom, we just got here."

"This is not a negotiation."

"But Mom, I want a puppy for Christmas instead of a Nintendo Switch."

"That's not a negotiation, either. That's for Santa to decide."

"But Mom—"

Helen turned to Lila with a laugh. "Run. Save yourself. Once these two start in on the 'But Mom' brigade, you've already lost half the battle. Besides, I owe you another one now." She winked. "Patrick and I are going out next week."

A wide smile broke across Lila's face. She couldn't have been more pleased if Patrick had asked her out herself. Actually, she *was* more pleased than when Patrick had asked her out herself. "Helen, that's fantastic."

A rosy blush highlighted Helen's freckles. "It's all thanks to you. A man like that would have never looked twice at me under any other circumstances. Well, he didn't. He admitted to not really noticing me at the school. I'd be sunk into a depression if he hadn't apologized so nicely and promised to make it up to me."

It was on the tip of Lila's tongue to tell her that Patrick was likely not to notice any number of things about a woman he was dating—up to and including how she looked when Jeeves didn't follow orders the first time around, exactly how she stood when trying not to let her emotions show, and how her lips twitched whenever she was trying not to laugh.

But that wasn't fair to either Patrick or Helen. Patrick had never seen her the way Ford did. She doubted anyone had.

"Is he still here?" Lila tilted her head toward the door.

"Yeah. He said something about wanting to talk to you." Helen hefted the pile of coats in her arms. "Would you think me awful if I sneak out the back with the boys? I hate to run the poor man off before we've even had a chance to go on one date. These two would scare a polar bear out of its den. It's better to ease him into them."

"Aw, they're not so bad. I like them. They're sweet."

"Gross," proclaimed Byron, overhearing this last part.

"Double gross," agreed Neil, but he remembered to thank Lila for letting them play with the dogs.

After seeing them out and ensuring the puppies were comfortably put away, Lila traipsed back into the house. Patrick was making himself useful by double-checking all the areas where she'd hung the lights and garland, reassuring himself that she hadn't hammered in a nail crooked or left a piece of wire exposed.

And by useful, she meant annoying.

"I've been putting holiday decorations up in this

house for five years, Patrick," she said and leaned against the wall. "I promise it'll remain standing until Christmas."

He paid her little heed. "Over two hundred house fires are caused by holiday decorations every year in the United States alone. It's important not to overload the outlets."

"Don't be such a fun sponge."

He paused in the act of testing a twinkle light. "A what?"

"A fun sponge. The void of happiness. A black hole of delight."

"Uh, did you and Helen get into the wine already?"

Lila laughed, feeling lighter than she had in years. She wouldn't say that she was ready to tricycle off the back deck or anything yet, but she might, should the situation call for it, tricycle anywhere else the wind took her.

"I'm not drunk, Patrick," she said. "Just happy."

Patrick broke into a sudden smile. She could have sworn she caught a glimpse of her reflection in his molars, but she let it slide. That dazzling brightness was Helen's problem now—or it could be, if he'd let it.

"I'm glad, Lil," he said with genuine warmth. "It couldn't have happened to two better people. I hope you know I mean that. A shame, though, about Seattle. I've done the long-distance thing before, and it's tough."

She was about to accuse *him* of getting into the wine when he laughed and rubbed a hand on the back of his neck. "Then again, Ford did say it was still up in the air. I can guess why. You're not an easy woman to leave. It took me two months to screw up the courage to do it."

There were several different layers to unpack in that statement. The one that got her bristles up the highest— that he had to *screw up the courage* to have an open and honest conversation with her about their relationship— was quickly set aside as the rest settled in.

Seattle. Long distance. *Leaving*.

"Do you think he'll end up taking the job?" Patrick added, oblivious to the way his last words were still clanging about inside her head. "There are great doctors there, of course, but I'd miss Emily. It's crazy how attached you can get to patients you've known almost their whole lives. Pediatrics can be tough that way—in a lot of ways, when I come to think of it. Helen's kids seem nice, don't they?"

Lila could only be grateful for the anxious way he voiced that question. He was so caught up in his own affairs that he hadn't noticed how still she'd gone.

"I don't have nearly as much of a say in Ford's future as you think," she managed after only a brief struggle. "What he and I have is just for fun. Naturally, he has to put Emily's needs first."

"Of course," Patrick agreed. His brows lifted at the terse way Lila spoke, but he didn't press the issue. "What was it you wanted to see me about, by the way?"

In all the bustle of taking care of the boys, Lila had forgotten that she'd lured Patrick here under false pretenses. Thinking fast, she decided on, "We've acquired a new puppy that I think will make a good hearing service dog, but I wanted your opinion on her temperament first."

"*My* opinion?" Patrick glanced around as if searching for another person whose advice she might be soliciting. "I don't know anything about dogs."

No, he didn't—and a fortunate thing it was, too. If he did, he'd walk into that kennel and see through her ruse in an instant. Each puppy was categorized and cataloged long before they walked through the door. With the amount of time and resources that had to go in to training them, Lila left nothing to chance.

"Maybe not, but you do have an unerring eye for detail." It was underhanded of her, she knew, but flattery had always worked well on this man. "I'd appreciate your input. My sisters, too. We're at something of a loss with this one."

His chest—and his ego—practically swelled before her eyes. To be called in to swoop to the rescue of not one, not two, but *three* damsels was just the sort of thing that got Patrick's blood going.

Ford would never have fallen for it. Ford would have laughed at her and demanded to know where she was hiding the real Lila Vasquez.

She'd have an answer for him, too. *I'm hiding her somewhere safe. I'm keeping her protected in case you leave and take all her chances of happiness with you.*

"Anything for a friend," Patrick said and followed her out to the kennel. "Well, that's not strictly true. Anything as long as it's not asking me to clean up after them."

chapter
16

"Hello, Ford." A seductive, sleepy voice sounded on the other end of the phone, sending a thrill down Ford's spine. "I don't recall asking you to set any alarms tonight."

Despite the fact that there was nothing fun about this phone call, he felt a strong urge to answer in kind. It wasn't his fault—the sound of Lila's low laugh awakened a Pavlovian response in him, heating his body and thickening his blood.

"You didn't," he said, wrenching his thoughts away from the image of her curled in bed, her body soft with sleep. "This isn't a social call."

"Business, then? How efficient of you. Let me make it easy. I'm not wearing a single, solitary scrap of fabric. There's something so indulgent about being naked when you slip between the sheets, don't you think? All that squirming and sliding…"

He groaned and pinched the bridge of his nose. It didn't do much to draw attention away from the interested twitch of his cock, but he had to do *something*. "Whatever you plan to say next, do me a favor and record it for later. Something is wrong with Jeeves."

It said a lot about Lila that she dropped the pretense of seduction in an instant. It would take much longer for his own body to recover, but he supposed that was the price of dating the most gorgeous woman in the world.

"Jeeves?" she echoed. "What happened? Is he hurt? Is he gone?"

"The puppy is fine. It's Emily I'm worried about. He, uh… I don't know how it happened, but he bit her."

"He *bit* her?"

Ford glanced over to where his daughter lay sleeping on her bed, her hand wrapped up in a white bandage. She'd fallen asleep just a few minutes after he'd administered first aid, exhausted from both her tears and the lateness of the hour.

"I bandaged her up and shut the puppy in the bathroom, but I don't know what to do next. Is this normal? I can't think what could have caused it. She woke up screaming."

"Of course it's not normal." The distress in Lila's voice was easy to hear. "Don't go anywhere. I'm coming over."

Don't go anywhere? He almost laughed. It was midnight on a cold winter night, and he'd just spent a terrible half hour trying to calm a child who'd been betrayed by the best friend she'd ever had. He hadn't slept a full night through since Lila and Jeeves had entered his life, and he owed an answer to Giles in less than a week. He was exhausted just thinking about putting on shoes.

"Please hurry," he said, hoping he didn't sound as desperate as he felt. "I need you, Lila."

She hesitated before answering in an even more

clipped tone than before. "I'm on my way. I'll be there in ten."

True to her word, Lila appeared on his doorstep in exactly nine and a half minutes, looking as though she routinely answered late-night calls from gentlemen in distress. She was fully dressed and had pulled her hair back in a long braid, a workbag carried under her arm. In fact, the only indication that she'd been sleeping less than fifteen minutes ago was a pair of glasses perched on her nose—and even those were cute, the chunky black frames that made her look like a librarian begging to be ruffled in the stacks.

"Do we need to take her to the hospital?" she asked by way of greeting.

Ford was more grateful for her calm acceptance of the matter than he cared to admit. "No, it wasn't a bad bite. It only broke the skin in two places. I think she was more scared than anything else."

"And you say it happened while she was sleeping?"

"I assume so." He made a move to take Lila's coat and bag, but she was so used to his house by now that she came right in, fully at home in these surroundings. He felt a pang at how easily she'd slipped into his life, how neatly she fit, how much he'd wished that she'd been here when Emily had woken him up in a panic.

He *did* need her—and for much more than one emergency puppy house call.

"She was sitting up in her bed, crying and holding her hand."

"And Jeeves?"

"Jeeves?" he echoed blankly.

"Yes. When you went to her aid, what was he doing?

Was he still in the room? Was he aggressive toward you?"

To be honest, he hadn't given much thought to the puppy. His concern had been mostly for Emily. "Uh, yeah. He was in the room. In her bed, now that I think about it. He was curled up under her other arm—her uninjured arm. I remember now that he didn't want to move. He bristled when I lifted him out of the way."

Lila nodded once. "That was his support position. He was protecting her from you."

"From *me*?" He released a shaky laugh. "But I'm not the one who bit her."

Ford had no idea what he said or did to cause Lila to pull him into a crushing embrace, but he was never more grateful for a woman's touch—and that was saying a lot considering a hug was all it was. And a *good* hug, too, hard and fierce and long. Lila didn't say a single word or make a single demand. She only held him against her until his feeling of shakiness started to subside and his heartbeat slowed to match hers.

She was comforting him—the way a mother comforted her young, the way a woman comforted her man. The realization almost broke him. The women in his life had always been more than he deserved, lending him a helping hand whenever he needed it, but this took things to a whole new level. Lila was an anchor, a *rock*. The seas could storm and the waters batter, but she'd never waver. She'd just hold him and let him feel overwhelmed and then remind him that there was work still to be done.

As if to prove it, she pulled back just enough to brush a lock of hair from his forehead and replace it with a soft kiss. And then she said, "If the bite broke the skin, then we need to put Jeeves in quarantine for ten days."

"Quarantine? Like...a plastic room and hazmat suits?"

She laughed. Like the hug, that warm chuckle did much to restore his equilibrium. "Not quite that bad. It's more like he needs to be isolated from other animals and watched for signs of rabies. I doubt that's the case, but it's standard procedure for all dog bites. We can either do it at the kennel or here at your house. It'll depend on what I find."

She didn't have to tell him what she meant by that. It depended on whether or not they were going to have to give Jeeves up—if he was a danger to Emily and other kids.

It was going to break his daughter's heart, he knew. Even with her hand clutched to her chest and huge tears in her eyes, she'd been determined that Ford put Jeeves somewhere safe until Lila could be summoned.

"Princess Lila can fix it," she'd said. "Princess Lila can fix anything."

Ford was inclined to agree. Lila could solve every problem he'd ever had—both in his home and in his heart. The trouble was, how was he supposed to repay her? All he had to offer was the occasional orgasm and the pages of a graphic novel no one wanted to read but her.

"What could have caused him to act out?" Ford asked as he followed Lila toward the bathroom. "Did she maybe roll on top of him in her sleep?"

"It's possible," she said, but not very convincingly. "There's also a chance he might be feeling sick or insecure. Did anything happen in the last few days to upset him? Did he show any signs of distress?"

Ford shook his head. "He's been nothing but his usual placid, soldiering self."

"All right, little guy." Lila pushed open the bathroom door. "Let's see what's bothering you."

To all outward appearances, the answer to that question was nothing. Ford had a strong suspicion that if someone had locked *him* up in a bathroom away from the girl he was supposed to protect, he'd have thrashed himself against the door until he made his way through— especially if that girl was Emily or Lila.

Not so with Jeeves. The dog was clearly unhappy about his banishment, but he sat on the bath mat as if resigned to his fate. His eyes were dark and full of woe, but his posture was serene.

Oh, that I had a tenth of that animal's dignity.

Lila dropped to the puppy's level the same way she did with Emily. She also spoke in the same low-toned, soothing voice that seemed to work so well on his daughter. He sat on her command, rolled over so she could push and poke at his various internal organs, and even opened his mouth so she could inspect his tongue and teeth. After about five minutes of this, Lila sat back on her heels and glanced up at Ford.

"Well, he's physically sound, at any rate. Can I see Emily, do you think, or is it better to let her sleep?"

"*Sleep*," came Ford's unequivocal reply.

"Oh. Okay." Lila took his proffered hand and allowed him to lift her to her feet. The telltale pink tinge to her cheeks told him that he might have uttered that response more harshly than he'd intended.

He didn't release her right away. "It's just that she's already had a pretty upsetting night, and the wound isn't serious." He spoke much more carefully this time. "Trust me. It'll be much worse for all of us if she doesn't get her full eight hours in. Children don't bounce back nearly as quickly as puppies do."

"That makes sense." A small, wistful smile twisted her lips. "I guess I'm still not very good with kids yet."

Ford had been on the verge of letting go, but at that, his grip tightened—not because she was once again shortchanging her ability to work with children, but because of that small word at the end. *Yet*. *Yet* implied there was more learning to be done. *Yet* meant she wanted to stick around long enough to try.

"Stay the night," he said. It was more of a plea than a request.

She attempted to yank her hand out of his grasp, but he was anticipating it and held her firmly. "Ford, you know I can't do that. Not with... Not when..."

Yes, he did know it. Not with the air crackling between them. Not when all he wanted to do was lower her to his bed and pin her there until they were both slick with sweat and desire.

"Not with me," he amended. "You can have the bed. I'll sleep on the couch. It's just that Emily will feel so much better about this whole thing if she wakes up to find you here. We both will."

Lila's struggle with herself was clear. She bit her lip and cast anxious glances down at the puppy, sneaking a covert look or two at Ford as she did. As he was once again wearing nothing but pajama pants, he couldn't help but think his bare chest was swaying her either for or against the plan.

"I promise to maintain decorum and dignity at every turn," he said.

"You *say* that, but—"

"I won't picture you naked or even in a mild state of undress. Starting right...now."

Her lips twitched. "That's not the point."

"I'll even give you a pair of my pajamas to wear so you can see for yourself why I never take them off. One night with this well-worn flannel between your legs, and you'll never go back to lace and satin. We'll have to trade. I don't mind. I rather liked those white ones you wore the other night. I think I could get used to them with a little time and practice, don't you?"

She outright laughed that time. "None of this is helping your case."

"I know, but it's the only way I seem to get anything out of you. You refuse to believe in my sincerity. You always have." Her hand was still clasped in his, so he brought it to his lips. Under any other circumstances, he'd have felt ridiculous—this gallant gesture more suited to the suave gentleman in the tuxedo than a man standing barefoot in his five-by-five pink-tiled bathroom—but Lila had a way of making even the most commonplace activity seem like an opportunity in seduction. "I'd really like for you to stay the night tonight, Lila Vasquez. Not because I want to *f-u-c-k* you, even though I do, but because having you here seems to make even my biggest problems seem like nothing. You're capable and warm and loving, and I don't know how you've gone through three decades of life and not been snatched up by every single man who's crossed your path."

Lila's lips fell open. She stood and stared at him, not moving—not even to blink. Her usual look of incredulity was there, but so was something else, something distant. Something *new*.

"Emily feels that way, Jeeves feels that way, and you know I sure as *h-e-l-l* feel that way." Ford finally dropped her hand, which fell like a deadweight to her side. "Will you please stay?"

That new, distant look didn't go entirely away, but Lila softened enough to nod. "Of course I will. Until the six weeks of training are up, being on call is part of the job."

It wasn't nearly the answer he'd been hoping for after the declaration he'd made, but it was enough. It had to be.

Until the six weeks of training was up, it was literally all he had.

chapter
17

For the first half of the day, Jeeves showed every sign of being a puppy reformed. Lila was careful to keep a vigilant eye on the cockapoo, her notebook out so she could jot down any aspect of his behavior that troubled her. Jeeves wouldn't be the first puppy to reject a placement this far into the training, and she was sure he wouldn't be the last. Dogs were like that. They loved and trusted without question, but the strain of long-term stress could still one day force them to their breaking point.

People were like that, too. No matter how much laughter and sex and camaraderie there might be, happiness was never guaranteed. It could all snap in an instant.

"Maybe it was just a fluke after all?" Ford sidled up next to her as she stood watching Emily and Jeeves work through their basic routine in the backyard. With the exception of Emily's hand, which was still bandaged and had to be encased in one of Ford's oversize gloves, Lila could detect nothing about the previous night's altercation. The puppy showed no signs of anything except placid happiness and a determination to stay close to Emily's side. "I haven't seen any sign of aggression out of Jeeves all day."

"Me either," Lila admitted. "I'm wondering if your theory about her rolling on top of him might be true. Is she a restless sleeper?"

"Not really, no."

"Huh." The word came out in a puff of white breath. She wished she had something more academic—more professional—to offer than that, but *huh* was the best she could come up with. She'd called both Dawn and Sophie that morning with the case notes, but her sisters hadn't been able to find an explanation for the puppy's behavior, either.

"Huh, indeed," he agreed.

There was a note in his voice that she didn't quite trust. "Whatever you're going to say next, fight the urge," she warned him. "It'll have to wait. I'm going home to shower and change my clothes."

He cast an obvious look over his shoulder back at the house. "I have a perfectly good shower right here. I promise you'll feel exactly like you're naked and lathered up at home. Don't be afraid to make use of the detachable showerhead."

"Nice try," she said, but with a visible effort. She knew it behooved her to tread warily where this man was concerned, but he made it so freaking *difficult*. Why, oh, why did he have to smile at her like that? And why, oh, why, did her body react so strongly to it? "This is one of those official on-the-clock moments."

His rumble of interest warned her away—both from him and from the topic at hand.

Instead of giving in to the pull of flirtation, into the

pull of *him*, she whistled for the puppy's attention. Jeeves alerted Emily and waited for her to join him before drawing close, a picture-perfect service dog from start to finish.

"Very good work this morning, you two," Lila said as soon as Emily came near enough to both see and hear her. "I'm going to head home, but I'll be back next week at the usual time. You're both so close to the finish line. As soon as Christmas is over, I think you'll be ready to move on without me. Isn't that exciting?"

"Very exciting," Ford agreed as he swept down to pull his daughter in his arms. His quick actions meant that he missed the look that crossed the little girl's face, an expression so full of dismay that Lila's chest clenched to see it. But when Ford turned his back toward her so she could see Emily again, the girl was nothing but calm. Her thumb was in her mouth, and all the lines wiped from her face.

"Bye, love," Lila said as she swooped down to kiss Emily's cheek. The term of endearment was one her own mother often used when talking to her daughters. It came out so naturally that Lila barely noticed it leaving her lips.

She had just gathered her things and made it all the way to the driveway when the scream sounded. At first, she thought someone had broken a leg or, at the very least, suffered a severe stab wound. She dropped her bags and ran back into Ford's house, prepared to put her annual CPR and first aid training to the test. *Always be prepared* might seem like a lackluster motto to some, but Lila had never been gladder to know the steps to applying a tourniquet.

Except that no one was bleeding when she entered the house. All she saw was Emily clutching her father's legs and a bewildered Jeeves sitting at attention a few feet away. His head was cocked, the long curls of one ear almost sweeping the floor. He was always a serene little thing, but this seemed to be taking things a touch too far. If something bad had happened, he should have been on full alert. That was the whole purpose of him—to keep Emily safe, to protect her from harm of all shapes and sizes.

Her heart was pounding so heavily in her ears that she didn't hear Emily's rushed explanation at first. She could, however, make out the gist of it.

"He did it again."

"He growled and came after me."

"He tried to run away."

"He jumped this high."

None of those garbled phrases seemed to fit the cockapoo, whose dark eyes were deep with worry but not fear.

"Princess Lila, Princess Lila!" The girl transplanted herself from her father's legs to Lila's. There was something so pathetically desperate in that clinging grip that Lila's heart felt wrenched from her chest. "You can't leave. Jeeves tried to eat me."

Casting another look down at the puppy, Lila found it difficult to believe that he was capable of eating anything other than his usual bowl of kibble and maybe a treat or two. Then again, there was no denying Emily's hysteria. Instead of dropping to the girl's level, as was her custom, she adopted a page from Ford's book and lifted her in her arms instead.

"Emily, love, I'm not going anywhere, okay? Just breathe very slowly and very deeply, and then you can tell me exactly what happened."

Emily nodded and struggled to follow her instructions, but her sobs had given over to hiccups, which racked her little body. Lila started to count aloud in an attempt to get the girl to breathe more evenly, but she had to give up. For one, it wasn't working. For another, Emily rested her head on Lila's shoulder and clung tighter around her neck. It was almost enough to make Lila start sobbing along with her.

She caught Ford's eye over Emily's back. He didn't look at all like a man whose child was being endangered by the animal who was supposed to be taking care of her. In fact, there was a tightness to his jaw, the sharp angles of his cheekbones more pronounced than usual. His concern, if concern it could be called, was focused on the back of Emily's head, which gave an occasional shudder against Lila's shoulder.

"I don't understand," she said softly. "They were doing so well this morning."

"Yes," Ford said, though his mind seemed elsewhere. "They were, weren't they?"

"Did you see what happened?"

He wrenched his glance back toward her. "No, unfortunately. I was checking my work email, so I didn't see anything. Do you think…?"

She paused, waiting for him to finish his question, but he shook his head and sighed. "Never mind. It's not important. If you need to get home, you can hand her over to me."

He held his arms out to take his daughter, but she

only clung tighter. Even if Lila could have found a way to physically detach the child, she wouldn't have had the heart to give her up. No one had ever shown such a fierce determination to hold her fast, such a reluctance to let her go. Not even her sisters.

"It's okay," she said. "I couldn't leave now. Not when she's so upset and when Jeeves is so…"

She paused again, unsure what came next. Jeeves was curious, yes. He was concerned, sure. But that curiosity and concern was to be expected of a service dog facing an unknown situation. Especially a well-trained service dog like that one.

"What should I do with him?"

It was on the tip of Lila's tongue to have Ford call Dawn or Sophie to come pick up the animal so she could reassess his training in a neutral environment, but she held off. "Let him stay where he is. You don't mind, do you, sweetie?"

Emily's head was still buried against her neck, so Lila wasn't sure if she'd heard her or not. She doubted the girl would mind, anyway. She seemed to have forgotten just about everything except that snuggling embrace.

"Is her thumb in her mouth?" Ford asked in a voice low enough that Emily couldn't hear him. Lila peeked over her shoulder and nodded.

"Does that mean something?"

He heaved a sigh. "Yes. *Dammit*."

At the sound of that mild profanity, uttered in such despairing accents and not spelled out in the slightest, it took all of Lila's resolution not to draw Ford close to nestle him against her other shoulder. Call it a maternal instinct, but if it had been at all possible to absorb the whole of this pair's woes, she'd have done it in an instant.

"I'll stay as long as you need," she promised instead. "One of my sisters can always bring a bag over for me later."

Ford nodded, but with such a despondent air that Lila didn't feel much better. Nor did her mood improve as he picked the puppy up and sat petting him with a distracted air.

"She always sucks her thumb when she's feeling out of her element," he explained in a low voice. "It's how she copes with stress. I thought... Oh, I'm not sure what I thought. For the past few weeks, she seemed to have been getting over it. Ever since Jeeves came into her life, she's been gaining so much in the way of confidence. But I guess it was silly of me to think it'd be that easy."

"I'm sure this is temporary," Lila said, even though she was sure of no such thing. In fact, if she was going to stay true to her children-are-just-like-puppies theory, she believed the exact opposite. A dog could overcome great challenges in its life, but some nervous tics never went away.

"Maybe," Ford agreed. His eyes met hers, his anxiety causing extra lines to branch toward his temples. "I don't know. It's times like this I really wish Janine hadn't left the way she did."

"How did she leave?" Lila found herself asking. *And why?* Relationships didn't work out sometimes, obviously, and you couldn't force affection you didn't feel. If nothing else, Patrick had taught her that much. But to abandon a daughter? To say goodbye to this sweet girl and never look back?

"I told you already. She went to the North Pole." Ford glanced at clock on the wall and swore again. That made twice in as many minutes. Lila was starting to worry for his sanity, especially since people didn't actually go to the North Pole.

"Speaking of, we have a video chat with her in five minutes. Emily, honey?" Ford put a finger under his daughter's chin and lifted her gaze to his. "Your mom should be calling pretty soon. Do you think you'll be okay to talk to her, or do you need me to reschedule?"

Emily's eyes still glittered with tears, but the mention of her mother had her perking up in an instant.

"Today is her phone day?" She wriggled and squirmed until Lila put her down. "Oh, goody! Can I show her Jeeves? He'll be a good boy, I promise."

"I don't know," Ford said with a wary look at the curly bundle in his arms. Emily, however, had no such qualms. All fears and tears forgotten, she took the puppy from her father and planted a kiss on the top of his head.

"You get to meet Mommy today, Jeeves. It's very 'portant to sit still so she can see you. Sometimes the picture comes in all fuzzy. It's a'cos she's so far away." To Lila, and with an importance she carried well, she said, "My mommy lives at the North Pole, but not Santa's North Pole. She's at the other one. There are two."

Lila could only blink—first, at how quickly the child had seemed to get over her fear of the puppy, and second, at the fact that Ford's nonsense was starting to sound a little less nonsensical.

A lot less, actually.

"One is for the elves, and the other is for the scientists. My mommy is not an elf."

Next to her, Ford chuckled. "It took a long time for that one to sink in, unfortunately. Come on, moppet. Let's get you set up. When you're done chatting, make sure you stay on the line for me, okay? There are a few things I need to talk to your mother about."

Lila could only watch, slightly bewildered, as Emily pulled a stool up to the computer desk in the kitchen and Ford settled her on it. Both of them seemed to have forgotten Jeeves's attack, all fears of the animal pushed aside to make way for the incoming video chat. Lila was profoundly curious what the woman looked like, but she was careful to keep out of sight in the living room. Some intrusions into this family she wasn't willing to make. Meeting the woman who'd once captured Ford's heart was one of them.

Still, she couldn't help a quick peek into the kitchen as Emily's squeal of delight sounded. Her glance wasn't nearly long enough to allow her to make out all the woman's features, but what she saw was a young, attractive blond with Emily's adorably pert nose and a pair of wire-rimmed glasses perched at the end of it.

"They should chat for at least half an hour," Ford said as he returned to the living room. "Reception on Ellesmere Island is tough this time of year, and Emily can't make out half the things she says, but they like to be in the same room together, figuratively speaking."

"Ellesmere Island?" Lila echoed, somewhat at a loss.

"The North Pole." Ford grinned. "The *magnetic* north pole, that is. You have no idea how heartbroken Emily was when she finally realized there was a difference."

"But…" Lila blinked. She was still floundering for her footing, but at least she could *see* a path by this time.

"I thought you were kidding. When you said she ran off to the North Pole to escape you, I assumed it was a joke."

One of Ford's brows lifted in a perfect arch. "I joke about a lot of things, I know, but my ex-wife isn't one of them. She's got another year there, and then who knows where they'll send her. Somewhere equally remote, I'm sure. She digs core samples."

"She digs core samples." This one wasn't uttered as a question. It was a statement, oddly flat as it escaped Lila's mouth.

"I told you I've always had a thing for women who are above my reach." Ford laughed and ran a hand over the back of his neck. "We met in college. I should have known, when I took her to the planetarium and she went on to recite the all names and locations of the nearest two dozen stars, that our paths had different endings."

Lila had no response for this, either. She could have started parroting his words again, but she was too busy trying to process what he was telling her.

"We didn't plan to have Emily—not so soon into our marriage and definitely not while Janine was still getting her doctorate—but the little sneak took us by surprise. Janine managed to hold on to domestic bliss for almost a year after Emily was born, but there's not a whole lot of room for a family in the kind of places she works." He smiled ruefully. "Whereas I, on the other hand, have nothing but room for family. My ambitions have always been a lot lower than Janine's. *H-e-l-l*, if it comes to that, they're lower than most of humanity's."

"Don't," Lila snapped.

Ford jumped at the sharp retort. "Oh, *s-h-i-t*. I'm sorry. Did you not want to hear about my ex? I have so little emotional attachment to her anymore, I forget that other people might think differently. It was rough at first, but I promise I don't feel anything for her except a kind of lingering nostalgia. I'll always be grateful that she gave me Emily, but that's as far as our relationship goes."

"Of course that's not what I'm upset about," she said. Considering the strange truce she and Patrick had just reached, she was hardly in a position to judge anyone's relationships. "I wish you'd stop selling yourself short, that's all. You don't have low ambitions—and even if you did, so what? Not everyone needs to be in charge of running the world. You're good at a lot of other things."

His startled look turned to one of melting interest. "Oh, really? Like what? I'd love to hear your thoughts on my various…skills."

"And if you turn this into a *s-e-x* thing again, I'll never forgive you," she added severely. "Ford, I didn't know your ex-wife was *really* in the North Pole. I thought you made that up to mess with me."

"To mess with you?" His lips pulled down at the corners. "Why would I do that?"

Lila stopped. The answer should have been an obvious one. *To get under my skin. To make me feel as though the world is tipped upside down. To ensure that this thing we have never goes beyond the line.*

"That's what you do, isn't it?" she said, summing it up in one easy package. "That's what you've always done."

"What are you talking about?"

"Come on," she said. "You know how you are. You laugh and you flirt and you make me feel like a teenager having her first crush, but you're hardly a trustworthy source of information."

He stared at her, the tightness back in his jaw. "That's what you think? Even now? Even after we—?"

"Please don't finish that sentence," she interrupted. She didn't think she could bear to hear him reduce their time together to a four-letter word. Not like this. "I'm right about this—you know I am. Half the things you say to me are utter nonsense. You told Helen you fell for me the first time we ever met, for crying out loud."

"That's because I did."

"*Ford*." She was perilously close to stamping her foot at him. "You did not. You're still trying to mess with me, trying to throw me off-balance. That sort of thing doesn't happen in real life."

"It's no use telling me it doesn't happen, because it *did* happen." For a man asserting his love for her, Ford looked an awful lot like he was about to accuse her of perfection and throw her out the door. "I'm George Washington, remember? I cannot tell a lie."

She could only blink at him.

"I told you that you'd realize it someday. I just assumed it would be a happy realization." His laugh was bitter, his smile self-deprecating. "From the look on your face right now, I guess I was wrong. I know I'm not perfect enough for you, but I always thought—"

And there it was. That word. That insult. Lila's heart gave a plummeting lurch before stopping cold.

"*Don't*," she warned. She couldn't take that again—not from him, not like this.

But he gave it to her anyway. "At least I was good for

a few things in the meantime, right?" he said. "Laughs and a *f-u-c-k*? The real dynamic duo?"

She held a hand to her head, unable to stop the sudden whirling that was threatening to pull her under. "Could you please stop that for five seconds?"

"What? Laughing? Or *f-u-c-k*—"

This time, she really did stamp her foot. The action did nothing to make her feel any calmer, and probably made her look like a fool in the bargain, but she had to do something to ground herself, to keep herself from spinning out.

"That's not what I mean, and you know it," she hissed. "You can't stand there and pretend to be the most honest man in the world, or act like this is all inside my head. Maybe you told the truth about some things, but not everything."

His whole body stilled, the smile falling from his lips. He looked to be about as old as Emily—and twice as vulnerable.

"Everything, Lila," he said. "Every last word."

It wasn't fair. When he spoke so earnestly like that, a plea underscoring his voice and shining in his eyes, she actually believed him. That he loved her and that he had from first sight, that she was his whole world and always would be. But she knew better.

"What about Seattle?" she asked. "What about the fact that you're going to pack up your entire life and leave, and you never once thought to tell me about it?"

She had the doubtful satisfaction of seeing the dashing Ford Ford at a loss for words. He opened his mouth and closed it again several times in succession, almost as though his vocal cords had been cut clean through. Her own throat felt equally raw.

By the time he did find his voice, his words weren't the ones she'd been hoping to hear. "How did you find out about that?" he asked.

No denial. No apology.

He's leaving.

"Does it matter?"

"To me, yes." Ford paused just long enough to come up with the answer on his own. "Dammit. It was Patrick, wasn't it?"

Lila could only give a helpless shrug. The source of the information didn't matter nearly as much as the fact that he wasn't denying it—not even a little. Even that curse had been uttered without heat or violence. It was more weary resignation than anything else.

"You saw him? When?"

The timing seemed much less important than the fact that Ford and Emily were about to exit her life as easily as they'd come into it, but she indulged him anyway. "A few nights ago. Don't blame him for it. He thought I knew already."

"I see," Ford said slowly.

She doubted it. If this man knew even a fraction of what was going on inside her heart right now, he wouldn't hold himself aloof like that. He'd whisk her into his arms and promise to stay forever. He'd tell her that not even a trip to the North Pole could keep them apart.

"So it's true?" she asked hollowly. "You and Emily are moving? How long have you known?"

"The job offer came in not long after the puppy

training started. It's a good opportunity—a great one, in fact. I was lucky to get it."

Bullshit, she wanted to say. The company would be lucky to have him. All of Seattle would be lucky to have him. She might not be so deluded as to consider him perfect—no one was that—but he was an amazing artist and an even better man.

Unfortunately, it was impossible to say any of that while he stood there looking at her like that. "Congratulations" was all that came out of her mouth.

"Thank you," he said with an obvious lack of enthusiasm. "It'll be good for Emily, too. Bigger schools, better hospitals, the whole show. She deserves more out of this life than what I've given her so far. I only wish—"

What he wished would forever remain a mystery. Lila would have liked to say that he'd been leaning toward sweeping her into his arms and begging her to go with him, or even just asking her to tackle a long-distance relationship, but that wasn't what his face said. His face said that any love he felt for her was secondary to his work, that his daughter must—and should—come first.

The worst part was, she couldn't fault him for it. In fact, she downright admired him. One of her favorite things about this man was his dedication to his daughter, the way he'd built an entire life with her at the center. It was exactly what she'd done for her sisters—what she would do for them a thousand times over, should they need it.

"Daddy, I'm all done with my call." Emily burst into the living room heedless of the somber note that had taken over. "Mommy said she only has a few more minutes, so you hafta hurry."

"Okay, moppet." Ford signed his thanks and turned to Lila with a wince. "I have to take this call. This is one of my only chances to talk to Janine, and I need to tell her about—"

He broke off suddenly, but there was no need for him to finish. He had to tell his ex-wife about his upcoming move. He had to make arrangements for his family, for his future, and Lila was only in the way.

"That's okay. I really should get going." Even though Emily showed every sign of flinging herself at Lila's legs and demanding that she stay in place, Lila was determined to go before she started screaming—or worse, crying. "I know you want me to stay, love, but I've got to get back for at least a few hours. If you want, I can send Princess Dawn over to check up on Jeeves instead, okay? You like Princess Dawn."

"I don't want Dawn," Emily said. "I want *you*."

"I know you do, but—"

"You promised to stay with me."

"I know I did, but—"

"You said you'd be my friend. Don't you want to be my friend anymore?"

Lila didn't know how to respond in a way that wouldn't break either Emily's heart or her own. She cast a helpless look up at Ford, but he was glancing distractedly over his shoulder at the computer. When he finally did notice her distress, he came to her rescue, but not in any way that counted.

"Emily Ford, you are being very impolite. Lila is not our servant. She has other places to go and other people to see. She'll be back to work next week on the puppy training, but that's all either you or I have a right to ask of her. Got it?"

Emily didn't get it—at least, not from what Lila was able to gather—but she picked up on her father's expression just fine. With a resolute sniffle, she nodded once. Had Emily said one more word to get her to stay, had Ford asked her to stick around long enough to talk things through, Lila would have parked herself in place forever.

But she had people to see and places to go.

And so, apparently, did they.

chapter
18

"Lila? Are you still at home? Oh, thank goodness. You just saved my life." Helen rattled off her sentences in one string, pausing neither to draw a breath nor to let Lila get a word in edgewise. "Would you be a dear and pick up some ice on your way? I've been filling my ice-cube trays and stockpiling all week, but wouldn't you know it? The boys decide to make snowballs with ice cubes at the center. Apparently, you can cause much more damage that way. I confiscated three bucketsful from the backyard already."

Lila stared at the cell phone in her hand.

"Two bags should do the trick. Oh, and if you're going to the grocery store on Fifth, could you also grab the cake? It's supposed to be Santa dressed up as a pirate. I was going to make one last run, but Danica arrived early. Danica *always* arrives early, the beast. If you ever invite her to your house, make sure you tell her to come at least two hours late, or she'll end up on your doorstep before you've had a chance to shove the laundry under the bed. Dirty laundry, too. I was never so embarrassed in my life."

The running dialogue gave Lila a chance to gain

her bearings, but she wasn't at all sure she liked where she ended up. *The holiday party. The entire block in attendance.*

Ford.

"Actually, I—"

"You know what? Make it three bags of ice. My house is already starting to feel like an oven. I may have to let the boys in with those buckets of snowballs, after all."

With that, Helen hung up, as sure of her conquest as Charlemagne setting out on his first campaign. For the longest moment, Lila could only continue staring at her phone, her whole body growing heavy with dread. In all the hustle of last-minute holiday plans and the situation at the Ford house, she'd somehow forgotten that Helen's holiday party was to be held this evening—the same holiday party she'd promised to attend in a wench costume that no decent woman would wear in public.

For an even longer moment, Lila toyed with the idea of sending one of her sisters in her stead. Maybe she could plead a headache. Or pneumonia. Even rabies might work. That way, she could quarantine herself alongside Jeeves, the pair of them hiding away until this whole thing blew over.

"Lila Vasquez, you are a lot of things, but a coward isn't one of them." She forced herself to rise from the couch where she'd been laid out all day. It had been her intention to unwind and relax, maybe even take a nap, but all she'd done was count the paint specks on the ceiling.

She still had that in common with Emily. Naps were the worst. What was the point of steeping in your own woes for hours at a time? She could have accomplished a lot of work in that time—gone to the mall and purchased a new pirate costume, for example. One that contained a lot less cleavage and a lot more weaponry. She needed an arsenal if she was going to make it through this event alive.

It was with that honorable intention that Lila started to get dressed for the party with much less care than she usually took over these things. She was going to have to hurry if she wanted to get Helen her ice and cake on time.

Her rush was what she blamed, anyway, for failing to notice her sisters' arrival. She was putting the finishing touches on her thick, smoky eyeliner when she looked up and noticed the mirror's reflection of Dawn and Sophie, both of whom were staring at her in a manner that could only be described as *agog*.

"Uh, Lil?" Sophie asked. "Is there a reason you're dressed up like an extra from Pirates of the Caribbean?"

Lila blinked a few times to clear her vision and stepped back to survey her handiwork. She'd been a trifle heavy-handed on the mascara, perhaps, but not in a bad way.

"And I'm assuming there's a plastic sword tucked into your belt for a perfectly good reason?" Dawn added.

"Of course there's a reason," Lila said.

Her sisters did it again—shared that look, that sideways glance that was somehow a roll of the eyes and a laugh wrapped up in one.

"There's also a plastic knife stuck into my boot and two butter knives strapped to my right thigh, but the dress does a pretty good job of concealing them." She ruffled her skirts to get any wrinkles out. "Well? What do we think?"

"That you've finally cracked," Dawn replied without a moment's hesitation.

Lila almost laughed. Her sister was a lot closer to the truth than she knew. "The dress is mine, but the weapons were borrowed from Byron and Neil. Well, I confiscated them, actually. I was afraid they might try to stab a puppy if I left them unattended. Will one of you please tighten the laces on this corset? I need to get going, or I'll be late to the party."

"Oh dear. You wouldn't want to be rude," Sophie murmured, but she came forward and gave her sister's laces a hefty tug. Lila grunted a protest, but since Sophie had managed to bring her waist in a good extra inch, she didn't mind too much. "Does this mean you got all those kinks with Jeeves worked out?"

"Nope." Lila tested her ability to twist and turn, pleased to find that all of her body parts stayed under wraps. "It's a disaster. In fact, we're probably going to have to cancel the Auditory Guild contract."

Her sisters shared another look.

Lila had no idea what it was about that second glance of theirs that caused her to snap, but snap she did. She was tired, she was sad, and she was being forced to wear a smile and a corset for the sake of a man who had no intention of sticking around long enough to enjoy them. She'd spent most of her life doing the right thing and saying what everyone wanted to hear, and it didn't seem to make them like her one bit more. Her beloved, well-trained service puppy had bitten the little girl he was supposed to protect, and all her professional goals were going up in smoke.

So, yes. She snapped.

"I can see you guys, you know," she said, whirling on them. "You're standing two feet away from me, and there's a mirror right here."

As though connected by an invisible—and very strong—string, their eyes started to move toward each other once again.

"Yes, that!" Lila cried, pointing an accusatory finger at them. "Right there. That thing you do whenever you think I'm being ridiculous. I can see it. I've *always* been able to see it."

Dawn gave a discreet cough and looked away, but Sophie made an attempt to maintain her innocence. "We don't think you're being ridiculous, Lil."

"Yes, you do. You think I'm ridiculous and uptight, and that I have no idea how the real world works. Everything is a huge joke, and I'm the only one who doesn't get the punch line. Or maybe I do get it, but you're sure as *s-h-i-t* not going to admit it, because then who would you have to laugh at?"

True to form, Sophie started to giggle.

"I know. It's hilarious. *I'm* hilarious." She was trying not to let her emotions get the better of her, but it wasn't working. Her voice had reached a higher pitch than normal, her throat tight with trying to keep it all in check. "Go ahead and laugh. At this point, I can't even blame you."

"I'm sorry, Lil," Sophie said, giggling again. "I know it's not funny, but you just spelled out the word 'shit' instead of saying it."

Dawn nodded. "Rolled it off your tongue like it was nothing."

Lila stared at them. "So?"

"I've just never heard you do that before, that's all. It's very maternal of you."

That word—*maternal*—acted like a bucket of the Griswold boys' snowballs over her head. "Ford doesn't like to swear around Emily," she said tightly. "I picked up the habit while I was there."

"Yeah, but you're not at Ford's house now," Sophie pointed out. "This is your own bathroom. You can swear all you want."

"And I think you should," Dawn agreed. "You look like you could use it."

Lila had no idea what had come over her sisters, but she didn't much care for it. She was having an emotional breakdown over here, or hadn't they noticed? After all her years of supporting them and loving them and just freaking being there when they needed it, this was how they were going to repay her?

"I don't want to swear, thank you very much," she said hotly. "What I want is to go to this party with three bags of ice and a pirate Santa cake. What I want is to get this whole sorry mess over with so I can go back to the cold, lonely life I've always led. And I swear on every piece of La Perla underwear you own, Dawn, if you so much as twitch your eyes over toward Sophie, I'm going to barge into your room and rip every single five-hundred-dollar panty to shreds."

Dawn's eyes grew wide, but they didn't shift in either direction.

"I can't think of what you own that's equally

valuable, Sophie, or I'd threaten you, too. He's leaving, you guys." Her voice wavered. "He's moving to Seattle and taking Emily with him, and I won't even have the benefit of work to distract me because I think I broke Jeeves, too."

Both her sisters had their arms around her in an instant. Lila had no way of telling if they shared any knowing looks, but there definitely wasn't any laughing this time around. All she could hear were clucks of sympathy and soothing susurrations. She also received quite a bit of conflicting advice.

"Just sit right here and put your feet up."

"Tip your head between your legs and breathe."

"This calls for pie, I think. And wine."

"No, this is definitely a pizza situation. With extra cheese."

Lila neither sat nor tipped her head, and she stopped Sophie before she could run to the kitchen and pull out every fattening food she could find.

"Don't go, Soph," she said instead. "It's not that bad. I don't need to be babied."

Her sister halted on the threshold. "Then what *can* I do?"

Nothing. There wasn't anything under the bleak winter sun that would make this situation anything other than what it was. Not even a pile of puppies—all nine of them this time—would change the fact that Lila's world was falling apart around her. She'd thought, when Patrick had accused her of perfection, that nothing could ever feel worse.

She'd been wrong.

Insults from a man she'd never really cared about

hurt, yes. But what she hadn't known was that declarations of love from one she *did* were so much worse.

"Please, Lila," Sophie begged. "Let me do something. I can't bear seeing you like this."

It was as good a rebuke as any. As was always the case, Lila needed to be strong. She had to carry the weight of her family on her shoulders. Causing her sisters pain had never been an option.

Even though Lila's knees felt like buckling underneath her, she forced a smile and stood her ground. "It's fine. I'm fine. I'm just tired, I think. And premenstrual."

Although it seemed like the cruelest thing her sisters could do at that moment, their eyes moved toward each other. Lila saw it and felt her insides crush in on themselves. Even now, even when she was holding herself together with nothing but the barest thread of dignity, they couldn't help but treat her like a sideshow attraction.

Step right up, folks. Come see the woman with the heart of a lizard. See how it keeps beating long after she's been trampled underfoot.

Before she knew what was happening, her sisters were on top of her again. This time, Dawn pressed a hand on her shoulder and pushed so hard that Lila had no choice but to sink to a seated position on her bed. Sophie planted herself in front of her and crossed her arms, providing a physical barrier so Lila couldn't stand again.

"Oh, no you don't," Sophie warned. "You're sitting right there until I say you can leave."

"You aren't the least bit premenstrual," Dawn added. "You know very well that we've been on the same cycle since we were teenagers. If I want you to sit there and eat pie, you'll sit there and eat every slice I bring you."

Lila stared up in wonder at her sisters, who'd taken on such a fierce appearance that it was like looking up into a pair of twin volcanos. "But I don't want pie," she said feebly.

He sisters laughed again, but it sounded much less ominous this time around.

"Do you have any idea how many times you've force-fed me comfort food?" Dawn demanded. "There was that entire spell in my early twenties when I couldn't look at a cake without going into sugar shock."

"And you used to bring me hot-water bottles even when it was like a hundred degrees outside," Sophie added. "I still don't understand what they were supposed to do. Sweat the sadness out of me?"

"It's well documented that applications of heat can be very soothing…" Lila began, but it was no use.

"Is this where you tell me that three thousand calories of buttercream frosting contain mood-enhancing endorphins?" Dawn laughed. "My trainer at the gym used to make me do hours of squats to work them off. *Hours*."

"You should have told me you didn't want cake," Lila said, feeling hot and stiff with embarrassment. How was she only hearing about this now? "I thought I was helping."

"Lil, you know I love you, but you can be the biggest blockhead sometimes." Dawn sank down on the bed next to her. "Of course you were helping."

"But you said—"

"It wasn't about the cake, stupid." Dawn wrapped her

arm around Lila's shoulders and squeezed. "It was about *you*. It's always been about you. There hasn't been a single Vasquez crisis that you haven't overseen—and without a word of complaint or judgment. I don't think I know how to get through a breakup without you there to hold my hand."

"Or the opposite of a breakup," Sophie said. "You're one of the main reasons Harrison and I are together today, you know. I still remember how amazing you were when I broke just about every professional protocol in place to get through to him."

Lila's warm flush of mortification didn't abate any, though it was taking on a different tone. "I didn't do anything during your Harrison case," she protested.

"I know. That's what I mean. You could have very easily swooped in and taken over—and rightfully so—but you didn't. You realized I needed to do it on my own and stood back to let me. There aren't many sisters who would do that. Especially since our business was on the line."

"You take good care of us, Lil," Dawn added softly. "You always have."

Sophie took Lila's hand and held it in her own. "Always," she agreed, somewhat mistily. Lila knew, without her saying so, that she was thinking far beyond their romantic woes to those years of her hospitalization. "But you never, ever let us pay you back—not in any way that counts. That's why we look at each other like that, why we're always sneaking glances at each other. It's not because we think you're ridiculous. It's because we're hoping that finally, *finally*, you need one of us the way we need you."

"But…" Lila allowed her words to trail off, thinking back on all the times she'd seen that look and felt her blood boil. It always seemed to appear just when she was feeling the most vulnerable, when she wasn't sure of her footing or how to proceed.

In other words, exactly when she'd needed her sisters most. She just hadn't been willing to admit it.

Until now.

"Of course I need you guys," she said, her voice thick. "I've always needed you. You're my sisters."

She was suffocated under yet another wave of sisterly affection. Like the pile of puppies, it was warm and exuberant and comforting—and with a lot fewer tongues in her face. She might have allowed herself to indulge in it, too, if not for the plastic sword that suddenly poked her back. With a yelp, she jumped up from the bed. Dawn and Sophie showed every sign of fearing for her intellect her again, so she pulled the sword out and tossed it onto the bed.

"I was stabbed," she said by way of explanation. She fingered the sore spot on her back and found that the plastic left a scrape behind. "And I don't think I'm going to give it back to Byron until Helen knows how sharp this thing is. How is this safe for children to play with?"

Sophie giggled and flicked Dawn on the arm. "See? I told you she'd be just as good with children as she is at everything else."

"I'm not really surprised," Dawn agreed. "After taking care of us for all these years, how could she be anything else?"

Lila found herself staring at her sisters through damp

eyes, surprise holding her in place. "Wait... You guys thought I'd be good with kids? This whole time? You weren't afraid that I'd make Emily cry?"

Sophie's wide-eyed incredulity spoke much louder than her next words, which were plenty vehement on their own. "Are you serious? You dressed up like a princess every day for a month, Lil."

Not to be outdone, Dawn added, "You made me spin plates at a tea party. Before noon. On a weekday."

"You willingly allowed Patrick Yarmouth to cross this threshold again."

"You asked our mother—*our mother*—to babysit an adorable child, and now she won't talk about anything else."

Sophie softened. "You're sitting here, devastated and determined not to show it, because you might not ever see that little girl again. If that's not being good with kids, I don't know what is."

"I..." Lila swallowed, her eyes misting up once again. The portrait they were painting wasn't one of warmth and fuzziness, but she liked it all the same. It showed a woman who got things done. A woman who told people what to do and how to do it. A woman who *cared*, even if she didn't bake cookies and speak in soft, dulcet tones to prove it. "You mean it? You're not just saying that to be nice?"

"When have you ever known me to be nice for no reason?" Dawn demanded. "You're good with kids, Lila. Amazing with them. Men, however..."

"Wait—what?"

"Oh, yeah. She's terrible with men." Sophie nodded soberly, but there was a laugh lurking in her eyes. "Just think. She has the most gorgeous man in the world on a string, and what does she do?"

"Lets him walk away without a fight." Dawn tsked. "It's sad, really. I always thought Lila had more nerve than that."

"Excuse me. I have nerve."

"She'd rather sit here and preserve her dignity than tell him how much he means to her."

"It's not that simple. He has Emily to consider."

"She gave up on that poor puppy, too," Sophie heaved a sigh. "One tiny slipup, and she's ready to throw him back in a cage rather than face Anya Askari's disapproval. Our reputation may never recover. We'll be bankrupt by the year's end."

Lila rose to her full height. She knew her sisters were goading her on purpose—helping her the best way they knew how—but their words still rankled. Of course they did. These two knew her better than anyone, knew exactly how to rile her up and bring her back down again.

Sisters were the absolute worst. And the absolute best.

"You know that's not true," she said, firing up in her own defense. "This deal with Anya is important, yes, but it's not everything. We survived without it before. We'll survive without it again."

Dawn broke into a grin. "I'm glad you realize that."

"Yeah," Sophie agreed, answering Dawn's grin with one of her own. "It took her long enough. Maybe *now* she'll be as slovenly and unprofessional as the rest of us. Put love first for once, Lil. Work can wait."

"That's a terrible way to run a business," Lila pointed out.

Dawn placed a hand over her heart and gave a romantic swoon. "True. But even you have to admit that it's a hell of way to run a life."

chapter
19

"She's not coming, is she, Daddy?"

Ford glanced down at Emily's tightly controlled face and felt his heart clench. He'd seen that look so many times—the lonely determination, the disappointed acceptance—that he could draw it in his sleep.

He *hated* that he could draw it in his sleep.

"I don't know, moppet. She might be resting this evening. It's been kind of a rough week."

Emily shook her head and popped her thumb into her mouth. It was a look ill-suited for the red-and-white-striped tights and ruffled black skirt that proclaimed her a Christmas pirate of the finest order. Even her hair was done up for the evening in one of the more complicated of Lila's princess braids, all tumbling curls and devious twists.

He was proud of that braid, dammit. He'd be even prouder if he could show it off to the woman who'd taught him the steps.

"She's not resting," Emily said around her thumb. "She doesn't like us anymore. Is it a'cos Jeeves is bad?"

The clenching in Ford's chest turned viselike. "No, moppet. It's not because Jeeves is bad."

"Is it a'cos *I'm* bad?"

"Emily Georgiana Ford, you are in no way, shape, or form responsible for—" he began, his voice dangerous. Yelling at a child whose heart was a fair way toward being broken wouldn't win him any parent-of-the-year awards, but he couldn't help himself. His own heart was in a fair way toward being broken.

"Oh, thank goodness!" Helen pushed her way past the pair of them, a smile parting her bright red lips. It seemed that in her world, dressing up as a pirate meant liberal applications of lipstick—though, to be fair, most of the moms at this party seemed to have interpreted it the same way. "You're finally here. I was beginning to despair of my ice. Thank you so much, Princess Lila. And Patrick. I'm glad you could make it, too."

Ford whirled, struck as much by Patrick's name as by Lila's. As he turned to see them standing in the doorway, he was equally struck by the vision they presented. Two more perfect specimens of humanity had never existed. Lila looked, as she always did, as though nothing could touch her. Unlike the rest of them, who were sweating in their costumes and regretting all that cheap polyester, she was like a model who had stepped away from a photo shoot highlighting the latest in swashbuckle couture. Her head was high and her hair in perfect waves around her bare shoulders, nary a line of worry on her gorgeous face.

Patrick wasn't dressed as a pirate, but instead of putting him at a disadvantage, the doctor only made it work to his advantage. He wore a suit jacket but no tie, the very picture of casual—and comfortable—chic. In his ruffled shirt and regrettably tight pants, Ford could only feel like a fool.

Again. *Always*.

The ease with which Helen drew forward and took the bags of ice in Patrick's arms indicated that she'd been expecting the doctor. That same ease was showcased by Patrick as he used his now-free hands to lift a cake from Lila's hands and carry it to the kitchen.

"Let me get that for you, Lil," Patrick said. "I don't mind."

And a good thing he didn't, because Emily launched herself at Lila as though she'd been parted from her for months rather than days. She hit Lila's legs at a dangerous pace, almost knocking her over in the process.

It should have made Ford happy to see his daughter so easily restored to good humor, her happiness back in her heart where it belonged, but the suffocating tightness of his chest only grew worse.

If only I were six years old. Then I could throw myself at Lila in ecstasy, too.

"You came!" Emily cried, her words coming out in a half sob. "And you're wearing the dress."

"Of course I did," Lila said. She dropped to the girl's level, her tone low and soothing, and planted a kiss on her forehead. "And how could I wear anything else? This is what I always wear when I'm fighting evil, remember?"

Emily giggled obligingly, but Ford found little to laugh at. There was no evil at this party. There never had been—that was the whole problem. As much fun as it had been to turn Patrick Yarmouth into a slobbering, toothy Krampus who wanted to steal Christmas, the reality was that he was a perfectly ordinary man. A perfectly ordinary man with a good job and an even better heart. The way he reached into his pockets and handed both of Helen's sons a small, wrapped package was an obvious clue. He was even good at parties, the bastard.

"How's Jeeves been holding up?" Lila asked. "I don't see him anywhere. I hope he hasn't been misbehaving again."

This question seemed to be directed more at Ford than Emily, so he had no choice but to swallow his jealousy and answer. "No signs of trouble, but we left him at home anyway. You said he had to be in quarantine, and we weren't sure if that included parties like this one. We'd have asked you, but you left in such a hurry the other day…"

Lila's body went still. "I thought you could use some privacy."

Right. Privacy. His five minutes with Janine. Five minutes in which she told him to do what he felt was best about Seattle, to give Emily her love, and to keep her updated on their change of address. He'd never been so close to losing it with his ex-wife. Her lack of interest in the day-to-day details of their life was nothing new—and in many ways, he appreciated that she didn't second-guess his decisions—but damn, he'd hoped for something more.

What about our daughter's health? What about her happiness? What about her heart?

"No Jeeves?" Neil came bounding forward, dressed from head to toe in black and with an eye patch slipping down his cheek. "Aw, man. I was hoping you'd bring him. I love playing with puppies."

Emily's face took on a look of haughty condescension.

"Jeeves von Hinklebottom the Third is not for playing. He is a servistus puppy. That means—"

"I know all about that," Neil interrupted. He didn't seem the least put off by Emily's expression. "Princess Lila taught me. They have to do work when it's time for work and can only play when it's time for play. Did you get to meet Andromeda?"

It was the longest conversation Ford had ever seen his daughter hold with a child her age, and he found himself staring openmouthed at the pair of them. The feeling of pleasant surprise didn't abate any when Emily lowered the thumb that had been moving toward her mouth and said, "No. Who's that?"

"Oh, man. She was the best puppy I ever saw." Catching sight of Emily's expression, he hastily amended this with "Except for Jeeves, of course. She had long hair and blue eyes and thought I was a sheep."

Emily giggled. "She did?"

"I drew a picture of her. It's in my room. D'you want to see?"

As she usually did when presented with situations like these, Emily looked to Ford for an answer. Instead of appearing wary of the offer, however, with her eyes desperately begging him to give her an out, she glinted up at him with a hopeful expression. "Can I go see, Daddy?"

"Absolutely, moppet."

It was all she needed to hear to go bounding off after Neil, the pair of them winding through legs and over furniture and almost knocking over three different adults in the process.

Ford had no idea when or how Lila had managed to

teach Neil about service dogs, but he could have kissed her. Hell, he could have kissed her for any number of reasons—including the way she watched Emily go with as much delight as he felt. Maybe it was part of the standard training package to introduce friends and neighbors to the nuances of service-puppy ownership, but he doubted it. From the day Lila had entered their lives, she'd gone above and beyond to make his daughter feel comfortable.

It was everything he'd ever dreamed of. She cared about Emily's health, she cared about her happiness, *and* she cared about her heart. The only problem was, he wanted her to care about his, too. It was terribly selfish of him, he knew, but what else could he do? He didn't want Lila for six weeks. He wanted her forever.

"Lila, I—"

"So this is the famous Princess Lila!" A laughing voice hailed him from behind, stopping any untimely confessions short. Ford turned to find himself being accosted by Danica DeWinter and Maddie Thomas. Under any other circumstances, he would have been happy to see his friends looking so ridiculously over-dressed and already wine-drunk, but not today. Today, he wished them at the bottom of the ocean—or, at the very least, on a pirate ship far away from here.

"For once, Helen didn't exaggerate. You're gorgeous. Ford, she's *gorgeous*." Danica extended a hand, which jangled under a long chain of gold bracelets. "I'm Danica, and I wouldn't have relinquished this man to anyone less, I hope you know."

Lila's face flushed with color.

"And I'm Maddie. Maddie Thomas. My daughter,

June, is around here somewhere, but with any luck, she won't surface for hours. Are you really from Canada?"

Lila sent an accusing look Ford's way—so fierce and so familiar. "No, I'm not. I've never even set foot outside the United States."

Maddie laughed. Like Danica, she'd interpreted the pirate theme to include an excess of jewelry, which meant her long, gold earrings clanked as she did. "I always suspected he made that up just to screw with us. He does that, you know."

Once again, Ford pictured a deep, tumultuous ocean in which he could cast these two well-meaning women. She couldn't have picked a worse comment to make—or a worse woman to make that comment to. Lila caught his eye and held it, her stare making him feel as though he'd just been pierced by the plastic sword she carried under the belt of her skirt.

"Believe me," she said. "I know."

"Helen has been singing your praises for weeks," Danica said and wound an arm through Lila's. "I'm dying to hear more about you and Ford."

With that ominous statement, she started dragging Lila away from the living room toward the kitchen, where several more women of his acquaintance and a literal cask of grog awaited. That particular combination was one Ford feared more than life itself. Those women would confirm every last one of his bad qualities, and at considerable length. He was frivolous and untrustworthy. He flirted with every single mom at school functions. He once ran a kissing booth at the school fair and made over five hundred dollars in under an hour.

And worst of all—he lied.

Oh, not about anything that mattered, and not to hurt people, but there was no denying it any longer. Since the day Janine had packed up and left, he'd never been perfectly honest with anyone. He spoke the truth, yes, but never in a way that would open him up to censure. Not in any way that would open him up to pain. By hiding his real self behind laughter and flirtation, he'd avoided the one thing that had the power to hurt him the most.

How was that for irony? He'd spent almost six years avoiding this soul-rendering pain, yet here he stood, suffering each agonizing twinge.

"There seem to be an awful lot of women at this party." Patrick sidled up next to him and stood surveying the gathering. As was Helen's custom, she'd packed her house to capacity and made no attempts to stem the festive air. Ford guessed there was about a ninety percent chance that the tree would end up toppled before the night's end. Last year, it had been a seven-foot cardboard T. rex that took the fall. "Kids, too."

"Welcome to my world." Ford took the red plastic cup being offered him and held it up in a mock toast. "Or my world as it now stands, anyway."

Patrick chuckled. "Will you miss it?"

The question surprised him—and not just because it was coming from a man he'd never considered a close friend. He'd been so caught up in what the move to Seattle would mean for Emily that he'd forgotten what it would mean for him. Not just leaving Lila behind, but leaving all these women behind, too. For so long, they'd been his only support system, his only *friends*. They were a more valuable resource than the gold they'd decked themselves out in for the night, and he had no idea what he'd do without them.

"Like you wouldn't believe," he confessed. "I can't tell you how many times these women have come to my rescue, and with no thought of anything in it for themselves. It's strange. I know I'm supposed to want stability, especially for Emily's sake, but I'm starting to wonder if all that economic prosperity is overrated. Why would anyone give this up?"

He cast a look around the hot, crowded room as he said this. To someone unfamiliar with these women and everything they had to offer, it might seem strange that he would prefer a tiny house on a tiny street where he could live a tiny life of his own making, but he did.

Even a tiny life could be a happy one, provided it had the right people in it.

Patrick must have considered the question a rhetorical one, because he didn't answer. Instead, he steered the conversation gently off course. "By the way, I ran into Lila on the way in, and she told me that Emily and Jeeves had a bit of a scuffle a few days ago," he said. "Since I'm here, would you like me to take a look at her hand? Lila said you didn't want to take her to the hospital, but it never hurts to get a professional opinion. Bites can turn nasty pretty fast."

"That would be great, actually," Ford said, taken aback. Not only was the gesture a kind one, but the way it was phrased caused his heartbeat to stutter. *He and Lila hadn't arrived together?* "Are you sure you don't mind?"

"Of course not. I like Emily. I always have."

It was yet another example of what Ford had been

talking about—of good people doing good things for no reason other than it being the right thing to do—but he didn't have time to consider the other implications. Without waiting to see if Ford followed, Patrick started heading in the direction of the bedrooms.

"I hate to interrupt what looks like a rousing game of Candy Land, but would you two mind pausing for a moment?" Patrick stood on the threshold, waiting until the two children seated on the circular rag rug looked up. "I'd like to look at your hand, Emily, just to be safe. It won't take more than a minute."

Emily paused in the act of flipping over a card. "No, thank you."

"Double purples! Gah! How are you so good at this game?" Neil leaned forward and began moving Emily's piece for her. "I bet you cheat. Byron always cheats."

Emily either didn't hear him or planned to take the stricture in stride. "Your turn. I hope you get a yellow."

As delighted as he was to see his daughter playing with Helen's younger son, Ford adopted his most fatherly air. "Emily," he said and waited until she reluctantly met his gaze. "Please let Dr. Yarmouth see your bite. We don't want it to get infected."

She tucked the bandaged hand under one armpit. "It's all better now."

"Emily…"

"Pinkie promise, Daddy. I'm okay. Ha! A yellow. I knew it."

"Here. Why don't you stay right where you are and play your game, and I'll unwrap your bandage?" Patrick sat on the bed next to Emily. She showed every sign of keeping her injured hand tucked in place, but Neil sighed.

"You'd better do what they say. They'll never leave us alone until you do. Grown-ups are the worst."

Emily considered this for a moment. "My daddy isn't too bad," she said. "Princess Lila is good, too. And I like Grandma Louise and Princess Dawn and Princess Sophie, and *their* mom, who is the queen, but she doesn't look like one."

"I see I don't figure on the list," Patrick said dryly, but he used Emily's monologue as a way to extricate her hand. Emily looked as though she'd like to voice further protest, but she'd spent enough time around doctors to know that it was useless to fight them for long.

Ford had cleaned the wound before they headed over to the party, so he wasn't worried too much about it. The puncture marks were small and healing well, and nothing about Jeeves seemed to indicate he was planning on repeating the experience.

Which was why he was so surprised when Patrick cast a sharp look up at him. "The puppy did this?" he asked.

"Yes. A few nights ago. Emily woke up bleeding."

Patrick turned her hand over and peered closer at the two broken spots, which were surrounded by a half-ring of bruised skin. "What did Lila say?"

"Just that we'd have to keep an eye on Jeeves for a few weeks. He's officially in quarantine, but she doesn't think there's any lasting harm."

"Did she look at the wound?"

"No. I didn't think there was a need." Ford thought about the puppy, bereaved and gated in the kitchen at home, and felt his heart sink. "Why? What's wrong? Is it bad?"

"On the contrary, it's healing nicely." Patrick began to carefully rebind the wound before giving Emily her hand back again. He made the motion of his thanks. "Thank you, Emily. That wasn't so bad, now, was it?"

Emily sighed and agreed, but she was clearly done with the doctor. Ford would have been, too, but Patrick tilted his head toward the door in a gesture that was impossible to ignore.

"What is it?" he asked as soon as they were out of earshot. They didn't have to go far, since the sounds of the party muffled their voices. "What did you see that I missed?"

Patrick cleared his throat and cast a look through the door at the two children playing on the rug. Neither one of them was paying him the least bit of attention, but he lowered his voice all the same. "Just that there's no way those marks were caused by a dog. That's a human bite, no question."

"What?" Ford stepped backward until his shoulders hit the hallway wall. "What do you mean, it's a human bite?"

"I mean, she was bitten by human teeth, not canine ones. *Small* human teeth."

With a sinking heart, Ford recalled his suspicions the day after the attack, when Emily had frantically called Lila back from the driveway. He'd never actually *seen* Jeeves do anything wrong, and had even wondered if his daughter had exaggerated her fears to get her own way, but this went far beyond crying wolf.

"Six-year-old teeth?" Ford asked.

"If I had to make a guess, yes." Patrick took one look at Ford's face and nodded. "I can see this isn't a total surprise." Raising his voice loud enough for Neil to hear him, he said, "Neil, will you let Emily know that her father wants to speak to her? I think we should give these two a moment alone."

"Aw, man. But the game was just starting to get good," Neil protested.

"Yes, but I, uh, need your help."

"My help?" Neil echoed suspiciously. "With what?"

The doctor thought fast. "I appear to be the only person at this party not in costume. Your mom didn't warn me to dress up. Do you think you can help me come up with something?"

"I guess so," Neil said as he forced himself into a standing position. He surveyed the doctor through critical eyes. "You're too big to wear my hat."

"Er, yes. Probably."

"But we can tape some knives to your stomach."

"Tape some knives…?" Patrick drew a deep breath and caught Ford's eye. "As long as your mom doesn't object, I guess it can't hurt. The things we do for *l-o-v-e*, eh?"

"Gross," Neil announced, but he followed Patrick out of the room anyway.

As delighted as Ford was to have the mystery of what Patrick was doing here cleared up, he felt no delight at the prospect of confronting his daughter. The look of innocent inquiry she shot up at him indicated that she had no idea what was coming.

"Emily." Ford tried to keep his expression as neutral as possible, but he must not have done a very good job.

Her innocent look slid into suspicion. "You and I are going to have a talk about your hand."

The suspicion changed almost immediately to crossed arms and a mulish tilt to her chin. She didn't speak, either, and turned her head away from him in an effort to avoid the conversation.

"I need you to look at me when I'm speaking to you." Ford lowered himself to a seated position on the floor and waited. "Emily, I'm not leaving this room until we talk, so you might as well give in."

Even if she couldn't make out the words, she knew he was speaking. He could tell from the way she kept sneaking covert glances at him, as if hoping he might suddenly disappear or be replaced by someone she liked better.

Someone like Lila.

"You have to tell me the truth," he continued, ignoring the way that thought made his chest squeeze. "Did you bite your own hand? Did you lie about Jeeves attacking you?"

Emily didn't move.

"I'm not mad, moppet. I just need you to talk to me. I need you to tell me what's going on." He reached and took her uninjured hand, those tiny, trusting fingers slipping easily between his own. "Do you not like Jeeves? Is that it? Do you want to trade him for a different puppy?"

Emily snatched her hand out of his the moment the words *trade him* crossed his lips, but at least she was looking at him now.

Encouraged by this, he continued along in the same vein. "It's okay if you've decided you don't like Jeeves. Remember what Lila said that first day—you're going to be with this dog for a long time. If you don't want him, we need to figure something else out."

"But I do want him," she said.

"Well, that's a good first step. If he's dangerous, though, we can't have him in the house."

"No, Daddy." Her voice wobbled. "*Please*."

"I don't like it, either," he admitted. He didn't like his daughter's wobbling frown or the series of events that had brought them to this point in the first place. "But we might not have a choice."

"Don't make him go back. Don't make him go away." A small sob escaped Emily's throat. "I love him. He's my first real friend."

As tragic and painful as her confession was, Ford forced himself to push harder. "Then why did you bite yourself and blame it on Jeeves?"

She sniffled, one large tear gathering in the corner of her eye. She didn't bother to wipe it away as it fell. "He's a very good boy, isn't he?"

"The best," Ford agreed.

"And I'm a very good girl?"

Ford nodded, his throat so tight he could barely swallow. "Absolutely. But even very good girls make mistakes sometimes. You bit yourself, didn't you?"

She nodded, and with such a woebegone expression that Ford would have forgiven her for biting every single person at this party, if it came to that.

"Can you tell me why?" he prodded.

She shook her head. For the first time in his life, Ford feared he was going to have to take a hard line with his daughter, become one of those parents who laid out punishments that only ended up hurting him more than they hurt his child, but she lifted her eyes to his and blinked.

"I wanted... I thought..." She took a deep breath that rattled in her chest. "Daddy, where's Seattle?"

"*F-u-c-k*," he swore. Emily's eyes grew wide at the sound of it, as though fully aware of its meaning. It seemed Lila had been right about that—about a lot of things, actually. Spelling out the violence of his feelings wasn't going to work for much longer. He was going to have to confront them instead.

"Did you hear me talking to Dr. Yarmouth that day in his office?" he asked. "When I said I got a job offer there?"

Emily sniffed and nodded.

"And were you afraid I'm going to make us move?"

She nodded again.

"And *that's* why you bit yourself?"

A few more trails of tears joined the one already on her cheek. She didn't brush those away, either. She didn't have a chance to, since Ford pulled her into his lap and did it for her.

He had to. He needed something to help his chest from caving in altogether.

"I don't want to leave Princess Lila," she said as she wrapped her arms around his neck. Her damp cheek pressed against his. "If Jeeves is bad, then we have to stay, right? So she can fix him? Or maybe train me a brand new puppy?"

Ford recalled her words the night of the attack and felt the last of his resolve give way. *Princess Lila can fix it*, she'd said. *Princess Lila can fix anything*.

He pulled back from his daughter so she could clearly

see his lips. "You did all that to keep Lila around? You even risked losing your puppy?"

"Jeeves is my first friend," Emily said, her voice barely above a whisper. "But Lila is my *best* friend. I love her, Daddy. I don't want to go away."

"I love her, too, moppet," he replied. His own voice sounded hoarse, the strain of trying to keep it all together almost too much to bear. But it was the truth, and it needed to be said. Whatever else happened, he and Emily would always share this reality. Lila had changed them. Lila had forced them to remember what was really important in life. "And I don't want to go away, either."

She gave a small jump. "You don't?"

He shook his head. "Not even a little. Not even for all the money in the world."

Although the tears showed signs of abating, Emily still hadn't lost the wary look in her large, blue eyes. "Does that mean we can keep Jeeves?"

He nodded.

"And Princess Lila? We can keep her, too?"

He hesitated. Every part of him longed to nod and agree and reassure his daughter that they would keep Lila forever and ever. But that wasn't fair to her—or to any of them. Without that Seattle job offer, he had literally nothing to offer that woman but his heart.

It wasn't much, but it was everything he had.

"People aren't like puppies, moppet. We can't force them to stay with us. The best we can do is love them and hope that's enough."

As he spoke the words aloud, he realized how true they were. There were no guarantees in this world. Jobs would come and go. Money was fleeting. People left. But that didn't make life any less worth living.

"Mommy didn't stay with us, did she?" Emily said with painful insight.

"No, she didn't," he agreed. "And we miss her every day, but we still love her, don't we?"

Emily thought about it for a moment before nodding. "But I don't love her as much as I love you."

It was all he could do to resist squeezing his daughter in his arms until his strength gave out. "Me too, moppet," he said and kissed the top of her head. "Me too."

They stayed that way for a moment before Emily added, "I'm sorry I pretended about Jeeves."

Ford remembered, belatedly, that his daughter had told one whopper of a lie and should probably be punished accordingly. But how could he punish his little girl for loving someone too much? How could he teach her that it was wrong to throw all caution aside and fight for what you wanted?

He couldn't. In that moment, bedecked in a pirate costume and holding his child in his arms, he knew there was nothing he wouldn't do for her. *Or for Lila*. He'd already learned so much from having Emily in his life, but nothing she gave him would be greater than this gift right here. If a six-year-old would bite her own hand to keep Lila in her life, then the least Ford could do was own up to the truth.

He loved Lila so much that the idea of moving on without her sliced him like a pirate's blade straight to the gut. As ridiculous as it sounded, there was nothing to laugh about in that. No joke that could gloss it over and make it okay.

Lila was right about that, too.

As hard as it was for him to drop every pretense, she deserved to hear the truth with no varnish on it. She deserved to see Ford Ford exactly as he was.

A little lonely. A lot uncertain.

And one hundred percent in love.

chapter
20

D o you remember that day at Tilly's pool party last summer? He wore an honest-to-goodness Speedo, Lila. I kid you not. He forgot to pack his own suit, so he had to borrow one of her son's. He's a competitive swimmer, so his suits are all tiny."

"I missed that one, but Helen took pictures. I still have them on my phone somewhere. Do you want me to pull them up?"

"Um, who cares what Lila wants? Pull them up anyway." Danica grinned at Lila to show she meant no harm. "We sound like creeps, I know, but the day Ford Ford moved onto our street was one we won't soon forget. I don't know if you've noticed, but there's a dearth of attractive men around here."

Lila could only blink at the circle of women standing around her in the kitchen. They were all lively, funny, and pretty—and, if half their stories were true, had once been married to men who had failed to appreciate any of that. They were also die-hard members of the Ford Ford Fan Club, which was a thing she had no trouble believing. She was ready to run for president herself.

"Well, there *used* to be a dearth of attractive men,"

Maddie countered. "Helen, who is that handsome hunk of a man your sons are making walk the plank over by the punch bowl? I'd like to wrap him up and put him under my tree."

Helen blushed up to the roots of her hair, which Lila noted had been recently touched up. "That's Patrick. Patrick Yarmouth." She colored even more. "He's, uh. Um. Well, he and I have started seeing each other."

There was so much squealing and hugging that Lila felt as though she were in the middle of a PTA mosh pit.

"It's not serious or anything yet, you guys," Helen protested, trying—unsuccessfully—to quiet them. "We're just trying things on for size. Lila introduced us."

All eyes turned her way.

"How many more of those do you have hiding in your pocket?" demanded a woman whose name Lila couldn't remember.

"Does he have any brothers?" asked another.

"You're coming to my game night next week," announced a third. "I won't take no for an answer. How are you at charades?"

Maddie wrapped an arm around Lila's shoulder and squeezed. "Ford is such a great guy, Lila. He deserves to be happy. I'm so glad you're together."

"Oh, we're not togeth—" Lila began, but it was no use. Helen winked and announced to the group that until the puppy training was over, all talk of relationships was to be kept to a low murmur.

For professionalism, of course.

The ease and delight with which the women agreed to this spoke volumes about them. So did the fact that the talk immediately turned to the snowplow schedule and whose turn it was to shovel Mrs. Bates's walkway until her hip had finished healing. These were nice women, *good* women, and their romantic rivalries were conducted almost entirely in jest.

Lila liked them. She liked them a lot.

She was also starting to appreciate the approach Ford had taken with them for all these years. To an outsider, his flirtatious demeanor bore all the hallmarks of a man who took nothing seriously and dallied with any female who crossed his path. But these women *liked* that he wasn't serious with them—encouraged it, even. It gave them something to look forward to without requiring them to invest their already-damaged hearts.

"Ahem."

Lila whirled at the sound of that voice. Her own heart, which was well on its way to being irreversibly damaged, gave a heavy thump.

"Ladies, if you'll excuse me, I'd like to whisk this woman away for a private moment or two." Ford stood less than a foot away from her, looking like a roguish pirate from head to toe. Lila had no idea what the real Blackbeard was supposed to look like, but the version Ford had chosen was decidedly *s-l-u-t-t-y*. There was no other way to describe the billowing white shirt that opened in a deep vee at his chest or the tan pants so tightly molded to his thighs that they looked like a second skin.

Lila could only be grateful that her sisters weren't here to see this. Or her mother, for that matter. There was no coming back from a man who looked like this one. *She* certainly wouldn't be able to.

"You can't have her until you promise to come to charades for my New Year's party." The woman who'd invited her to game night crossed her arms. "I need more bodies, and Lila has promised to bring me a date."

"Has she, now?" Ford asked with one arch of his brow. When matched with the rest of him, the result was even more debonair than usual. "I'm starting to wonder how many backups she keeps on hand."

"Sixteen," she lied.

The speed with which she answered caused Ford's brow to shoot up even more.

Emboldened, Lila added, "So you'd better watch your step, because there are plenty more where you came from."

Ford didn't, as she'd hoped, treat this as the cavalier piece of nonsense she meant it to be. "I know," he said in a perfectly serious tone. "But I'm hoping you'll choose me anyway."

If the flutter of sighs that erupted from behind her were any indication, his words had their intended effect. The women swooned where swooning was called for, adored when adoration fit.

And why wouldn't they? These women had only seen the fun, flirtatious Ford Ford—the man who'd wear a Speedo at a pool party just to give them something to ogle, and who could be counted on to make a pirate costume look amazing. They didn't know that he struggled to get his work done every day, sitting down at his desk whenever he could squeeze in a few minutes. They didn't know that he constantly worried about Emily's well-being, putting every single one of his own needs behind hers. They didn't know that he was an amazingly talented artist who was too afraid and too humble to do anything but dream.

But Lila knew. She also knew that swooning and adoration weren't what he needed. What he needed was someone who saw him for what he really was: strong and scared, fallible and funny, and most of all, incredibly protective of his heart.

He's just like me.

When she glanced up at him again, she expected the earnest expression on his face to be gone, once again replaced by the charming smile that characterized him. She was wrong. Not only did he remain perfectly serious, but his hand was held out in a gesture of supplication, his palm up and waiting for hers.

"Will you come with me for a minute? Emily has something she'd like to say to you." He drew a deep breath that swelled his chest and made his ruffles flutter. "For that matter, so do I. But I think I should let her go first."

Lila might have been able to withstand the request if he'd laughed or joked or done something intensely piratical, like winked at her, but he didn't. All he did was hold his hand flat and add, "Please."

There was nothing for Lila to do but give in. As her palm touched his, his fingers closed tightly around hers, clutching as though she were the only thing keeping him from plunging off the edge of a cliff. If that wasn't alarming enough, the fact that he said nothing more than a terse "Thank you" as he pulled her toward the bedrooms would have been.

"What is it?" she asked, trying to keep the sharp note of worry out of her voice. "Is it about Emily's hand?"

"Yes, but not in the way you're thinking." He cast a look over his shoulder back at her, his face relaxed despite the urgency of his grip. He even managed a smile. "She has a confession to make."

Ford led Lila to a bedroom almost identical to Emily's, but crammed with a bunk bed and shelves full of action figures in every possible shape and size. It was incredibly messy, although a space had been carved out in the middle of the floor where Emily stood over an abandoned board game.

Lila couldn't help but laugh as her gaze landed on the color squares and candy-coated figurines on the game box. *Candy Land*. Of course. Her pink dress really did look like it could preside over a field of those lollipops.

The laugh didn't last long. As soon as her gaze landed on the little girl, all thoughts of joy fled. Emily's eyes were wide and wet with tears, her hands clasped behind her back. Lila had seen far too many puppies stand exactly like that—hurt and dazed—to react any other way.

"Oh, love." She dropped to her knees and held out her arms. "Whatever it is, it's okay. It's going to be okay."

Emily didn't, as she expected, come running into her waiting embrace. With a shuffle of her feet and an even more stricken glance at Lila, she said, "It was me."

The words came out barely above a whisper, but in addition to sign language, Lila's skills in lip reading were also growing by leaps and bounds. "What was you, Emily? What happened?"

Pulling her injured hand from around her back, Emily held it out to Lila. She looked over Lila's shoulder toward her father and gulped before continuing. "Jeeves didn't bite my hand. And he didn't growl or bark or jump or do anything bad."

It took everything Lila had not to turn toward Ford and demand a more concise explanation, but she did it. Emily was obviously taking this very seriously, which meant Lila would, too. If there was one thing she remembered well from her own childhood, it was feeling annoyed whenever an adult acted like her problems didn't matter.

Emily mattered. She mattered a lot.

She took the proffered hand and held it lightly, careful not to press on the injury but unwilling to let the girl go. "Why don't you tell me all about it?" she said.

That earned her a hug. Emily came tumbling in to her, her arms winding up around Lila's neck and holding on with a desperation that hooked on her heart. "I bit myself," she said, the words coming out in a rush. "I bit myself and then I got Jeeves in trouble, only now he's all locked up and I don't want him to be."

"Of course you don't," Lila murmured, but she doubted Emily heard her. She must have felt the soothing rumble of her voice, though, because she only burrowed deeper into Lila's chest. "He's your trusty steed, isn't he? Your valiant knight? You need him. A princess always knows *that*."

Ford cleared his throat. Lila glanced up to find him watching them with a furrow between his eyes. "That's not the whole story, I'm afraid," he said. "The part she isn't telling you is *why* she did it."

Lila didn't want to jostle Emily out of her embrace, so all she did was lift an inquisitive brow. Ford sighed and ran a hand along the back of his neck before gesturing at the space on the floor next to them. "May I?"

Lila nodded, scooting over just enough to make room for Ford to join them. Emily noticed the shift and turned around to face her father. As though it were the most natural thing in the world, she settled herself in Lila's lap, those warm little legs pressing against Lila's own. For a moment, Emily made a move as if to put her thumb in her mouth, but she decided against it.

She took Lila's hand instead.

"Tell her, Daddy," she said. "Tell her that we don't want her to go."

For the first time since they entered the room, Ford relaxed enough to chuckle. It was such a familiar sight— that gorgeous smile of his, the easy way he allowed joy to spark his life—that Lila found herself gripping Emily even tighter.

"Well, I was going to segue in a little more delicately than that, but Emily's not wrong," he said. "She doesn't want you to go, Lila. *I* don't want you to go."

"*Me*?" she said, somewhat taken aback by the direction the conversation had taken. She wasn't the one who'd been offered a job three hundred miles away. She wasn't the one about to pack up and move her heart to the other side of the state.

"Her methods were a little drastic, I'll admit, but her intentions were pure." Ford bestowed a smile on his daughter and leaned in to give her nose a tweak. "She thought that if Jeeves had to be retrained, we could hold on to you a little longer. How much longer, I don't know. A few weeks, a few months... Maybe forever."

"Forever," Emily announced sharply. But with one

look at her father's warning glance, she amended this with "'Cept you can't make people stay. You can only love them." She twisted in Lila's lap until they were face-to-face. "I love you, Lila."

"Oh, sweetie." Tears sprang to Lila's eyes. "I love you, too. And I do want to stay with you, I really do, but—"

Ford cleared his throat again. "I think this is where it's my turn. Emily?"

Emily leaped out of Lila's lap, still pale and a little stricken, but doing her valiant best not to cry. She looked so much like Jeeves—proud and determined to see things through no matter what it cost her—that Lila couldn't help but sniffle. That little puppy was strengthening this girl in so many ways. She was so *glad* they could continue being together.

Before she could say as much out loud, Ford grabbed her hands, snatching at them like a desperate man. It might have been to keep her from speaking, but she liked to think it was because he couldn't go another second without touching some part of her.

She certainly couldn't.

"We're not moving to Seattle, Lila. Emily and I are going to stay right here, regardless of what happens between you and me. I think a part of me always knew that." His voice was low, his gaze serious as he stared into her eyes. "I know I should have told you the second the job offer came in. I wanted to—so many times, I wanted to—but I was scared of coming on too strong, of scaring you away. We've only known each other a short time, and I wasn't sure how involved you wanted to be in my future."

She knew the answer to that. *Fully involved. All the way in.* Their hearts and lives moving as one.

"To be honest, I'm *still* not sure," he said, swallowing heavily. "But it doesn't matter, because I want you to hear this—no joking, no lies. I love you, Lila Vasquez. I've loved you from almost the moment we met. I know you have no reason to believe me, and that I've been hiding like a chicken *s-h-i-t* behind a silly facade the whole time we've been together, but it's the truth."

"Oh, Ford," she said.

But he wasn't done. "I don't have much in the way of worldly goods to bestow on you. Almost nothing, in fact. Starting on the first of the year, I'll be an unemployed stay-at-home dad who lives in his ratty pajama bottoms and eats peanut butter straight from the jar. But everything that I do have—my home, my heart, my stacks of half-finished drawings and unfinished dreams—is yours for the taking." His lips lifted in a rueful smile. "Some offer, huh?"

That showed what he knew. It wasn't just *some* offer. It was the best offer Lila had ever received. The idea of being a part of this man's life—of Emily's life—in any capacity was everything she never knew she wanted.

And he was giving it to her with no jokes and no playful lies. He was giving her his heart.

Finally.

"That depends," she said, unable to keep the smile from her face any longer. "Which pajama bottoms are we talking about?"

Laughter lit Ford's eyes from within. "Lila! I'm trying to be serious over here."

Emily must have sensed the sudden lightness in the air because she looked back and forth between Lila and Ford, her hands clasped to her chest. "Princess Lila?" she asked, an excited vibrato underscoring her voice. "Daddy?"

Ford took this as his cue to continue. He rubbed his thumbs over the backs of Lila's hands, sending a delighted shiver straight through to her spine. "I don't have much, but I do love you—more than I ever thought possible, more than any man has a right to love a woman. I'd marry you right now if you'd have me. But you've seen my life—*our* life—up close and personal, so it has to be your choice. It's not going to get much grander than that anytime soon."

"Do you promise?" Lila asked.

The question took him aback, but not so much that he didn't make a quick recovery. His eyes twinkled. "Of course I do. Like George Washington, I cannot—"

"Ford! You know how I feel about that man."

"*Fine*. You're a tough woman to please, but I'm willing to put in the work." He took a deep breath and started again. "Like Abraham Lincoln, I cannot tell a lie. I want you, Lila Vasquez. For richer and, most likely, poorer. In sickness and, with any luck, health—"

"Jeeves!"

Emily's sudden squeal of happiness was broken by an even happier bark. Lila barely had time to register what was happening before the curly-eared cockapoo landed on them. Literally. Her exceptionally well-trained puppy—the same puppy who would sit still for hours at a time, who could tell the difference between a fire alarm and the sound of a microwave buzzer going off—tumbled in with all the enthusiasm of a scrappy mutt without an ounce of obedience training.

And to top it all off, he had an arrangement of plastic mistletoe affixed to the back of his collar.

"But Mom!" Lila recognized Neil's voice in the hallway, followed almost immediately by an indistinguishable murmur from Helen. "You're the one who made me go get the puppy. And it's *my* room."

There was a pause as Jeeves began frantically licking Emily's face. His whole body wriggled with delight, but Ford managed to get hold of him before her training went *too* much in reverse.

"Fine," Neil grumbled from the hallway. "But as soon as they're done kissing, I'm going in. *Gross*."

Which was why, when Ford finally pulled Lila to her feet, she was laughing. She had no choice. Jeeves had given up on licking Emily's face and decided to make do with Ford's. Emily was demanding to be lifted up so she could admire the decoration on her puppy's collar. Ford was trying to hold everything together in his barechested pirate ruffles. And unless Lila was very much mistaken, the entire party was crowded in that hallway waiting for the inevitable.

"Well, Lila?" Ford asked, a mocking lift to his brow. "I told you that everything I have is yours for the taking. Here it is in all its loud, squirming, undignified glory. What do you say?"

"Yes, please," she said, blushing harder than she'd ever blushed in her entire life. Which, considering that she'd spent the last six weeks with a man as outrageous as Ford Ford, was saying a lot. "There's nothing I'd like more."

The smile that broke out on Ford's face was enough to light every Christmas tree from here to Seattle and back again. Emily, seeing it, matched it with one of her own.

Lila would have done the same, but a voice from the hallway interrupted her before she could manage much more than a quirk of her lips in the right direction.

"Oh my God. Would you just kiss her already?" it demanded.

That was all the prompting Ford needed. With both of them breathless from laughter, they shared what had to be the most public kiss of Lila's existence. It wasn't dignified or proper, there was a puppy and a child wedged between them, and it ended to a crash of applause in the background.

It was, in a word, *perfect*.

Epilogue

Y ou have to promise me you won't read it until I'm out
of the house."

Ford held the book just out of Lila's reach. Such a
taunting gesture would compel any other woman to
make a dive for it, to wrestle him to the floor with promises of extracting a painful—and pleasurable—torture
until he gave in.

Not so with *his* woman.

"I can just go to the bookstore and buy my own copy,
you know," she said, holding herself with a dignified air.
"They ordered like five dozen."

"Yeah, but the bookstore is miles away."

"I'm sure the woman who does the ordering wouldn't
mind bringing a copy around. I saw what she wrote on
your Facebook page." A slow, careful, smile worked
across Lila's face. She went from a beautiful temptress
to a beautiful, *evil* temptress in less time than it took
him to blink. "In fact, if I promise her you'll be shirtless
when she arrives, I bet she'll bring all sixty."

Ford glanced down at himself. He was, for once in
his life, fully clothed—and *nicely* clothed, if he did say
so himself. He still preferred to work in his pajamas,
but there were actual buttons and a logo on his shirt
today.

"And how, exactly, do you propose to get me *n-a-k-
e-d*?" he asked.

Her evil smile didn't abate any. "Oh, the usual way."

He was about to follow up on this intriguing piece of

information when Lila gave a piercing whistle. "*Now*, Emily. Release the hounds!"

The hounds in question were only one animal, but Jeeves had been trained well. *Too* well, if the way the dog came dashing into the kitchen and sat at his feet was any indication. He was followed not too long after by Emily, who planted herself next to her service animal and looked up at Ford through wide, adoring eyes. Lila, laughing at how well both her protégés performed, stood next to them.

"Please, Daddy?" Emily asked with her hands clasped angelically in front of her. "Pretty please with sugar on top?"

"Please, Ford?" Lila chimed in. "Please will you give us a copy of your book?"

"*Rrrrroowww*," Jeeves put in at a quick hand signal from Lila.

It wasn't fair. Since the day Lila had moved in, bringing with her a parcel of neatly folded clothes, a huge organizational calendar to tack on the wall, and enough dog treats to see them through the next century, Ford had been lost. When it had been just him and Emily, he'd won the occasional battle of wills. Nowadays, it was three against one, and he didn't stand a chance.

"Don't make us resort to bribery," Lila warned. "Helen promised to bring over a batch of cookies later, but I can call her up and tell her to give them to Patrick instead."

"Cruel fate," Ford said. He turned to Emily. "You're really going to side with this dictator? I thought I raised you better than that."

Emily giggled. "I want to see the pictures, Daddy. I've never been in a book a'fore."

There was nothing more he could do after that but hand over the graphic novel he'd been guarding. It was titled, after much deliberation, *The Misadventures of the Lizard Queen*, but it would have been just as appropriate to call it *Emily's Tale*. Or *Tail*, considering how prominently Jeeves figured in the pages.

"I don't know why I even bother," Ford said as he tossed the book down. "Since the day you married me, you've had me under your thumb." He didn't add that he rather enjoyed his position there—usually because he was also under the rest of her at the time.

Lila softened, her eyes melting into his. "We're just proud of you, Ford, that's all. You've worked so hard on this book."

He had. It had taken months to fit it in around his freelancing work, and there'd been a long period of rejection in which he'd been sure nothing would come of it, but the results had been well worth it. He had an actual graphic novel in his hands. And more importantly, Lila and Emily had it in their hands, too.

The contract had hardly turned him into a rich man overnight, but he didn't mind. Lila's business was thriving, thanks to a successful partnership with the Auditory Guild, and she showed no signs of discontent in the cozy house they all shared. This was where Emily had grown up—was still growing up—making friends and playing in the street and enjoying the active, busy childhood he'd always wanted for her.

It was home.

"I still don't see how it's fair for you three to gang up

on me all the time," he grumbled. He had to do *something*. Lila was peeking over Emily's shoulder at a particularly sentimental scene in which her lizard twin was teaching the peasant girl how to braid her hair. "You could at least pretend I get a say in how things work."

"I could," Lila agreed, "but one of the best pieces of advice Helen gave me was not to run my family like a democracy."

He turned his head to look at her, struck, as he always was, by how beautiful she was when she laughed. It was dangerous for a lot of reasons, but none so prominent as the fact that these days, she was *always* laughing.

Partly because Emily was starting to get to the good part of the book, and partly because he'd never been able to resist Lila's low, sultry chuckle, he swooped in and wrapped his wife in a tight embrace. He kissed her long and slow, refusing to give in to her mild protests that their daughter was watching. Emily was far too wrapped up in her first literary appearance to care.

"Your family, huh?" he asked, breathless as he held Lila in his arms.

"Yes, Ford," she replied, her eyes crinkling up at him. "My family. *Our* family."

*Keep reading for a sneak peek at
book three in the Forever Home series!*

PUPPY
Kisses

Stealing a dog turned out to be much easier than Dawn had expected.

"Wait. So that's it?" She glanced down at the animal in her arms. The shaking, shivering golden retriever puppy whimpered and tucked her head into the crook of Dawn's elbow. "We just walk out that gate, and the deed is done?"

"Well, we could climb over that section of fence with the razor wire if you really want to," her coconspirator said. He didn't even whisper, which went to show how anticlimactic this whole ordeal was. "But if it's all the same to you, I'd rather not. I like my fingernails where they are."

"It seems a little tame, is all I'm saying." Dawn ran a soothing hand over the back of the puppy's neck and contemplated their two exits out of the dusty backyard. Even if they *had* been forced to take the more perilous route, they could have easily tossed a piece of canvas over the top of the razor wire and come out unscathed. There was a whole stack of it sitting on the ground. "I always assumed that theft came with higher stakes. Geez. If I'd have known it was this easy, I'd have started a life of crime years ago. Here—grab the keys out of my front pocket, will you? You'll have to be our getaway driver. I don't want to let this poor honey go. I can feel every last one of her ribs."

Only a flicker of a frown for the dog's thin, scabbed body crossed Zeke's face before being replaced by a more pronounced expression of horror. "You want me to put my hands *where*?"

"Oh, don't look so worried," she said, laughing. She also jutted out her hip to give him better access. "I promise not to like it."

"You owe me for this," he grumbled, but he did as she asked. And was none too pleased about it, if the way he tentatively poked one finger in the tight fit of her jean shorts pocket and fished around for the key ring was any indication. "I don't know why I let you talk me into these things."

Dawn did. "Because you love me and I'm the only reason you have even a semblance of a social life. Now, come on. The sooner we get this sweet girl to a veterinarian, the better. People who treat animals like this deserve to be in prison."

It was a subject on which Dawn would have gladly expounded—and at considerable length—had the situation allowed for it. She'd driven by this house at least half a dozen times in the past week. Each time, regardless of the hour of day or the fact that the summer temperatures were soaring well into the hundreds, the undersized puppy had been hooked onto a short, heavy chain in the backyard.

One time was unfortunate, but six was nothing short of animal cruelty—especially since it looked as though the chain weighed more than the animal did. The poor dog couldn't reach either shade or water, and had done her feeble best to dig a hole in the dirt to cool herself off. But she clearly hadn't been fed in some time, and she barely had the strength to stand up, let alone carve out a space where she could be comfortable. Just thinking about it started Dawn's blood running hot again. It always tended on the warm side, quick to boil over and liable to scald, but this went beyond anything.

Dawn drew a deep breath and adjusted the puppy until she was more comfortably encased in her arms. As much as she would have loved to get up on a soapbox and shout at this house until someone came out to face her, this was neither the time nor the place for such a tirade.

Especially since a light in the upper story of the A-line house flickered on before she could take so much as a single step toward freedom.

"Oh, crap!" Dawn clutched the quivering bundle tighter. She cast an anxious—and slightly accusatory—look at her friend. "I thought you said you rang on the doorbell and no one answered."

"I did." Zeke finally managed to get hold of her keys and yanked them out of her pocket. "Twice. Maybe the guy was taking a nap."

"Hey!" A window was thrown open and a head appeared. From her vantage point, Dawn could just make out a gray, scruffy beard and the top of a filthy white t-shirt. "This is private property. What the hell do you think you're doing?"

"Running," Dawn said, and did just that.

She didn't wait to see if Zeke followed. As a full-time ranch worker and competitive triathlete, he was in far better shape than she could ever hope to be. In fact, he took a nimble leap over a pile of broken-down lawn furniture and passed her within the first ten seconds of their flight. Since he also paused to make sure she got through the gate and even opened the car door for her, she wasn't too insulted.

"Step on it," she urged as she swung the car door shut and slammed her palm on the lock. She caught sight of the man struggling into a pair of brown sweatpants at the front door to the house. He seemed to be having some trouble getting his second leg into the proper hole— most likely because of the shotgun clutched fervently in his right hand. "And step on it hard. I think he's going to start shooting at us."

It said a lot about her friendship with Zeke that he only sighed and muttered something about his inevitable death at her hands before following orders.

"It's moments like these that I wish you'd bought that Tesla," Zeke said as he shifted the car into drive and hit the gas. Her little Jetta was cute but not very powerful. A crunch of gravel kicked up behind them, followed by a slow, almost painful whip of the tail end of the car before they started moving forward. "I could use some zero-to-sixty action right now."

Dawn cast a look in the rearview mirror. "We both could. He's given up on the sweatpants and is going straight for the truck in his underwear. It's not an attractive sight. *Move*."

Zeke didn't have to be told twice. He hit the gas with a heavy foot and pulled them out of the drive.

It wasn't an ideal place to make a getaway. The house where the puppy had been tied up was in the middle of semi-rural area just north of Spokane, where pockets of houses were broken up by long, empty stretches of highway. It took them all of thirty seconds to pull out of the neighborhood and find themselves surrounded by the vast nothingness of rural eastern Washington. Unless they barreled the car into a field of corn or one of the many haystacks dotting the landscape, there weren't many places to hide.

Dawn suggested one of the latter, but Zeke just gripped the wheel and showed a tight-lipped determination to outrun the shotgun-wielding man.

Since the pickup truck was already starting to smoke in the distance, and Zeke knew this area better than if Google Maps and Apple Maps had a baby, Dawn settled back and turned her attention to the puppy in her lap. She'd never been one to worry about the things she couldn't control—mostly because her life had mostly been one long series of things she couldn't control. If she took it into her head to get into a pucker every time someone tried to chase after her, she'd never leave the house.

"You poor honey," she murmured as she settled the animal more comfortably across her bare thighs. "Let me take a good look at you."

The golden retriever had stopped shaking by this time, opting instead to balance her head on Dawn's knee. As if sensing a kindred spirit, the animal showed no desire to fight back against Dawn's gentle pokes and prods. This, in and of itself, was a good sign. Dawn wasn't the expert in the family when it came to dog behaviors—her older sister Lila was the one with the master's degree and an incredibly analytical mind—but she hadn't spent the last six years training service puppies for nothing. Abuse and neglect often caused animals to show their teeth and stop at nothing to protect themselves. And rightly so, if you asked her.

This little darling, however, only offered a feeble tongue and sighed contentedly, even when Dawn's hand moved over the silken fur on her stomach to find numerous neglected sores.

"I hope you run that bastard off the road," she said as she poked gently around the edges of the wounds, all of which must have been there for quite some time. One, in particular, seemed to have become infected sometime in the past few days. "I hope you aim for a cliff and propel him right off the end of it."

Zeke didn't look over. He was too busy gripping both hands on the wheel, the fields a blur around them. "There aren't any cliffs around here, but there's a good chance we'll end up turned over in a ditch before this is over. Are you wearing your seat belt?"

"Yep."

"Airbag is on?"

"Check."

"You've made peace with your maker?"

"Um." Dawn was forced into a laugh. "That depends on who you ask. I mean, *I'm* okay with most of my life choices. If you were to ask my mother, however…"

"Uh-oh. Hold that thought, D. We've got more company."

Since both her arms were wrapped around the puppy, there wasn't much for her to hold on to. Not that it would have been of any use to cling to the dashboard or those weird hanging handles that people used to carry their dry cleaning. Just when the frenetic, wheezing pickup was becoming nothing more than a blip in the rearview mirror, their tail was replaced by a sleek green-and-white car with a whir of colorful lights up top. Unlike the truck, this new car managed to keep pace with them just fine.

"Oh dear. Is that—?" Dawn began.

Zeke finished for her. "Sheriff Jenkins? Yes. *Fuck.* I was going at least ninety. He's not going to like this. I hate to say it, but I think we'd have been better off with No-Pants Shotgun back there."

Dawn disagreed. She'd had enough encounters with the legal system in her lifetime to feel wary where they were concerned, but she'd take her chances with a back-woods officer of the law over an irate man without pants any day.

"Don't worry about the sheriff," Dawn said with a toss of her head. She bit down on her lips to bring the blood to them and gave her t-shirt a not-so-discreet tug. She'd dressed for the day's heist in functional jean shorts and a ratty shirt, but the top had been worn so many times that it was practically sheer. The deep plunge of the v-neck didn't hurt matters, either. Her boobs were far and away her best feature—too big for everyday comfort, but ideal when trying to bend men to her will. Whenever she got annoyed with the former, she tried very hard to focus on the latter. "I'm sure I can convince him to let us go with a warning."

Zeke snorted as he pulled the car over to the side of the road. "You obviously haven't met Harold Jenkins. The only thing he hates more than people who speed is *women* who speed."

"But I'm not the one driving," Dawn pointed out. She dropped a kiss on the golden retriever's dusty head. "Besides—who would give a ticket to anyone holding such a sweet little love as this?"

The answer, as it turned out, was Sheriff Harold Jenkins.

"That makes the third time this month, Mr. Dearborn." The sheriff—a short, balding man with a swagger in his step and nothing but disdain for Dawn's cleavage—was every bit as disagreeable as Zeke had promised. He examined the driver's license in his hand as if inspecting the edges for lines of cocaine. "I told you last time that I'd suspend this if I caught you speeding again."

"Yes, sir."

"I clocked you at eighty-nine. That's an eight and a nine. Together. In one number."

"Yes, sir."

"Last I checked, we hadn't made any changes to the speed limit around here."

"No, sir."

It was almost more than Dawn could take. Meekly accepting one's fate was a thing she never could and never would understand—especially in a world as flawed as this one. They'd just saved this poor animal's life, for crying out loud, and her white knight was quaking more in fear over a traffic violation than the man who'd been chasing them with a gun.

Since it appeared she was on her own for this fight, she leaned across the driver's seat and plastered on her brightest smile. "I'm so sorry about this, Officer. But it wasn't Zeke's fault—honest, it wasn't. This one was all me."

"Sheriff."

She blinked, somewhat taken aback by the gruff note in his voice. She also noted her error at once. "Yes, um. Of course. That's what I meant, *Sheriff*." She batted her eyelashes for good measure. "Zeke was only going so fast because it's an emergency."

The sheriff's eyes narrowed as they ran over the car's interior. "Doesn't look like much of an emergency to me. Is there a reason you have the dog up front like that?"

"Yes." Dawn saw her chance and latched onto it. She was nothing if not opportunistic. "This puppy is in desperate need of medical attention. Look how frail and underweight she is—and at these sores on her stomach. The poor dear is in a lot of pain."

She thought both she and the puppy sold it pretty well. Not only did the animal give an appropriately pitiful blink of her sleepy brown eyes, but Dawn followed up with one of her own. No man would be able to stand up to the pair of them. She was sure of it.

At least, she was until the sheriff chuffed out a breath and handed Zeke a ticket. The ID he kept firmly in hand. "Then you're going in the wrong direction, young lady. Marcia Peterson is the best veterinarian in twelve counties—a thing Zeke Dearborn has known since his cradle. She's also located a good fifteen miles the other way."

Dawn's heart sank. That had been some of her best work, too.

"I'll have to see the lady's license, if you please," the sheriff added in a clipped tone. "Seeing as how she'll be the one driving you home. If she's unable to take the wheel, then I'll be happy to escort all three of you in the back of my car. This ID is no longer valid."

"But Harold, you can't—" Zeke began with an agonized glance at Dawn. She knew what that look meant. His athletic training sessions had to fit around his ranch work schedule, which meant he was on the road more often than not. To lose his driver's license would be to lose his only means of transportation in and out of here—his only escape. He freaking loved those triathlons.

"We're not taking her to Marcia's," Dawn said, grasping at the only straw she could see. And she meant that literally. They were so far from civilization out here, not even that Google Maps and Apple Maps baby could save them. "We're taking her to the ranch."

"The ranch?" Sheriff Jenkins echoed doubtfully. He paused, though, which was the most important thing, the driver's license hanging fatefully in the air. "What for?"

"Well... You see... The thing is..." Dawn heaved a deep breath to give herself strength. This next part was going to hurt, but she had to do it. "This is Adam's dog."

Despite the pang that filled her at such blasphemous words, she had the benefit of seeing a flicker of hesitation in Sheriff Jenkins's eyes. Of course, that flicker then moved to the puppy, taking in that hunched, traumatized form with a disbelieving chuff of air.

"Mr. Dearborn owns *this* dog?" he asked. "What for?"

"She's a service animal." Zeke was quick to pick up on the train of her thoughts. "To help Adam around the ranch and stuff when Phoebe and I can't be there."

The idea that this starving bundle of a puppy could be of service to anyone was ludicrous, but Zeke went on, driven by the silence greeting him on all signs. "Dawn here is a dog trainer," he said. "Didn't I mention that? She owns a company—a real business that trains and places puppies for the blind. You have some business cards on you, right, Dawn?"

Dawn saw nothing for it but to pull out her wallet and extract a business card. She was, in fact, exactly what Zeke was making her out to be. She worked with her sisters Lila and Sophie to take bright, eager puppies and train them to provide services to people of all kinds. Hearing service dogs, vision service dogs, emotional support animals—if a dog could do the work, they found a way to make it happen.

"Here you go," she said as she handed over the business card. It was a little ragged around the edges from being wedged in her wallet for so long, but the gist of it was there. "Our company is called Puppy Promise. We specialize in training young dogs so we can make sure they grow up to be a perfect fit. My sister Lila is the brains behind it."

Sheriff Jenkins took the card and eyed it carefully, almost as though he suspected her of carrying them around just in case she would someday get pulled over for speeding while in the care of an emaciated golden retriever. "That so?"

Zeke held up three fingers in a Boy Scout salute. "On my honor."

For a long, suspended moment, Dawn thought it was going to work. The sheriff glanced back and forth between them, taking in the driver and the passenger, the puppy and the card. *Let us go*, Dawn willed him. *Send us on our way*.

Her hopes reached their zenith when Sheriff Jenkins gave a curt nod and returned her business card. He even handed Zeke back his ID. "Then of course you're free to go on your way."

"Thank you, Sheriff," Zeke said, not wasting a moment as he turned the keys in the ignition. "And it won't happen again, I promise. You won't regret—"

Sheriff Jenkins coughed, cutting Zeke short. "I'll go ahead and follow you two to the ranch. You'll want a police escort. An animal like that one should be seen right away. We wouldn't want you to run into any more setbacks on the road."

Dawn could only open her mouth and close it again, watching as the sheriff turned on his heel and walked away. She continued her silent vigilance in the rearview mirror as he lowered himself into the driver's seat of his patrol car, said something into his handset, and checked his mirrors.

And then waited—patiently and calmly—for Zeke to pull out onto the road.

"We're in for it now," Zeke accused. The engine gave an ineffective roar as he stepped down on the accelerator before he remembered to remove the car from park. "Have you lost your ever-loving mind? We'd be better off going to jail than facing Adam. What in the hell made you introduce my brother into the conversation?"

Dawn gently massaged the puppy's silken fur, struggling to come up with a reasonable excuse. *Desperation. Stupidity. An overwhelming desire to see Adam again.*

"I'm sorry," she eventually said. "I panicked."

"Yeah, well, you might want to hold on to that panic a little bit longer." Zeke glanced over his shoulder before pulling out onto the highway. The sheriff was visible behind them, keeping an exact six car lengths back. "The second we walk in that door with your stolen puppy and a sheriff in tow, Adam is going to eat me alive. No—he's going to eat *you* alive while I'm forced to stand by and watch. Isn't that how the best torturers do it?"

"Don't be so dramatic. I'm not scared of your brother."

Zeke snorted a laugh. Now that no one was pointing a shotgun at him and his ID was safe in his wallet, he was back to his usual carefree self. "Yes, you are. You're terrified of him. That and bees—the only two things in the world capable of bringing you down. And at least you have an EpiPen to fight the bees."

"I could probably use the EpiPen on Adam, too," she pointed out. "If it came down to hand-to-hand combat."

He snorted again. "My brother? Felled by one tiny needle? You've got some strange ideas, Dawn, but I draw the line at that one." He cast an obvious glance down at the puppy. "One of these days, those ideas are going to be the death of you. And me, probably."

"I'm not scared of your brother," she echoed, more firmly this time. "I can handle him."

"The same way you handled Sheriff Jenkins?"

She didn't bother answering. Okay, so the good officer had proven himself impervious to her charms—it happened sometimes. Not often, but sometimes. Zeke, for example, regularly told her that he'd rather sleep with a tiger on fire than get anywhere near the disaster that was her romantic life. Clearly, the honorable Sheriff Jenkins was formed from the same mold.

Adam Dearborn, however, wasn't impervious. Not to her *physical* charms, anyway.

"Now that I'm thinking about it, you weren't too adroit with No-Pants Shotgun back there, either," Zeke added. "For a woman who claims to be so good at handling men, you seem to have a pretty terrible track record lately."

"At least when an angry man runs after me with no pants on, I know what's on his mind," she retorted, nettled. That had been some of her best work, too. "It's when they keep their clothes on that I start to worry."

About the Author

Lucy Gilmore is a contemporary romance author with a love of puppies, rainbows, and happily ever afters. She began her reading (and writing) career as an English literature major and ended as a die-hard fan of romance in all forms. When she's not rolling around with her two Akitas, she can be found hiking, biking, or with her nose buried in a book. Visit her online at lucygilmore.com.

LOVE AT FIRST BARK

The digital clock on the dashboard of Ben's Jeep placed him a solid forty-five minutes ahead of schedule for a client meeting. This morning, he'd be presenting a series of designs to a family who was converting a hundred-year-old church into a home. He'd poured hours into the designs, manipulating ways to enable the family to modernize and add warmth while keeping the majority of the stained glass, archways, coffers, and even the belfry.

Showing up this early at a client's home wasn't ideal. Ben told himself this was the reason his foot seemed instinctively to ease off the gas pedal as he neared the exit leading to the house in Webster Groves where Mia had been living since August. He'd resisted shooting off a text to check in with her before leaving this morning. Most likely, if he asked if she needed anything, she'd thank him but say no, just as she'd been doing the last few months. She wasn't one to ask for help. Or even accept it when it was offered.

But he remembered the way she'd leaned against him in a rare moment of surrender at Brad's funeral.

It was over before he'd been able to react or even savor the soft smell of her perfume or her toned but ample figure pressing into him. Too soon, she'd stood straight and locked her shoulders, the Atlas of her small world.

What if he just showed up? If he knocked on the door instead of texting. He'd done that dozens of times without a thought when she'd been married. Just because she was on her own now didn't mean he wasn't still Ollie's godfather. And more than any time in his young life, Ollie needed him.

She's probably in a rush to get Ollie to school. Ben tapped his thumb in indecision on the steering wheel but took the exit anyway. Two blocks in, he passed Ollie's favorite bakery. Seeing that the parking lot wasn't crowded this morning, he pulled up and ran in for a couple of their favorite mini-quiches—ham and cheese for Ollie and spinach and fontina for Mia—and an assortment of scones and muffins. Mia had mentioned they froze well the last time he sent Ollie home with a bag of them after an outing with him and Taye.

Ben pulled into an open spot in front of the home where Mia had grown up. It was a quaint brick bungalow. The dark streaks on the roof and some erosion on the chimney pots showed it was in need of some TLC. Seeing it reminded him of just one more way he'd like to help her if she'd let him. If.

As he headed up the path, he spotted her through the bay window. She was at the counter in the kitchen, grabbing something from a cabinet. Through the darkened window, it wasn't easy to make out much, but his insides twisted all the same. She was the only woman he'd ever met who caused his chest to tighten and his gut to burn hot at the same time.

And that was before she answered the door in fleece pj's that were only half successful in hiding her lack of bra, no makeup, and hair still mussed from sleep. He locked his gaze on her face to keep it from straying south.

"Hey. Morning. I, uh… Did you call? My phone's in the bedroom." A blush lit her cheeks, and she clamped one arm over her chest as she pulled the door open wide.

"Morning. I was about to, but I figured if I did, you'd shoot me down," he said with a smile.

Ben heard a flush and splash of water from the opposite end of the small house; then a familiar golden-haired head popped around the corner. "Ben!" Clad only in a long-sleeved pajama top and Spider-Man underwear, Ollie charged down the length of the living room and locked Ben in a bear hug around the waist. A dog, a hefty-set Lab that Mia must have been fostering for the night, trotted over and sniffed his shoes and pants with hesitant curiosity, a slow pump to its tail.

"Hey, buddy!" Mia reached for the bakery bag that Ben held out. After she relieved him of it and both hands were free, he scooped Ollie into the air and held him high overhead, sending Ollie into a familiar fit of laughter. Ben knew Ollie's emotions ran the gamut since losing his father, and it was good to see him in a moment of easy bliss again. "How's it going, little man? You're getting so big, pretty soon I'm going to be wearing you when I do this."

His godson had Mia's face shape and her smile, but the rest of him was all seven-year-old boy.

"I don't care if you wear me." Ollie locked his arms around Ben's head and laughed some more. "I'll be a hat, and you can wear me all day."

"Something tells me you'd be the squirmiest hat I've ever worn."

Mia joined in, tickling Ollie's exposed belly. "I think Ben would need the world's best chiropractor if he wore your wiggly body all day, Ol."

"So who's this?" Ben asked when he set Ollie down.

"Clara Bee. She's been at the shelter for a couple months. She's pending adoption, and this is a bit of a home-living test before she goes out at the end of the week. She was featured in the last newsletter. She's got quite the story."

Ben held out his hand, and Clara Bee gave him a tentative lick. He sank to the balls of his feet and, when she didn't shy away, gave her a thorough scratch under the chin, burying his fingers in her soft, golden fur. "Clara Bee, huh? After Clara Barton, right? Yeah, I remember reading about her."

She was a middle-aged dog who'd been living in subpar conditions and had had litter after litter before being taken from her home and brought into the shelter. She'd needed hip surgery but had come through it fine.

As if in thanks for the scratch, Clara Bee pressed in and swiped her tongue over Ben's ear. He'd never have guessed she'd had very limited human interaction for the majority of her life. Dogs, Ben figured, were simply hardwired to be good companions. He'd seen that in places like Nepal where most dogs were either free-roaming or strays. Even with minimal care and food, their bond with humans was inspiring.

"Thank goodness for the shelter, huh?"

As Mia agreed, Ollie lifted the brown paper bag from her hands and peeked inside. "Yes!" With his free hand, he rubbed his stomach vigorously, sending his pajama shirt up and exposing his trim belly and bony ribs.

Ben chuckled and stood up. "Did you eat yet?"

"I was just trying to get him to the table," Mia said. She gave Ben a hopeful glance. "But this certainly is more enticing than a soggy bowl of cereal. Can you stay?"

"For a little while. What time do you head out with him?"

She turned to check the kitchen clock. "Twenty minutes or so." A hint of her flush returned when she met Ben's gaze again. "I'm glad you came by. And I'm good if we're a few minutes late. It's not like they'll stick him in lockdown."

"Oh, can we be late? Please can we be late?" Ollie looked from his mom to Ben. "I hate journal time."

"How about instead you make quick work of this breakfast, and I drive you to school but try to get you there on time?" Ben said.

Ollie's eyes opened wide, and he dashed to the window. "You're in the Jeep. Sweet! Mom, please can he drive me? Please?"

Mia laughed and shook her head. "That's fine by me." She took a step toward the kitchen, then stopped and glanced downward, drawing Ben's attention toward the body he'd been doing his best not to notice. "You guys start without me. I'll throw on some clothes."

The flannel gown she was wearing was unbuttoned just to the point that it accented the rise of her breasts, and her fuzzy socks highlighted her toned, smooth calves.

"Ol, show him where the plates are, 'kay?"

"Come on, Ben," Ollie said, heading for the kitchen. "Do you like coffee or orange juice? My mom likes coffee, and I like orange juice. But I only get to have it if I also drink a glass of water."

Clara Bee followed Ollie into the kitchen, sniffing the bag of bakery items in his hand. Ben trailed along behind them, very glad he'd listened to his instincts and stopped by. It felt a bit like old times, when everything was easy between them, only it was different too. It was a new road, a new path they were blazing, one that was somehow as familiar as it was foreign.

And Ben was more than ready to head farther down it.

Mia stepped out of the shower and was sliding the glass door closed when her phone beeped from the bedroom. After knotting her hair in a towel and tying a second towel around her torso, she headed over to the dresser to check the new text.

Clara Bee hopped off Mia's bed and trailed behind her, tentatively licking the back of one still-wet calf.

Ollie had been begging for a puppy for Christmas, but Mia was secretly hoping he'd fall in love with one of the adult foster dogs they'd been bringing home each weekend. She had a feeling he might've with this sweet girl, had there not already been a family ready to bring her home sometime this weekend.

Having reached the dresser, Mia swiped her hands

across the front of her towel and lifted her phone. Ben. She'd hoped the text was from him.

Made it with 2 minutes to spare.

Her hands froze over the digital keypad. A handful of unworthy replies swam through her head. Why was coming up with a response so difficult?

Great. Thanks!

She groaned. He'd dropped off a delicious breakfast and driven his godson to school, not delivered the mail.

Thanks for the food and for coming by.

Still too generic, and you know it. Unsure what else to say, she shot off the text anyway.

Before this summer, it had been easy to talk to Ben, easy to be in the same room with him without blushing. He was Ollie's godfather, and he'd helped her keep Brad together during the harder times in her marriage. She'd counted on him in a hundred different ways.

And he'd never let her down.

Anytime. It was good to see Ollie. Good to see you too.

It was good to see her. Mia's heart thumped in her chest. Did he remember that night on his balcony? She'd hardly seen him since then, and whenever she did—like this morning—she could feel her cheeks burning hot.

As if Mia's indecision was palpable, Clara Bee paused her licking to glance up at her. Mia scratched the top of Bee's head, then turned back at her phone.

> Good to see you as well.

She was about to say "thanks again" when another text arrived.

> That's good. Because I've decided to take a more proactive approach to overcome your resistance to help.

Mia bit her lip as a smile spread across her face.

> Hmm, if this proactive approach comes with spinach-and-fontina mini-quiche, I'm good with that.

She debated adding a wink back but turned it into a regular smiley face instead.

> So I had you at quiche, huh? Well, I'm good with that.

"I think this is Ben fixing things," she said aloud, laughing. Clara Bee pricked her ears and cocked her head. "Thank goodness, because I didn't know how to do it."

Mia thanked him again for driving Ollie to school and set her phone down to get dressed. Ben wasn't to blame for the awkwardness that had been between them the last four months. She was.

The team at his firm had held a surprise party at Ben's downtown loft on his return from Everest. It had been a remarkable night and a late one. Ben didn't crave being the center of attention, but when he'd realized there was no way around it—he'd summited Everest and his friends wanted more than the single picture and snippet of information he'd posted on Instagram each day—he regaled his guests with some of the wilder things that had happened up there. One story, about Ben's ladder slipping from under him and him hanging over an impossibly deep crevasse until he could be pulled up by his team, had shaken Mia to the core.

She'd stepped out onto the balcony after getting Ollie to sleep on Ben's bed and sucked in a deep breath of summer night air. The party had continued in the main loft, but out there she could no longer hear Brad's voice booming across the room, and she willed the silence to soak into her pores. She'd stared out at the night skyline, contemplating the impending end of her marriage.

She hadn't been in love with Brad for a long time. It was just so much more obvious to her when she was around Ben. She wanted a chance to love someone who was whole and complete and wouldn't drain the energy out of her. And even though she'd never seen him in a committed relationship, it was obvious Ben could be that for someone.

And a part of her she'd done her best to ignore had wanted that someone to be her.